BBC
DOCTOR WHO

FIFTEEN DOCTORS
15 STORIES

PUFFIN

BBC CHILDREN'S BOOKS

UK I USA I Canada I Ireland I Australia
India I New Zealand I South Africa

BBC Children's Books are published by Puffin Books, part of the Penguin Random House
group of companies whose addresses can be found
at global.penguinrandomhouse.com.

www.penguin.co.uk
www.puffin.co.uk
www.ladybird.co.uk

Original stories first published as ebooks 2013
First published in one volume as *11 Doctors, 11 Stories* 2013
Published with Twelfth Doctor story as *12 Doctors, 12 Stories* 2014
Published with Thirteenth Doctor story as *Thirteen Doctors, 13 Stories* 2019
This edition published with Fourteen and Fifteen Doctor stories as *Fifteen Doctors, 15 Stories* 2024
001

Set in 13.3/18pt Bembo MT Std
Printed and bound in Great Britain by Clays Ltd, Elcograf S.p.A.

The authorized representative in the EEA is Penguin Random House Ireland,
Morrison Chambers, 32 Nassau Street, Dublin D02 YH68

A CIP catalogue record for this book is available from the British Library

ISBN: 978–1–405–96525–5

All correspondence to:
BBC Children's Books
One Embassy Gardens, 8 Viaduct Gardens
London SW11 7BW

CONTENTS

THE FIRST DOCTOR:

A BIG HAND FOR
THE DOCTOR

EOIN COLFER

1

THE STRAND, LONDON, 1900

The Doctor was not happy with his new bio-hybrid hand.

'Preposterous. It's not even a proper hand,' he complained to Aldridge. 'There are only two fingers, which is rather fewer than the traditional humanoid quota.'

Aldridge was not one to put up with any guff, even from a Time Lord.

'Give it back then. No one's forcing you to take it.'

The Doctor scowled. He knew Aldridge's bartering style, and at this point the Xing surgeon usually threw out a red herring to distract the customer.

'Would you like to know why I closed my practice on Gallifrey?' Aldridge asked.

Red herring delivered as expected. Every time he turned to Aldridge for help, this story was trotted out.

'Was it our title perhaps?' the Doctor enquired innocently.

'Exactly,' said Aldridge. 'Call yourselves Time Lords? How pompous is that? Someone previously registered Temporal Emperors, had they? A pity, you could have shortened it to Temperors.'

Temperors, thought the Doctor. *That's almost amusing.*

Amusing because a Time Lord known as the Interior

Designer had once famously suggested that exact title at a conference and been nicknamed Bad Temperor for the rest of his quantum days.

But the Doctor could not allow even a glimmer of a nostalgic smile to show on his lips – firstly because smiles tended to look like a death rictus on his long face and secondly because Aldridge would exploit the moment to drive up his price.

'Five fingers, Aldridge,' he insisted. 'I need an entire hand just to do up my shirt in the mornings. Humans put buttons in the most awkward places even when they are quite aware that Velcro exists.' He checked his pocket watch. 'Or rather, will exist in half a century or so.'

Aldridge pinged one of the curved ceramic digits with a scalpel. 'The exoskeleton has two fingers, I will grant you that, Doctor, but the glove has five, including the thumb, all controlled by signals from the exoskeleton. A bloomin' bio-hybrid miracle.'

The Doctor was impressed, but would not allow himself to show it. 'I'd rather have a bio-bio miracle if it's all the same to you. And I am in a dreadful hurry.'

'Come back in five days,' said Aldridge. 'Your flesh and bone hand will be ready by then. All I need is a sample.' He thrust a specimen jar under the Doctor's nose. 'Spit if you don't mind.'

The Doctor obliged, feeling more than a little relieved that spittle was all Aldridge needed from him. Some time ago, after the whole Inscrutable Doppelgänger fiasco, he'd been forced to part with two litres of very rare TL-positive blood from which to work up plasma.

'Five days? You couldn't get the job done with a little more urgency, could you?'

Aldridge shrugged. 'Sorry. I have a cluster of amphibi-men in the back, all hissing for their tail extensions. It's setting me back a fortune to hire a fire truck to keep 'em lubricated.'

The Doctor stared Aldridge down until the portly Xing surgeon relented.

'Very well. Two days. But it's gonna cost you.'

Ah yes, thought the Doctor, preparing himself for bad news. 'How much exactly is it going to cost me?'

Although *how much* was perhaps the wrong term to use as Aldridge usually dealt in commodities rather than currencies.

The surgeon scratched the bristles that dotted his chin like the quills of a porcupine. If ever one of Victorian London's cads, scoundrels, dippers or muck snipes stepped inside Aldridge's Clockwork Repair and Restoration hoping to light-foot it down the Strand with a couple of glittering fobs, they would have had a nasty surprise. For Aldridge could balloon his cheeks and expel one of those venom-laden bristles with a speed and accuracy comparable to that of the rainforest nomads of Borneo wielding their blowpipes. The villain would wake up six hours later, chained to the Newgate Prison railings with very fuzzy memories of the previous few days. Prison warders had taken to calling these occasional deliveries 'Stork Babies'.

The Doctor pointed pointedly at Aldridge's chin. 'Are you trying to intimidate me, Aldridge? Is that a threat?'

Aldridge laughed and his beard rippled. 'Oh, come on, Doctor. This right here is the fun of it. The barter and such. Our little game.'

The Doctor's face was unreadable. 'Even if I hadn't lost one of my hands, I would not be smiling like an idiot. I don't laugh. I don't play games. I have a serious mission.'

'You used to laugh,' rebutted Aldridge. 'Remember that thing with the homicidal earthworms? Hilarious, was it not?'

'Those earthworms excreted nitrous oxide,' said the Doctor, 'known on Earth as laughing gas, so I was laughing against my will. I do not usually indulge in merriment. The universe is a serious place and I left my granddaughter watching a house.'

Aldridge spread his fingers on the desk. 'Very well, and I only make this offer because of the wonderful Susan. What I require for the rental of the bio-hybrid and the growth of a new hand in my vat of magic is . . .' He paused, for even Aldridge knew what he was about to ask would not be swallowed easily by a Time Lord who did not possess a sense of humour. 'One week of your time.'

The Doctor didn't understand for a moment.

'One week of my time?' Then the penny-farthing dropped. 'You want me to be your assistant.'

'Just for the week.'

'Seven days? You want me as your assistant for seven whole days?'

'You hand over your time and I hand over . . . a hand. I have a really important repeat client that needs a job done. Having a smart fellow like yourself at my elbow would help a lot.'

The Doctor pinched his brow with his remaining hand. 'It's not possible. My time is precious.'

'You could always regenerate,' suggested Aldridge

innocently. 'Maybe the next guy will have a better sense of humour, not to mention sense of fashion.'

The Doctor bristled, though not as dramatically as Aldridge did on occasion.

'This outfit has been chosen by computer so that I may blend in with the locals. Fashion has nothing to do with it. In fact, fashion obsession is the sort of frivolous distraction that gets people –'

The Doctor did not complete his sentence and the surgeon chose not to complete it for him, though they both knew that *killed* was the missing word. The Doctor did not want to say it in case putting voice to the word would bring death itself, and there had been too much death in the Doctor's life. Aldridge knew this and took pity.

'Very well, Doctor. In return for four days of your time, I will grow a hand for you. I cannot and will not say fairer than that.'

The Doctor was grudgingly mollified. 'Four days, you say? I have your word on that, as a fellow visitor to this planet?'

'You have my word as a Xing surgeon. I can drop the hand at your TARDIS if you like. Where are you parked?'

'Over in Hyde Park.'

'You keeping your nose outta the smog? Actually I think I've got a few noses here if you fancy something less . . . pronounced.'

This was veering towards small talk and the Doctor had never cared too much for small talk or chit-chat. As for gossip and prattle, he loathed them both.

'Four days,' he repeated. The Doctor raised the stump of his left wrist upon which used to sit his left hand and without another word pressed the bio-hybrid claw-like fingers into the Xing surgeon's chest.

Aldridge regarded the action in silence and raised his bushy eyebrows high until the Doctor was forced to ask, 'Could you please attach the temporary bio-hybrid hand?'

Aldridge took a sonic scalpel from his belt.

'Careful with that,' said the Doctor. 'No need to get carried away.'

Aldridge spun the scalpel like a baton. 'Yessir. Careful is my middle name. Actually Clumsy is my middle name, but that doesn't encourage clients and it makes me sound like one of those dwarfs that are going to be so popular when moving pictures get going.'

The Doctor did not respond, or move for that matter, as Aldridge was already working on his arm, attaching the temporary hybrid hand to his wrist and slicing away the burned nub of flesh and seeking out nerve endings.

Incredible, thought the Doctor. *He seems to be barely paying attention and I can't feel a thing.*

Of course, that was the trademark of Xing-Monastery-trained surgeons – their incredible speed and accuracy. The Doctor had once heard a story about how acolytes were woken in the middle of a dark night by the pain of their own big toe being amputated by a professor. They were then timed on how long it took to reattach the toe using only the innards of a dental-floss packet, three lizard clips and a jar of glow-worms.

Hogwarts, it is not, thought the Doctor, realising that no one would appreciate this reference for almost a century.

Within minutes the surgeon was tugging on the

thought-responsive plasti-skin glove and stepping back to admire his work.

'Well, give 'er a wiggle.'

The Doctor did so and discovered, to his embarrassment, that the fingernails were painted.

'Would this, by any chance, be a lady's hand?'

'Yep,' confessed Aldridge. 'But she was a big lady. Very manly like yourself. Hated laughing and such, so you two should get on very well.'

'Two days,' said the Doctor, pointing a finger tipped by a curved nail coated with ruby lacquer.

Aldridge tried so hard to hold back a fit of giggles that one of his bristles thunked into the wall. 'Sorry, Mister Time Lord, sir. But it's really difficult to take you seriously wearing nail polish.'

The Doctor curled his fake fingers into a fist, straightened his Astrakhan hat and resolved to acquire a pair of gloves as soon as possible.

Aldridge passed the Doctor his cane.

'You never said how you lost the hand?'

'No,' said the Doctor. 'I didn't. If you must know, I was duelling a Soul Pirate who wounded me with a heated blade. If the blade hadn't cauterised the wound, I think you'd be looking at a different Doctor right now. Of course, I managed to compartmentalise the pain through sheer concentration.'

'Soul Pirates,' sniffed Aldridge. 'I won't even serve those animals. They're barred on principle.'

'Hmmmph,' said the Doctor, pulling his army greatcoat close to his throat. He might have said *bah humbug*, but that catchphrase already belonged to somebody else.

The Strand was filled with crowds of hawkers, and feral children who trekked daily from London's rookeries to follow moneyed gents the way iron filings follow a magnet, and red-cheeked revellers spilling on to the street outside the infamous Dog and Duck pub. If anyone had noted the elderly curmudgeon striding along towards Charing Cross, they would have noticed nothing strange about this gent, apart from the fact that he was staring at his own left hand with some surprise, as though it had spoken to him.

A retired army man they may have guessed, nodding at his overcoat and his measured gait.

A world traveller perhaps people might have surmised due to his Russian hat.

Or *an eccentric scientist* – this inferred from the bolts of white hair crackling in his wake, not to mention the ivory handle of a magnifying glass poking from his pocket.

No one would have known that there was a Time Lord in their midst that evening. Nobody except his granddaughter, Susan, who was possibly the only person in the universe who could make the Doctor smile at the mere thought of her.

There were numerous things that did not make the

Doctor smile: chit-chat, answering questions in times of emergency, answering questions in times of complete calm, the paintings of Gallifreyan Subjunctivists (confidence tricksters the lot of them), the Earth spread known as Marmite, the human TV show *Blake's 7*, which was patently ludicrous, and the clammy, pungent squeeze of a Victorian London crowd. Londoners endured a signature aroma composed of two parts raw sewage, one part coal smoke and one part unwashed-body odour. The great stink knew no master and was sniffed from queen to washerwoman. This stink could be exacerbated by summer heat or prevailing winds and the Doctor thought that there was not a smell that he despised more in the entire universe.

By the time he reached Charing Cross, the Doctor could stand the stench no longer and so hailed a hansom. He refused the cabbie's offer of half a sandwich, pressed an air-filter mask concealed behind a kerchief to his face, and hunched down low on his bench to discourage the cabbie from asking any further questions. The Doctor ignored the journey, including the detour round Piccadilly where a milk truck had overturned, spilling its load across the avenue, and he gave his mind to the problem that had cost him many nights' sleep and, more recently, his left hand.

The Soul Pirates were abominable creatures: a rag-tag rabble of the universe's humanoid species with only two things in common. One, as mentioned, they were approximately human in appearance; and, two, they cared not a jot for the lives of others. The Soul Pirates had a very specific *modus operandi*: they chose a planet where the inhabitants did not yet have hyperspace capabilities, then hovered in the clouds above and sent down a jockey, riding an anti-gravity tractor beam loaded with a soporific agent into the rooms of sleeping children. The anti-grav beam was clever, but the soporific agent in the beam was genius, because, even if the victims did wake up, the sedative would allow their brains to concoct some fantastic fairy tale and so they would willingly allow themselves to be spirited away. They believed themselves able to fly, or saw the beam jockey as a glamorous adventurer who desperately needed their help. In any event, there was no struggle or hoo-hah, and, most importantly, the merchandise was not damaged. When the kidnapped children were drawn into the pirates' ship, they were either sent to the engine room and hooked to brain-drain helmets, or chopped up for organ and body parts, which the pirates would transplant on to or into themselves. Nothing was wasted, not a toenail, not an electron, hence the bandits' moniker: the Soul Pirates.

The Doctor had relentlessly hunted the pirates across time and space. It had become his mission, his obsession. According to his galactic network, the crew who had taken his hand were the only ones still operating on Earth. He had last tangled with them in this exact city and now the TARDIS had detected their anti-grav signature here again. For the pirates it would be twenty years since their captain sliced off the Doctor's left hand, but for the Time Lord, having jumped years ahead in the TARDIS, it was a very fresh wound indeed.

This was what Susan would call a *break*. Soul-Pirate ships often eluded authorities for centuries because they had impenetrable shields, making it difficult to track them down.

They must have lost one of their protective plates, surmised the Doctor. *And that had made the pirates visible for a few minutes, before they effected repairs. Plenty of time for the TARDIS to find them. Well done, old girl.*

Unfortunately, whatever hole had allowed the pirate ship's signature to leak had now been plugged and the Doctor couldn't know if the pirates were still hovering above Hyde Park, hidden in the cloud banks, or off to their next port of call. A typical pirate crew had over a hundred streets that they revisited in random order. But the pirates had a tendency to revisit good harvesting sites. So if someone really wished to track them down, all they needed was determination and lots of time.

And I have both, thought the Doctor. *Plus a resourceful granddaughter.*

Sometimes too resourceful. Perhaps it would be wise to check in on Susan, after all. Sometimes it seemed as though she wilfully ignored specific instructions because, as she put it, *it seemed the right thing to do.*

And, while it often *was* the right thing to do morally, it was rarely correct from a tactical standpoint.

Just as the Doctor thought to call Susan, she must have thought to contact him as his wrist communicator vibrated to signal the arrival of a message. Surprisingly it buzzed a second time, then a third. Several more urgent buzzes followed.

The Doctor checked the small screen to see a dozen messages all from Susan coming through at the same time. How could that be? He had designed and built these communicators himself. They could broadcast through time if need be.

Then it hit him.

Stupid. Stupid. How could he not have foreseen this?

Aldridge was off-radar in this city. He would obviously have set up a series of jamming dishes. Anyone scanning the planet would find no trace of the surgeon or his gadgetry.

Susan had been trying to get through all evening, but he had been inside the jammed zone.

The Doctor scrolled to the last message, which had come through only seconds before, and clicked *play*.

'Grandfather,' said Susan's voice, breathy and he could hear her feet pounding as she ran. 'I can't wait any more. The beam has hit number fourteen as you predicted. Repeat, number fourteen. I have to help those children, Grandfather. There is no one else. Please come quick. Hurry, Grandfather, hurry.'

The Doctor cursed himself for being a fool, threw some coins in the cabbie's general direction and shouted at the man to make haste for the Kensington Gardens end of Hyde Park.

She was supposed to wait. I told her to wait. Why must she be so foolhardy?

As they neared the row of terraced townhouses at the end of the park, the Doctor played through the rest of Susan's messages hoping for some information that might help him rescue her and the children.

From what he could gather, Susan had befriended three children in the park and managed to glean that their parents had gone to Switzerland to a revolutionary new spa because of the father's nervous problems. Fearful of the curse, they had left one Captain Douglas, a soldier of the Queen's own guard, in charge of the children to protect them.

The curse. The family, like many others, believed that children went missing because of a curse.

The Doctor could see the signature tawny orange light of the pirates' beam entering the house. He jumped out of the hansom cab, then ran along a footpath lit by the firefly glow of gas lamps, and up the steps of number fourteen. The door was typically Victorian: solid and unbreakable by a shoulder charge.

How about my bio-hybrid hand? thought the Doctor, deciding to put Aldridge's technology to the test.

With barely a pause he punched the door with his left hand, middle knuckle striking the brass-ringed keyhole, and in spite of the circumstances he felt a moment's gratification when the metal lock crumpled beneath the blow and the surrounding wooden panel literally exploded into splinters. One of his fake glove fingers did split like an overcooked sausage but the Doctor knew that Aldridge would understand. Susan's life was at stake after all.

He barged into the hall and straight up the stairs, looking neither right nor left. The pirates would come in on the top storey, directly into the bedroom. The Doctor knew which bedroom because of a glow emanating from under the door, and he heard a dull buzz like a far-off, agitated beehive.

The anti-gravity beam.

I am too late. Susan, my dear.

With a cry that was almost animal, the Doctor split the fake thumb smashing open the bedroom door, and what he saw in there nearly stopped both of his Time Lord hearts.

It was the type of bedroom one would expect in a normal upper-class Kensington townhouse: patterned velvet wallpaper, prints framed on the wall – and an orange beam retreating through the bay windows like a spooked snake. Perhaps in the world outside the Doctor's, the orange beam was less than normal.

Susan was suspended in the air, floating out through the window, a dreamy smile on her lovely young face.

'Grandfather,' she called to him. Her movements were slow as though underwater. 'I have found Mummy. I am going to see her now, do come with me. Take my hand, Grandfather.'

The Doctor almost took the proffered hand, but to do so would have meant entering the beam, just as Susan's compassion for the children had caused her to do, and it was too early because the minute he took a breath in the beam the soporific agent would affect him too, and even Time Lords can only hold their breath for so long.

Beyond Susan, the Doctor saw a cluster of figures suspended by the beam.

The children and guard have been taken. I must save them all and somehow end this tonight.

And so the Doctor skirted the beam, ignoring Susan's pleas, though they were breaking his heart, and climbed through a side window on to the roof where there was a Soul Pirate with a large sword waiting to catch a ride back to his ship on the tail end of the anti-grav beam. The pirate was huge and bare to the waist, his skin a patchwork of grafts and scarring. His too-large head was completely shaved apart from a braided lock, which stood erect on his crown like an exclamation mark.

Mano-a-mano, thought the Doctor grimly. *And that pirate is a much bigger mano than I am.*

3

The Doctor and the Soul Pirate faced each other across an expanse of slick grey slate. The wind churned the mist into maelstroms and the great expanse of space yawned overhead. The Doctor's hat was snatched from his head and sent spinning over the hotchpotch of pitched roofs into a coal bunker ten metres below.

Where I shall probably soon follow, the Doctor realised, but he had no alternative but to engage this pirate fellow. After all, the grotesque creature stood between him and his granddaughter.

'Igby kill white-hair,' said the foul creature from between clenched teeth. He was presumably referring to himself in the third person, and referring to the Doctor according to his hair colour, not randomly informing the Doctor of the existence of a man called Igby who had something against white hair.

'Release your prisoners,' the Doctor shouted into the wind. 'You don't have to live this way. You can be at peace.'

And even though the Doctor had always abhorred weapons, he wished he had something a little more substantial than a walking stick to fend off the blows that were coming his way.

'I like white hair. He funny,' shouted Igby, his own booming voice penetrating the elements. 'Come die, old man.'

There is an excellent chance that I will do just that, thought the Doctor grimly. *But despite the odds I simply must not lose. Sometimes there is more to life than the odds.*

The orange anti-grav beam pulsed, scorching a cylinder through the London fog, silhouettes of brainwashed abductees floating in its depths, dreamily certain that they were flying to their own tailor-made heavens.

Jolly adventures, trees to climb, heroes all.

How long would that fantasy sustain them before the reality of the Soul Pirates' ship manifested?

The Doctor advanced cautiously, picking his way along the slick ridge, keeping his cane extended all the while. As soon as he stepped out from behind the chimney, the full force of the elements battered him with sideswipes of wind and tacks of icy rain. He struggled to keep his balance on the treacherous slating, and each time a loose tile slipped from its moorings and smashed on the cobbles below the Doctor remembered the danger he was in.

Though one is hardly likely to forget.

Igby waited for him, his eyes ablaze with bloodlust, twirling his sword in complicated patterns that deflated the Doctor's optimism with every revolution.

This alien is an expert killer. A mercenary. How can I, a pacifist with a stick, hope to defeat him?

The answer was obvious.

Igby was a beam jockey, that much was clear from the faint orange tinge to his skin, which reminded the Doctor (if one can be reminded of the future) of the pungent, toxic goo twenty-first-century ladies chose to slather on their skin in the name of tan. Beam jockeys were impervious to the soporific agent inside the anti-grav beam but long-term exposure did give their IQs a bit of a battering.

So, Igby appeared to be strong and fast, but maybe a little dim.

So, thought the Doctor, *I use tactics*.

Do the unexpected.

Closer they drew. On the face of it, the Doctor was totally outmatched. The pirate Igby was in his prime and packed solid with muscle. Igby's teeth were golden and the heavy slab of his naked chest bore a tattoo of the Soul Pirates' motto: *We Never Land*.

The Doctor noticed Igby's shadow flicker and shift, and realised the anti-grav beam was retracting towards the ship. If that happened, all hope would be lost. Even if Susan survived and he did find her again, she would be a different person – her wonderful spirit broken.

'No!' he cried. 'I will not permit it.'

Igby laughed, jerking his head at the Doctor as if informing an invisible friend that this old man was crazy. Then he too noticed the beam retracting, and realised that he had better finish up here or he could find himself stranded on Earth.

'Sorry, old man. No play now, just kill dead with sword.'

Igby rushed the Doctor, covering the space between them in two strides. The Doctor held his cane in front of him protectively, but Igby bashed it away with his silver wrist-guard.

'Fool,' spat Igby, spittle spattering through layers of teeth, craggy as a mountain range.

He lifted his blade high and brought it down with terrific force towards the Doctor's head. No time for subtleties. The pirate obviously intended to cleave one of the greatest frontal lobes in the universe with an almighty blow. Though the Doctor could not know it, this particular move was a favourite of Igby's, and the tattooed lines on his arms did not represent a record of days spent in prison, but rather the number of heads he had split, properly witnessed by a minimum of two crewmates.

As he swung, it occurred to Igby that none of his mates was present to credit the killing, so he turned his head towards the ship just to check if any of the camera stalks at the ship's front were focused on him, and to give the camera a clear shot of his face so there would be no cause for debate.

'Look,' he shouted in the direction of the camera stalks. 'I kill white hair. No problem.'

Igby felt a *thunk* as expected, but it was somehow different from the signature skull-splitting *thunk* that generally followed a fatal blow to the noggin.

Igby turned his gaze to the Doctor, and was more than surprised to find that the old man had caught Igby's sword in his left hand.

'Igby,' said Igby. It was the only word that would come to him.

The pirate yanked the sword, but it was trapped in the grip of the Doctor's bio-hybrid hand, so Igby tugged again, this time with all of his considerable strength. The Doctor was lifted off the ground for a moment, then the temporary binding polymer, which secured the bio-hybrid glove to the Doctor's wrist and was never meant for rooftop shenanigans, simply split with a noise like the twang of a rubber band. Igby's yank sent him past the point of correction and over backwards.

The Doctor reached out the exposed curved ceramic digits to save the pirate, but Igby was beyond his reach. All he could do was blink at the appendage stretched out towards him and utter the last word of his despicable life.

'Hook,' he groaned and slid on all fours down the roof and tumbled into the darkness below.

The Doctor regretted the loss of any life, however vile, but there was no time to mourn Igby's death. The orange tractor beam was withdrawing into the cloud and in mere seconds it would be beyond his reach. Perhaps it already was.

Oh, how I wish I had already regenerated to become the tall one with the dicky bow, thought the Doctor, who occasionally had visions of his future selves. *He is always so fit and agile. I suppose all that incessant running down corridors that he does . . . will do . . . may do, in one of my possible futures . . . is good for something.*

'Stupid blasted sequence of events,' he shouted at the heartless elements. 'Isn't a person supposed to have a reasonable option?'

If the elements did have the answer, they kept it to themselves.

'S'pose not,' muttered the Doctor. 'Better take the unreasonable option then.'

He trotted along the ridge to the nearest chimney, going as quickly as he could before his subconscious caught on to his lunatic plan and tried to stop him. Up on to the chimney he scrambled, dislodging two clay pots and a bird's nest from its perch. And from there he dived out and was lifted up into the fading glow of the pirates' tractor beam.

4

The anti-gravity beam sucked the Doctor into its belly and he supposed that this was how being eaten must feel. Indeed it was more than mere supposition. He had been eaten twice before, on the same holiday, by blarph whales in Lake Rhonda who thought it was hilarious to gulp down bathers then pop them out through their blowholes. Then all the whales would surface-high-five each other and have a good old laugh at the bather's expense. The bather would generally take the whole thing in good spirits – after all, who's going to take issue with a twenty-tonne blarph whale?

The Doctor banished these memories because they were for another time when he was not suspended in the anti-grav beam of a Soul Pirate frigate.

The Doctor knew he had only moments of total consciousness left before the beam's soporific agent lulled him into a peaceful sleep, when it would seem as though all his dreams were on the verge of coming to pass. The Doctor shook himself vigorously to stay awake, while at the same time holding his breath.

Suddenly he was back on Gallifrey, with his family, safe at last.

'*That's right,*' *said his mother and she smiled down at him, her long hair brushing his forehead.* '*Stay here, my little Doctor. Stay here with me and you can tell tales of the worlds you have visited. I so want to hear your stories.*'

She is so pretty, he thought. *Just as I remember her.*

'D'Arvit!' swore the Doctor aloud. 'I am being drugged.' He began to describe what was happening around him just to stay alert.

'There are half a dozen souls trapped in the beam. Three children and three adults, counting Susan as an adult, which I am not sure I should considering the fact that she wilfully disobeyed my instructions. All able-bodied. The pirates need youth and strength to power their ship. I cannot see Susan's face, though I can feel her joy. I wonder what she sees in her dreams?'

The beam was more than light. It offered resistance when touched and was heavily charged to allow suspension of dense matter.

'I know we are moving,' continued the Doctor, narrating his journey. 'Yet there is no sensation of movement. No friction whatsoever. I can honestly say that in spite of the ominous circumstances, I have never been so comfortable.'

A slender shape flitted past and the Doctor knew, even from the briefest glimpse, that it was Susan. He recognised her as surely as an infant recognises the voice of its mother.

'Susan, my dear!' he cried, releasing more precious breath, but Susan's smile never wavered, and she did not answer.

The Doctor saw in her expression how optimistic about the universe Susan was and he realised how utterly she would collapse in the Soul Pirates' hands. That could not be allowed to happen.

They passed through the folded-pastry layers of a puffed-up cumulus and emerged looking at the stars. The second star on the left winked and crackled suddenly as its cloaking shield was powered down, and where sky had been now hovered the hulking pirate factory ship.

The beam drew them towards the specially modified bay of the mid-size interplanetary-class frigate. The underside was scored from many close calls with asteroids and weapon fire. The Doctor could clearly see the spot welds where a new plate had recently been attached.

Space gates were cranked open and the Doctor saw that the anti-grav beam had been modified to fire from inside the ship itself, which was incredibly dangerous if not properly calibrated, but it did allow the Soul Pirates to draw their victims directly into the hold for processing.

'The anti-grav cannon fires from within the hold,' said the Doctor, but he could feel himself losing the battle to stay alert. 'The subjects are drawn inside and often spontaneously and in perfect synchronisation sing every word of the Monzorian opera *Grunt the Naysayer*.'

Stop it! The Doctor chided himself. *Draw your wits about you. Say what you see.*

'The Soul Pirates' ship works on the same principle as those despicable Orthonian whaling factories,' he said, feeling a numbness buzz along his arms. 'Once the subjects have been deposited inside the Soul Pirate ship, they are scanned by computer and the ship decides how best to use each one. Most are hooked up to battery rigs and drained of their electricity, but some are sent directly to dissection for their parts. Soul Pirates are humanoids, mostly but not exclusively from the planet Ryger. Their systems are extremely robust and can accept all manner of transplants, even ones from different species, such as Earthlings. With timely transplants a pirate can reasonably expect to live three to four hundred Earth years.'

The giant gates yawned wide and sucked the subjects into a vast abattoir. Rows of meat hooks hung from the metal ceiling and a couple of pirates stood in rubber aprons ready to hose down the new arrivals with water cannons. They wore curved heat blades attached to battery packs on their belts in case the computer recommended an instant amputation.

The beam was powered down and its cargo dropped with a thump into a pit on the deck. The Doctor confirmed that there were four others besides Susan and himself.

Six to save, he thought. *And those pirates have the high ground.*

As soon as the last gloopy globs of the anti-grav beam had faded, the Soul Pirates cranked up their hoses and turned them on their latest victims, blasting Susan, the Doctor and the four others into a heaped hotchpotch of limbs and torsos in the corner of the pit.

The pirates laughed. 'They so stupid,' said one. 'Look, I spray them again.'

Pummelled by water on two sides, the Doctor could barely breathe. He was effectively blind and couldn't have fought back if he wanted to. But he didn't want to. When your enemy believes you to be unconscious, let them continue to do so until you gain a tactical advantage.

Or plainly put: play dead until they come close.

The second pirate dropped his hose and checked a computer console with big coloured buttons.

'Ship say beep, Gomb,' he said, puzzled. 'What beep mean?'

What beep mean? Obviously the pirates kept the slower members of their crew on the lower decks. In the case of Igby, probably below decks.

Gomb clipped the hose nozzle on to a special hook on his belt and hurried to check the screen.

'Special beep!' he exclaimed. 'We got Time Lords. Computer say Time Lords. Brains worth many money pieces. Big blobby brains.'

Even buried under a mound of bodies in an abattoir, the Doctor found a moment to take offence.

Blobby brain, indeed.

Gomb squinted at the heaped pile of sleeping bodies. 'Which one?'

'Lay them out,' ordered his companion. 'I tell Cap'n face to face and maybe get grog bottle for we two. You find Time Lords.'

The Doctor tried to pull his limbs from their entanglement so he would have some chance in a physical struggle, but he was stuck fast, pinned at the bottom of a body pile, his face a metre from Susan's. Her eyes were open now, and he could see her consciousness return.

She is frightened, he thought. *I cannot allow her to die here.*

But Susan was not dead yet and neither was the Doctor.

'Grandfather,' she whispered. 'What can we do?'

'Shhhh,' said the Doctor gently, wishing he could give her some encouragement, but if anything there was worse to come before things got better, which they probably would not. 'Dream a while.'

Pirate Gomb jumped down into the pit, his boots striking

the deck with a clang. He sauntered across the closed space doors to where valuable Time Lords were waiting with blobby brains. Gomb sang in a surprisingly pure tenor as he walked, which was about as unexpected as hearing a quantum physics lecture from the mouth of a lemming.

> 'Grog, grog,
> Swallow it down,
> She cures constipation
> She up-turns yer frown.'

The Doctor thought that maybe Gomb had composed this classic himself.

Up-turns?

Gomb reached the body pile and hauled off two sleeping children, laying them out side by side and straightening their clothes.

'Yer going to meet Cap'n,' he said. 'Look yer best for Cap'n and maybe he just drain yer soul 'stead of slicing you up for parts.'

The pirate returned to the pile and bent towards Susan.

This was as far as he got because the Doctor had reached up and yanked the release switch on the hose on Gomb's belt. This was not as precise a plan as the Doctor would have liked, but if he had estimated the hose's pressure correctly, and providing the pirate's belt did not break, the result should be advantageous for the prisoners.

Advantageous was one way of putting it: Gomb had barely a moment to register what was happening when the hose bucked as water pressure ran along it, then lifted Gomb bodily into the air, wrapped its coils around him and sent him spinning down a corridor, out of sight.

The Doctor knew that he had seconds before their escape attempt was known to everyone on the ship. They were probably under video surveillance right now.

He crawled out from underneath the sleeping humans and turned to Susan.

'My dear,' he said, wiping her eyes, 'are you hurt?'

'No,' she said, but she was terrified. The Doctor could see it dawn on her what happened here as she stared raptly at the meat hooks swaying from the ceiling.

'Susan, listen to me,' said the Doctor, taking her face in his hands – well, one hand and a claw. 'I will get us out, but you need to help me. Do you understand?'

Susan nodded. 'Of course, Grandfather. I can help.'

'That's my girl. Drag the others into the centre of the space gates. Inside the circle.'

'Inside the circle.'

'As quick as you can, Susan. We have mere moments before reinforcements arrive.'

Susan began her task of pulling the other captives inside the circle. They slid across the slick deck easily enough, even the adult, who was clad in a soldier's uniform.

The Doctor's sodden greatcoat made him feel as though he was wearing a bear, so he shrugged it off and hurried up the steps to the console. The controls were set to Rygerian, which the Doctor could understand well enough, but he switched the language to Earth English and locked the preferences, which might give them another second or two when they needed it.

The Doctor had always been a finger-and-thumb typist so working with a claw didn't hinder him too much. He ran a search of the vessel for captives and found none besides his own group. Yesterday's abductees had already been disposed of, which made the Doctor feel a lot better about the action he had decided to take.

He circumvented the pirate craft's basic security codes and quickly reset the anti-grav beam parameters and door controls. Once the computer had accepted his overriding commands, the Doctor set such a complicated password that it would take either ten years or a miracle to get this computer to perform any task more complicated than playing solitaire.

The pirates did not have ten years, and the universe certainly did not owe them a miracle.

Susan had managed to gather the prisoners on the circle in the centre of the bay doors. The soldier was attempting to stand and the smallest child, a boy, was being violently ill on his own shoes. The Doctor swept him up in his arms, ignoring the squeals of protest.

'Quickly,' he said. 'All together now. You must lay your hands on me.'

He may as well have been talking to monkeys. These humans were in the middle of a transition from paradise to hell. If they were fortunate, it was possible that their minds would heal, but at the moment it was all they could do to breathe.

Only Susan had her wits about her. She hugged the Doctor with one arm, the soldier with another and gathered a boy and a girl who might have been twins between her knees.

'Good girl,' said the Doctor, hoisting the ill boy on to his shoulders. 'That's my girl.' They were all connected now: a circuit.

'Whatever happens, we do not break the circuit!'

Susan nodded, hugging her grandfather fiercely. 'I won't let go.'

'I know you won't,' said the Doctor.

Seconds passed and the Doctor began to fret that he had allowed too long on the timer. The pirates would be upon them at any moment. In fact the approaching ruckus echoing down the corridor suggested that this moment had arrived.

A dozen or more pirates fell over each other to access the cargo bay, training their weapons on the Doctor and his fellow captives. But they did not fire. Why would they? These prisoners represented a night's work. By the looks of it they had managed to surprise Gomb, but a jack-in-the-box could surprise Gomb, he was so stupid. And what could the prisoners do now? Outnumbered, surrounded and unarmed? There was nothing for them to do but accept their fate.

The Captain elbowed his way to the front of the pack. He was a fearsome specimen. Three metres tall with a flat, grey-scaled face, deep-set glittering eyes and a long scar vertically bisecting his face.

'The Time Lord,' he bellowed, and it sounded as though someone had taught a rhinoceros to talk. 'Where is the Time Lord?'

'I am here,' said the Doctor, checking by touch and sight that the band of Earthlings was still connected.

The Captain's laugh was uncharacteristically high-pitched for such a large person.

'It is you, Doctor,' he said, touching the scar on his face. 'You should not have come back.'

The Doctor noticed that the Captain wore a shrunken hand on a cord around his neck.

That is my hand, the fiend!

'I had unfinished business,' said the Doctor, counting down from five in his head.

'We both have unfinished business,' said the Captain.

Generally the Doctor was not in favour of rejoinders or snappy one-liners but this captain was a vile specimen and so he treated himself to the last word.

'Our business is now finished,' the Doctor said, and the space doors opened beneath them, dropping the Doctor and his group into the black of night, three thousand metres above the glowing gas-lights of London.

The Captain was disappointed that he would not get to personally enjoy harvesting the Doctor's organs, but the fact that the Time Lord would be dead in a matter of seconds cheered him somewhat. There was one little thing that niggled at him, though: if the Doctor had set the space doors to open, what other computer settings could he have fiddled with?

He barged to the nearest screen and was greeted by complicated unfamiliar text running in ever-decreasing circles.

'Doctor!' he bellowed. 'What have you done?'

As if to answer his question, the anti-grav cannon fired off one short fat squib through the closing space doors. Just one burst that grazed the doors on its way out before they clanged shut.

Lucky for me, thought the Captain. He did not think *lucky for us*, as he was a selfish and tyrannical captain who would sell his entire crew to a body farm to buy himself an extra minute of life.

Because if the anti-grav cannon was ever fired when the space doors were closed it would be the end of the entire ship.

Again it seemed as though the computer could read his mind as it diverted every spark of energy into the cannon and unloaded it directly at the sealed space doors.

The Doctor and his party plummeted to Earth, although it felt as though London was rushing upwards to meet them. There was no room in their lives for thought now. Life had been reduced to the most basic of urges: survival. And if they did survive tonight, any of them, then their lives would never be the same. They would have been to the brink, peered into the abyss and lived to speak of it. Only the Doctor maintained something of his faculties, as near-death experiences were more or less his speciality.

They fell in a ragged bunch, held together by death grips and tangled limbs. Somehow in the middle of the jumbled chaos, the Doctor and Susan came face to face. The Doctor tried to smile, but air rushed between his lips and ballooned his cheeks.

I cannot even smile for my beautiful granddaughter.

He saw it coming from the corner of one eye, an orange bloom in the sky above them.

Physics, don't fail me now, he thought. Then: *Physics cannot fail, but my calculations could be flawed.*

The bloom blossomed and became a bolt, which shot towards them with unerring accuracy, leaving a wake of fairy sparks behind it.

The Doctor pulled everyone tight, hugging them to him.

Live or die. This moment decides.

The anti-grav pulse enveloped the small band, and slowed their descent in a series of jarring hops and sputters. The Doctor found himself floating on his back watching the pirate ship list from the side of a large cloud bank. Eight storeys of wounded metal.

They deserve this, he told himself. *I am saving the lives of children and avenging many more.*

But still he turned away when the anti-grav ray he'd instructed the computer to fire began to eat the ship from the inside, changing the very atomic structure of the craft until its molecules disbanded and became at one with the air.

Susan hugged him tight and cried on his shoulder.

They would survive.

They would all be fine.

Aldridge was mildly surprised.

'The Doctor defeated a whole crew of Soul Pirates? Single-handed, if you'll pardon the expression?'

Susan flicked her nail against something on Aldridge's work bench that looked very much like a miniature TARDIS.

'Yes, my grandfather took care of them. He coded the ship's anti-grav beam to his own DNA so the blast from the beam locked on to him and therefore us. Genius, really.'

Aldridge moved the tiny TARDIS away from Susan's fingers. 'There is a giant octo-shark in there and I don't think he'd be impressed with you flicking his box.'

'An octo-shark, really?'

'For all you know. Please stop touching things.'

Susan was filling Aldridge in on their adventure while they waited for the Doctor to wake after his operation.

'So we put the children back in their house and left the soldier on guard outside the door. With any luck they will think the whole episode was a dream.'

'The curse is broken,' said Aldridge. 'I don't know why that family didn't just move. There's not exactly a shortage of houses in London town, especially for rich folk.'

Susan began putting rings from a tray on each finger, eventually managing to fit thirty rings on her hands. 'Tell me, Mr Aldridge. How do you do that trick with your beard bristles?'

Aldridge bristled, as he usually did when bristle comments were passed.

'The beard *trick* is a discipline. All you need to do is practise and drink a very diluted glass of poison every night. Now will you please put those rings back on the tray? I'm running a business, you know, not a toy shop.'

Moaning drifted from the back room followed by a long bout of coughing.

'Where is she?' said the Doctor's voice. 'Susan?'

Susan quickly stripped off the rings and dumped them in the tray.

'It's Grandfather. He's awake.'

She hurried behind the screen to find the Doctor already sitting up on a soldier's cot, surrounded by an array of highly sophisticated equipment, which had been disguised as everyday Victorian objects.

Someone once tried to use what he thought was a commode, Aldridge had told Susan in an attempt to stop her touching things. *And had the two sides of his bottom sutured together.*

'Here I am, Grandfather,' said Susan. 'Everything is fine.'

The Doctor's panic disappeared as though blown away by a gust of wind.

'Good, child. Good. I had such dreams under the anaesthetic. Such nightmares. Now I wake to find you beside me and I can hardly remember what those nightmares were.'

Aldridge appeared around the screen. 'Such poetry, such effusiveness. It's enough to make an old surgeon shed a tear.'

The Doctor scowled. 'I presume the transplant was a success, Aldridge?'

'That hand will last longer than you, provided you don't let some pirate slice it off,' said Aldridge.

The Doctor held up his left hand, examining it closely. The only sign of surgery was a thick pink line around the wrist.

'It was touch and go there for a while,' said Aldridge. 'You nearly regenerated twice.'

'Hmmm,' said the Doctor, and then: 'Hmmmmmm.'

Aldridge elbowed Susan. 'He does the whole *hmmmm* routine when he's looking for faults, but can't find any.'

The Doctor sat up, then stood, holding the hand out to Susan for inspection.

'Tell me, Granddaughter. What do you think?'

Susan pinched his palm and pulled on the fingers one by one.

'Honestly, Grandfather,' she said. 'It looks a little big to me.'

EPILOGUE

On that bitter night when the Doctor battled Igby on the rooftop overlooking Hyde Park, a man sat alone on a bench in Kensington Gardens. He was sombre-faced with a high forehead and large kind eyes.

An author by trade, he'd found some little success in the theatre, but had not yet found the spark of a magical idea that could elevate him to the status of his friend Arthur Conan Doyle.

The young writer tugged on his moustache, a nervous habit, and looked to the stars for inspiration. What he saw there lasted for the merest blink of an eye and he would often wonder if it had indeed happened or if his imagination had brewed it up to set him on the road to literary immortality.

What he thought he saw was this:

Children surrounded by stardust flying into the night.

Two people fighting on a rooftop.

One was perhaps a pirate and the other seemed to have a hook for a hand.

The writer sat stunned for perhaps half an hour until the cold seeped through the seat of his trousers, then he pulled some scraps of paper from his pocket, chewed the top of his pencil stub, and began to write.

THE SECOND DOCTOR:
THE NAMELESS CITY

MICHAEL SCOTT

PROLOGUE

We are old now.

Our age is not measured in centuries or millennia or even aeons.

We have seen the rise and fall of solar systems. We have observed galaxies spin and turn, and, once, we watched the entire universe die, only to be instantly reborn in music and light.

Before the Doctor, before the Master, before Gallifrey and the Time Lords, our race ruled the universe. Gone now. All gone. Just we few remain.

But while the rest of our race faded, their atoms mixed amongst the stars, we clung to a semblance of life, dancing to the Music of the Spheres. Our rage kept us in existence, and our loathing sustained us. We will have our revenge. We will rule again.

We are the Devourers of Worlds, the last of the Old Ones.

We are the Archons.

Decrypted data burst recovered from the TARDIS records.

1

LONDON, 1968

A shout: high-pitched, terrified.

The sound was nearly lost in the noise of the busy Saturday-afternoon traffic and the crowds bustling along Charing Cross Road. A few people glanced up and looked around. Seeing nothing wrong, they went on their way.

A second shout rang out, almost completely drowned by the blare of car horns.

Only a tall dark-haired young man standing outside a shabby antiquarian bookshop continued to look, head tilted to one side, eyes half closed, listening intently. None of the passers-by paid him any attention and, since this was London and the city was awash with the latest fashions, no one even blinked at his oversized black turtleneck sweater or the fact that he was wearing a red Scottish-tartan kilt, complete with sporran.

The young man used a trick his father had taught him when they'd been hunting grouse in the Highlands. He deliberately focused on the sounds — first, the cars and buses; next, the street clatter, the dull hum of shouts, the buzz of laughter — and then he tuned them out. He waited for something out of the ordinary, something odd, alien. Something like . . .

The slap of leather on stone.

It had come from behind him.

Moving quickly now, he followed the sound. It led him to the mouth of a cobbled alley. He glanced down: it was empty. However, he knew with absolute certainty that this narrow tube of stone would have carried any sounds out into the street beyond. Ducking into the alleyway, he blinked, allowing his eyes to adjust to the gloom, before darting forward. The alley curved slightly to the left and as he rounded the corner he discovered the source of the noise.

A bearded grey-haired man lay sprawled across the filthy stones, surrounded by a scatter of antique leather-bound books. An enormous greasy-haired thug crouched over the figure, searching through a battered satchel, pulling out books and tossing them to one side.

'Please . . . please be careful,' the old man groaned as each leather-clad volume hit the ground with a distinctive slap.

'Where's the money?' the huge thug snarled. 'Where's the shop's takings?'

'There is none . . .' the old man said quickly. 'We sell antiquarian books. But some days we don't sell anything . . .'

'I don't believe you. Empty your pockets.'

'No,' the old man said defiantly.

'Yes!' The thief smiled, thin lips peeling back from yellowed teeth.

Anger flashed in the young Scotsman's eyes. He knew he shouldn't get involved. He'd been entrusted with a critical mission and had promised not to delay, but he'd also been raised to a strict code of honour, which included protecting the weak and respecting elders. Keeping close to the walls, he hurried forward, well-worn soft-leather-soled shoes making no sound on the cobblestones.

'I said, *Empty your pockets.*' The thug tossed the satchel to one side and loomed over the man lying on the ground.

Suddenly, a shout cut through the air: a guttural snarl that shocked the thief into immobility. He caught a glimpse of a shadow in the corner of his eye the instant before a tremendous blow to his side sent him crashing into the alley wall. His head cracked against the old stones, and red and blue spots of cold light danced before his eyes as he sank to his knees. The thief blinked, watching a figure in a red skirt – no, a kilt – swim into focus. Scrambling to his feet, he threw an unsteady punch and then something hit him in the centre of the chest and he sat down hard, spine jarring on the cobbles.

'If you know what's good for you, you'll run away now. And you won't look back.' Although the Scotsman had spoken in little more than a whisper, the threat was clear.

Bending double, with both arms wrapped round his bruised chest, the thief backed away, then turned and ran.

The Scotsman knelt, offering his hand to the old man and gently easing him into a sitting position. 'Are you hurt?'

'Only my pride . . . and my trousers.' The grey-haired man struggled slowly to his feet, brushing his hair back off his high forehead. 'And my poor books.' He moved to pick them up, but the Scotsman was already darting around, collecting the scattered volumes. 'You're very brave,' the man said, his deep voice echoing off the alley walls.

'Well, I couldn't just walk away, now could I?'

'Yes, you could have. Others did.' The older man stuck

out a leather-gloved hand. 'Thank you, thank you very much.' He smiled through a neat, grey-flecked goatee beard, his eyes dark and curious beneath heavy brows. 'I'm Professor Thascalos.'

'I'm Jamie, Jamie McCrimmon.'

'Scottish. I thought I recognised a Gaelic war cry. *Creag an tuire*. What is that – "The Boar's Rock"?'

Jamie handed over the books. 'You mean the kilt wasn't a clue?' he asked with a grin.

The old man smiled. 'Fashions nowadays.' He shrugged. 'Who knows what you young people are wearing?'

Jamie picked up the satchel and held it open as the professor carefully brushed off each book and returned it to the bag. Some of the leather bindings had been scuffed and torn when they'd hit the cobbles and one cover had come away entirely. 'You were in the military?' the professor asked.

Jamie shook his head. 'Not really.'

'You reacted like a soldier,' Professor Thascalos said. 'A shout at the last minute to disorientate the enemy, followed by an overwhelming attack. That only comes with experience. You've been in battle.'

The young Scotsman nodded slightly. 'Aye, well, it was a long time ago,' he said, his accent suddenly pronounced. 'And it didn't end well.' He wasn't going to tell the professor that the last battle he'd been in had taken place over two hundred and twenty years ago. He handed the final book to the professor. 'Is there much damage?'

'I can have the worst ones re-bound. I should not have come down this alleyway, but I was taking a short cut to my shop. I'm a bookseller on Charing Cross Road,' he added, and then lifted the bag of books. 'But you probably guessed that.'

'I did.' Jamie grinned. 'Will you report this to the police?'

'Of course.'

'If you're all right then, I'll be on my way.'

The professor reached into an inside pocket and pulled out a wallet. 'Here, let me give you something –' He stopped suddenly, seeing the look on Jamie's face. 'Not money then, but here . . .' Rummaging in the bag, he found a small book, wrapped in a black silk handkerchief.

'I don't want payment . . .'

'Not payment – a gift,' the bookseller said. 'A thank-you.' He handed the package to Jamie, who took it and turned it round in his large hands, folding back the silk to trace a curling outline embossed into the book's dark leather cover.

'It looks old.'

'It is. It is one of the oldest books I possess.'

Jamie opened it. The thick pages were covered in blocky black print in a language he thought might be German. 'It must be very valuable.'

'It is,' the professor repeated, 'but I want you to have it. You saved my life today, young man,' he said gruffly. 'It is the least I can give you.'

'I cannot read the writing.'

'There are few who can. But keep it. I insist. You can always give it as a gift to someone you think might appreciate it.' He suddenly reached out and shook Jamie's hand. 'Now I have delayed you and taken up far too much of your time. Thank you. You are a credit to your clan.' The professor stood back and swung his satchel on to his shoulder, then turned and strode down the alley. He raised his gloved hand and his voice echoed off the stones. 'Take care, Jamie McCrimmon,' he called. 'Enjoy your book.' And then he rounded the corner and vanished.

Jamie looked at the black book, rubbing his thumbs over the surface. The leather felt oily and slightly damp. He guessed it had fallen in a puddle. Bringing it to his nose he breathed in slowly. He thought he smelled the faintest odour of fish and sea air from the pages. Shrugging, he wrapped it back in its silk and shoved it in his belt as he hurried away. Maybe the Doctor would like it.

Professor Thascalos paused at the end of the alley. He could hear Jamie's footsteps fading away in the opposite direction. He turned his head to look at a huge figure lurking in the shadows. The greasy-haired thief stepped forward, mouth wide in a broad, gap-toothed grin.

'You did well,' the professor said quietly. He pulled out a wad of money from an inside pocket of his greatcoat. 'We agreed on fifty, but here's sixty.' He peeled off six crisp ten-pound notes and handed them across. 'A bonus for getting hit.'

The man looked at the thick bundle of notes and he licked his lips.

'You're thinking foolish thoughts now,' the professor said quietly again, his face settling into an implacable mask. 'Dangerously stupid thoughts,' he added icily.

The thug looked into the professor's dark eyes, and whatever he saw there made him step back in alarm. 'Yes . . . yes, fifty. And the bonus. Very generous. Thank you.'

'Good boy. Now, go away.' The professor tossed the bag of books at the big man. 'Here, get rid of these for me.'

'I thought they were valuable.'

'Only one,' the professor muttered to himself, looking back down the alley. 'And that was invaluable.'

Stepping into the shadows, the professor watched as the thief slid unnoticed into the throng of people walking past. Then he pulled a slender metal cylinder from his pocket, twisted it counter-clockwise and held it to his thin lips. '*It is done,*' he said in a language that had not been heard on Earth since the fall of Atlantis. '*I have completed my half of the bargain. I trust, when the time comes, you will honour your part.*'

A thread of faint ethereal music hung on the air.

The professor snapped the cylinder closed and strode away, a rare smile on his lips.

2

There was a blue police box almost directly opposite the statue of Henry Irving at the back of the National Portrait Gallery. None of the tourists gave it a second glance, though a few of the local traders were a little bemused by its sudden appearance. It had recently been announced that London's police boxes would soon be phased out and demolished.

Jamie McCrimmon slowed as he rounded the corner of the gallery and then stopped. There were tourists everywhere; some were even taking photographs using the blue box as a background. A family of what could only be American tourists in florid shirts, matching shorts and sandals was standing right up against the door.

'Ah, there you are!'

Jamie whirled round.

The Doctor was standing behind him, looking his usual rumpled and dishevelled self. Polly, one of the Doctor's companions who had known him before he'd *changed*, once described him as looking like an unmade bed. Jamie thought it was a good description. The Doctor's mop of thick black hair was uncombed, his collar was rumpled and a bow tie sat slightly cock-eyed round his neck. He was wearing a black frock coat that had gone out of fashion decades ago over black-and-white checked trousers, which managed to be both too large and just a little too short. It was impossible to put an age on him: he looked to be in his mid-forties, but the Scotsman knew that the Doctor was at least five hundred years old. Jamie still hadn't decided if he was a genius or a madman. Or both.

The Doctor was licking an ice-cream cone. 'What kept you?'

'There was a wee spot of bother . . .' Jamie began.

'Did you get everything on my list?'

'Nothing,' Jamie said ruefully. 'I went to all the chemists I could find – none of them had even heard of the stuff on your list, except the gold and mercury.'

The Doctor bit off the top of the cone. 'Then we have a problem,' he said, frowning, deep lines etching into his face. 'A serious problem.'

Jamie nodded towards the police box. 'I know. How are we going to get inside?'

The Doctor silently handed Jamie the half-eaten cone. He reached into an inside pocket and pulled out a slender wooden recorder decorated in swirls of blue. 'When I say run, *run!*' he said. 'Oh, and you might want to stick your fingers in your ears,' he added, raising the recorder to his lips.

Even with his fingers jammed in his ears – and with cold ice cream dripping down the side of his neck from the cone clutched in one hand – Jamie could still hear the sound vibrating through the air. Pressure built up in his ears and all the nerves in his teeth protested. Birds nestling in the trees and pecking on the ground erupted into the air in an explosion of flapping wings.

'Run!' the Doctor instructed. He darted forward, head tilted towards the sky, finger pointing upwards. 'What is that?' he shouted. 'There . . . just there.'

Everyone looked up, following the wheeling, darting birds.

The Doctor brushed past the staring tourists, stepped up to the police box and quickly unlocked it. He opened the door just wide enough to slip through and pushed it closed promptly after Jamie squeezed inside.

'We don't want anyone peeping in now, do we?' The Doctor grinned and clapped his hands in delight. 'See? Simplicity itself! There are very few things that a good diversion won't solve.'

No matter how many times he travelled in the extraordinary machine, Jamie knew he would never get used to the idea that the Doctor's ship – the TARDIS – was bigger on the inside than it appeared on the outside. He had no idea how many rooms, galleries, museums and libraries were housed in the extraordinary craft. There was even supposed to be an Olympic-sized swimming pool somewhere in the basement, but he'd never managed to find it. Jamie stopped, suddenly conscious that the beautiful and ornate central console, which was at the heart of the machine, had been dismantled and lay strewn in pieces around the hexagonal room. The floor was scattered with coils of wire, glass panels and hundreds of oddly shaped cogs and wheels.

The Doctor tiptoed his way through the mess. 'Touch nothing,' he warned. 'I know exactly where everything is.' His foot struck a squat metal cylinder, sending it spinning into a little pyramid of ball bearings, which scattered in every direction, ricocheting around the room. 'Well, almost everything.'

'You can fix it, can't you?' Jamie said carefully. When he'd left a few hours earlier, the Doctor had been lying flat on his back, head buried under the central console, whistling softly to himself.

The Doctor stood in the centre of the mess and spread his arms wide. 'Not this time. I'm afraid we're stuck,' he said ruefully. 'The Time Rotor is damaged; I daren't take us back into the time stream with it in its present condition.'

Jamie stepped over a coil of cable, which writhed on the floor trying to follow him. The Doctor had once told him that these ships were not made but grown, and were actually sentient in their own way. 'Stuck. Now, when you say *stuck* . . .?'

'As in stuck. Unable to move. Trapped.' The Doctor's humour changed in an instant. 'Are you sure you couldn't find anything on my list?' he asked irritably.

'Nothing,' Jamie said. He carefully skirted round a wire honeycomb filled with tiny winking stones.

'Can't we buy the gold?' enquired the Doctor absent-mindedly.

Jamie pulled the handwritten list out of his sleeve and unfolded it. '*A ton of gold,*' he read. 'Doctor, unless we rob the Bank of England, we're never going to find a ton of gold. And, even if we bought it legally, it would cost a fortune. I checked this morning's *Financial Times*. Gold is priced at around thirty-seven American dollars an ounce. I don't know how many ounces there are in a ton . . .'

'Thirty-two thousand,' the Doctor said immediately.

Jamie tried to do the maths in his head and failed.

'One million, one hundred and eighty-four thousand dollars,' the Doctor said in exasperation. 'Didn't you learn anything in school?'

'I never went to school.'

'Oh.' The Doctor suddenly looked embarrassed. 'No, of course you didn't. Silly me.' He waved an arm vaguely in the direction of the roof. 'Money is not a problem. There's plenty upstairs in one of the bedrooms. And there's lots of jewellery we can sell. I've still got the pieces Tutankhamen gave me. I'll never wear them.' He nudged a spring with his foot. It bounced a metre into the air, pinged off a wall and danced around the room. 'Oh dear, oh dear.' He patted the gutted remains of the central console, then turned, leaned against it and slowly sank to the floor, legs stretched in front of him. 'There's only so much I can do for the old girl. I can put the bits back together, but if she's going to heal, she needs the equivalent of a blood transfusion: gold, mercury and Zeiton-7.'

'No one has even heard of Zeiton-7,' Jamie said, scanning the list again. He sat on the floor alongside the Doctor. 'Can't you . . .' He paused. 'I don't know . . . do something?'

'I'm a doctor, not a magician.' The Doctor looked around the control room and slowly shook his head. 'We're trapped in London, Jamie. We'll be forever stuck in this place and time,' he added softly. 'And there was so much I wanted to see and do, so much I wanted to show you.'

They sat in silence for a long time. Jamie shifted on the hard, uncomfortable floor and something dug into his side. He reached into his belt and his fingers touched the soft silk wrapping round the strange little book.

'I've got a present for you,' he said, suddenly remembering. 'Maybe it'll cheer you up.'

The Doctor looked up. 'I quite like presents.' He frowned. 'You know, no one has given me a present for a very long time. Well, not since my three-hundredth birthday, or was it my four-hundredth? What is it?' he asked.

'Well, I was given this as a reward for something I did this morning. It's a book and I know you like books. I was told it was very old.'

'A bit like me,' the Doctor said, smiling. 'Aged, like a fine wine . . .'

'Or a mouldy cheese,' Jamie murmured with a grin. 'Here, I'd like you to have it.' He slid the book out of the silk wrapping and handed it over. The leather felt slightly greasy and flesh-warm. The Doctor's long fingers closed round the scuffed black cover. Almost automatically, his thumbs began to trace the raised design. 'Interesting. What is that?' he wondered aloud, tilting the cover to the light. 'Looks like a type of cephalopod . . .'

'A seffle-a-what?'

'Octopus.' Resting the book on his knees, the Doctor opened it to the title page, the thick parchment crackling as it turned. 'I don't quite recognise the language,' he murmured, index finger tracing the individual letters. 'This looks like Sumerian, but this here is certainly one of the Vedic scripts, while this is Rongorongo from Easter Island. No, no, I'm wrong. This is older – much, much older. Where did you say you got it?' But before his companion could reply, the Doctor's index finger, which had been following the words in the centre of the title page, stopped, and he automatically read it aloud: '*The Necronomicon . . .*'

With a shriek of pure terror, the Doctor flung the book away from him.

'*The Necronomicon.*'

In a place abandoned by time, in the heart of an immeasurably tall black-glass pyramid, the words rang like a bell.

'*The Necronomicon.*'

The sound hung in the air, trembling, vibrating off the glass to create thin ethereal music.

Three sinuous shapes wrapped in long trails of ragged shadow rose from a silver pool to twist through the rarefied air, moving to the gossamer music. Two more pairs detached from the four cardinal points of the thick darkness and joined the intricate mid-air dance. The seven curled and wound round one another, folding and bending to form arcane and ornately beautiful patterns, before they finally settled into a perfect black circle. The tower's mirrored walls and floor made it look as if the darkness was alive with huge unblinking eyes.

'*The Necronomicon.*'

'Oh, Jamie, what have you done?' The Doctor's voice was shaking.

'I don't know . . . I mean, it's just a book.'

'Oh, this is more, much more, than a book.'

The Doctor and Jamie stared at the leather-bound volume on the floor. Caught in a tangle of wire and cogs, it was pulsating with a slow, steady rhythm.

'It's like a heartbeat,' Jamie whispered. 'Doctor, I don't . . . I mean, I just . . .' the young Scotsman said in confusion. He leaned forward. 'Do you want me to throw it out?'

The Doctor raised his hand. 'Don't touch it!' he snapped. 'If you value your life and your sanity, you'll not touch it again.' He opened and closed his right hand into a fist. The tips of his fingers where they had touched the book were bruised and blackened.

The book's cover suddenly strobed with dull red light and a tracery of thin lines flickered across it, briefly outlining the shape of a tentacled creature etched into the black leather. The heavy cover flew open and the thick pages lifted and flapped, blowing in an unfelt wind. It finally fell open at a page showing a black-and-grey illustration of narrow pyramids and towers. Abruptly, a series of tiny golden lights – like windows – appeared on the image. A spark leaped from the pages into the tangle of wires cradling it. A second spark – like a tiny yellow cinder – billowed up and hung in the air, before see-sawing into a spider's web of fine silver wire on the floor. The wire immediately twisted and trembled, pulsating red and black. A fountain of sparks then erupted from the book and scattered across the floor, bouncing like tiny sizzling beads. Wires quivered and shifted with a surge of power; cogs and wheels turned and spun of their own accord.

And then the control console coughed.

It was an almost human sound, a cross between a breathy sigh and a wheeze.

'Oh no, no, no, no, no, no . . .' The Doctor scrambled to his feet and reached for the lever in the centre of the console.

He pulled hard – and it came away in his hand. He looked at it blankly. 'Oh! Well, that's never happened before.'

The TARDIS breathed again: a rasping gasp.

The Necronomicon had now turned into a sizzling rectangle of sparks and the usually dry, slightly musty air of the TARDIS became foul with the stink of rotting fish.

'What's happening, Doctor?' Jamie asked. He watched, wide-eyed, as the mess of wires, cogs, wheels and dismantled instruments was drawn back towards the central console, as if pulled by a magnetic force. He scrambled out of the way as a cable was sucked back under the desk, writhing like a snake. 'Doctor?' Jamie shouted.

But the Doctor was incapable of speech. The air was full of components, winging their way to the control unit. He danced out of the way as a thick tube of metal whipped towards him, plunging deep into the interior of the console. Black smoke filled the room.

'I think we're OK,' the Doctor said, as the incredible movement died down. He grinned and shook his head. 'For a moment there, I thought we were going to take off,' he added shakily, 'but there's no power, there's no way we can –'

The TARDIS lights flickered, dimmed and then blazed. And the ship wheezed again. A dry, rasping intake of breath, then a sighing exhalation. And again, faster this time. Then – a familiar, unmistakable sound. The TARDIS was taking off.

'Impossible!' the Doctor shouted.

'I thought you said we were trapped?'

The Doctor waved his hands at the remaining knot of wires on the floor. 'We are. We shouldn't be able to go anywhere. We shouldn't be able to move!'

The main lights dimmed and all the dials on the console lit up with a strange, sickly green glow. The faintest vibration hummed through the floor.

Jamie felt a shifting in his inner ear and then sudden pressure in his stomach. 'We're moving,' he said.

'And fast too.' The Doctor rested his fingertips against the metal, feeling it shiver. 'Very fast. I wonder where we're going?' He looked down at the book on the floor. The sparks had died away and the book had snapped shut. The black cover was leaking gossamer-grey smoke. The edges of the white paper were burned black, but the book seemed to have suffered no other damage. He made no move to touch it. 'Where did you get the book, Jamie?'

'I tried to tell you. I rescued an old man who was being robbed. Well, maybe he wasn't that old. He gave me this book as a reward. I did tell him I would not be able to read it . . .'

'. . . and so he told you to give it to someone as a present.' Jamie nodded. 'It was meant for you, wasn't it?'

'It was.'

'Have you any idea who it was?'

The Doctor shrugged. 'When you've lived as long as I have, then you make the odd enemy or two.' He nodded towards the book. 'Though not that many who would be this powerful. However, there is one who was always fascinated by this terrible book . . .' A thin thread of pain crept into the Doctor's voice. 'I've not seen him in a long time. The Necronomicon is the Book of Dead Names. It is a collection of dark and terrible lore. And it is . . . old.'

'Even older than you?' Jamie asked with a shaky laugh.

'Older than the Earth. Even older than my homeworld.

Older than most solar systems. It was written by one of the races who ruled the galaxy in the very distant past. This is the sum total of their knowledge and speaks of the Time before Time.'

'And this race,' Jamie said quietly, 'I'm guessing they are not your friends?'

'Oh, they are long dead. They exist only in the memories of a half-dozen scattered worlds, where they are still worshipped as gods. I've come up against their worshippers, though,' he added softly. 'They didn't like me very much.'

'Have you any idea where we're going?'

'None.' The Doctor knelt and peered at the smouldering book, his nostrils flaring. 'It stinks of old power and foul secrets.' Then he sat back, dusting off his hands. 'I'm reluctant to lay my hands on it again. My touch obviously activated it.'

'I was able to handle it.'

'But you're just a human. Tell me,' he said, 'when you were given the book, was it wrapped in a cloth?'

Jamie reached into his belt and sheepishly held out the square of black silk.

The Doctor leaned forward until his nose almost touched the material. He breathed deeply and his eyes closed. 'Ah, now there's a familiar scent. This old man: tall, dark eyes, goatee beard touched with grey, black gloves.'

'Yes, that's him. And gloves, yes, he had gloves. He said his name was Professor Tas– Tascal?'

'Thascalos,' the Doctor whispered.

'That's it. Who is it?'

'Someone I've not encountered in a long time. But at least we now know where this is taking us,' the Doctor said grimly.

'Where?'

The Doctor focused on gingerly wrapping the black silk cloth round the smoking book. 'Why, to our doom, Jamie. To our doom.'

And the book pulsed in time with his words.

3

'It feels like we've been travelling for days,' Jamie grumbled.

'Eight hours as you measure time,' the Doctor said absently. He was staring intently at a small globe that looked like an oversized light bulb as he carefully twisted two wires – silver and gold – round its base.

'I thought the TARDIS could move instantly into any place or time.'

'It can, and usually it does,' the Doctor grunted.

'So what's taking it so long?'

'During our time together, we've never travelled this far before.' The globe flickered, faded, then blinked alight. 'Ah, success! You do know I am a genius?'

'So you keep telling me,' Jamie muttered.

The globe was now glowing with a pale-blue light. The Doctor stared intently at it, turning it slowly with his fingers. 'I've managed to connect this to the exterior time and space sensors. Now, let us see . . .'

The globe turned black for an instant and then was suddenly speckled with silver dots. A long misty white streak appeared across its centre.

The Doctor gasped in horror. 'Oh my giddy aunt. Oh crumbs.'

'What is it? What do you see?' Jamie demanded, peering at the image.

'This! *This!*' The Doctor pointed to the globe.

Jamie stared and then shrugged.

'The dots are stars . . .' the Doctor said in exasperation.

'And the white streak across the middle –' Jamie began, but almost immediately knew the answer to the question. 'That's the Milky Way.'

'It is.'

'It seems very far away.'

'That's because it is.'

As they were speaking, the long cloud of the distant Milky Way faded and vanished into the blackness of space. Then, one by one, the stars winked out until nothing remained but complete darkness.

'Has it stopped working?' Jamie asked.

'No,' the Doctor said glumly. 'It's still working.'

'But what happened to all the stars?'

'They've gone. We're heading to the edge of space.'

A sudden explosion shocked Jamie awake and he realised he'd fallen into an exhausted sleep in a nest of wires. The interior of the TARDIS was filled with noxious white smoke. Coughing, he scrambled to his feet as another detonation ripped a panel off the ceiling. As it came loose, it dangled on a long curl of transparent tubes. The Doctor was lying on his back under the central console, and Jamie could hear the distinctive whirr of what the Doctor called his sonic screwdriver. Jamie wasn't entirely sure what it did, but he was sure it was definitely not a screwdriver.

Suddenly all the dials on the console lit up with cold blue-green light and began to spin and dance.

'Are you doing that?' Jamie asked.

'Doing what?' The Doctor's voice was muffled and distorted. Jamie guessed he was holding the sonic screwdriver between his teeth.

A shower of multicoloured sparks skittered across the surface of the console. Two of the dials bubbled and melted. 'Setting the control panel on fire?' Jamie shouted, darting away.

The Doctor pushed out from under the console and scrambled to his feet. Hopping from one foot to the other, he waved his hands at the blue-green flames now licking up through the panels. Jamie reappeared with a red fat-bodied fire extinguisher, which bore the words *Property of London Underground* stencilled on the side.

'No . . .' the Doctor squeaked.

'Yes.' Pointing the nozzle at the flames, Jamie pressed the lever and doused the control panel in water. A huge gout of flame shot up to the ceiling, where it was swallowed in thick white steam. When the smoke finally cleared, the central panel was a blackened mess.

'Now look what you've done,' the Doctor said accusingly. 'You've ruined it!'

'Ruined it? I didn't start the fire –'

The Doctor suddenly held up his hand and turned away. 'Do you hear that?' he asked in a hushed whisper.

'I can't hear anything,' Jamie said, looking around.

'Exactly.' The Doctor spun back to Jamie. 'We've landed,' he said grimly.

4

'It looks like every other barren rocky planet we've landed on,' Jamie murmured. He peered round the edge of the TARDIS's door, a breathing mask pressed to his face.

The Doctor brushed past him and strode out on to black sand. It billowed up around him.

'Hey, how do you know it's safe to breathe?' Jamie's voice was muffled behind the mask.

'I don't. But I'll wager we've not been brought all the way out here to suffocate.' Putting his hands on his hips, the Doctor craned his neck back and looked up into the night sky.

Jamie pulled away the mask and breathed in quickly. The air was dry and bitter, tasting vaguely of rotten eggs.

'Sulphur,' the Doctor said, answering the question the Scotsman was about to ask.

'I hate it when you do that,' Jamie muttered. Standing beside the Doctor, he looked up into the night as well. There were very few stars visible and they were little more than distant specks. Rising low on the horizon was a thin vertical strip of gauzy stars. 'That's the Milky Way,' he said in awe. 'But it's wrong,' he added, tilting his head to one side. 'The Milky Way does not look like that.'

'It seems we have travelled very far indeed,' the Doctor said, looking about them. He wrapped his arms round his body and a shiver ran through him. 'We're at the edge of known space, in that place known as the Great Desolation.'

'And I'm guessing this is one of those places no one ever returns from?' Jamie asked.

'No one,' the Doctor replied. 'This is the place where myths go to die.'

Deep in the silent heart of a black-glass pyramid a sound reverberated off the sloping walls.

Slow and sonorous, the noise washed across the circular silver pool set into the floor and the fluid within trembled. A series of thick concentric circles spread out across its surface and then a shape appeared, rising up into the blackness. Hooded and wrapped in dripping grey robes, it was joined by a second and a third, and then the liquid boiled as four more rose from beneath the silver. In a ragged V formation, the seven tall shapes turned to face the pyramid's only door.

The noise boomed out again, growing and intensifying until it became identifiable: the sound of laughter – insane and malevolent laughter.

'Is this planet inhabited?' Jamie asked.

The Doctor was lying prone on the ground, staring intently at the black sand through a huge magnifying glass. 'Remarkable.' He looked up. 'Inhabited? Once, perhaps, but not now. This world is ancient beyond reckoning.' He patted the ground and a cloud of fine black particles rose to envelop his head. 'This sand has the consistency of talcum powder,' he said, coughing. 'Some of it is already dust. Why do you ask?'

Crouched on the brow of a low hill, Jamie pointed. 'Well, unless I am very much mistaken, I'm looking at a city.'

The Doctor scrambled to his feet and dusted himself down. 'Nonsense, this place has been uninhabited for aeons,' he began. 'Probably just an oddly shaped mountain range. Oh! That's a city.'

Jamie bit his lip and said nothing.

The Doctor dug into an inner pocket, pulled out a long brass telescope and focused. 'It's a city,' he repeated.

'Why is it so shiny?'

'It's made of black glass.' The Doctor handed over the telescope.

Jamie pressed the instrument to his eye. The distant cityscape shifted into sharp focus: a vast metropolis of towering ebony-glass buildings razor-etched against the starless sky, each one outlined and traced with threads of gold. They were all tall and slender, triangular and pointed, some bent into odd, irregular angles. He couldn't see any windows. The young Scotsman pulled the telescope away from his face as the image shifted and blurred. He blinked hard, eyes watering. 'It's difficult to look at.'

The Doctor nodded. 'It was built by creatures who did not live completely in this dimension.'

'You've seen it before.'

'No. I doubt there is a single creature alive today who has seen this place. My people told stories of it. This is the Nameless City: the home of the Archons.'

'Friends . . .?' Jamie suggested hopefully.

'The enemies of every living thing.' The Doctor took the telescope and put it to his eye again. 'I cannot see any signs of life,' he murmured. He tapped the telescope against his bottom lip. 'I seem to remember something about the Nameless City.' He shook his head. 'It is a curse having a memory like mine: to have seen so much and not remember all of it.'

'Would there be something about it in the TARDIS's library?' Jamie asked.

'Ah! The library. Genius, Jamie, just genius. If I can activate the TARDIS's archive, it is sure to have something about the Nameless City.' He passed the telescope to Jamie before turning and darting back into the ship.

Jamie was about to follow when he spotted movement in the distance: a swirl of black cloud heading out from the city. 'Doctor, I think we may be about to have company.' He trained the telescope on the fast-approaching cloud, but could only make out vague shapes in the gloom. None of which looked human.

The Scotsman slapped his hand against the side of the TARDIS and stuck his head through the open door. 'Doctor, something's coming. We need to go now!'

The Doctor was hunched over the console, desperately weaving a handful of wires together. 'Give me a minute. I just need to push a little power into the library. There's something at the back of my mind about the Nameless City.'

'We don't have a minute.'

Jamie looked over his shoulder. The cloud was closer, and he caught a dull reflective flash – weapons!

'Now, Doctor. Now!' he cried, rushing into the TARDIS.

'*The . . . Name . . . less . . . City.*' Low and rasping, the sudden sound sent both the Doctor and Jamie scrambling backwards. The drawn-out syllables echoed off the interior of the TARDIS.

'*The Nameless City.*'

The Doctor attempted a shaky laugh. 'Why, it quite startled me. The TARDIS's voice is usually female.' He twisted a wire from the bundle on the burnt-out console, pulled his sonic screwdriver out of a pocket and focused it on the wires. The screwdriver hummed and there was a sudden stink of burning rubber and molten metal.

'*The Nameless City.*'

The voice started low and slow, and then speeded up to become sweet and unmistakably female.

'*Home to the Archons –*'

'Stop,' the Doctor commanded. 'We don't need a history of the Archons. Why is the Nameless City so important? Why does it stick in my memory?'

With a glance at the door, Jamie moved over to where the Doctor was standing.

The female voice continued. '*The only description of the Nameless City occurs in the Necronomicon, the Book of Dead Names. Harnessing the Music of the Spheres, the Archons raised their city over a pool of gold, surrounded by canals of mercury and Zeiton-7.*'

The Doctor's fingers bit into Jamie's arm. 'That's it. That's our ticket home!'

'How?'

'The TARDIS is not a machine,' the Doctor said. 'These old TT Type-40 Mark-III machines are organic; they were grown, not made. If we can get the old girl to the city, we can treat her with the gold, mercury and Zeiton-7. Then the self-repairing mechanism will take over.' He clapped his hands. 'She'll be as good as new.' He looked up at the black monitor. 'What is the location of the Archon world?'

'*The Archon homeworld is on the Prohibited List. Data has been struck from the records.*'

'Why?' Jamie wondered aloud.

'Now that, my young Scottish friend, is the question.' The Doctor nodded towards the door. 'Go and see how close our friends are.'

Jamie hurried outside. And ran straight into a huge black shape.

'Doctor –'

Jamie's cry of warning was cut off as a massive three-fingered claw gripped his sweater and jerked him forward and up. Suddenly he was cartwheeling through the air. He caught an upside-down glimpse of dozens of huge black metallic ape-like creatures converging on the TARDIS before he hit the ground hard in a billowing explosion of powdery sand.

'*The Nameless City . . . The Nameless City . . . The Nameless City . . .*'

'Yes, yes, yes, I know.' The Doctor pulled apart the wires and the ship's voice crackled and faded.

A metallic thump echoed against the ship.

Then another, and another.

Something was hammering on the outside of the craft.

When Jamie had been dragged outside, the Doctor's first instincts were to go to his aid, but he knew he would be of little help and it would leave the interior of the TARDIS open and exposed. Throwing himself on the ruined console, he'd pushed the manual lever and the door had shuddered and then squealed shut. 'I'm sorry, Jamie. But I think you will be safer out there than in here.'

The Doctor was beginning to formulate the theory that someone like Jamie – a human – would be of no interest to the creatures, who had obviously gone to a lot of trouble to bring him and the TARDIS to this long-forgotten place. He nudged the Necronomicon with his toe. None of this was accidental.

Snatching a length of wire from the mess on the floor, he wrapped it round his sonic screwdriver and then pushed the other end of the wire into the monitor. An image formed, dissolved into snow, then slowly re-formed to show the exterior of the TARDIS.

'Oh crumbs.'

The TARDIS was surrounded by what he first assumed were black metal robots. There were dozens of them, shifting and moving around the craft, three-fingered claws scraping the blue surface. Measuring them against the outside of the TARDIS, he calculated that they were at least two metres tall. They had two squat legs and four arms: these were creatures that could stand on two legs and run on six. Despite their size and bulk, they would be fast. Their heads were smooth featureless domes with a single long, glowing red oval where the eyes should be. They had no mouths. As they moved, the Doctor saw that they were semi-transparent. Then he realised that they were not made of metal: these were creatures of glass.

The TARDIS lurched, sending the Doctor crashing to the floor. The last image he saw before the monitor's picture dissolved into static fuzz was of the huge creatures toppling the ship on to its side and hoisting it on to their backs.

'Well, I did want to get to the Nameless City,' the Doctor said, sliding across the floor and ending up in a heap against the wall. Turning his head to one side, he saw the Necronomicon caught like a fly, in a spider's web of wire. Pulling a crumpled spotted hankie from his pocket, he wrapped it round his right hand and reached for the ancient book. He wondered what else it could tell him about the Archons and the Nameless City.

When Jamie awoke he had no idea how much time had passed – it could have been minutes, it could have been hours. Rolling over, he hauled himself slowly to his feet, biting back a groan. He'd banged his elbow and the fingers of his left hand were still numb. The entire left side of his body was going to be one enormous bruise, he decided, probably the same colour as the black sand. He looked around: the creature had flung him into an almost circular crater. A thick layer of soft powdery sand at the bottom had saved him from serious injury.

The Doctor!

With a little difficulty, Jamie scrambled up out of the crater, the fine dust swirling around him, getting in his eyes and nose, and coating his tongue. Once he reached the lip of the crater, he saw the Nameless City ahead in the distance, which meant that the TARDIS should be right behind him.

He spun round.

The TARDIS was missing.

His gaze followed a mess of tracks in the dust . . . and there, now a long way off, was a billowing cloud of dust heading towards the city.

'Oh, Doctor . . .' Jamie sighed, and set off after the cloud.

The black-glass apes carried the TARDIS towards the city on their backs. Inside the ship, the Doctor had precariously balanced a stepladder on the ruined console. He was standing on top of a wooden stool, which he'd wedged into the top rungs of the ladder. The contraption brought him close to the door, which was now directly above his head. Slowly and carefully, he ran the sonic screwdriver round one of the circular wall panels. It dropped to the floor, bouncing like a ball. The Doctor grinned; the roundels were practically indestructible. Directly in front of him were the square windows set into the TARDIS's outer door. He carefully undid the hermetic seal and peeled off the glass-like membrane. Shoving the film into his deep pockets, he popped his head out of the opening and looked around.

He was within the walls of the Nameless City.

The Doctor's eyes immediately started to water. The angles, shapes and perspectives of the buildings were *wrong* and almost painful to look at, while the gold-trimmed black-glass pyramids reflected one another in endlessly dizzying iterations.

Blinking hard, trying to focus, the Doctor turned to face the direction the TARDIS was being carried.

Directly ahead of him, in the centre of a vast square, was a towering gate: two massive black-glass pillars rising hundreds of metres into the dark sky supported a golden lintel that was easily two hundred metres across.

'A Time Henge,' the Doctor murmured in awe. He had come across these ancient gates scattered across hundreds of worlds, including Earth. Millennia past, the Time Lords had rendered them inert and useless, but, once, they would have been used to transport people and goods between fixed places in space and time.

The Doctor looked around. Glass apes poured out of the nearby twisted alleyways and irregular streets. There must have been thousands – tens of thousands – of them. They ebbed and flowed round the TARDIS, reaching up to touch it as it was carried aloft towards the largest building in the centre of the Nameless City: an impossibly tall windowless triangle of shimmering, gold-etched ebony glass.

'Like a trophy, or a relic,' the Doctor murmured. As he watched, a vertical seam split the glass triangle and an opening appeared at the top of a series of uneven steps. The doorway was a series of ragged lines, tilted at an angle. Beyond the doorway, there was nothing but thick impenetrable darkness.

The Doctor gingerly climbed down off the stool and ladder. The TARDIS tilted, sending him staggering left and right, then forward. 'Looks like we're heading up the steps.'

Replacing the window membrane or the roundel in the wall was clearly impossible, so, wrapping his hankie round his hand again, he slumped to the ground and lifted the Necronomicon off the floor. The book fell open to the illustration of the Nameless City. Focusing on the text, the

Doctor began laboriously translating the arcane languages. Almost unconsciously, he started to whistle.

Jamie discovered that the gravity on this ancient planet was a little bit less than Earth's. He ran in long loping strides, covering a lot of ground quickly, racing towards the Nameless City, which grew out of the desert floor in jagged, irregular blades. He could still just about make out the billowing cloud of dust . . . and then it suddenly disappeared.

They had gone into the city.

'Doctor, you will be the death of me yet,' he muttered. He crouched, then took off at a flat run and launched himself into the air in a soaring jump. He had to get to the Doctor; he would never forgive himself if anything happened to him. And he was also keenly aware that this was all his fault. He should never have taken the book; the Doctor had warned him countless times about talking to strangers.

Jamie's relationship with the strange little man was complicated. The Doctor had saved his life on more than one occasion, and he'd repaid the compliment by saving the Doctor's life in return. In their time together, Jamie had come to accept the Doctor as his laird, and as a clansman he owed undying loyalty to his chieftain. Jamie knew the Doctor was not human: he didn't know exactly *what* he was, though when he was growing up, he had heard tales of the legendary fairy creatures of the Unseelie Court who haunted Scotland's deepest valleys. He suspected the Doctor might be one of the dark Sith. He also knew that humans rarely came away from their adventures with the fairy folk unscathed.

★

Silence.

The TARDIS had been righted and the Doctor had slid off the wall into a tangle of wire and metal. He'd crouched on the floor for a long time, listening intently, but hearing nothing. He finally stood up and peered through the empty square in the door where he'd pulled out the glass-like membrane. It took his eyes a few moments to adjust to the gloom. He saw another TARDIS and then a second and a third; he was surrounded by hundreds of blue police boxes.

Reflections.

He was looking at reflections.

The Doctor was within the enormous black-glass pyramid, and the mirrored walls reflected and distorted everything around him. He could see the massed ranks of thousands of crystal apes standing still, their 'eyes' now just dark panels. Almost directly in front of him, a few metres away, a huge triangle was traced in gold on the floor, and at its centre was a gold-encircled pool of shimmering silver liquid. Lifting his right hand, the Doctor pointed his sonic screwdriver at the pool, thumbed the button, then examined the result. Just as he suspected: mercury.

He cracked open the door and popped his head out, looking quickly left and right. There was no movement. He breathed deeply: the air smelled stale and sour, but with a definite tang of dead fish.

The Doctor squeezed out of the half-open door, ducked through the ranks of unmoving crystal apes and crouched at the edge of the mercury pool. He stared at its metallic surface and then looked back at his poor damaged craft. He needed to get the TARDIS into the pool. The Doctor wrapped his arms tightly round his chest and rocked to and fro: if only he could take control of the apes, he could get them to carry the damaged craft . . .

A droplet of mercury, a metal bead the size of his thumb, popped up on the surface of the pool. It vibrated and then floated upwards.

Another appeared. It drifted up into the air.

And another.

A shimmering thread of music hung in the air, a single humming sound.

Suddenly, long strings of metal streamed up towards the unseen roof and slowly, slowly, slowly a head appeared out of the silver. A second head emerged, a third, then four more.

'Archons,' the Doctor breathed in amazement.

With a swirl of sound, the seven figures rose from the mercury.

5

The Nameless City was empty.

Jamie raced through the streets, his reflection rippling off the glass walls. He was looking for any signs of movement, any clue as to where the Doctor had been taken. But the city seemed deserted.

He ran into a vast square and stopped before a huge black-and-gold gateway. He looked around; all the streets of the city converged on this point. And they all led to one building.

Directly in front of him rose the tallest of the black-glass pyramids. It was the only one with a door – and it was open. Without a moment's hesitation, Jamie raced towards it. It was at times like these when he wished he had his claymore, though he wasn't exactly sure what the great Scottish sword could do against glass apes.

The Doctor watched in horror as the rulers of the glass city appeared out of the mercury in a swirl of ethereal music.

In his long life the Doctor had seen creatures both monstrous and hideous, but nothing like these. The stink of stagnant water and rotting fish filled his nostrils. Each creature was wrapped in long, trailing rags, which concealed most of their flesh, but he caught hints of their true appearance as they floated up into the air. One, bigger than the rest, resembled an octopus, with twisting, writhing limbs, while a second had an eel's sloping head peering from within its hood. Another had a suggestion of a crab claw half hidden in its sleeve, and everywhere he caught glimpses of barbed squid suckers and albino flesh.

'You are the Gallifreyan. We will not honour you with your title.' The words were liquid and sticky. The Doctor could not be sure which creature spoke.

Hanging in mid-air, rags blowing in a foul breeze, the seven creatures began to move in a beautiful, intricate dance. Circling one another and undulating in time to the shimmering music, they crawled all over each other in a writhing mass – tentacles sliding over claws, fins interlocking with suckers – until they finally all slotted together, fitting into place to form one huge entity. A tentacled, beaked and clawed monstrosity. The Doctor stared at it in awe; it was simultaneously hideous and mesmerisingly beautiful.

'Once we were many, now we are all that remain. We are seven; we are one. We are the Archons.'

The Doctor backed slowly away from the pool. He needed to get to his ship. If he could just get inside . . .

An enormous milk-white eye at the centre of the grotesque being glared at the Time Lord. Beneath the eye, a beak – ringed with waving tentacles – opened and closed. The head dipped forward and the huge black pupil dilated until the Doctor felt he was looking into a bottomless pit.

'We've waited a long time for you.' The voice was fluid and gurgling and full of menace. 'And the TARDIS. Our TARDIS.'

Made dizzy and nauseous by the bizarre angles, Jamie stepped through the doorway and looked down into the heart of the pyramid. It took his eyes a few moments to adjust and when they did he took a quick step backwards. The pyramid was filled with the huge semi-transparent six-legged apes. There were thousands of them, maybe more, but it was hard to be sure with the confusion of never-ending lines and reflections. They were standing immobile in long irregular ranks facing the centre of the pyramid where the tiny figure of the Doctor crouched before a silver pool.

Jamie's breath caught in his throat: floating in the air over the pool was a monstrous squirming nightmare waving octopus tentacles in the Doctor's face.

Jamie knew he had to get down there. He stepped up to the nearest ape and poked it gently with his finger. The glass was smooth and cool to his touch, but the creature didn't react. Growing bolder, Jamie stepped up and waved his hand in front of the ape's face. There was no response.

'You're not so scary,' he said with a grin. Dropping flat on the ground, he began to crawl and slither between the apes' legs across the smooth floor towards the Doctor.

'*Your* TARDIS?' the Doctor snapped, rising to his full height. 'I think not.'

'We created TARDIS technology.' The sticky, bubbling voice crackled and long strings of liquid dripped from its beaked mouth. Music swirled around the creature. 'The original TARDIS seeds were created by Archon science-mages.'

The Doctor shook his head. 'I think not,' he repeated. 'The secret of Time Travel was created by my people.'

'And your people stole those seeds from us. The Time Lords cloned them and grew their own ships. And then, in order to keep the mystery of time to themselves, your race declared war on us.' The music rose and fell as the Archon spoke. 'They abandoned us here and left us to rot.'

The Doctor continued to shake his head, but without his previous conviction. The early history of Gallifrey and the Time Lords was shrouded in mystery.

The Archon leaned down, tentacles and claws waving in the Doctor's face, spattering his cheeks with rancid mercury. 'Do you know what it is like to spend an eternity in isolation? Have you any concept of the loneliness of millennia of solitude?'

The Doctor nodded. 'I have known loneliness,' he said quietly.

'We are the last of the Archons. Trapped here in the Great Desolation, we have watched our people die. But they will not have died in vain if we can avenge them.'

The Doctor started to back away from the edge of the pool. If he turned and ran, could he make it to his ship?

'Do you know what we have needed all these millennia?'

The Doctor shook his head, though he already had a good idea of the answer.

'A TARDIS,' the Archon continued. 'And, just when we had despaired, one of your kind appeared before us. He made us an offer. He was not foolish enough to land. Orbiting the planet, he told us of a damaged TARDIS, a craft without a Time Rotor, blind and defenceless. And he could bring it here.'

'No doubt you paid him well.'

'When the Archons return in fury and vengeance, we will make good our promises to him. He will rule galaxies.' The creature's tentacles waved, suckers opening and closing like tiny barbed mouths. 'He must hate you very much.'

'He does.'

The Archon drifted out over the heads of the crystal apes and hovered above the TARDIS. Dozens of hooked tentacles dangled from beneath its ragged grey robes. They wrapped round the battered craft and lifted it effortlessly into the air.

The Doctor watched in amazement as the Archon brought the TARDIS back to the mercury pool and then slowly, almost delicately, lowered it into the silvery metal liquid.

'The time of the Archons has come again,' the huge creature announced. 'The TARDIS is the key to our escape. Once the ship is repaired, we will fuse it into the Time Henge and activate the gate. All the galaxies and all the time streams will be ours to command. We will lead our army back through time to Gallifrey, back when it was still a fledgling world, and we will turn it into a barren rock. When we are finished, your race will never have existed.'

'You cannot –' the Doctor began.

'We will.'

'If Gallifrey falls and if the Time Lords do not police and protect the time streams, then the history of many galaxies and times will be altered. Countless millions of worlds will die,' the Doctor said desperately.

A shudder ran through the Archon and the creature seemed on the point of splitting apart. 'We will rebuild the Archon empire.'

The Doctor watched as the mercury pool shrank. The ship absorbed the liquid metal, draining the pool and soaking it up like a sponge. He saw it leach colour from the gold perimeter, turning it to grey stone. One by one, the scrapes and scars on the blue surface of the TARDIS faded and vanished.

With the falling level of mercury, the Archon was forced to dip lower to keep the TARDIS submerged in the liquid.

The Doctor edged closer to the pool and peered down. He could see the distinctive green glow of Zeiton-7 on the floor of the pool. Gold, mercury and Zeiton-7: all the nutrients necessary to revive the ailing TARDIS. The ship already looked sleek and gleaming: 'well fed' was the phrase that came to the Doctor's mind.

He caught a flicker of movement in the corner of his eye and glanced sidelong to see Jamie crawl out from between the legs of the crystal apes. The Doctor turned his back on the Archon.

'And what will you do with me?' he asked.

The rippling laughter was disgusting. 'Why, Doctor, we will eat you. You will be a tasty snack.'

'I'll give you indigestion,' he snapped. 'And what will you do with this new Archon empire?' he continued, his voice rising and echoing slightly. Looking directly at Jamie, he mouthed, *Get ready*. He held up his hand, five fingers spread open, then folded down his thumb: four . . . three . . .

The beautiful music rose to a crescendo and the creature rippled in its intricate dance. 'We will rule again. It is our destiny. We are the Archons.'

Still with his back to the creature, the Doctor pulled out his recorder, put it to his lips and played the first few bars of 'The Skye Boat Song'.

The TARDIS doors hummed open.

'Now, Jamie! Now!' The Doctor flung himself forward and leaped through the open door of the craft dangling over the now empty pool. A huge suckered tentacle instantly wrapped round his leg, pulling him back. Jamie sprang on top of the squirming tentacle. He ripped the Doctor's leg free, just as the TARDIS door slammed shut, slicing the writhing limb in two. Leaking green gore, the dismembered appendage flapped helplessly on the metal floor of the TARDIS like a fat green worm.

'Och, man, that's disgusting!' Jamie muttered.

The interior of the craft was pristine and the Doctor scrambled to the gleaming central console. 'Oh, it is good to have you back, old girl,' he murmured, pushing two levers and bringing the ship to roaring life. The TARDIS growled and tore free of the Archon, soaring into the air. It floated in the centre of the pyramid, swirling round the creature.

'Everything is new again.' The Doctor danced from foot to foot.

All the monitors lit up, showing the Archon splitting up into seven separate parts, each creature attaching itself to the blue box, claws and tentacles snatching and holding on. The ship lurched and sank down.

Jamie looked knowingly at the Doctor. 'You have a plan,' he said.

'Is that a question or a statement?' the Doctor asked.

'A statement.' Jamie grinned. 'You always have a plan.'

'Get your bagpipes, Jamie. It's been a while since you played them.'

'My pipes?'

'Your pipes.'

Without another word, Jamie hurried away.

'You are trapped here, Gallifreyan,' the Archons boomed, seven voices speaking in unison. 'There is no escape.'

The Doctor hit a lever on the console and then flopped cross-legged on the floor. 'I have no intention of escaping.' Magnified, his voice echoed and re-echoed throughout the glass building.

Jamie reappeared, settling his bagpipes under his arm. 'What'll I play?' he asked.

'Something loud. Maybe a *ceol mor*?'

'You once told me a *ceol mor* sounded like fingernails being pulled down a blackboard.'

'Exactly.' The Doctor grinned. 'Play, Jamie.'

Settling the bag under his arm, and slipping the mouthpiece between his lips, Jamie started to blow and pump the bag.

'Make it loud, Jamie,' the Doctor said, pulling out his recorder. 'I think I'll join you.'

The sound was indescribable.

Shrill, high-pitched and screeching, it bounced warbling distortions around the interior of the pyramid, completely swamping the fragile delicate music that the Archons moved to.

Hissing and spitting, the creatures fell away from the spinning TARDIS.

The sounds rose higher and higher to an incredible crescendo. The new music caught the Archons, sending them twisting in a frenzy, crashing into the glass walls and blindly bouncing off one another. They tried to reunite into the one enormous creature, but the distorted wailing of the bagpipes curled their shapes into ragged ugly spirals.

The Archons threw themselves on the TARDIS again, claws and beaks tearing at the exterior, tentacles trying to prise the door open.

'Try "Scotland the Brave",' the Doctor suggested. His hands danced across the console as Jamie played, altering the output, subsonics and high harmonics screeching out through the ship's hidden speakers and sending the Archons into a paroxysm of ugly random movement. One, a thickly shelled clawed crustacean, smashed blindly into the side of the pyramid, and a frost-white crack spider-webbed along the black surface.

'Louder, Jamie!' the Doctor called. 'These creatures have spent an eternity dancing to the Music of the Spheres. Let them dance to a new tune.'

A howl of feedback sent two of the Archons soaring high into the glass pyramid, smashing them against its apex. Another crack appeared and, even above the caterwauling bagpipes, the sound was like a thunderclap. It was followed by a second and a third. And then a huge slab of glass sheared away. It smashed into the two Archons and drove them down to the floor in a tangle of ugly fins and razor teeth. Massive shards of glass fell with the Archons on to hundreds of apes, cutting a swathe through their massed ranks and reducing them to powder.

The entire building started to tremble. A network of cracks radiated across the surface, creeping out into the adjoining buildings. The surviving Archons darted away from the TARDIS and desperately tried to escape, but it was too late: the pyramid suddenly exploded in a detonation of glass. A deadly rain of enormous razor shards fell, completely burying the hideous creatures and pulverising the crystal apes. The explosion rippled out through the Nameless City, setting up a chain reaction as buildings toppled on to one another.

The TARDIS spun up through the opening in the shattered roof, and the Doctor and Jamie watched in silence as the entire city shattered and crumbled into black dust. Soon, only the glass-and-gold Time Henge remained, standing tall amid the ruins.

The Doctor put his recorder to his lips and whistled a single screeching note. Fractures radiated along the length of the henge's black supports. They snapped like cracking ice and the golden cross-beam fell and splintered into a dozen massive pieces.

The Doctor spread his arms out across the restored console, pressing his cheek against the warm metal. 'I was worried about you for a while,' he whispered.

'It worries me when you talk to the ship,' Jamie said.

'Sssh, you'll hurt her feelings.'

'How did you know how to defeat the Archons?' Jamie asked.

With his foot, the Doctor nudged the Necronomicon lying on the floor. 'The book they sent to destroy us proved to be their undoing. It tells of their origins. The Archons have their roots in the oceans of long-dead worlds. They were once deep-sea dwellers, living in vast undersea kingdoms where they would have hunted and communicated by sonar. You saw them dance in the air, moving to the beautiful music created by the faintest ghost winds blowing across the sharp edges of the city. You just gave them something else to dance to, something to disorientate and confuse them. They'd never heard the bagpipes before. And, of course, I tweaked the sound. It must have been agony for them.'

Jamie started to nod and then stopped. 'Hey! Are you saying my music's not beautiful?'

'Dear boy, it helped us escape, didn't it? That makes it the most beautiful music in the world.'

'What about the professor who gave me the book?' Jamie asked. 'What do we do about him?'

'Nothing. We'll not chase trouble, Jamie. And we'll meet him again,' the Doctor said. 'Sooner or later, he'll turn up. He usually does,' he added, twisting the recorder in his fingers. 'Come on now – let's play!'

Spinning in the light of a thousand suns, blue and now sparkling new, the TARDIS flew back towards the Milky Way, leaving the faintest trail of 'Scotland the Brave' in its wake.

THE THIRD DOCTOR:
THE SPEAR OF DESTINY

MARCUS SEDGWICK

1

'You're being very mysterious, Doctor.'

The Doctor raised an eyebrow.

'Let me rephrase that,' said Jo, stabbing his shoulder with her forefinger. 'More mysterious than usual.'

The Doctor grappled with the gear-lever of Bessie, the bright-yellow vintage roadster he was so fond of driving. He frowned. The gearbox answered with the sound of cogs trying to eat each other, but soon lost the fight as the Doctor moved up into third. He smiled, looking ahead along the bustling street of Piccadilly. It was a warm day and the hood of the car was down. A few people stared and pointed at them as they trundled past.

Jo sank a bit further back into her seat as the Doctor waved at a couple of passers-by.

'You know what I love about London?' he said, turning to her briefly.

She sighed. 'I'm sure I can't guess.'

'It's the only city in the universe where you can drive around in a car that's seventy years old and get away with it.'

'Who says you're getting away with it?' muttered Jo.

The Doctor waved again, and Jo shut her eyes. 'We couldn't have taken the Tube, I suppose?'

'Now come on, my dear. Where's your sense of style?'

Jo stared, open-mouthed, at the Doctor.

The Doctor was dressed in a green velour smoking jacket over a purple frilly shirt, the collar of which was large enough to sail a small yacht. It was eye-watering fashion, even for 1973, but, in all honesty, it was quite restrained. For the Doctor.

Jo shut her mouth. At least he wasn't wearing the Inverness cape for once. But she hated it when he didn't tell her what was going on. 'Doctor!' she wailed. 'Will you please tell me what we're doing?'

The Doctor turned up Dover Street, scuffled briefly once more with Bessie's gearbox and then brought the car to a halt at the top of Hay Hill.

'We're going to a museum.'

'You told me that much. A private collection. To look at something?'

'No,' said the Doctor, grinning. 'To steal something.'

2

'I never had you down as an art thief,' said Jo.

They stood looking at the noble frontage of the museum: just one of many magnificent Georgian three- and four-storeyed houses in Mayfair.

'Not art,' said the Doctor. 'Antiquities.'

'There's something in here that interests you?'

'Right,' said the Doctor. His eyes scoured the building as if he were trying to see through it.

'Something dangerous?'

'Right again.'

'And UNIT sent you here,' said Jo triumphantly.

The Doctor rounded on her. 'My dear girl,' he said. 'UNIT do not *send* me anywhere.'

Jo decided to tease the Doctor a little. 'But you do work for them, don't you,' she said, her eyes twinkling. 'Just like I do.'

The Doctor glared at her. 'I have offered my services to them during my . . . time here as a scientific adviser, and in a purely unaffiliated manner. I am not employed by them, and if at any time I choose to leave I will do so. Now come on. Let's get inside and have a look at this thing.'

'What thing?' called Jo, but the Doctor was already striding ahead and up the steps.

Maybe now wasn't the time. He did seem to be very preoccupied, and, really, she knew better than to tease him about working for UNIT, the United Nations Intelligence Taskforce. She also knew better than to remind him that he had only agreed to work for them since he had been exiled to Earth by the High Council of the Time Lords, having been found guilty of violations of time. And, although the High Council had now allowed the Doctor freedom to travel in time and space once again, she certainly knew better than to mention his exile.

Jo hurried up the steps, out of the bright day and into the cool dark of the museum.

The Doctor had disappeared inside. Fumbling for some money, she bought a ticket from a small desk in the foyer and pushed through heavy glass doors into the exhibition itself.

Various rooms stretched away in front of her. People wandered around in the dreamy, irritating way they do in museums. A security guard lifted his head and looked at her. She walked on.

The ticket seller had pushed a leaflet into her hand, and only now did she stop to read the front.

The Hoard of the King

Early Scandinavian treasures recently uncovered in Sweden
Presented by the Moxon Collection

Jo found the Doctor on the second floor of the museum. He was staring through the glass of a cabinet in the centre of the room. Inside the cabinet was an unbelievably beautiful helmet with a face mask attached. It appeared to be silver and gold, and was polished so fiercely it shone like a small sun under the bright lights.

'Is that what we've come to steal?' whispered Jo as she stepped up beside him.

The Doctor shook his head almost imperceptibly. He nodded through the glass of the cabinet in which the helmet sat to another, taller, case in the corner of the room. Inside that case was a spear.

Its shaft was simple enough – of wood that had done well to last the best part of two thousand years – but the head of the spear was another thing of wonder and beauty. Made of a long tapering piece of gold, it too glowed brightly in the beam of a small spotlight.

'Do you see it?' asked the Doctor.

'Can we take a closer look?' whispered Jo.

The room was emptying of people. A guard sat in one corner, almost asleep in her chair.

The Doctor nodded. 'Yes. But don't linger.'

They took a circuit of the room and tried not to dawdle as they passed the spear. Now they were closer, they could see small markings cut into the flat parts of the golden tip.

'Runes,' said the Doctor. 'In Elder Futhark from the look of them.' He turned to Jo. 'The runic alphabet of the Norsemen.'

Jo bent to peer through the glass at the gold. 'What does it say?'

'There are no doubt more markings on the other side, but those we can see from here say *Gungnir*.'

'I beg your pardon?'

'It's a name.'

'Of the man who owned it?'

'No. Of the spear itself.'

'The spear has a name?'

The Doctor nodded.

Jo suddenly straightened. 'Is it a good idea to be seen at the scene of the crime?' she whispered, glancing over her shoulder.

'It's not a crime scene,' said the Doctor. 'Yet.'

He winked, allowing himself one more close look at the spearhead, then took Jo by the arm. 'Time to go, I think,' he said, and they headed for the stairs, hurrying down to the ground floor. 'Did you enjoy the exhibition?'

'What exhibition? I saw one helmet and one spear.'

Jo smiled brightly at a security guard on the door, who was staring openly at the Doctor's clothes. 'Fascinating!' she declared loudly, and then they emerged from the darkness into the sunshine, blinking their way back into the modern world.

3

'We believe that the spear is not all it seems,' explained the Doctor as they headed back to UNIT headquarters. 'There have been a few temporal anomalies in the area.'

'What kind of anomalies?' asked Jo.

The Doctor turned Bessie into the drive that led to UNIT, and she chugged happily over the gravel as if eager to be done for the day. It was getting late, the sun starting to dip behind the tall trees that lined their way.

'Small things. Like several watches all losing time at once; a rash of people getting a feeling of déjà vu; a clock striking thirteen. Small things, so small that they might have gone unnoticed, were it not for the fact the museum is opposite the bridge club of a friend of ours. He told me; I spoke to the Time Lords; and here we are . . .'

'And who's this friend of ours?'

The Doctor smiled. 'The Brigadier. Ah! There's the old greyhound now. Shall we make our report?'

Brigadier Lethbridge-Stewart was just walking out of the front doors as they pulled up, tugging his cap on to his head as crisply as ever. He saw Bessie and strode towards them. 'Doctor! Miss Grant!'

'You were quite right, Brigadier. The spear has every indication of being a PTN.'

'A what?' asked Jo, but neither the Doctor nor the Brigadier were listening.

'You've informed the High Council?' asked Lethbridge-Stewart.

'I already have their authority to remove the object for analysis. Immediately.'

'But why not just ask them for it?' said Jo. 'The museum, I mean.'

'We tried,' said the Brigadier. 'They refused. This chap, Moxon, the owner of the collection. Total recluse. Billionaire. Not used to taking orders.'

'But can't you make him?'

'Private collection. We have no power to order him to do anything.'

'But surely if you explain what it's all about . . .?' Jo asked. She stopped. 'What *is* it all about, anyway? What's a PTN?'

'Physical Temporal Nexus,' said the Doctor. 'Very dangerous things indeed. Their origin is unknown, but they are certainly alien and certainly ancient. There are believed to be only a few in existence, and the High Council is – how shall we put it? – more than keen to keep them out of circulation.'

'I see,' said Jo, 'I think. We'd better get on with it then.'

'Well put,' said the Doctor.

They headed into the UNIT building. 'What's the plan?' asked Jo. 'Do you have a nice black burglar suit in your wardrobe, Doctor? One with frills?'

The Doctor paused briefly, started to raise a wagging finger towards Jo, then thought better of it. 'The museum stands between a bank and an embassy building,' he said. 'Both of which will be well protected. However, with all due respect to my friends here, this *is* 1973.' He smiled at the Brigadier and then walked on. 'The room in the museum is without CCTV, laser sensors or other motion detectors. It would be child's play to walk in and out, with a minimum of broken glass, but there are simpler ways of entering and exiting a building without being noticed . . .'

They'd stopped by a certain familiar police box. The Doctor patted the side of the TARDIS. '. . . if you have one of these.'

Jo laughed.

'What is it?' asked the Brigadier.

'I just realised,' she said. 'Banks. Safety-deposit vaults. Museums. Art galleries. You could get very rich in a week with this.'

'Some of us have nobler aspirations,' said the Doctor sternly.

'Oh, me too, me too,' said Jo, grinning. 'Really noble. The noblest. It was just an idea. So, we materialise in the room on the second floor of the museum, smash the case, grab the spear and dematerialise again, yes?'

'Not quite,' said the Doctor. 'If I may make one small adjustment to your otherwise excellent plan, Jo? I took the trouble of getting the UNIT boffins to prepare this.'

He stepped inside the TARDIS and reappeared a moment later with a spear that looked just like the one they were going to steal – with one small difference.

'It has no runes on it,' said Jo.

'Quite so,' said the Doctor. 'We made this from photographs in the exhibition catalogue, but the runes were unclear — hence the need for our visit today. As soon as we complete the work on the spearhead, we can be off. Later tonight, I hope.'

'And we replace the spear with this copy!' said Jo. 'That's brilliant. They won't even know they've been robbed!'

The Doctor smiled. 'Well, as long as we don't break any glass, they won't.'

4

'Well, here we are!' announced the Doctor. 'Second-floor exhibition room of the Moxon Collection. *Voilà!*'

He threw the TARDIS door open theatrically, smiling broadly at Jo, who frowned and gave a little prod of her finger to the air, pointing outside.

The Doctor turned. 'Blast!' he said loudly, then more quietly, 'Couldn't you land where you're supposed to, old girl? Just once?'

Jo peered out and surveyed the view. 'We appear to be on a roof. The roof of the museum actually. Not bad.'

'Well, really,' said the Doctor.

Outside was the night skyline of London. They could see the lights of Piccadilly Circus and, a little further on, Nelson's Column striking up into the darkness.

'Fair enough!' declared the Doctor. 'It is still only 1973, after all. We can slip inside from up here just as easily.' He fished in his pocket and pulled out the sonic screwdriver. 'There must be some kind of skylight for access to the roof,' he added.

Jo tugged his sleeve. 'There. Look.'

'Excellent,' said the Doctor. 'Jo, would you mind bringing our decoy?'

A short way away on the roof of the building was a small door leading into the roof space. The Doctor held the sonic screwdriver against the lock for no more than a second, and the lock clicked open.

They made their way down a cramped, darkened stairwell. At the bottom was another, larger door. Once more, the screwdriver did its work, and they were into the museum itself.

'One floor down,' said the Doctor quietly. 'Keep your ears open. Just in case.'

Jo nodded, clutched the fake spear a little more tightly, and they started down the stairs, which were wide and thick with plush carpet.

Near the bottom of the staircase, the Doctor paused, then pointed to the door to the room they'd visited that afternoon. He stood still on the bottom step, tense, listening hard. Then he relaxed and smiled. 'Well,' he said. 'I think the coast is clear.'

He stepped down on to the landing and the wail of an alarm broke upon them, deafening and shrill.

Footsteps rang out across the marble tiles of the ground floor and then, much closer, a voice shouted at them. 'Stay exactly where you are or I'll fire!'

They spun round to see a guard levelling a pistol at them – not one of the dozy security guards from their afternoon visit but one dressed in almost military uniform, adopting a stance as if he meant to shoot at any second.

'What do you mean, you'll fire?' roared the Doctor. 'Don't be preposterous! This is a museum, not a rifle range!'

He turned to Jo. 'Come on. I think we should leave.'

'Do not move!' bawled the guard. There was the sound of more guards running up the stairs, and the Doctor grabbed Jo's hand.

'I'll shoot!' shouted the guard.

'He won't,' said the Doctor with great certainty, taking a step back up the stairs.

The wall behind their heads exploded in a mess of plaster that seemed to reach them before they were aware of the gunshot itself.

'Run!' cried the Doctor, and they sped back up the stairs, heading for the roof. More gunshots sounded and the wall above their heads erupted as they ran, crouching, for the door to the small stairwell.

The pistol fire was suddenly overwhelmed by the harsh metal sputter of a sub-machine gun. 'Preposterous!' cried the Doctor as they took the metal stairs to the roof two at a time. There were more shouts and the sound of boots ringing on the stairs clattered after them.

Shots pinged off the ceiling as they ducked out of the tiny door and back into the cold night air.

'Into the TARDIS, Jo!' shouted the Doctor. 'Quick!'

They burst inside and flung the door shut. The Doctor pounced on the central console and locked them safely inside. The distant sound of gunfire breaking on the outside of the TARDIS came to them, like bees pinging off the glass of a thick window.

'Let's not outstay our welcome,' said the Doctor, busily setting coordinates.

'I'd say we already have,' said Jo. She set the spear beside the door and rushed over to the Doctor.

The sound of gunfire was replaced by the familiar grinding sound of dematerialisation, and Jo felt relief rush over her. She turned round and perched on the edge of the console.

'Yes, that was rather close,' said the Doctor. 'Still, it proves one thing.'

'Which is?'

'That the spear is something unusual. No one would go to such lengths to protect it if it was just an old piece of wood and a lump of gold.'

'Maybe Moxon is just very protective of his collection.'

'Sub-machine guns? That's taking museum curation a bit far, don't you think?'

'I suppose so,' said Jo. 'Anyway, where are we going?'

The Doctor smiled. 'A very good question.'

'With a very good answer, I hope.'

'We can't steal the spear *now*, but we can steal it in the past. We are therefore travelling back to its only other confirmed location in space–time.'

'Which is?'

'Didn't you read the notice by the case?'

Jo shook her head. 'Too busy trying to understand Futhark.'

'Well, do you still have the leaflet from the museum?'

Jo fished in her back pocket and pulled out a crumpled piece of paper. She found the short description of the spear.

Ceremonial spear. Found in Gamla Uppsala, Sweden. Believed to have been used in festivals around the vernal equinox, second century AD. Inscription upon the head reads GUNGNIR. In Norse mythology, Gungnir was the magical spear of Odin.

'You're taking us to see the Vikings?' asked Jo incredulously.

'I know! Wonderful, isn't it?' said the Doctor with a grin.

'That's not the word I'd use,' Jo said. 'Hey, wait a minute, how do you know where to go?'

'*Where* is easy,' said the Doctor. 'Just look at your leaflet. Uppsala, central Sweden. Or Old Uppsala to be exact. Centre of power of Swedish kings for over a thousand years till the Christians turned up. That's *where*. *When* is a little harder. We know we should head for the spring equinox . . . Nice of the Vikings to date things around astronomical phenomena. Makes life so much easier.'

'But in which year?'

'Well, there I'm guessing a little. In the British Museum there is a rune stone that bears the only other known reference to Gungnir. It refers to a ceremony in Old Uppsala and mentions the passing of a second sun across the heavens. Scholars have always assumed that to be a reference to Halley's Comet, whose *only* known appearance in the second century was in 141 AD – according to the old Julian calendar that was on the twenty-second of March, the very next day after the equinox. So that's when, and where, we're going.'

'Oh,' said Jo. 'I see.'

'Good.'

'I have just one question.'

'Fire away!'

'Oh, Doctor, please. Not after that business at the museum.'

The Doctor held up his hand. 'Sorry. What's your question?'

Jo swallowed. 'So, listen. This spear. The magical spear of Odin. I might have got this wrong, but wasn't Odin a god?'

'That's what they say.'

'Well, doesn't that worry you at all?'

'On the contrary. Rather fun, I'd say.'

'Fun?' asked Jo, eyeing the spear by the doorway nervously. 'Do you really think the owner of Gungnir was a god?'

The Doctor smiled again. 'I suppose,' he said, 'that we're about to find out.'

5

With an almighty groaning the central column of the TARDIS came to rest. They had landed.

'Of course, the Vikings are much misunderstood.'

'Is that right?' asked Jo.

'Come on, you must have done some history at school.'

'Doctor, we did the Romans. Every year. Ask me about the Punic Wars and I'm your girl.'

'Some other time maybe,' said the Doctor. 'The point is that people often see the Vikings as violent marauders and nothing else, when the truth of the matter is that by and large they were farmers, fishermen.'

'By and large . . .?'

'They were great explorers, too. They discovered North America five hundred years before Columbus thought he had. They got as far as the Mediterranean, Russia. You have to remember that most accounts of the Vikings are written by the Christians who displaced them. Somewhat biased accounts.'

'You know this for a fact?'

The Doctor gave Jo a hurt look. 'What I do know *for a fact* is that they're the only humans ever to name a day of the week after bathtime. Washing once a week was pretty advanced stuff two thousand years ago.'

Jo laughed.

'Well,' said the Doctor. 'Shall we look around?'

Jo nodded. 'Let's.'

The Doctor brought up the outside view on the TARDIS's scanner screen. They were treated to the sight of a peaceful forest, with snow deep on the ground and thick on the branches of the trees, although it appeared to be a bright and sunny day otherwise.

'Seems quiet enough,' said the Doctor.

He shut down the screen, opened the door and they headed out.

'Cold,' said Jo.

'Will you be warm enough?' asked the Doctor. 'I could always fetch my Inverness cape for you?'

'I'll be fine,' said Jo hurriedly. She shot a quick smile at the Doctor so as not to hurt his feelings.

Their feet crunched noisily into the snow, which was frozen hard.

'Which way do we go?' asked Jo.

'I'm not sure,' said the Doctor. 'Let's circle around. It can't be far. There should be a large temple complex. And a village serving it.'

Jo stopped and looked back over her shoulder. 'Will the TARDIS be all right?'

'She's tougher than I am,' said the Doctor seriously. 'And, anyway, I have a theory.'

'Yes?'

'Yes. You see, the whole nature, shape and even the modern

blue pigment of the TARDIS is so deeply unfamiliar to the primitive mind that, although the optic nerve registers its presence, the brain cannot decode what it is seeing. The primitive visual cortex is unable to relay information about it consciously to the viewer. In effect, even though her chameleon circuit is still damaged, she's as good as invisible. She'll be just fine.'

'That's remarkable,' said Jo.

'She is a remarkable old girl in many ways,' said the Doctor. 'Let's move, shall we? We'll be warmer if we walk a little faster.'

They made their way deeper into the forest. As long as there wasn't another snowfall it would be easy enough to find their way back to the TARDIS from the trail of their footprints in the snow.

The woodland was on sloping land, and they headed gently downhill through a mixture of birch and ash and conifers until, finally, they saw the trees thinning out a little in front of them.

'I hear a river somewhere,' said Jo.

'Yes,' said the Doctor, nodding. 'That way.'

Very soon they glimpsed clear green water flowing rapidly in a wide and strong river, whose banks were covered with snow and ice.

'This way,' said the Doctor.

'How do you know?'

'Because rivers mean settlements sooner or later.'

'Sooner, I hope. I'm freezing.'

'I could still go back for my cape . . .'

'Look, Doctor! What's that?'

Jo pointed downstream to the opposite bank, where there was a huge wooden construction. As they moved closer, they saw what it was – a vast waterwheel fed by a channel from the river. Then they saw that beyond it was another one, exactly the same, and beyond that, more – six of them in total – and all drawing water from the channel underneath the heavy wooden wheels, which turned slowly but with a power that was somehow threatening.

'Fascinating.'

'Is there a way across?'

'Let's head downstream. Maybe there's a bridge. I wouldn't want to cross that river, even on a summer's day.'

The river was deep and moved in eddying currents. Ice crusted its banks, and even looking at it seemed to sap the warmth from Jo's blood. She shivered.

As they approached the first of the waterwheels a bridge came into view beyond it, but before they could get any further they heard shouts from across the water and quickly threw themselves in the snow behind some tree stumps on the riverbank.

The Doctor lifted his head. 'It's all right. They haven't seen us.'

'Who?' Jo couldn't hide the worry in her voice.

'There's a group of men on the other side, beyond the wheels.' The Doctor took another look. 'It's safe, Jo. Have a look.'

Jo peered across the water. 'What's going on?'

'I don't know,' said the Doctor. 'I think there are two groups. They don't seem to like each other.'

Jo saw what he meant. There were definitely two groups

of warriors facing off in a clearing between the waterwheels and the forest. They wore leather and furs: boots up to the knee strapped round with cloth bindings, thick furred tunics and fur-lined caps.

They were shouting at each other and waving metal – swords and axes. Not actually fighting, but clearly no love was lost between them, and they appeared to be on the verge of a scuffle at the very least. One man in the left-hand group waved an enormous hammer above his head, roaring like thunder as he did so.

'Posturing, that's all,' said the Doctor. 'Although . . .' He hesitated. 'Maybe more to come.'

He was right. Without warning, one of the hammer-man's group charged forward, wielding a war-axe above his head, screaming.

There was sudden silence from all the other men, a silence into which one voice rang out. It sounded like a shout of warning, but it came from *behind* the charging man.

He alone ignored it.

And then, whistling through the snow-still air, a spear came from nowhere. A huge throw, an impossible throw, and the spear stuck into the man's back.

He took one more step and then pitched forward into the snow, as dead as the landscape around him.

There was silence. No one moved on either side.

'Gungnir?' whispered Jo.

Before the Doctor could answer, the thrower of the spear came into view, walking out of the trees. It was hard to be sure at the distance they were looking from, but the Doctor and Jo could see he was a tall man, taller than the others. He appeared to be older too, with a long beard, but no less powerful for that.

His own men moved away from him as he approached; their enemies backed away too, heading for the bridge back across to the side of the river where the Doctor and Jo were hiding.

The spear-thrower walked slowly up to the man he'd killed – his *own* man – and, putting a boot on his back, pulled his spear free. He shouted a word to his men, and they turned to go.

'Oh my –' said Jo, but she didn't finish because hands grabbed her.

She tried to scream, but a hand clamped across her mouth and as she was pulled to her feet she saw the Doctor being grasped by two men, who were dressed like the ones they'd just seen. They dragged him towards the river.

The Doctor struggled to fight his way free, and Jo managed to bite the hand over her mouth. She got a cuff to the back of her head, and her vision swam. As she struggled to stay conscious, Jo saw the Doctor wrench free of one of his attackers and dispatch a firm blow to the man's neck, sending him to his knees.

Then the other man swung at the Doctor, who ducked. The man flailed past him, catching the Doctor's jacket as he fell. Jo watched in horror as both he and the Doctor tumbled into the fast and icy river, and were swept away.

Jo fainted, and her attacker allowed her to fall limply to the ground.

6

When Jo woke up, the world was upside down. It also seemed that there was an earthquake in mid-rumble. It took her a moment to realise that she was hanging, her wrists and ankles tied, over the shoulder of one of the Vikings, and that he was jogging with her through the trees as if she were a paper doll.

The second thing she noticed was the smell. The most terrible stink she'd ever had the misfortune to come across, so bad it made her want to retch. *Must be bathtime tomorrow then,* she thought, wrinkling her nose.

The third thing she thought was that it was actually terrifying being pressed so close to a hot and sweaty Viking. She could feel the muscles in his shoulder working, pushing into her stomach, and at that point she screamed and tried to wriggle her way off.

Jo thought she heard him laughing, but, either way, his arms tightened round her legs and she knew she was going nowhere.

She could see other men running beside her, though upside down it was hard to tell how many. They were silent for the most part, though from time to time one of them would bark a single word that she didn't catch.

And then, finally, she remembered the Doctor.

She'd seen him washed away into the powerful currents of the river, a river so cold there were plates of ice tumbling along in its waters.

She told herself not to panic. He'd be all right. He always was. Wasn't he?

Apart from those times he'd told her about when he sort of died and then sort of turned into another version of himself.

Another version of himself who might not even know who she was, and here she was almost two thousand years before she'd been born.

She started to panic.

Get a grip, Josephine, she thought. *Get a grip on yourself.*

He'll be OK.

He'll get out of the river somehow.

He'll see these tracks in the snow and he'll come and find you.

He'll be fine and the TARDIS will be fine because these ignorant savages can't even see it, just like the Doctor said.

7

From a distance the Doctor watched as a group of about twenty men loaded the TARDIS on to the back of a large low wagon pulled by four sturdy oxen. Then it trundled away through the trees.

'Well, it was just a theory,' he said.

He'd fought with the man in the river for a long time, but finally the poor human had succumbed to the cold and had been washed away to Valhalla.

The Doctor had managed to fish himself out of the river and had stood dripping on the riverbank, but within minutes the water had begun to freeze, threatening to turn him into a living ice sculpture.

The cold didn't worry him unduly. Given that his normal body temperature was way below human levels, the dip in the river had been no more than refreshing, certainly not deadly.

But it was a nuisance being damp and icy, so he began to walk briskly back along the bank, trying to pick up Jo's trail. One of the advantages of having a binary vascular system was that he could always pump his blood faster than normal if he chose to, raising his body temperature at will. Very soon his clothes were steaming as he walked along, and in twenty minutes he was as dry as a good martini.

'As I always say,' he said, 'two hearts are better than one.'

He soon came back in sight of the waterwheels and the bridge, and hesitated for a moment. He had to find Jo. But something wasn't right about these waterwheels, and he knew he should investigate.

He hesitated a little longer. The most important thing was to find the spear. But then there was Jo. Jo Grant. Loyal, funny, quick-witted Jo. If anything happened to her . . . He'd had other companions before, of course, and all wonderful people, in the various weird ways humans could be, but none of them was quite like Jo . . .

'Five minutes,' he said to himself.

A quick look at the waterwheels and then find Jo. If they'd wanted to kill her she'd be dead already, and five minutes wouldn't help that.

He crossed the bridge to the far side of the river, and as he approached the closest waterwheel he saw something in the distance they'd missed before.

Through the forest, up and away on a hill, was a clearing, and in the clearing stood a wooden temple, towering and vast.

He felt a strong urge to go and take a look; even from this distance and looking through the trees he could see it was covered in fantastic carvings that he longed to examine, but Jo had been taken the other way, and there were the wheels, and the spear, and . . .

He hurried on.

There was no one in sight, but he approached the first waterwheel cautiously – being shot at and dunked in a river was quite enough fun for one day.

The wheel was a heavy undershot device: a long wooden leat channelled water from the river to the bottom of its fins, which turned constantly in the flow.

He moved on to the next wheel, and the next, and now, in the far distance, he heard the sounds of axes and saws, of wood being chopped in the forest. He squinted towards the direction of the sounds and watched as part of the forest trembled, and then a gap appeared in the canopy as a tree came down.

'They're making more . . .' he said, wondering why they needed all these wheels, all this potential power – power that was useless unless it was feeding something.

But what?

The axle of each waterwheel entered a wheelhouse, and the Doctor approached the nearest one. The door was locked; a big iron keyhole was set into the heavy wood.

The Doctor pulled his sonic screwdriver out of his pocket and, once inside, his eyes widened.

There was no primitive set of cogs and drive-shafts, no trip-hammers or cam-wheels. No milling or grinding stones. Instead, the axle of the wheel went straight into a large metal box, from which heavy-duty electrical cable emerged and then disappeared into the dirt floor of the wheelhouse.

Neither the cable nor the box looked like they had anything to do with Earth in the second century AD.

★

It was as he'd left the wheelhouse that he'd heard the snort of an ox from across the river, and that was when he'd seen the TARDIS being towed away.

The Doctor put his head down and made for the bridge.

'Hang on, Jo,' he said. 'Hang on.'

8

Jo knelt on a hard earth floor.

In front of her stood a huge warrior, his face almost obscured by a thick beard, though his eyes were clear enough to see and burned down at her, making her want to melt into the ground and disappear.

Around them were the men who'd brought her, and around *them* was a vast dark hall. A fire-pit at its centre sent smoke curling up into the thatch of the roof.

She'd been carried through a village – a series of small huts and some larger houses – and then brought before this man, who was evidently the chief.

'I,' announced the man, 'am Njord.'

Jo understood him perfectly. She knew the telepathic circuits of the TARDIS had a certain range, and, although the Doctor had never said how great that range was, she knew the TARDIS must be close enough for it to make her hear the ancient Norse dialect as English.

Njord stepped a little closer to Jo and began walking round her. Her wrists and ankles were still bound. She longed to stand and give this old goat a piece of her mind, but she knew she'd most likely fall over if she tried, which wasn't the effect she was after.

Njord grunted in satisfaction. 'Everything is as Frey said.'

'Frey?' asked Jo. 'Who's Frey?'

Njord ignored her. He clapped his hands and gave a short laugh that sounded more like a bark. Then he stopped in front of Jo and bent down, putting his face right up close to hers.

Her nose wrinkled.

'Where is the Healer?' he said.

'The who?' asked Jo.

'My men say he drowned. He fell in the river. But Frey says not to believe what you see with the Healer.'

'The Healer? You mean the Doctor?'

'The Healer, the Doctor. Yes. Is he drowned?'

Jo hung her head. 'Oh, I hope not,' she said quietly.

Njord straightened. 'My men are looking for him. They will find him if he still lives.'

Staring hard at the earth in front of her, Jo fought the urge to weep.

'You are the Healer's woman? His wife?'

Jo lifted her head. 'I am the Doctor's companion,' she said proudly, and held Njord's gaze for as long as she could, until her nerve failed her.

A smile spread slowly over Njord's face. It was not a nice thing to see. His lips parted and Jo almost winced when she saw his blackened teeth.

He put his boot on Jo's shoulder and with a shove sent her to the floor, where she lay on her side, wondering how accurate the Doctor's lecture about peaceful Viking farmers had been.

Njord stared coolly down at her. 'Today there was almost a fight. Everything is as Frey said it would be. Old One-eye killed one of his own to stop the war from starting. He is scared. He is weak. Full of bluster and noise, yes, but in reality he is weak. And when *Skithblathnir* returns to our shores with Frey at her helm, carrying more warriors to swell our army, we *will* go to war with the Aesir. And we *will* win.'

Jo lay still, trying to understand everything she had heard, knowing it might be important, knowing it would be good to be able to tell the Doctor everything she'd learned. If only he was still alive.

Hands grabbed her again and dragged her out of the hall and through the village. She saw a wagon being pulled by four oxen. On the wagon was the TARDIS.

She was about to yell when someone pulled her back so hard the breath was knocked from her. Before she knew it, she was taken into a small but solid hut, where she was tied to the post that held up the roof, and left to shiver.

9

Darkness fell, and as Jo's shivers turned to great shudders of cold, she wished she'd taken the Doctor up on the offer of his cape.

It was *that* cold.

She'd lost track of how much time had passed. All she'd heard were the sounds of the village: footsteps coming and going, the occasional chatter of voices, the clang of metal somewhere and the barking of dogs.

Then there was the scrape of the door opening. Jo looked up, blinking in the light of a burning torch being held by one of the warriors, and saw the Doctor being ushered into the hut. Two more men tied him to the post, so that he and Jo sat back to back on the cold ground. Then the door shut and they were left alone in darkness once more.

'I've just been talking to your friend Njord,' said the Doctor.

'I'm fine,' said Jo. 'Thanks for asking. And how are you?'

'Very well, my dear. Thought I'd find you here somewhere. Are you warm enough?'

'You're joking,' said Jo. 'I'm freezing!'

'Well, sit as close to me as you can. I'll warm us up. Three hearts are better than two, after all.'

In spite of herself, Jo laughed. 'Doctor?' she said. 'Who is Njord? He kept speaking about someone called Frey, too. I don't think he's here now, though. He's away, fetching warriors on his ship. It had a funny name.'

'*Skithblathnir*.'

'Yes! That's it! How did you know? Gosh, Doctor, have you got a fever? It's like sitting next to a log stove!'

'Well, you did say you were cold. Jo, do you remember we spoke about Odin?'

'What about him?'

'You know him as a god of Norse mythology, correct?'

'Yes. There's Odin, and Thor too. He has a hammer and makes thunder. I think he was Odin's son.'

'That's right. And Odin was supposed to have the spear, Gungnir . . . and he only had one eye.'

'Doctor! Njord spoke about someone he called One-eye, like a nickname.'

'We saw him earlier today, Jo. He killed one of his own men. And there was a man with a hammer, too.'

'Thor! But they're supposed to be gods!'

'We've arrived at a most interesting time. Some scholars, and myself, I might add, have a theory about certain myths and legends.'

'A theory, Doctor? Like your one about the TARDIS being invisible . . .?'

'Yes, thank you. I think that one might need a bit more consideration. No, this theory is that many stories that scholars of your time believe to be myths, legends and mere tales were, in fact, originally based on real events, and the characters in them based on real people. Even those we now consider to be gods were just great men of the past. Jo, this is so fascinating! We are witnessing the origin of Norse myth!'

'You're not serious.'

'I'm absolutely serious, my dear. Odin is the king of all Sweden. His people are called the Aesir.'

'Njord spoke about them. He said they're going to fight them.'

'Quite so. What we witnessed by the river today was just an early skirmish. Odin had to kill one of his own men to stop the fight from escalating. According to the great Norse sagas, there were two races of gods: the Aesir, ruled by Odin, with his sons Thor and Balder, and the Vanir, ruled by Njord, with the assistance of Frey.'

'Thank you, Doctor, I'm much warmer now.'

'What? Oh good. I'll turn the central heating down.'

'Thanks,' said Jo. 'Go on with your story.'

'Yes, the Aesir and the Vanir. They had been squabbling for some time, and then they all gathered at a great meeting, an assembly of some kind. Odin grew angry and threw Gungnir over the heads of the Vanir. And so the great war between them began.'

'You think that's about to happen?'

'I think it is, yes. Be that as it may, we have to get Gungnir and get away from here.'

'Gungnir? Why? You still haven't told me why it's *so* important.'

'I am now absolutely convinced that Gungnir is a Physical Temporal Nexus. A PTN. In the Norse legends it was said that Gungnir was magical, that it would hit whoever the thrower wished it to hit, without fail. We saw that for ourselves today. That throw was impossible – far too far. But once thrown, Gungnir cannot miss its target.'

'Well, that's pretty neat for a Viking weapon, but still not much of a match for a machine gun. Or a nuclear bomb.'

'Jo, let me finish. Always hitting its target is nothing to a PTN. That's just a party trick. But the *way* it does it is the point. In order to perform such a feat a PTN forms a link with the mind of whoever is holding it. At a quantum level the PTN joins with the brain patterns of its owner and then it does a remarkable thing. You are, of course, aware that there are an infinite number of possible universes?'

'Of course,' said Jo.

'I thought so,' said the Doctor. 'So what the PTN does is shuffle through all possible states of the universe in a fraction of a second, and it selects the one that its owner desires the most. That is why it is so powerful. So dangerous.'

'Because whoever owns it can literally make their wishes come true.'

'Exactly! The High Council of the Time Lords has spent a great deal of time tracking them all down. One was found on Usurius, two more on Kirith. There are perhaps no more than six in all, and even the Time Lords don't know who made them or where they came from. And, trust me, the Time Lords know a great deal about the universe. A very great deal.

'So now it seems we have another in our reach. I doubt very much that Odin knows what he has in his hands – Gungnir's true power. To him it's just a spear with which he seems to hunt rather well . . .'

'I can see why they think it's magic, though.'

'Not only that. Another thought occurs to me.'

'Which is?'

'Gungnir is not the only famous spear in history. There is another, even more famous. Or perhaps I mean infamous. As Jesus hung on the cross, a Roman soldier called Longinus wanted to see if he was really dead, and drove his spear into Christ's side.

'That spear became known as the Spear of Destiny, but it soon went missing. We simply don't know what happened to it. But, despite that, stories about its power began to circulate. It was said that the army that possessed it would be invincible. Not so very long before your own time, Jo, another man craved the Spear, which by then had turned up in a museum in Vienna. That man was Adolf Hitler. The very day he invaded Austria in 1938 he drove straight to the museum to capture the Spear. He took it back to Berlin and believed he was, from that time on, invincible.'

'But the Nazis lost the war,' said Jo. 'It didn't work.'

'There are two possibilities. First, some people believe that the spear he captured was a thirteenth-century fake, not the real thing. Or, second, there is a simpler explanation: the spear *was* the real thing, but Hitler made a mistake. In order for a PTN to work, you have to actually *hold* it. Hitler put it in another museum in Berlin and then got on with invading the rest of Europe.'

'My goodness!' said Jo. 'If he'd only known . . .'

'Quite so, my dear, quite so.'

'But wait a minute. What's this got to do with Gungnir?'

'Jo, I believe Gungnir and the Spear of Destiny are one and the same.'

'But we're in Sweden. How did the Spear end up here?'

'I told you, the Vikings raided far into the Mediterranean. Odin must have got lucky and found it there.'

'I see,' said Jo. 'That makes sense. But if Hitler had the Spear in the war, how was it dug up in Sweden just now and put in the Moxon Collection in London?'

'Yes, well, that's what's worrying me the most,' said the Doctor, and his voice sank dark and low. 'We only have the word of that leaflet that it *was* recently found in a dig in Sweden, don't we?'

'You mean the museum was lying? Why would they do that?'

'Why indeed, Jo? And how do we know that the spear in the museum is not, in fact, another fake?'

'There were temporal anomalies. Small disturbances in time.'

'There were indeed. But those can also sometimes be the result of the presence of a poorly shielded TARDIS.'

'Doctor?'

'Jo, this man Frey that Njord spoke about. He has a ship called *Skithblathnir*, yes? Do you know what Norse myth says about *Skithblathnir*?'

Jo shook her head, and suddenly didn't feel so warm any more.

'It was said that Frey could make his ship any size he wanted. That he could fit as many men on board as he wished. Does that sound familiar? A ship that's bigger on the inside?'

'Doctor! You think. . .?'

'Jo, the name Frey. In Old Norse it means Lord. Or —'

'Master!' cried Jo. 'Frey is the Master!'

Before the Doctor could reply there was a laugh from outside the hut's door. It was pushed open, and in he came, laughing and clapping his hands.

'Oh,' he said, 'it's been such fun listening to you two work it out. Well done! Well done!'

He stood over them, looking down, leering.

The Master.

10

'You've been busy,' said the Doctor.

The Master stood in the doorway. In his hand he held a burning torch that cast a flickering fiery light across his face.

'You know,' said the Doctor. 'I always thought you looked a little like the Devil with that beard. Now I know it.'

'Doctor, Doctor,' said the Master mockingly. 'Such a bad loser. Come on now, admit it! You've been plodding around in the dark. Talking of which, the sky tonight will be illuminated most wonderfully by the comet. You'll enjoy that.'

'Yes,' said the Doctor. 'Yes, I see now. You could have just gone to Judea in 33 AD to find the spear. Taken it right out of Longinus' hands, no doubt. But that date is not accurate. Calendars have changed and, besides, all we really have to go on are dates made up hundreds of years later by the men who wrote the apocryphal Gospels.'

'Precisely, Doctor. Whereas here, tonight, the comet marks the equinox, so neatly recorded on that rune stone in the British Museum. These Vikings are such wonderful people. Do you know they wash once a week?'

'Could have fooled me,' muttered Jo.

'And now, Doctor, you're here. You join me just as I planned. So nice of you to turn up to order. Because I need you, Doctor. Or, rather, I need your ship.'

'Something wrong with yours, old boy?'

'Not at all. It's quite well. I've been making lots of trips in it. Finding warriors for Njord. He's most impressed. So is Odin, and that's why I need your TARDIS. I'm giving it to him.'

'And Njord's men have already relieved me of the key, along with my screwdriver. I can guess what you want in return.'

'Quite right, Doctor. Odin and I have made a bargain. He wants a ship just like mine. And he will get one in return for the Nexus. The Spear of Destiny.'

'But he can't operate the TARDIS.'

'No, but then he doesn't know that, does he?'

'And meanwhile you've set the Aesir and the Vanir at each other's throats, pushing them towards war, while you've been cooking up your own little plans.'

'Now will you admit how stupid you've been, Doctor?'

The Doctor said nothing, but clenched his jaw and stared at the wall of the hut.

'It gets worse, I'm afraid,' said the Master. 'You see, I've told Odin all about you. Both of you. He was very interested to hear about the Doctor, some sort of magician, or wizard. And his young and attractive assistant. So you're to be made guests of honour. Tonight. At the blessing. In fact you could say you'll be the main attraction.'

He turned to go, then hesitated. 'I do have a few problems with the Vikings, though,' he said. 'I quite clearly told them to put you in different huts. And now here you are together.

I'll send someone to separate you. Miss Grant, Doctor, goodnight.' And with that he ducked out of the low door and was gone.

'We have to escape,' whispered the Doctor.

'Now?'

'No, after we've been separated. That will buy us some time. If you get free, find the TARDIS. It's here somewhere. Close by, I'm sure.'

'But how will I escape? How will you escape for that matter?'

'I'm more of a thief than you imagine me to be. While I was talking to Njord I pinched a couple of knives. Can you reach my right-hand pocket?'

Jo squirmed and managed to find a knife in the Doctor's jacket.

'As long as they don't search us,' said the Doctor, 'we'll be fine. As soon as you're tied up again, get yourself free. Find the TARDIS.'

'And what are you going to do?'

'I'm going to talk to Odin.'

'Oh,' said Jo. 'Fine. But what's the big hurry? The Master said we'll see him tonight, anyway, at the blessing. That doesn't sound so bad.'

'Jo, you should know your own language better. A blessing isn't what you think it is. It comes from an ancient Norse dialect, in which to bless means to sacrifice. We're to be the sacrifice at tonight's ceremony.'

11

The Doctor made his way out of Njord's settlement towards the river and the temple, and, beyond it, Odin's village.

He moved quietly and, though the night should have been dark with the last quarter of the month's moon dying overhead, the sky was lit by an eerie glow. Looking up, he saw the comet in the sky and knew how much store the Vikings put against such portents: the perfect moment for Odin to make a sacrifice to ensure victory in the war that everyone knew was brewing.

He hurried onwards, down the slope, through the trees and across the river. In the gloom, the waterwheels were still turning on and on, and now the Doctor knew they had some hideous purpose of the Master's making, but there was no time to stop and investigate. In the distance the lights of Odin's village twinkled, and he pressed on.

As he came towards the hilltop where the temple stood, he stumbled over something. He looked down. More of that heavy electrical cabling, snaking its way through the trees, and though time was against him he followed it.

It wasn't long before he saw where it was going. It headed

into a small tunnel cut into the hillside, right underneath the side of the temple.

He crawled in and, although it should have been totally dark, light came to him. Hand over hand he edged further along the cable and down the tunnel until, suddenly, it opened up into a small man-made cave. At its centre sat another blank metal box, like the one in the wheelhouse, but this one pulsed with lights set in its side, and it seemed to throb from the power within.

Jo had managed to slice through her bonds easily, remarking that Viking table knives were more like lethal weapons than cutlery.

The night was still and the village strangely quiet, although she could hear the sounds of people in various houses as she passed by. She knew where she was going. Since the chameleon circuit of the Doctor's TARDIS was still broken, his ship had to be in a building large enough to house a 1963 police box, and there was only one of those: the hall in which she'd met Njord earlier.

She crept towards it and saw that it was in darkness. She found a door and slipped inside, finding that the central hall was in fact surrounded by corridors and galleries. She began to make her way along the first of these, looking for the familiar shape of the TARDIS.

She turned one corner, and another, but found nothing, and then came to a room where a little of the weak moonlight spilled down from a glassless window set high in the wall.

The light showed her something very beautiful – a large wooden model of a Viking longship, almost as long as she was tall. It was open-decked, low and sleek, and very finely detailed, and despite herself she found herself staring at it as if it had some magical attraction that pulled her in.

She reached out a hand to stroke the carved dragon's head that served as the prow, and saw there was even more detail inside the model: the benches on which the oarsmen would sit, the tiller that controlled the rudder. She couldn't resist the temptation to touch the tiller, and as she did so she gasped, because the thing snapped off in her hand.

'You!' cried a voice in the dark. 'You! What are you doing there?'

Someone was approaching.

She spun round and hastily shoved the small piece of wood in her back pocket, turning a guilty face to a large Norseman glaring at her.

'Oh no,' she said.

'I just tied you up,' said the Viking. He grunted. 'Come with me. Njord and Frey will want to know of your escape.'

The Master laughed.

'Didn't like your quarters, Miss Grant? No matter, I was about to fetch you and the Doctor, anyway. Sadly, it seems that he has also seen fit to leave us. For the time being only, no doubt. You wouldn't like to tell us where he is, would you?'

'I have no idea,' said Jo, wondering if that were actually true.

'Oh, I doubt that,' said the Master. 'But it needn't matter. His time is very nearly run, no matter what. And you will make just as good a sacrifice as him. Come along. We should be going.'

Two men grabbed Jo.

Njord stepped forward and clapped his hands, and suddenly a host of Viking warriors appeared in full battle gear.

The Master pointed to the corner of the hall behind Jo. She turned, and there she saw the TARDIS.

The Master slipped the key from his pocket, strode over to the blue police box and opened the door. He beckoned to Njord, and then he and his men and Jo all followed him inside.

'I always was a better pilot than the Doctor, you know,' said the Master, his hands on the controls of the central console as the TARDIS began to dematerialise. 'I have no idea why he makes such a fuss.' A few seconds later they had materialised.

The Master left the console and the press of Viking warriors silently stood to one side to give him access to the door. He sauntered over and opened it. 'Or maybe she just likes me better than she likes the Doctor, hmm?'

Outside the TARDIS was a vast room, even bigger than Njord's hall, which seemed to Jo to be like a church or a cathedral.

The space was full of people and, although a few seemed alarmed by the sudden arrival of the TARDIS, most seemed unconcerned by it, as if they had seen something similar before.

Jo looked around. There he was. The one-eyed king. The living god. Odin, High King of all Sweden. He was holding Gungnir and was flanked by his sons. There was Thor with his hammer, and another man, whom Jo guessed was his younger brother, Balder. Ranks of Odin's warriors stood on either side of them, and so the Aesir and the Vanir faced each other.

In between them stood a man alone, dressed from head to foot in a floor-length white robe. In his hands he held a long and wicked-looking knife; he was both the priest and the executioner, ready to make his sacrifice.

'So!' roared Odin. 'You come, Njord, to observe our ancient and noble blessing here in the temple, tonight of all nights.'

Njord stepped forward. 'I do.'

Odin smiled, but there was treachery in that smile. 'And have you, Frey, also come? Have you come to keep your promises to me?'

Njord flicked his head sideways at the Master questioningly.

The Master nodded. 'I have.'

'What is this?' cried Njord. 'What have you agreed with this man?'

Odin laughed. 'And yet we should still have a sacrifice! Yes!'

There was a roar from his people, and then his men parted as the Doctor was led forward into the middle of the assembly.

'You, Healer!' declared Odin. 'The owner of the magical ship that is now mine!'

Njord roared, a great cry of betrayal and anger. 'What? What is this?'

He waved to his men, but, before they could react, more of Odin's warriors emerged from the shadows of the temple and surrounded them, weapons drawn.

'And now, Odin, O great king!' said the Master. 'It is time for you to keep your side of our bargain. The spear, if you please.'

Again, Odin laughed. 'You foolish little man! I have the ship. And I have the spear. What need have I of you any more?'

The Master's face darkened. 'You! How dare you! You know nothing! You need me. And you will give me the spear, or I will not show you how to operate the ship.'

'You *will* show me!' Odin shouted. Then his voice dropped to a low, menacing whisper. 'Or I shall kill you, along with the Healer and the woman.'

The Doctor looked at the Master. 'Nice work, old boy,' he said, then turned to Odin. 'Now, look here, my dear sir, you need to listen to me. You need to listen to me very carefully.'

Odin turned to face the Doctor, surprise and amusement spreading across his face. 'I do? And why is that?'

'Because this man has betrayed you, just as you have betrayed him. But his betrayal is *far* more potent than yours. Those waterwheels he's had you build. No doubt he told you they would benefit you in some way?'

Odin's eyes narrowed. He glanced from the Doctor to the Master, who now stood helpless, his arms held firmly by two of Odin's men.

'He told us it was some great power. Power that would light and heat our houses and halls.'

'And so it will, just not in the way you imagine. What you have created for him is sending power to a box hidden underneath this temple. This device has been storing the power from the wheels for a very long time, and it will explode when he wants it to, at his command. If it does so, it will not only destroy you and everyone here, your temple and your village, but also create a wound in the time stream, preventing anyone from ever travelling in and out of here ever again. No doubt that was his intention: to steal the spear and cover his tracks.'

Odin stared at the Doctor. 'You are talking nonsense, Healer.'

'I speak the truth. You may not understand everything I'm telling you, but understand this: Frey has betrayed you! Do not trust him!'

'Enough of this,' cried Njord. 'It is Odin who has betrayed *us*!'

'No!' roared Odin. 'You and Frey have been angling for war from the very start, and you shall have it!'

He waved Gungnir above his head and seemed about to hurl it at the Vanir.

'Doctor!' cried Jo. 'It's the start of the war!'

'Not yet, it isn't,' he said. 'Odin! Aren't you forgetting something? Shouldn't you make your sacrifice for victory before going to war? That must come first, correct?'

Odin wheeled round, his eyes wide with rage, but he lowered his spear as he spoke to the Doctor. 'Yes,' he said. 'You are right. You are right . . . Very well! And which of you shall I sacrifice first? The traitor, Frey? Or your woman?'

'No!' cried the Doctor. 'You will take me. I give myself to you, upon one condition.'

'Which is?'

The Doctor waved a hand at the priest. 'Do not insult me with this man. If I am to be a sacrifice, I request – no, I *demand* – the honour of dying at the hand of the king, and by the power of Gungnir itself!'

'Doctor! No!' screamed Jo, fighting but failing to break free of the men who held her.

Odin stared at the Doctor as the seconds ticked by, and then he began to chuckle. He lifted his spear high above his head and bellowed its name: '*Gungnir!*'

His shout was taken up by his men, and Odin stepped forward. The Doctor began to edge sideways, backing away, backing away. Odin smiled, relishing the game – the cat and mouse, the hunter and hunted – as the Doctor opened up some distance between them.

'No!' cried Jo again. 'No!'

And then she fell silent, because she saw what the Doctor had done, and where he was now standing.

Odin pulled back his arm and flung Gungnir with all his might. The spear flew from his hand and headed straight for the Doctor. It could not miss. It would not.

Jo screamed as she saw the Doctor watch it for a split second. Then he took two neat steps backwards and pushed through the unlocked door of the TARDIS, disappearing from sight.

The spear hurtled in after him, it too vanishing.

Everyone gasped, and then fell silent.

Nothing and no one moved for three long heartbeats, and then the Doctor stepped out of the TARDIS, holding the spear.

His voice was deep and strong. 'You threw the spear that cannot miss, Odin. And you missed. Now it is my turn.'

He pulled back his arm, then paused and grinned. 'Or, I can give you Gungnir back on one condition.'

Odin began to roar his displeasure, but the Doctor again made as if to throw the spear. 'Are you so sure I will miss, too?' he asked.

Odin's roar settled into a rumble, and through clenched teeth he hissed, 'What is it that you want, Healer?'

The Doctor turned to Jo and smiled.

12

Safely inside, the Doctor closed the door of the TARDIS, and Jo ran to his side. 'We can't leave the spear!' she cried. 'It's more important than I am!'

The Doctor held her by the shoulders. 'My dear girl,' he said. 'That is very noble of you. You were right. Your aspirations *are* the very noblest. But you're wrong about something. Nothing is more important than you.'

'Oh, Doctor. I . . . But the spear . . .'

'Yes, the spear,' said the Doctor. 'The spear. But which spear?'

He nodded towards the door of the TARDIS, where the spear was leaning.

'But you just gave that back to him.'

'No, I gave him the copy we were going to leave in the museum. That one is the real one – I hope. It was all such a rush.'

He winked and Jo burst out laughing. 'That's brilliant!'

'Thank you. One of my better improvisations, I'd say. Bit of a nuisance.'

'But, anyway, why didn't the spear hit you?'

'Temporal grace,' said the Doctor. 'No weapons can function inside the TARDIS – even something as simple as a spear. Once I was inside, I was safe. It was easy enough to sidestep it and catch it. Then I simply swapped the spears and walked back out of the old police box.'

Jo smiled. 'And what about the Master?'

'Oh, well, they'll find the capacitor I was talking about under the temple, and then they might take me, and the Master, more seriously. But you know him. He'll talk his way out of it in the end. Though it might take a little longer than usual. The only thing I can't work out is where his TARDIS is. Or *Skithblathnir*, I should say.'

Jo fell silent.

'What is it?' asked the Doctor. 'Is something wrong?'

'The Master's TARDIS. You think he made it look like a Viking ship?'

'That seems likely. It must be where the legend comes from. It would have made it easier for the Norse to understand if it looked like one of their own ships.'

'Oh,' said Jo. 'And how big would it be?'

'Any size at all. Why?'

Jo rummaged in her pocket, looking for the piece of wood from the model that she'd snapped off: the tiller. Instead, she found a strange metallic device.

'Doctor, is this something important? I found it. I . . . well . . . I broke it.'

The Doctor took it from her, studied it briefly, and then laughed so hard it almost drowned out the sound of the TARDIS materialising at UNIT HQ once more.

'My dear girl,' he said. 'You appear to have removed the dimensional stabiliser from the Master's TARDIS. He'll have a hard time time-travelling without it. Jo, you are quite superb! Even I would be hard put to make a new one.'

'What, even you, Doctor?' said Jo, laughing.

'Well,' he said, 'using Viking-age technology – yes.'

And with that he pushed his way out of the TARDIS, and back into the safe warmth of the British summer in 1973.

THE FOURTH DOCTOR:
THE ROOTS OF EVIL

PHILIP REEVE

PROLOGUE

Above the dead surface of a nameless world, far out among the Autumn Stars, the Heligan Structure hangs alone in the hard, cold light of space. A tree that has never known the tug of any gravity, except its own, it has grown immense, stretching out its massive branches in all directions. Among its glossy leaves the people build their homes and halls and galleries, but the tree does not notice them. It is sleeping, as it has slept for centuries, dreaming its long, slow, bitter dreams of vengeance . . .

1

As he walked down the steep trunk-roads, which generations of his people had bored through the living wood, Ven could hear the great tree creaking, shifting, muttering. He hated those noises. He hated the shadows that the dim bio-lamps on the ceilings cast. These deep places had always made him uneasy. But someone had to go there. Someone had to check the central trunks for canker and seek out the honey-hives and meatberry bushes, which the people needed to supplement their food supply. Ven was fifteen now – in the first year of his manhood. Even the Justiciar's son had to take his turn among the inner branches.

Nervously he made his way along the twisting passages, shining his glow-beetle lamp into crevices, listening out for the buzzing of the small black bees that might lead him to a honey-hive. He found an out-sprouting of woody shoots that would soon block the road if they were left to grow: he marked the place with a red thread and made a note in his bark-book to report them to the pruning squads.

The creaking of the tree grew louder. It was restless tonight, Ven thought, grumbling in its sleep. And then – just when he had almost made himself believe that those noises were nothing to be frightened of – a new one reached him. A roaring, snoring sound, like some vast saw tearing at the tree: a wheezing that grew louder and louder, as if some terrible thing was rushing towards him out of the Heartwood.

Ven dropped his lamp and covered his ears with his hands. One of the lamp's precious glass panes broke and the beetles inside escaped, circling his head in a storm of dizzy little lights before scattering away into the shadows.

The noise grew louder and louder and . . . stopped.

Ven took his hands from his ears and listened. The mumblings of the great tree were all that he could hear now. They seemed quiet and comforting after that terrible new sound.

His first thought was to run back to the out-branches. But what would he say when they asked him why he'd left his work unfinished? That there had been a scary noise? He could imagine how the others would tease him about that. He was the Justiciar's son. It was his duty to show courage, and to set a good example.

So instead of hurrying away, he went towards the place where the noise had come from, around a bend of the passage and down a flight of shallow carved stairs to where a hollow space opened among a mass of vast trunks.

Ven had been to this place before. It was directly above the digestion chamber, and was used for funerals. He remembered, as a small boy, watching the shrouded body of his grandfather being lowered down through one of the dark openings in the floor to become one with the tree. The place had been empty then, nothing but the ring of mourners. Now something waited in the dim, silvery light.

It was more than man-high, and a colour that Ven had seldom seen before; a rectangular thing, with windows and a door, like a small, lost room. Or a *box* . . .

Ven's mouth felt dry. *It can't be!* he thought. Not *now*, not *here*! Not appearing to *him*, after all the years of waiting . . .

Yet here it stood, solid, impossible and terrifying: the Blue Box.

2

'Leela!' shouted the Doctor. 'We're here!'

He was in one of his excitable moods. Leela threw aside the furs she slept under and went out of her cabin to find him. She had travelled through years and light-years with him, but she still didn't understand the turnings that his temper took. Sometimes he was like a child, sometimes a god. Often he seemed to be both at once.

'Come on!' he shouted, his voice echoing as he strode ahead of her somewhere through the strange, too-big spaces of the TARDIS. 'Don't you want to take a look?'

She hurried past the swimming pool, up the long spiral of a staircase and down a corridor to the control chamber. The rising-and-falling thing that told her when the TARDIS was in motion was still, so she knew that they had landed somewhere. The Doctor waited by the door, his long scarf wrapped three times around his neck, his hat pushed back on his brown mop of curls, a wide grin on his face.

'Where are we?' Leela asked.

'Surprise!' the Doctor said. 'You know you were complaining that you missed trees?'

'I did not *complain*,' said Leela. Though it was true: she

was a forest-dweller, a warrior of the Sevateem. But since
the Doctor had taken her from her jungle home, their
travels had mostly been to treeless places: the crystalline
cities of Ix, the steel hives of the Sun Makers on Pluto. Part
of her longed for the dappled light of forests and the smell
of growing things.

'Of course you complained!' said the Doctor. 'And you
were quite right to. It reminded me that I've always meant to
visit this place. It's called the Heligan Structure.'

'And there are trees here?'

'Oh, better than that! The Heligan Structure *is* a tree; one
enormous, genetically engineered tree, the size of a small
moon. Earth people in the twenty-fourth century use these
things to help terraform alien worlds.'

'Terror . . . what?'

'Terraform: to make Earth-like. I've seen whole forests of
Heligans hanging high in the upper atmospheres of planets
in the Cygnus Sector, slowly breathing in carbon dioxide,
breathing out oxygen. The leaves act as solar collectors. This
one's different though: much bigger, and all alone.'

He put a picture of it on the TARDIS's screen for her. It
did look like a moon, she thought. A moon of spiky green
leaves, with spires and windows and covered balconies and
jutting pointy bits poking out all over it. It was floating above
a world that looked as lifeless as a cinder.

'It doesn't look like a tree . . .'

'No,' agreed the Doctor. 'More like a giant Christmas
decoration built by squirrels. The tree's inside: root ball in
the centre, trunks and branches radiating out in all
directions. And people live on it! There's no life on the

planet below, but here they are, hundreds of them, living in this tree. A whole city of tree houses, slowly linked together over hundreds of years. It's a space station, Leela. A wooden space station!'

Leela stared at the thing. 'Why would people want to live there?'

'Do you know, I have absolutely no idea!' said the Doctor, his grin growing wider, as it always did when he arrived in some new place. 'Let's find out!'

He unlatched the door. Leela checked she had her knife, and looked round for K9. The robot dog was parked under the main console. Multicoloured wires trailed from one of his hatches to a port on the console's underside. He was motionless, his single eye unlit, but when Leela called his name he raised his head and the antennae on top swivelled towards her.

'Recharging batteries, mistress,' he said. 'Estimated time remaining: two hours, thirty-seven minutes, fourteen seconds . . .'

'All right, K9,' said the Doctor. 'You wait here. There's a good dog.'

'Affirmative, master.'

'But, Doctor!' Leela protested. 'What if we are attacked? The little metal one fights well!'

'I don't need K9 to look after me,' the Doctor assured her. 'I'm sure there'll be no danger here anyway.'

He might be sure, but Leela was not. She could never understand why the Doctor was so careless of danger. It was a good thing he had her to look after him, she thought, as he opened the TARDIS door and they stepped out together into dim, green light and the earthy, warm-compost smell inside the great tree.

The TARDIS had materialised in a sort of woody cave, its walls formed by thick trunks, which had twined and fused together over centuries. The floor was a latticework of roots. Here and there a dark hole opened between them. The Doctor bounded around this space delightedly, running his hands over the smooth silver bark, saying things like: 'Grown from heavily modified holly DNA, I think!' and 'Too small to create this much gravity on its own . . . They must have a generator somewhere. That's how they stop the atmosphere escaping into space . . .'

Leela ignored him. He might know about DNA and gravity and space, but she knew trees. She'd known each individual tree within a day's walk of her home village. Even as a child she'd understood that trees each had their own character, like people. She looked around her at the scarred and knotted trunks, and listened to the way that this tree creaked and stirred and shifted. It seemed to her that it was ancient – and evil.

And she could feel eyes on her. Someone was watching them. She turned, reaching for her knife. A narrow passageway opened between the trunks nearby, and from the darkness there a boy stared out: wide, scared eyes in a brown face.

'Doctor . . .' she whispered.

The Doctor saw the boy. 'Hello!' he said.

The boy seemed unable to move, unable to speak. He cowered a little deeper into the shadows as the Doctor walked towards him, but that was all.

The Doctor looked pleased to see the boy. He always looked pleased to see everybody. He reached into his pocket and pulled out a crumpled paper bag. 'Would you like a jelly baby?' he asked, holding it out to the boy.

The boy looked down at the bag, then up again at the Doctor's reassuring grin. He didn't look at all reassured. He said, 'You are really him! You are *the Doctor*!'

'That's right. And this is Leela. What's your name?'

'Ven,' said the boy.

'Ven? That's a good name. Catchy. Easy to remember.'

The boy said, 'It's short for "Vengeance-Will-Be-Ours-When-The-Doctor-Dies-A-Thousand-Agonising-Deaths".'

The Doctor's grin faded. 'Well,' he said, 'that *is* a bit of a mouthful. I can see why you shortened it . . . Are you *sure* you wouldn't like a jelly baby?'

A tremor rippled through the tree, making all the trunks and branches creak and whisper, shuddering the roots underfoot.

'There is danger here,' said Leela firmly. She turned back towards the TARDIS. But in the few seconds that her attention had been focused on the Doctor and Ven, the chamber had changed. New shoots were sprouting silently from the floor and twining around the TARDIS, enclosing it in a cage of living wood, which grew thicker with each passing instant. Leela ran forward and tugged at a shoot. It was young, green and pliable, but as fast as she pulled it away from the TARDIS another grew to take its place.

'Do something!' she shouted at the Doctor. 'Use your magic!'

'The sonic screwdriver, you mean?' The Doctor took off his hat and scratched his head, staring at the mass of branches

and tendrils where the TARDIS had been. 'It has no effect
on wood, I'm afraid.'

Leela gave a cry of frustration and drew her knife. The
thinner tendrils parted easily enough, amid sticky splatterings
of sap, but more were sprouting all the time. The ones that
had grown first were already thick and woody.

'You will never free it!' shouted Ven. Outraged by what
Leela was doing to the tree, he forgot his fear of the Doctor
and ran to her, struggling to pull her away. 'The tree has
awoken! You will never get your box back! You will die here!
Let justice be done!'

Leela wrenched free of him and spun round, cursing, ready
to drive her knife through him despite the Doctor's shout of
'No!' But before she could strike, another tremor shook the
tree, far worse than the first. Caught off-balance, she pitched
forward, and would have fallen had the Doctor not caught
her. Ven was not so lucky; stumbling backwards, he slipped
into one of the ominous dark openings in the floor and
vanished with a terrified scream.

As the shaking ceased, the Doctor and Leela ran to the
edge of the hole. It opened into a shaft, smooth-walled and
sticky with sap. Far below they could see a greenish glow. It
seemed to Leela that they were looking down into a lake of
thick green fluid. The composty smell came strongly up the
shaft, and so did the whimperings of Ven, who was clinging
to some tiny handhold halfway down.

'Don't worry!' called the Doctor. 'We'll soon have you out
of there!'

Leela could not see why they should help him – he was
their enemy! He had attacked them! – but she wanted to

please the Doctor, so instead of arguing she leaned into the shaft, stretching down both hands towards the terrified boy.

He was far beyond her reach. The Doctor pulled her out again. 'No, no, no . . . We don't want you falling in after him.' He peered down at Ven again. 'What's down there?' he called. 'Is there any way out at the bottom?'

The boy shook his head.

'Doctor!' said Leela, tugging at his sleeve. 'There are forest plants at home that trap small creatures and dissolve them in pools of slime among their leaves. This tree must be the same, but bigger!'

The Doctor looked at her, his eyes very wide, his expression deadly serious. 'Heligans aren't usually carnivorous. I suppose this one is just too big to sustain itself on sunlight alone. Someone has been monkeying about with its DNA sequences . . . That must be the digestion chamber down there. I expect they shovel all their waste into it. Their dead too. Making the tree stronger. Very efficient . . .'

'Doctor, what about the boy?'

'Eh? Oh yes . . .' He peered down the shaft again. Ven was still clinging there. 'How far down do you think he is?' the Doctor asked. 'I'd say about twenty feet; that's about six metres, or roughly . . . let me see . . . two and a half Rigellian floons . . . Yes, this should do it . . .'

As he spoke, he was unwinding the long, stripy scarf from around his neck. He tied one end firmly around a protruding root at the mouth of the shaft and lowered the other carefully down towards the boy.

'Catch hold of this, Ven!'

The boy looked as if he'd been asked to touch a poisonous snake. Perhaps he thought it *was* a poisonous snake, it occurred to Leela. 'It will not hurt you,' she promised. 'It is called a "scarf". It is like a cloak, only pointless. Take it! He is trying to save your life!'

The boy still looked just as scared. 'But the B-Blue Box,' he stammered. 'And he said . . . He's the *Doctor*!'

'Now catch hold,' said the Doctor cheerfully. 'There's a good chap.'

For a moment Ven just hung there, staring up. Then, with a yelp of fear, he let go of his precarious handhold and snatched hold of the scarf. He dangled for a moment, flailing for a foothold on the shaft walls. Little flakes of bark, dislodged by his boots, went tumbling down to splash into that green lake below.

'I hope he doesn't stretch it,' the Doctor whispered to Leela, as they watched him scramble towards them. 'Still, that's one problem solved. Now to think about untangling the TARDIS . . . There's always a solution to these little emergencies. You just have to think sideways at them.'

Leaving Leela to keep an eye on the boy while he climbed back up, the Doctor rolled over on to his back and clasped his hands behind his head. He always thought best when he was relaxing. But just as he was about to turn his mind to the problem of the TARDIS, he noticed that he and Leela were no longer alone. While they had been busy rescuing young Ven, three men and a girl had crept silently into the chamber behind them. All four wore what appeared to be wooden armour, and all carried spears. The girl, who seemed to be their leader, was pointing hers at the Doctor's throat.

The Doctor beamed at her. 'Hello! I think you'll get on rather well with my friend Leela here.'

Leela glanced round, saw the newcomers, and sprang up, reaching for her knife. The Doctor gestured at her to keep it in its sheath. If his young companion had a fault, he thought, it was this habit of hers of trying to stick knives in people as soon as she met them. Personally, he much preferred to get them chatting. People were generally much less inclined to want to kill you once you'd chatted for a bit, and if they weren't, well, at least you could use the time to think of an escape plan . . .

He touched a curious finger to the tip of the spear that the girl had levelled at him. 'Ouch! Wooden, isn't it? It seems very sharp.'

'It is,' said the girl, who didn't appear to want to chat. 'You'll find out just *how* sharp unless you tell me who you are and what you're doing here.'

'Oh, we were just passing, you know,' said the Doctor, smiling brightly. 'Thought we'd look in. I'm the Doctor.'

The girl glared. The men behind her looked terrified. One said, 'It *is* him!' Another warned, 'Be careful, Aggie! Remember, "The Doctor is a Master of Deceit".'

'Aggie?' said the Doctor thoughtfully. 'I wonder what that's short for?'

The girl's nostrils flared proudly. 'My *full* name is Agony-Without-End-Shall-Be-The-Doctor's-Punishment.'

'Ah,' said the Doctor. 'You know, Leela, just between ourselves, I'm starting to feel that I'm not entirely welcome here.'

'Chairman Ratisbon felt the tree wake, and sent me to find out what roused it,' said the girl.

'Chairman Ratisbon, eh?'

'You have heard of him?'

'No. Who is he?'

'He is the one who has been chosen to be the instrument of our people's vengeance,' said Aggie proudly.

'Well, good for him . . .'

'Watch out!'

It was one of the spearmen, pointing to the mouth of the shaft.

Ven was so dishevelled and smeared with sap that they did not recognise him at first as he came scrambling up, gasping with the effort of the climb. Then Aggie cried, 'Ven!'

'He is the Doctor!' said Ven, pointing. 'He arrived in the Blue Box, just as the legends tell, and the great tree awoke and captured it to stop him from escaping.'

'The great tree be praised!' said Aggie.

'But . . . He saved my life!' Ven untied the scarf and handed it back to the Doctor. 'I would have fallen into the digestion chamber, but he risked his scarf to save me . . . So can he really be the Doctor? The Doctor would not have done that, would he? And he looks unlike the carving.'

'Perhaps he has disguised himself,' said Aggie. 'Perhaps he saved you for some purpose of his own.' She looked at the Doctor again. 'The day we have waited for so long has come at last. We must take him to Chairman Ratisbon.'

'No,' said Ven. 'It is the Justiciar who leads us, not Chairman Ratisbon. You must take the Doctor to the Justiciar. She will decide.'

'And because you are her son, do you think that gives you the right to command the Chairman's guards?' asked Aggie.

'No, but . . . It is the ancient law: when the Doctor comes, the Justiciar will try him before all the people.'

Aggie nodded haughtily. 'Very well. We shall take him before the Justiciar, and send word to Ratisbon to prepare the Chair.' She beckoned one of her men over. 'Stay here; guard the Blue Box. The rest of you, bring the prisoners.'

An odd splashing sound came from down below; a strange, wet rustling from deep in the digestion chamber. 'What was that?' asked the Doctor, as Aggie's spearmen dragged him to his feet. 'Did anybody else hear that?'

Nobody was listening to him, except Leela. She knew what the noises meant. *The tree is angry*, she thought, but she didn't say so. He would only tell her that she was being unscientific.

Below them, unseen, something was happening in the complex of woody caves that formed the giant Heligan's digestion chamber. Dark growths studded the walls and roof down there. They had been no bigger than footballs until now, but they were starting to swell, bigger and bigger, thorny spines pushing through their outer skin. Already a few were so large that their own weight tugged them free of the sockets they had grown in. They rolled down into the lake of green broth and bobbed there for a few moments like floating mines. Then, unfolding, putting out roots and feelers, they began to drag their way ashore . . .

3

Leela was uncertain just how far they travelled through the endless windings and twistings of the Heligan Structure. Gradually the passageways through which their captors drove them began to be walled with planks and panels rather than simply hollowed through living wood, and finally they entered the tree-house city in the out-branches. Once or twice they crossed broad thoroughfares, and passed openings that gave glimpses into great chambers where food was being prepared, and bark-fibres turned into cloth. Sometimes they went through busy spaces where people came crowding round to watch the strangers led past. Leela heard the news passing from mouth to mouth, crackling like a brush-fire: 'It is the Doctor! The *Doctor*!' People shouted it in the wooden arcades, spreading the news to distant branches. But Aggie and her companions would not stop, just jabbed the prisoners with their wooden spears and forced them onwards.

'They're not very hospitable,' the Doctor whispered. 'But you can't help admiring them. They've built this whole world out of Heligan wood. Remarkable!'

Leela thought what was really remarkable was the way he could remain so light-hearted while they were being led to whatever awful fate these tree people had planned for them. He had that grin again. She supposed it was because he had lived so long and seen so many wonders. It must grow boring after a while. Anything new delighted him.

'I suppose your ancestors were stranded here?' he asked, looking back at Aggie and the spearmen. They would not answer him, so he tried calling out to Ven, who was still trailing behind. 'Space-wreck, was it? And you salvaged just one Heligan and managed to turn it into a sort of living space station . . . Ingenious! How long have you been here?'

'The great tree has been the home of our people for nine hundred years,' said Ven. 'Yes, our ancestors were trapped here . . .'

'But there was no wreck,' said Aggie fiercely. 'It was *you* who stranded us, Doctor.'

'Really? Me? No, I think there's been a bit of a misunderstanding . . .' the Doctor began, but the conversation was at an end, and so was the journey. One of the spearmen opened a carved door, and Aggie shoved the Doctor and Leela through it into a big octagonal room with carved panelled walls. That side of the Heligan Structure was turned towards the sun, and leaf-dappled sunlight came dancing through a window made from a single translucent sheet of cellulose. A woman waited for them there; handsome, grey-haired, the hem of her tea-coloured bark-fibre robes brushing the floor as she rose from her seat and came forward to study the Doctor.

Aggie and her men forced him to his knees.

'Mother,' said Ven. 'It is him!'

The woman frowned. 'He is not like the carving.'

'I saw the Blue Box,' said Ven. 'But . . .'

'He admitted himself that he is the Doctor,' said Aggie. 'I shall fetch the Chairman. Justice shall be done.'

'So you must be the Justiciar?' said the Doctor, smiling up at the woman as Aggie left. He pointed at the chair that she had risen from; a thing of plastic and metal, quite unlike the rest of this wooden world. 'That's the pilot's chair from a Wyndham-class starship, isn't it? An antique, by the look of it . . .'

'We have waited a long time for you, Doctor . . .'

The Justiciar's voice was stern, but she looked troubled. All her life she had known of the Doctor. She remembered as a little girl being told by her grandmother, 'Be good, or the Doctor will come and get you!' But she had never really believed in him. A man who travelled through space and time in a blue box? It sounded so unlikely! She had thought he was just a symbol; a useful myth that the founders had invented to bind the people together and help them to survive in this strange place. When she was elected Justiciar she had sworn solemnly that she was ready to sit in judgement on the Doctor if he should return – but a hundred Justiciars before her had sworn that same oath, and he never had. She had never imagined that it would fall to her to deliver sentence on him.

'For nine centuries our people have awaited their revenge,' she said, looking into his wide, intent eyes, and wondering still if it was really him. 'Their glorious leader, Director Sprawn, promised our forefathers that you would come one day, Doctor. He designed the Heligan Structure to lure you. An intergalactic nosy parker like the Doctor will not be able to resist such a thing, he told them. And here you are.'

'Now what is all this about vengeance?' The Doctor started to rise, but the spearmen forced him down again. 'Vengeance for what? I've never done anything to you!'

'Perhaps you have betrayed so many people that you have forgotten us,' said the Justiciar.

'The Doctor would never betray anyone!' said Leela angrily.

'Hush, Leela . . .'

'Nine hundred years ago,' the Justiciar went on, 'our forefathers were colonising a world called Golrandonvar. They were from Earth. Their forest of Heligan trees was transforming the atmosphere; mining and construction operations were under way. And then you arrived in your blue box . . .'

'Golrandonvar?' asked the Doctor. 'No, it doesn't ring a bell, I'm afraid. But then I've visited such a lot of places . . . Did it look a bit like a gravel pit? You'd be amazed how many alien worlds look just like gravel pits . . .'

'Mother,' said Ven. 'He saved my life. I would have fallen into the digestion chambers if it had not been for him. Why would the Doctor do such a thing?'

'Because he is a good man!' said Leela. 'That is why he saved you! That is why he stopped me killing the angry girl and these curs with their toy spears! He would never let anyone be harmed who did not deserve it!'

The Justiciar looked at her.

'I believe you are telling the truth,' she said. 'I believe you truly think he is good. But perhaps he has deceived you. Our people have a saying: "The Doctor is a Master of Deceit: even his smiles are stratagems." He *seemed* friendly enough when he arrived on Golrandonvar nine centuries ago. But then he sided with the natives of the planet; vicious, primitive, swamp-dwelling creatures called the Thara. He helped them to rise up against our ancestors, and drive them from that promising world. One ship, that was all he left them, and just enough fuel to make it to this rock we orbit now. That is why, for all these years, we have awaited the Doctor's return. So that he can be made to pay for what he did to us.'

'Yet he did save my life,' Ven said.

'And I am grateful,' acknowledged the Justiciar. 'It shall be taken into account at his trial.'

The door crashed open again. Aggie stood there. Beside her was a tall old man, gaunt and fierce-eyed, his white brows bushy as an eagle owl's. There were more people behind him; people with spears and clubs, peering nervously over one another's shoulders for a glimpse of the Doctor.

'There will be no trial!' the old man boomed – his voice was nearly as rich and deep as the Doctor's own. 'None of your so-called justice for the Doctor, Justiciar! Have you not felt the tree-quakes? The Heligan is awake! It knows the Doctor is here, and it does not want justice. It wants revenge!'

4

Down in the Heligan's rooty heart, the man who had been left behind to guard the TARDIS was growing bored. He walked all the way round that thicket of new trunks, peeking in through the gaps between them, but he could barely make out the Blue Box, and from the bits he could see it did not look nearly as scary or impressive as the old stories made it sound. It was supposed to be 'bigger on the inside', whatever that meant, but he could not see in through the windows.

Small noises came constantly now up the shafts in the floor: splashings and slitherings and strange, scratchy rustlings. He ignored them. The old tree was restless tonight, and who could blame it? It was trembling and shaking itself, full of new sounds.

Deep in thought, and studying the TARDIS, he did not notice the things that came squeezing out of the shafts all around him. As spiky as conker casings, as tall as men, they moved like crabs on their crab-leg roots, slow at first, then scuttling suddenly . . .

The tree was restless tonight.

No one heard his screams.

*

'Revenge?' asked the Justiciar, turning from her prisoners to confront the angry newcomer who had interrupted her. 'Yes, but it must be done honourably, Chairman. I am the Justiciar, and I say that we must have a trial. We must make certain that this really is the Doctor; he should be allowed to have his say before you put him to death.'

'You are not fit to be Justiciar!' sneered Chairman Ratisbon. 'You are like so many others nowadays; you think the Doctor is only a fairy-tale monster to scare our naughty children with.'

The Justiciar blushed angrily. 'Hasn't everyone wondered that? Everyone with any intelligence? Even fierce old men like you, Cut-Out-The-Doctor's-Living-Heart Ratisbon? But here he is, and he says that he is the Doctor, and by our ancient laws he must face judgement.'

'There is no need,' said Ratisbon. 'Judgement was passed on this traitor nine hundred years ago. The sentence is agony and death, and it is my duty to see that it is carried out. Take him to the Chair!'

And although the Justiciar held up her hands and commanded them to stop, there was no stopping the men who poured into her chamber, who seized hold of the Doctor and dragged him roughly away. Leela, while her own guards were distracted, snatched back the knife that one had taken from her and ran to rescue him, but one of Ratisbon's men felled her with a blow from a spear-butt. She landed on all fours, groggy, blood dripping from a cut on her forehead. Ven ran to her, and his mother came and knelt beside her, dabbing at the wound with a cloth.

'Leave me alone! It is barely a scratch . . .' Leela tried to fling them away, to run after the Doctor. They held her back. 'Where are they taking him?' she demanded. 'I thought you were leader here?'

The Justiciar said, 'I thought so too, but it seems not. Ratisbon is our executioner. It seems he is impatient to get to work.'

The room quivered. The whole tree seemed to be stirring restlessly, like some great animal troubled in its dreams. From outside the room came a rustling sound, like someone dragging a heavy bundle of twigs.

One of the men who had been lingering in the open doorway, not sure whether to stay with the Justiciar or follow Chairman Ratisbon, suddenly shouted out in fear. 'Justiciar!'

He stumbled back into the room and tried to shut the door, but something shoved it violently open. The rustling sound was very loud, and the room was suddenly filled with the compost smell that Leela remembered from down below. She looked at Ven and his mother, saw fear and incomprehension on their faces, and stood up, knife in hand, ready to meet this new peril face to face . . .

Except it had no face. A hard greenish shell studded with sharp spines, a cluster of busy, scuttling, claw-like roots, delicate tendrils that groped and fluttered, a thick hairy stem, but nothing anywhere that looked like eyes or a mouth.

Behind her one of the Justiciar's women shrieked, and the creature swung towards the sound. *It's blind*, thought Leela, *but it is not deaf* . . . She motioned to the others to be quiet. She did not know if she could fight this thing – not alone. A few of the men in the room had spears, but they looked too scared to use them. Anyway, where did you stab a thing like that? What would its weak points be?

Someone whimpered. The thing twitched, creeping forward on its skirt of roots, tendrils reaching out to feel the air ahead. Leela held her breath, trying not to tremble as a tendril-tip came within a hand's breadth of her face.

Then, from somewhere outside, there was another scream – *There must be more of them*, thought Leela – and the creature whirled around and scuttled out. More screams in the corridor; whispers from the huddled, frightened people in the room.

'What was that?' hissed Leela.

'I don't know!' Ven whispered back. 'I've never seen anything like it.'

'The Doctor,' she said. 'He will know what they are, what to do.'

'But Ratisbon has the Doctor!' said the Justiciar.

'Then we must save him!'

The Justiciar looked at her for a moment, then slowly nodded. To the people in the room she said, 'You who have weapons, come with me; the rest, gather at the Hall of Justice. Be careful of those . . . those whatever-they-ares.'

Leela was already at the door. She acted as if she had forgotten that she had ever been their prisoner, and they did not try to remind her. Outside, the wooden corridors were filled with the rooty rustling and wet vegetable smell of the creeping things. Leela gripped her knife more firmly.

'Where have they taken him?' she asked.

5

They had taken him down stairs, and through carved and polished wooden corridors, until at last they came to a heavy door. Chairman Ratisbon himself unlocked it and flung it wide. And there, in a big, shadowy chamber, stood the Chair.

The Chair was Ratisbon's own invention. For many years the executioner had sensed that belief in the Doctor was fading and the hunger for revenge growing weak. He had set out to remind his people of their old hatred, and show his own faith in the ancient legends, by preparing the device on which the Doctor would be tortured and killed when he finally showed up. Over the years he and his supporters had gathered wood and much of the remaining metal from the original colonists' dismantled starship, and they had built the Chair.

It was a metal and plastic chair much like the Justiciar's throne, but it was surrounded by a spiky halo of sharp implements mounted on articulated wooden arms. There were drills and blades and needles, syringes filled with the tree's own acids, rubber tubes and electric terminals, ingenious devices designed to peel and carve and crush.

'Did you think death would be quick, Doctor?' sneered Ratisbon. He gestured to the Chair. 'Please – take a seat.'

'Oh, that's all right,' said the Doctor. 'I'd rather stand, if it's all the same to you.'

The chamber lurched; the walls creaked. Some of the people who had gathered there cried out in fear, and from outside came noises; shouts and screams, the crash of something falling.

Ratisbon sniffed irritably. 'What now?'

The door opened. Aggie burst in, shouting, 'Chairman! There are . . . things! They are coming up out of the Heartwood! They are everywhere!'

More shouts behind her, then a strange noise, like someone dragging a big bundle of sticks. Ratisbon flapped his hands, waving the annoyance away. 'Then deal with it, Agony-Without-End. I daresay it is just some trick by the Justiciar. She hasn't the stomach to let real justice be done . . .'

But even as he spoke, the floor behind him bulged and split, its ancient planking splintering upwards as a great blow struck it from beneath. The Chairman's followers scattered as something large and spiny squeezed up into the chamber. Others were rising too, all around the room. They reached out tendrils to seize struggling and screaming men. One snatched Ratisbon, wrapping roots around him, dragging him backwards towards the hole it had emerged from.

The Doctor, forgotten by his frightened guards, ran to the Chair and broke off the arm that held the biggest, sharpest blade. By the time he turned back, Ratisbon was vanishing through the floor. The Doctor ran to him, slashing at the roots that held him. He grabbed one of the Chairman's flailing hands and shouted, 'Hold on, man!' and 'Aggie, help!' But Aggie was battling against another of the creatures. Roots wrapped around Ratisbon's throat and tightened, squeezing and crushing. His fingers slipped limply from the Doctor's grasp; the thing dragged his body down into the darkness under the floor.

The Doctor ran to help Aggie. Defending herself with her spear, the girl was managing to hold at bay the monster that was attacking her. When the Doctor joined her it retreated, waving its roots and tendrils threateningly, making fierce rustling noises, which sounded like wind in treetops.

'Come on!' the Doctor shouted. He and the other survivors fled from the chamber, and Aggie slammed the door behind them. The corridors outside were full of rustlings too, and shouts and shrieks, which told them that more of the creatures were loose all through the maze of the Heligan Structure.

'What are they?' asked Aggie.

'I should say they are some kind of mobile spore,' said the Doctor. 'That's how Heligans reproduce, normally. They should be setting off on their own to turn into new trees. But they've been altered, re-programmed if you like. Turned into warriors . . .'

Aggie nodded slowly, stupid with shock. 'The tales tell how when the Doctor comes, the tree itself will defend us from him. But why would its warriors attack *us*? We too are the tree's own children!'

'Well, I should imagine it's me they're after,' said the Doctor. 'That's the trouble with plants – they aren't always very bright. I expect we all look the same to them. They just grab anything that makes a sound . . .'

'Kill him, Agony-Without-End!' shouted one of the men nearby. 'He is in league with the monsters!'

'No!' said Aggie angrily. 'He helped me. He fought bravely, and tried to save the Chairman.'

The door behind them creaked, bowing outwards under the force of some heavy weight. They could hear the root-tips of the angry spores scrabbling against it. From the other direction more noises came – quick, furtive scufflings. Shadows moved where the corridor twisted. Aggie gripped her spear.

'No . . .' said the Doctor.

Around the turn of the passage came, not a spore-warrior, but another group of frightened human beings. Among them the Justiciar, Ven and Leela, who ran to the Doctor and hugged him tight. 'I knew you would escape! I came to save you! There are things, creatures . . .'

'We know, we know,' he said.

'They are everywhere!' said Ven.

'We must make our way to the Hall of Justice,' said the Justiciar. 'That is where our people gather in times of danger. Together, perhaps we can hold them off.'

She pointed down a broad corridor. They ran along it, pausing once in the shadows at an intersection while a cluster of spores went rustling by. When they reached the big double doors, Ven and one of the men heaved them open.

The spores did not yet seem to have found the Hall of Justice; it looked just the same as it had looked for all Ven's life, the same as it had looked for all the nine hundred years that there had been people in the Heligan Structure. There was the seat where the Justiciar would sit, the benches for the observers, the dock where the Doctor would stand, and behind that, towering over everything, the great statue, which the founders had carved so that their descendants would never forget their ancient enemy.

'Who's that supposed to be?' asked the Doctor, glancing up at it.

'That is you,' said the Justiciar, but she sounded uncertain. She looked from the face of the Doctor to the face of the carving, trying to detect a similarity. She said, 'That is how the Doctor appeared to our ancestors, nine hundred years ago.'

'It looks nothing like him!' said Leela.

'Oh, I don't know,' said the Doctor. 'There is a certain resemblance. Two eyes, two ears, one nose – I suppose you could call that a nose? – and it's true that I've changed a bit over the years. But I'm certain I've never looked like that.'

'He's so young!' said Leela. 'And so handsome!'

'I mean, he's wearing a bow tie!' the Doctor explained patiently. 'Ridiculous objects! I wouldn't be seen dead in a bow tie!'

'The Doctor told our ancestors "Bow ties are cool",' said Ven.

'Cool?' The Doctor blinked at him. 'I would never have said . . . Oh, wait! Hang on! Ah! I think I see what's happened. That fellow must be one of my *future* regenerations. These things you blame me for, the revolt of the Thara, your exile from Golrandonvar . . . they haven't happened yet. Not for me. And you can't hold me responsible for something I haven't done yet. Would that be justice, Justiciar?'

'I suppose not . . .'

'We should kill him anyway!' said one of Ratisbon's men. 'Then he will never be able to betray our ancestors and help the Thara.'

'No,' said the Doctor, 'that wouldn't do any good. If you kill me now I won't be able to visit Golrandonvar, the Thara may never revolt, this Heligan will never exist and you won't be here to kill me. You would all vanish instantly in a puff of paradoxes.'

Another great quake shook the hall; shook the whole wooden city. Carved panels dropped from the roof. The statue of the future Doctor swayed drunkenly.

'This tree is angry,' blurted Leela.

'You're right,' the Doctor said.

'Am I?' She blinked at him. 'Are you not going to say that I am being unscientific?'

'These tree-quakes, the way the spores are behaving . . .' said the Doctor. 'Justiciar, I don't think your founders were being honest with you. Your Director Sprawn didn't really trust his descendants to bring me to justice. He knew he couldn't rely on you to stay angry all those years. He knew you'd grow too reasonable, too merciful. He just needed you to keep the tree alive. To do a bit of light pruning and keep an eye out for greenfly until I returned. Then it would take its own revenge. Even if that means destroying itself – and all of you.'

There were moans and cries of woe from his listeners. 'What can we do?' asked the Justiciar.

The Doctor smiled that wide, delighted smile of his. 'Oh, we'll think of something! Now, an organism as complex as a Heligan, especially one this big, must be controlled from somewhere. There must be a central brain of some sort, which sensed the arrival of the TARDIS and triggered the release of those spores.'

'The root ball?' suggested Ven. 'It's down in the Heartwood, beneath the digestion chamber, at the very centre of the tree.'

'Can you show me the way?'

Ven looked at his mother, then back at the Doctor. He nodded.

'I am coming with you!' Leela said.

'No, Leela, you stay here; they'll need you if the spores attack. Don't worry; I'll be back in two ticks!'

'Doctor . . .!'

But he was already gone, loping after Ven to a small door on the far side of the hall and vanishing through it into shadows.

Leela turned to the others. 'How long is a tick?' she asked. But they didn't know, and hadn't time to answer anyway. The Hall of Justice was suddenly full of the sound of spore-roots battering against the doors.

6

The Heligan Structure was shuddering constantly now, as if the ancient tree were trying to shake off all the elegant wooden buildings that had been attached to it. The groaning of the thicker branches as they heaved and thrashed had a tuneless music, like the bellowing of huge animals. And down through it all Ven led the Doctor, hiding now and then from passing spores, down past the chamber where the TARDIS was embowered, to deep places where even he had never been.

'It is forbidden to go any further,' he warned, peering down the last passage that led into the root ball. Cobwebs hung like curtains, stirring softly in a wind that seemed to come from the heart of the tree. A faint, silvery light showed at the far end.

'Oh well, rules are made to be broken!' said the Doctor cheerfully, and then, seeing how afraid the boy was, added, 'All right, you stay here. Shout if any of those spores come poking about, eh?'

He went on alone, using his hat to sweep aside the cobwebs. The light grew brighter. He emerged into a space whose walls and floor and roof were made of ancient, interwoven roots. Tangled among the roots was machinery torn from the guts of an old starship; one of those twenty-fourth-century computers with the big dials and buttons, controlling the flow of chemicals through the Heligan's boughs. Wires and coloured flexes led from the machines, wrapped around the roots like strands of ivy leading up into the ceiling. The Doctor followed them, looking up into the shadows above his head.

Among the twistings and knottings of the wood, two eyes were watching him.

'Ah!' said the Doctor. 'Director Sprawn, I presume?'

He could make out a face around the eyes now, ancient, mutated, scarcely human, sprouting twigs and tendrils like a carving of the Green Man in a country church. There were the suggestions of a body, spreadeagled on the ceiling, almost engulfed in the web of roots. So that was how Sprawn had made sure the Heligan would do his bidding, even after all these years. He had become a part of it.

They barred the doors, but the spores burst through them. They piled up benches, but the spores shoved those easily aside. And then it was all fright and confusion and the hack and thrust of spears, the screams of the people snatched by the spores, the shouts of their comrades as they fought to tear them free, the squeals of children hiding behind their mothers at the far side of the hall. And Aggie and Leela sap-spattered, fighting side by side, spear and knife and desperate courage against the spines and tendrils of the spores . . .

★

'So, Doctor!' growled the face in the ceiling, root-muffled. 'We meet again!'

'Well, we're meeting for the first time, technically, Sprawn,' said the Doctor, looking quickly around at the machinery. 'Though we *will* meet again, nine hundred years in the past. Your past: my future. That's the trouble with time travel, you never know whether you're coming or going . . .'

He reached over and turned one of the knobs on the nearest control panel. It seemed to do nothing but draw an angry hiss from the face above him.

'The Heligan will tear itself apart rather than let you escape, Doctor! We shall be avenged at last for what you did to us all those centuries ago!'

The Doctor nibbled a fingernail, his eyes still on the controls. Absent-mindedly he said, 'Ah yes, about that. I can just about accept that I might, one day, in a moment of weakness, wear a bow tie, but there is no way I will ever take up arms against anyone unless they thoroughly deserve it. I don't think you and your fellow colonists on Golrandonvar were innocent victims of the Thara rebellion at all. I think you were vicious tyrants.'

'The Thara were vermin!' shouted the face in the ceiling. 'They opposed every improvement we tried to make to their benighted world!'

'Improvements like altering their atmosphere?'

'Golrandonvar had to be terraformed: turned into a world fit for people, not those methane-breathing swamp-monkeys. We had no choice but to exterminate them!'

'Now that's a word I've never liked,' said the Doctor,

starting to sound quite stern. 'I can see why my future self is going to help them to get rid of you. Just as I'm going to have to help your own people now, to save them from your suicidal rage.'

'Let them die!' screamed the mad face above him. 'What have they to live for? For nine hundred years they've scraped a living in this wretched weed, imprisoned by your moralistic meddling!'

'Wretched?' asked the Doctor. He tried another dial, and chuckled delightedly when it produced a beeping noise and a bubbling of amber fluid in a glass container buried deep among the roots. 'Oh, I think they've done rather well with the place, all things considered. They're ready to move on. Except you didn't exactly play fair with them, did you? This tree should have had offspring, a forest of Heligans that would have made the world below us habitable. But you didn't want that. If they'd had a new world to build, your descendants might have forgotten all about their vengeance. So you made some changes to the genome, didn't you? Stopped the Heligan producing spores at all, until now . . .'

'Doctor!' There were scrabbling sounds from the passage outside. Ven came hurrying in, bearded with cobwebs, still scared of the forbidden chamber, but more scared of what was outside it. 'There are spores coming!'

'I have called them here to kill you, Doctor,' said the head in the ceiling, and it began to laugh. Saliva pattered on the brim of the Doctor's hat.

'And that's another thing,' the Doctor said, while his hands went spidering over the controls and the machinery beeped and burped. 'Heligan spores aren't normally aggressive. You must have tampered with the chemical messages that control their behaviour . . .'

'Doctor!' Ven fled to the far end of the chamber as the first spore came pushing its way along the passage, reaching out with woody limbs.

'It's all right, Ven,' said the Doctor. 'The only things that Heligan spores naturally attack are parasites that threaten their parent tree. Now I've adjusted the chemical balance, they should start to behave normally again . . .'

The spore reached past the Doctor. Its tendrils took hold of the roots that formed the wall. It climbed awkwardly, like a land crab. Other spores entered, and also started climbing. The thing that had been Director Sprawn watched, wide-eyed. He tried to struggle free of the ceiling, but his limbs were roots, his flesh was wood, the stuff of the tree was woven through him. He shrieked as the spores clustered around him. Stone-hard root-tips rose and fell like axes, hacking and hewing, splattering thick sap. The shrieks did not last long.

'What are they doing to him?' asked Ven.

'He's being pruned,' said the Doctor. 'Cut out . . .' He felt sorry for Sprawn. In many ways it was a wonderful achievement, this great tree that he'd created. If only he had been able to enjoy it for what it was, instead of poisoning it with his need for vengeance.

'Will the Heligan be all right without him?' asked Ven.

'Oh, I should think so,' said the Doctor.

Some of the spores had now turned their attention to the machinery, driving their roots through the old computer casings, ripping out spaghetti-tangles of electronic innards in fountains of dazzling sparks. Blinking away the after-images of the explosions, the Doctor started to lead Ven back up the passageway towards the outer branches and the others.

'In fact,' he said, 'I should think it will be a great deal better off . . .'

In the Hall of Justice the spores had stopped attacking all at once, suddenly going still, as if they had forgotten what they were supposed to be doing – or remembered.

'It's the Doctor!' said Leela, wiping the sap from her knife as she turned to the others. 'He's done it!'

Her comrades were not so sure. They watched warily, holding their spears ready. When the spores all suddenly shuffled into life again a few moments later, they leaped hastily back behind their barricades of piled-up benches.

But the spores were not returning to the attack. Ignoring the humans, they rustled their way to the hall's huge, misty windows. The cellulose tore as they leaned their spiny shapes hard against it. They clustered on the windowsills, tensing their many legs, and then, one by one, they sprang out, releasing jets of pent-up gas to help thrust themselves free of the Heligan's gravity.

'There!' said the Doctor, sauntering in with his hands in his pockets, Ven close behind him. 'Look at that! Another ten years or so and that world we're orbiting should start to be quite habitable.'

'Ten years, Doctor?' The Justiciar turned to look at him. She still felt faintly that she was failing in her duty by not making him stand trial, but so much had happened since his arrival, so much had changed . . . 'What shall we do in the meantime?' she asked.

'Oh, you should branch out!' the Doctor said with a grin. 'Think about advertising this place. A tree of this size, surrounded by its own floating forest – it must be one of the wonders of the galaxy! You should try luring tourists instead of Time Lords . . .'

From every window of the Heligan Structure now the spores were taking flight, unfurling their first young branches as they spread across the sky. The humans stood wonderstruck, gazing at the airborne forest that they had seeded. Ven took Aggie's hand. The Doctor tapped Leela on the shoulder and nodded towards the door.

'So,' the Doctor asked, a while later, when they had managed to cut a way through the woody stems to the door of the TARDIS. 'Seen enough trees for a bit?'

'I do not care if I never see another,' said Leela.

'Excellent! Because I was thinking the sand-reefs of Phenostris IV might be worth a look. I haven't been there since . . .'

The door closed behind them. After a few moments, the TARDIS slowly dematerialised, leaving a TARDIS-shaped cage of branches to mark the place where it had stood. The noise of its going echoed and re-echoed through the passageways and chambers of the Heartwood, but there was nobody to hear it. All the people of the Heligan Structure were crowding at its windows, watching as the skies of the world below them filled with newborn trees.

THE FIFTH DOCTOR:
TIP OF THE TONGUE

PATRICK NESS

'Is it broken?' Jonny asked, frowning.

Nettie's face looked like she was ready for this. 'It can't *break*,' she said. 'It's alive. Or something.'

'Well, *sick*, then.'

'It's fine. Look, do you want it or not?'

Jonny again felt the money he had wrapped in a tight roll in his pocket. Two dollars. A king's ransom, almost six months of saving the nickel tips he got from his job as a busboy at Mr Finnegan's diner. He gave the bulk of his wages to his mother, of course; they needed every penny now that his dad was overseas fighting this war against Hitler.

But Nettie's family needed the money, too (went the argument Jonny had rehearsed a dozen times in his head for the inevitable moment his mother blew her top when she found out how much money he was about to spend). Nettie's dad had died just after she was born, but while Jonny's mother could find good war work at Temperance's local factory making shells for tanks, Nettie's mother couldn't. Nettie's mother was black, and even though this was Maine and not the deep south, Mr Acklin, the factory owner, had found ways to keep Nettie's mother out of a job. She was supporting herself and Nettie on a cleaner's salary that could barely keep Nettie in school clothes.

Jonny's mother knew this. She and Nettie's mother had been friends ever since Jonny and Nettie had met as five-year-olds at the town's one public school, their moms quickly coming together in the way that outcasts sometimes do. The mother of the town's only mixed-race girl and the Jewish mother of the small boy with the German last name.

She'll understand, Jonny thought, rolling the money between his fingers. *Won't she?*

'You're sure it'll work?' Jonny said.

Nettie sighed, sounding twenty years older than her own fourteen. 'It worked for Uncle Paul,' she said.

'He'll get mad that you sold it –'

'He's on a tropical island by Australia somewhere shooting at people in swamps.'

Nettie's young uncle had rented a room from her mother before he'd shipped out. There was a harsh anxiety in Nettie's voice that she wasn't altogether successful in disguising. 'He's got other things to worry about.'

Jonny was still hesitant. Nettie gave an exasperated *tut*. 'Try it!' she practically shouted. 'If it doesn't work, you don't have to buy it. We can forget the whole thing.'

'OK,' Jonny finally said, holding out his hand. Nettie placed the Truth Teller in his palm. It stared up at him balefully, its yellow eyes full of weary sadness. 'It looks depressed.'

'If it was a machine, I'd fix it,' Nettie said, impatiently. Which was true. She could fix nearly anything. Jonny's bike several times, a door at his house that had never hung properly. Her Uncle Paul had been great with his hands and a worshipful Nettie had mooned around him for years like the world's most devoted younger sister, almost accidentally learning how to repair toasters and change the oil in a Studebaker. 'All I can tell you is that Paul said it worked.'

Jonny gently poked the small frown in his hand. It said nothing, but gave him a look of unsurprised hurt feelings.

He blew out a long breath. The Truth Teller was real. It was the closest he was ever going to get to being able to buy one. It could be his for two dollars.

And it might finally, *finally*, get Marisa Channing to notice him.

He turned it over, opened the two prongs at the back and unfurled the long body. He'd never worn one and wasn't exactly sure how it was supposed to fit, but there were only so many ways it could go. He opened his mouth, put the two prongs on either side of his tongue, and rolled the body down over his chin and under his neck, draping it there like his face was wearing a tie.

'How's it look?' he asked, his tongue tripping a little over the prongs.

Nettie crossed her arms. 'Don't ask me. I hate those things. I don't approve of this transaction at all, remember?'

'I remember,' he said. 'How do you get it to say anything?'

'It should –' she said, reaching forward.

'*I like you only as a friend*,' the Truth Teller said, its eyes looking directly from Jonny's chin into Nettie's face.

She frowned. 'It works.'

★

After the two dollars was handed over and a bewildered but nervously happy Jonny went one way back to his job at the diner and a richer but somehow still irritated Nettie went the other way back to *her* job at Mr Bacon's gas station, a blond man dressed in what seemed to be a cricketing uniform with what seemed to be a stalk of celery on his lapel, stepped out of what seemed to be absolutely nowhere with a thoughtful look on his face.

But surely none of that could be possible.

'Surely none of this can be possible,' he said, almost cheerfully.

'None of what?' said a woman with long, curly hair, stepping out of the nothingness behind him. 'They seemed like nice enough children.'

'Yes, Nyssa,' the man said. 'But this is Earth, 1945.' He took in a deep breath. There was sea salt in the air. 'Maine, if I'm not mistaken.'

'And?'

'And the Dipthodat aren't supposed to arrive here for at least a hundred years. They should still be halfway across the galaxy at this point in the timeline.'

'So what are they doing here now, Doctor?'

'What, indeed, Nyssa?' the Doctor said, putting his hands in his pockets. 'That sounds like a question that needs answering.'

The fad had started just before summer, which made it awkward at first. There was no school to go to each day to check on what kinds of Truth Teller everyone else was wearing or what attitudes they were taking towards them or, most importantly, how fashionable they properly were. Plus, it was wartime: if you were more than twelve (and sometimes not even that), you had a summer job to go to, labouring on farms, working in local shops, even a few kids older than Jonny or Nettie taking up summer shifts in the weapons factory for Mr Acklin.

It was, in fact, Mr Acklin's daughter Annabelle who had shown up three days before the end of the school year, a dark blue Truth Teller mounted on her chin like one of those busty ladies on the fronts of pirate ships. Her father didn't just own the factory, he also owned Temperance's general store, which her mother ran, and so Annabelle was the first with every fashion that migrated its way up from the big cities to the south, from where, incidentally, the whole Acklin family had moved five years earlier and visited regularly, so she came with an inbuilt authority no other girl in Temperance could ever hope to match. She'd worn the first knee-length (instead of mid-calf) skirt the school had ever seen and was promptly sent home for it, though overnight every other girl in school had hemmed her own skirt right up to the knee and Principal Marshall, swamped with what he called 'an outbreak akin to the Bolshevik revolution', gave in. Annabelle was also the first to wear a real fur collar on both her winter and summer coats – coney, but dyed to look like mink, because 'There's a war on, you know,' she said – and the first to use make-up on her legs in place of stockings after the Japanese cut off the supply of silk to America. Not that any other girl in town could have afforded silk stockings anyway, but Annabelle's powdered legs led to a full week of school-wide stains at ankle level until the principal finally did put his foot down.

'What on *earth* is that *thing* on your *face*, Miss Acklin?' he said on the first day of the Truth Tellers, as always looking like he was only just fighting off a heart attack.

Annabelle raised her head proudly. She hadn't even made it to the front doors of the school, and the rest of the school population – including, Jonny saw, Marisa Channing – had its eye on her. 'What?' Annabelle said, affecting a what's-the-big-deal air and implying that any shock was entirely someone else's problem. 'This old thing?'

Principal Marshall's mouth opened and closed a few times as disbelief fought outrage and lost. 'Take it off this instant!'

And then it spoke.

The thing on her jaw opened its toothy mouth – edged just where the point of Annabelle's chin fell – and a gentle, sad voice, which put Jonny immediately in mind of a sorrowful cow, rang out, quiet but in a strange, impossible way that carried to every eagerly listening ear.

'*You are a bald man,*' the voice said, '*and your wife is not visiting her sister in Boca Raton. She ran off with Mr Edmundsen at the bakery. Everyone knows this, yes.*'

'You could have heard a mosquito burp,' Nettie said later of the silence that followed, and indeed you could have. Principal Marshall's face grew redder and redder until he finally shouted, 'How *dare* you!'

'It's only the truth,' Annabelle said, eyes bright. 'How can you punish anyone for the truth?'

Speechless, Principal Marshall's eyes opened wide and unfortunately that allowed a moment for everyone to reflect that, yes, Principal Marshall was, in fact, a bald man and it *was* widely known that Mrs Marshall had been the bakery's most enthusiastic customer before it mysteriously shut and she left for her sisterly 'visit' shortly thereafter.

Annabelle was suspended, of course, sent home immediately pending further disciplinary action, but not before telling everyone how there was a stock of Truth Tellers in her mother's shop for anyone who might be interested in buying one.

Further disciplinary actions never materialised. Annabelle's parents were the richest, most powerful, and frankly scariest people in town, and though no one actually *liked* Mr Acklin (How could you? The smarm, the big-city arrogance, the way he threw his money around, including tearing down the town's one big mansion to build a new one in its place. In wartime!), no one could afford to oppose him either. Although the Truth Tellers were never officially allowed on school grounds, that didn't stop crowds of people, young and old, man and woman, anyone who could afford them, really, and often even those who couldn't, from buying them in their droves.

'*Your posterior is demonstrably too wide for that dress,*' Jonny would hear from the sidewalk as he emptied the rubbish from the diner. The woman whose posterior was in question would turn around in horrified anger, but the man behind her would already be shrugging with a smirk not masked by the Truth Teller draped over his chin. 'These pesky things,' he'd say. 'Can't argue with the truth, huh?'

At which point the woman's own Truth Teller would say, '*Your breath has always smelled like that of a person long dead. And*

*no one believes your excuse of flat feet for not enlisting with the rest of
our brave soldiers.'*

Both parties would leave angry and frustrated and
somehow even more ready to inflict truth on somebody else.

Within two weeks of the sale of the first Truth Teller,
Temperance's small jail was full to bursting with minor
assault cases, some between people who had up until that
moment been lifelong friends. Its small courthouse was
hearing filing after filing of new divorces from couples who
had otherwise been happy since before the Great Depression.
The town's ineffective council begged Mr Acklin to stop
selling the 'damned things' but he said there was no reason
to, as it was, after all, 'just a passing fancy. We'll all move on
to the next thing soon enough. For instance, have you heard
of this thing called a hula hoop? Just a dollar ninety-nine
down at the shop . . .'

But like many fads misunderstood by the aged – i.e.
anyone over the age of twenty – the Truth Tellers found a
secondary, but thriving underground market in the school-
age population of Temperance. As mothers and fathers
returned the Truth Tellers to the shop at great speed (for no
refund, of course), an unofficial subculture developed. At
the Horizon, Temperance's only movie palace, hordes of
matinee youths would gather in their seats, wait for the
lights to go down, and then quietly slip on the Truth Tellers
abandoned by their older relatives or, in rarer cases, bought
second-hand with their own money under the counter in
Mrs Acklin's shop, never a woman to turn a blind eye when
there was cash to be made.

Hardly anyone would be watching the newsreel as a Truth

Session, as they came to be known, started in the first five rows of the balcony.

'*Troy Davis likes you but not as much as you think he does, nor in the manner in which you would wish.*'

'*You think your hair looks like the cinematic star Veronica Lake while everyone else comments behind your back on its resemblance to a horse's mane. This is not said in any way that might be taken as a compliment.*'

'*You are too selfish and loud and the spirits of your friends fall when you walk into a room.*'

'*Troy Davis's story about getting Debbie Madison in the family way so that she had to move is a lie.*'

'*You have a faint odour that people discuss behind your back.*'

'*Everyone knows your father is a drunk.*'

'*Your thighs are just as fat as you think they are.*'

'*You, Troy Davis, are saving your affections for another member of your basketball team in a way that would not be widely accepted by the societal attitudes of this time period and location.*'

The Truth Sessions were spearheaded by Annabelle Acklin, of course, who would choose whoever that day's victim might be. Well, not her, exactly, it was completely out of her hands, wasn't it? It was the Truth Teller who had all the truths to tell, and truth, after all, could neither be denied nor hidden nor defended against. And if sometimes after the Session, people withdrew from their social circle or decided to sit forever in another part of the classroom or even – like when Troy Davis lied about his age to enlist and was immediately shipped overseas – people left altogether, then perhaps Temperance could do without them, no?

Jonny had never been to a Truth Session. Not high enough up the school food chain. Plus, too short, too foreign-seeming – with that last name that hung on him like a sack of wheat – he was, frankly, too invisible to have even registered on the radar of someone like Annabelle Acklin.

That would change, though. Oh, yes, that was about to change.

Because Jonny knew that *Marisa* went to Truth Sessions, though he didn't think she'd ever been the focus of one, just contributed with the pearly pink Truth Teller her father had bought her for her birthday.

Beautiful, tall, elegant Marisa. With her one stray freckle and her flowing blonde hair and her otherworldliness that made her seem like an angel.

All words Jonny would have rather died than say out loud.

Still, wouldn't she be surprised when Jonny showed up in the balcony with a Truth Teller of his very own?

'This old thing?' he'd say.

He wouldn't say he'd bought it used from Nettie.

(For her part, Nettie had never been within a mile of a Truth Session and he knew she wouldn't have gone even if invited by Annabelle Acklin herself.

Sometimes he didn't understand Nettie at all.)

'The strangest thing happened today,' his mother said, hanging her coat on the hook in the kitchen. Jonny was peeling the two potatoes they would have for an early dinner before he went off to his evening shift at Mr Finnegan's Diner. His mother always came in from the factory smelling strongly of iron and oil, and by the time she'd washed – with the water he'd warmed for her on the stove – dinner would be ready. They'd eat, Jonny would go back to work and his mother would start the sewing she did for extra cash. Sometimes Nettie's mom would come over, too, and more than once he'd returned home to find them in their separate chairs, cups of 'war coffee' on the table between them, both completely asleep, sewing half-done in their laps.

'What strange thing?' Jonny asked, when she didn't continue. He sliced the second potato and dropped it into the boiling water.

'What?' his mother said, distracted. He glanced over. She was looking at the picture of his father she'd hung by the door, touching her fingers to it, not saying anything. Despite their last name and despite the fact that both sets of Jonny's grandparents were as German as could be, his father'd had no trouble finding a place in the US Army and was now over there in Europe, fighting people to whom they were probably distantly related. Funny what war did, huh?

'The strange thing?' Jonny said, gently.

'Oh!' she said, sitting down wearily at the kitchen table. 'Yes. We had an inspection.'

Jonny added a few ounces of peas to the boiling potatoes. Those and a little butter and salt would be their entire dinner. 'Why is that weird?'

'It was this man and woman. British, I think, which was strange enough, but she was wearing trousers, if you can believe it, and he wore all white clothes to inspect a factory!' She sat back in her chair as if the disbelief had pushed her there. 'He didn't seem to ever get dirty, though.'

Jonny kept cooking, trying to ignore the Truth Teller in his pocket, which in his mind blared there like a siren, shouting at the top of its lungs (did they have lungs?), and he'd been wondering since his mother entered why she hadn't been able to hear it.

But of course it made no actual sound. They didn't unless they were being worn. They didn't do *anything* unless they were being worn. You never needed to feed them, they never needed cleaning up after, they just watched you, sadly, until you put them on your chin and they told all the truths you weren't brave enough to say yourself.

Like, as a purely random example, telling your mother you'd spent two whole dollars on a Truth Teller when you could only afford meat once a fortnight.

'Mom,' he started.

'You should have seen Mr Acklin, though,' his mother chuckled to herself. 'I think I can be happy with anything that makes that man squirm.'

'Mom,' Jonny said again.

'Kept asking everyone about those God-awful Truth Tellers,' his mother said.

Jonny froze. His mother didn't. 'Oh, I hated those things,' she frowned. 'People being rude all the time and acting like it's brave, acting like it's *your* fault if you get upset that they've been horrible to you.' She looked up at him. 'I know you kids like them, but I'm so glad you never got one, Jon.'

Jonny said nothing. She brushed a strand of hair out of her eye. 'What was it you were going to say?' she asked, innocent as anything.

'Nothing,' Jonny said. 'Just . . . the washing water's ready. If you want it.'

'Thanks, *Liebchen*,' she said. She stood and kissed him on the forehead. He let her. 'You're a good boy.'

She took the pan of water out to the washroom and Jonny just stood there at the stove, letting the steam from his boiling dinner blow over him.

'So did it work?' Nettie asked him as they rode along. She'd caught up with him on his way to his evening shift. She was returning home from her day at the town's sole gas station. She was supposed to just run the till in the small store there, but with her Uncle Paul-inspired flair for fixing things, and in the absence of all the professional mechanics who'd been snapped up by the war, she ended up spending most of her time changing fan belts and replacing spark plugs. She smelled more of chemicals than his mother did. 'Did you get your truths told?'

'I haven't had time to properly try it yet,' Jonny said.

They rode along in silence for a moment, Jonny pedalling away, Nettie coasting skilfully and riding in easy curves as she always did.

'Don't be . . .' Nettie started, but didn't finish.

'Don't be what?'

Nettie stopped her bike. Jonny stopped his, too. They were a block away from the Diner, a block away from where Nettie would turn to the poorer part of town she and her mom called home.

'With Marisa,' Nettie said, not quite meeting Jonny's eye. 'Don't be surprised if it doesn't . . . get you what you want from her.'

Jonny felt every inch of his skin start to burn red. The sun was setting and he could only hope it was too dark for Nettie to see him blushing. 'I don't know what you're talking about,' he said, his voice only squeaking a little bit.

'Girls like that . . .' Nettie started, but didn't say what girls like that were like. All Jonny heard in her silence was '*never look at boys like you*'.

'I don't know what you're talking about,' he said again, more angrily this time and pedalled away from her, leaving Nettie to watch him go.

'I have a very large nose,' the Truth Teller said into the mirror. 'And my forehead is greasy and will undoubtedly fill with acne as I grow older.'

'Well, don't tell people *that*,' Jonny said, his tongue still tripping a little on the Truth Teller's prongs.

It stopped talking and looked at him sadly. Jonny wasn't on a break, and he could only really hang around the bathroom for maybe another minute before Mr Finnegan would come knocking loudly, yelling that there were tables to clear.

But Jonny had looked up from his crate of dirty dishes to see Annabelle Acklin and three of her friends come in to sit at a booth and drink milkshakes. Two of those friends were Virginia Watson and Edith Magee.

The third was Marisa Channing.

Jonny had bolted to the bathroom. In the small mirror, he'd tried to shape his unruly hair into something approaching normal, wiped stray mustard from his lips where he'd been stealing leftover French fries, and tried to calm his breathing to lower than hyperventilation.

Then he'd taken the Truth Teller out of his pocket and popped it in his mouth.

It wasn't going particularly well.

'*I am afraid that the war will not end in time,*' it said, '*and I will be shipped off to fight and I will die.*'

Jonny shifted from foot to foot. 'Well, everyone's afraid of that. Aren't they?'

'*Mr Finnegan is about to knock,*' it said.

'What are you doing in there?' Mr Finnegan said through the door, knocking on it with a hammer blow. 'These tables won't clear themselves.'

Jonny took out the Truth Teller and shoved it back into his pocket. 'I'll be right out,' he said.

Jonny neared the booth where the girls were sitting. They were all drinking their milkshakes through straws over the tops of their Truth Tellers.

'*You really should hide your ears more with your hairstyle,*' Annabelle's was saying to Edith Magee. '*They stick out.*'

'*I am afraid of you,*' Edith's Truth Teller said. '*I will do anything you say.*'

'Don't I know it?' Annabelle said with a smile. Then she saw Jonny. 'What are you staring at?'

'Nothing,' he stammered, only realising just then that he *was* staring. He held the crate of dirty dishes under one arm, but his free hand went into his pocket, reaching for his own Truth Teller.

'*You have a very large nose,*' Annabelle's Truth Teller said before he could get to it.

'*And very oily skin,*' Virginia Watson's said.

'*Are you not of the Jewish persuasion?*' Edith's said.

'*And definitely German,*' Annabelle's said. '*With your cumbersome last name, you could be a traitor to this country.*'

'I'm not –' Jonny started.

'*And how very short you are,*' Virginia's said.

'*And ugly.*'

'*And do you think those three hairs under your nose are a moustache?*'

'*And no one knows who you are.*'

'*And no one ever will.*'

Jonny turned and fled, the dishes in the crate jangling under his arm. He slammed them down on the counter in the kitchen.

'Hey!' Mr Finnegan shouted from the grill. 'You break any of those, you're replacing them out of your tips.'

Jonny just breathed heavily for a moment. His only small consolation was that Marisa Channing's Truth Teller hadn't said a word.

But was that a good thing? Or was it the worst thing of all?

'Two chocolate milkshakes,' Jonny said, moments later, placing the drinks in the corner booth without making eye contact with the people sitting there.

'He seems to be the only employee in this whole establishment,' Nyssa said as she watched Jonny go, 'aside from the proprietor.'

'There *is* a war on,' the Doctor said, sniffing his drink. 'Just chocolate and milk and frozen cream.' He took a sip. 'Delicious.'

'Doctor,' Nyssa said, slightly impatiently. She was

watching the booth of four girls two tables down. 'You said they were in terrible danger.'

The Doctor turned and followed her gaze. 'And so they are. The Dipthodat are merciless. They hide in plain sight, lulling a planet into accepting them. And then . . .'

He didn't finish.

'Oughtn't we do something?' Nyssa asked.

'In time,' the Doctor said. 'We need to find out their source. Ah.' The girls at the booth had risen as one. The Doctor didn't stop drinking his milkshake as he watched them put on their summer coats and go laughing out of the front door. 'Time to go,' he said, taking a last slurp and moving to leave.

He paused, then put down two dollars as a tip.

'Didn't it work?' Nettie said, from underneath the car, a shiny new one, even though they were as rare as hen's teeth in wartime.

'I don't know,' Jonny said, looking at the Truth Teller in his hand. 'Sort of. I guess.'

There was a pause in the clanking sounds Nettie was making. 'You didn't do it, did you?'

Jonny didn't answer. Which was an answer in itself.

'Why do you like her, anyway?' Nettie said. 'Marisa Channing barely even knows you're alive.'

'She knows it a little more now.'

Nettie scooted out from under the car. She had oil smudged on her cheek. 'You got your own little Truth Session, didn't you?'

Again, Jonny answered by not answering. Nettie shook

her head and rolled back underneath the car. He was visiting Nettie on his lunch-break the day after the unpleasantness at the Diner. He had to get back in a few minutes, but still he sat in the garage of the petrol station, the sun shining through the open door. The Truth Teller in his hand stared back up at him like it always did. Mournfully.

'Where do these come from anyway?' he asked.

'Europe,' Nettie said. 'Or South America or something. Paul said he thought it was a chemical thing they were trying out for the war —'

'Well, well, well,' a voice boomed from the doorway, shadowing it suddenly. 'What do we have here?' It was Mr Acklin himself, suddenly looming. He stepped inside, his expensive coat billowing out behind him in the slight breeze.

He wore a Truth Teller over his thin beard.

'*The town's mixed-race girl working on your automobile*,' it said, sadly, '*along with the town's only Jew.*'

'The town's only *German* Jew,' Mr Acklin sneered, looking at Jonny. 'Isn't that right, Mr Heftklammern?'

And there it was. The two-ton weight of his last name. It had been the bane of his growing up. So undeniably German, especially with the rise of Mr Hitler, as if small, Jewish Jonny Heftklammern didn't feel like enough of an outsider amongst the Protestant giants of Temperance, Maine.

It wasn't even a proper German name. His father's father had immigrated just after World War I and, given that that was another war fought against Germany, had been advised to anglicise the family name upon arrival in the United States. This had originally been intended as simply changing Mueller to Miller, but starving and sleepless after a lengthy, awful sea journey, Grandpa Dietrich had quailed at the stern face of the immigration clerk. Unable to remember his long-practised speech about his name, he had glanced at the clerk's desk and blurted out the first thing he saw.

Heftklammern was the German word for 'staples'.

Mr Acklin shook his head, an unpleasant smile hovering above the Truth Teller. 'How's your mother, Miss Washington?' he asked Nettie, who had scooted back out from underneath the car.

'This is your car?' was Nettie's only answer.

'Yes, indeed,' Mr Acklin said. 'Just bought it. And imagine my surprise to find the coloured daughter of a maid working on it.'

Nettie got carefully to her feet and swallowed nervously, wrench still in her hand. Jonny felt a sudden flash in his stomach, surprised at how much he hated seeing Nettie look nervous.

'It needs some work on the clutch –' she started.

'I wonder what the town would think if they knew who Mr Bacon had looking after its automobiles.'

'They've been fine with it so far,' Nettie said.

Mr Acklin smiled. 'Have they?' he said. 'Shall we find out for certain?'

He took a sudden step towards her. She – angry, defiant, but still a foot shorter – stepped back. 'Hey!' Jonny said, leaping to his feet, and when he turned to look, saw Nettie stumble. She fell back against the pearly black paint of Mr Acklin's car –

The wrench in her hand scraping a curlicue dent all the way down the side as she fell.

For a moment, there was nothing moving but the dust in the sunlight.

Then Mr Acklin smiled. Again.

'You're going to pay for that,' Mr Acklin said.

His Truth Teller added, '*I will make sure you never work here again.*'

'And that's the truth,' Mr Acklin finished. 'You can't argue with the truth, now, can you?'

He left, again momentarily blocking the sun streaming through the open door, calling out Mr Bacon's name.

'He can't do that,' Jonny said. 'It was an accident.'

'He can try,' Nettie said, angrily. 'And you know he'll get his way.' She picked up the wrench again and made to swing at the window of Mr Acklin's car.

'Don't!' Jonny said. Nettie stopped mid-swing. 'He'll only make you pay for the glass, too.'

She dropped the wrench to her side, sighing. 'What am I going to do now?'

Jonny suddenly remembered the two dollars that someone had amazingly, *bafflingly*, left him as a tip the night before. He took it out of his pocket and handed it to her. 'Take this.'

Nettie frowned at him. 'I don't need your *charity*.'

'Take it as a second payment,' he said, holding up his Truth Teller.

'That's not the price we agreed —'

'A *loan*, then.' He still held out the money. 'To pay for the dent.'

Nettie grunted and then took it. 'A loan.' She looked out through the door. 'But this isn't over. Mr Bacon can't just —'

She stopped, because Mr Bacon – as if the sound of his own name had conjured him up – entered, Mr Acklin striding in behind him.

'Nettie,' Mr Bacon said, and the look on his face was all the news anyone needed.

A bell rang at the door of Mrs Acklin's shop. She stood up from behind the counter, the smile on her face freezing as she saw the very oddly dressed man and woman coming through. Then she got a shrewd look. Maybe *other* women would like to wear trousers. Maybe it was something she could *sell* to these –

'Are you the proprietress?' the man asked.

Good Lord, was that *celery* he was wearing on his lapel?

'Yes,' said Mrs Acklin.

'Then I wonder if you could tell me where you found *these*, exactly?'

He held out his hand. In it were four Truth Tellers, including one she recognised as her daughter Annabelle's. She looked back up at him, fearfully.

Then she started to scream.

Jonny kept waiting for her to cry. Crying he was used to. His mother cried a lot, especially when she got a letter from his father, though that was mostly from an all-consuming relief that his father *could* write letters and hadn't been eaten by the war over in Europe.

He'd also seen a lot of crying around the town, as that same war claimed husbands and sons, brothers and boyfriends. He'd seen Nettie's mom cry when her brother, Nettie's Uncle

Paul, had shipped out for a second tour at the beginning of the summer, and seen her cry again when she shared news of him with his own mom during their sewing sessions.

He'd never seen Nettie cry, though. Not even when Paul left.

And she wasn't doing it now either.

Well, not really.

'I'm going to kill him,' she said, for the hundredth time. 'I'm going to take that wrench and I'm going to knock those racist brains out of the back of his head.'

She took a sip from the soda bottle Jonny had sneaked out from the Diner to share after his evening shift was over. He needed to get home; he'd worked all day and was beyond tired, and it was dark, and tomorrow was another day where he'd do the same all over again. But instead, he was sitting on the bus-stop bench across the street from the biggest house in town. Owned, of course, by the Acklins. The one they'd built right in the middle of a war, which seemed almost criminal.

'People would probably appreciate it,' Jonny said. 'But then you'd go to jail.'

'At least I wouldn't have to pay for food there,' she said, bitterly.

'He can't do it,' Jonny said. 'It wasn't your fault. I'll tell Mr Bacon, and I'm sure in a couple of days –'

'If you do, Acklin might decide he doesn't like Jews much either,' Nettie said, almost calmly. 'Your mom needs that job.'

'And you need *yours*,' Jonny said. 'We'll figure something out. I promise.'

'Oh, you promise, do you?' she said, but the sarcasm was

light and when he looked at her, her eyes were shining wet in the moonlight. When she saw him notice, she wiped them hurriedly with the back of her sleeve. 'What am I going to tell my mom? What are we going to *do*?'

'We'll figure something out,' Jonny said again. 'I mean it.'

Nettie looked at him. 'I know you mean it,' she said, quietly. 'You always mean it.'

And the way she said it made that sound like a very good thing. He looked at her now, turning her face away from him, taking another drink from the soda bottle. *I only like you as a friend*, his Truth Teller had said, and neither he nor Nettie had challenged that at all.

But seeing her now, seeing her wipe away more tears that she was hoping he didn't notice, he suddenly felt he'd very much like to take the wrench and bash the brains out of Mr Acklin himself, just for making Nettie look like that.

'Nettie —' he started.

'Someone's coming,' she said, sitting up.

He looked down the street. It was a group of girls, *the* group of girls, led by Annabelle Acklin. And there was Virginia Watson and Edith Magee. And, of course, Marisa Channing, looking like the moonlight was made just to illuminate her fresh, clear skin. They were in deep, fractured discussion, with Annabelle smiling that dangerous smile back at Virginia and Edith, who seemed to be both arguing and crying at the same time.

None of them were wearing their Truth Tellers.

'Now's your chance,' Nettie said.

Jonny started a little. For a second, he'd forgotten Nettie was there. He looked at her. Her eyes were a little defiant now, and maybe not in a nice way any more. 'Chance for what?' he said.

'Chance to impress your *Marisa*,' she said. She stood up from the bench, soda bottle still in her hand.

He looked at her for a moment more, then back at the girls still approaching up the street, obviously heading to Annabelle's house. 'You think?' he asked.

Nettie's shoulders slumped and she shook her head at him. He didn't like the look on her face at all now. '*Idiot*,' he heard her whisper.

'Why –?'

'Just put it on,' she said. 'Let's finally see what happens when Marisa Channing hears you tell her the truth. Come on, let's see how that goes, shall we?'

'Nettie, I don't under–'

'Because you really think it's just a matter of truth, do you? She'll see that you can afford one of those awful things and that you're not afraid to say rude and horrible stuff to everyone else, but when you look at her all your truth is about how pretty her skin is and how wavy her hair is and how the world stops smelling like farts when she walks by.'

Jonny blinked at her, blushing. Most of this was pretty accurate, though he wouldn't have thought of the farts thing –

'Honestly,' Nettie said, shaking her head again. 'The lies people tell themselves and call it the truth. Well, go ahead. What are you waiting for?'

The girls were almost directly across the street now. In a second, they'd turn into Annabelle's house and he'd have missed his chance. His stomach was pulling with how angry

Nettie seemed, and it was only just now dawning on him what might be going on and what he might himself think about that. But there was also the other voice in him, the one that had looked at Marisa Channing for so long with a yearning he couldn't really describe, and she was just about to turn up the path into the Acklin house –

He reached into his pocket and pulled out the Truth Teller. He ignored the look on Nettie's face as he fitted the prongs under his tongue and draped it down his chin. He pulled himself up to his not particularly impressive height, took a deep breath and stepped forward to cross the street.

Which was when the Acklin house exploded.

It wasn't just the windows blowing out or one room or a door or anything like that. The *whole thing* exploded, all three storeys of it, including the roof, outwards and upwards in a flash of fire and light. The four girls standing in front of it and Jonny and Nettie all screamed as the blast wave flung itself at them.

Jonny didn't even think. He threw himself in front of Nettie as the *whoosh* of flames and smoke rolled towards them and they fell together into the bus stop. The fire swept over them, but it didn't burn and was gone in an instant. Protecting Nettie as much as he could – she was several inches taller than him so he had a fleeting moment to wonder what good he was doing – Jonny kept expecting to be pelted with rubble and bricks –

But there was nothing.

'Get *off* me,' Nettie finally said, pushing him away. Across the street, the four girls were bundled together in a heap on the sidewalk, but looked as uninjured and confused as Jonny and Nettie.

The Acklin house was gone. Not even burning rubble.

Just . . . *gone.*

'What just happened?' Jonny said.

'They build their houses out of a kind of secreted polymer,' said an accented female voice behind them. 'It's remarkably similar to your sugar, actually, which is curious.' A woman with curly brown hair and trousers was reaching down a hand to help them up. 'Might actually be where some of the candy houses come from in your folk tales.'

Stunned, Jonny took her hand and allowed himself to be pulled up. Nettie did the same.

'Either way,' the woman continued, 'it only *looked* like a house. But when the polymer is fired upon with their own weapons, it more or less vaporises, burning quickly at a very low temperature and leaving little residue.'

Jonny and Nettie stared at her.

'Huh?' Jonny finally said.

'Are you British?' Nettie said, as if this was the most surprising part of the whole thing.

The woman simply smiled at them and then reached forward to touch a gentle finger to the Truth Teller Jonny was still wearing.

'*I am terribly confused,*' it said.

'I'll bet you are,' the woman said. 'But we've spent the day gathering up your brothers and sisters.'

'Nyssa!' a voice called from across the street. A man was emerging from the strange blank place where the Acklin house used to stand.

And he wasn't alone.

There was a small gasping sound as Virginia Watson fainted dead away. Everyone else just stood and stared, mouths agape.

The man was leading what looked a little bit like two very tall upright sheep, but sheep that had the faces of some kind of giant fish. But also mixed with a squirrel. And a pumpkin.

The pumpkin squirrel sheep fish didn't look happy at all. They both had their front feet/flippers bound, looking for all the world as if they were under arrest.

'I've put them under arrest!' the man called, leading them down the remains of the front path. 'I can do that, can't I?'

Edith Magee screamed as they approached and fled down the street, screaming all the way. Annabelle and Marisa stayed watching, frozen, with wide-open eyes.

The British woman started across the street towards the man. She beckoned to Jonny and Nettie. 'Come on,' she said. 'It's all right.'

Stunned, Jonny found himself following her. He looked back. Nettie was following too, her face as shocked as his. She was still clutching the soda bottle.

'And there's the last one,' the man said, looking at Jonny's chin as they neared him. The sheepfish made angry-sounding cries, but they went quiet again as the man looked at them sternly.

'What's going on?' Nettie asked, taking in Marisa and a wide-eyed Annabelle. 'Who are you?'

But before the man could answer, Jonny's Truth Teller spoke up.

'*You are the Doctor*,' it said.

'The who?' Jonny said.

'The what?' Nettie asked.

But the Doctor was talking to the Truth Teller. 'I am,' he said. 'And you, my little friend, are safe.'

'*I am safe*,' said the Truth Teller, and Jonny noticed that, for the very first time, it didn't sound sorrowful.

'Are those your parents?' a voice said. They all turned when they realised it was Marisa. Annabelle was still standing next to her, looking both furious and terrified.

'Mom?' said Annabelle. 'Dad?'

There was a pause as everyone realised she was talking to the sheepfish.

'I'm afraid you'll have to come with us, too, Annabelle,' the Doctor said.

The sheepfish made a snorkelling sound.

'But I *like* it here,' Annabelle said. 'Everyone obeys me.'

The two sheepfish made further snorkelling sounds that seemed to indicate they'd liked that part, too, but what were you going to do?

'I heard about the time-fracture accident,' the man said to Annabelle. 'Your parents explained it.' He looked back at the hole where the house used to be. 'Eventually. You got thrown here by accident, a hundred years before the natural timeline. And that will go some way to mitigating the sentences you'll be receiving.'

'Sentences?!' Annabelle said.

'Slavery is illegal,' the man said, suddenly more stern and, it must be said, a bit scary, too. 'In this solar system and every neighbouring system between here and the Dipthodat homeworld. And even worse for you –' he leaned down towards Annabelle – '*I* don't like it.'

Annabelle looked as if she was going to argue back, but the sheepfish made extensive snorkelling sounds and Annabelle, though still looking peeved, finally said, 'Oh, all *right*.' She sighed and shuffled off the coney-collared jacket she was wearing, and before their eyes she . . .

Changed into one of the sheepfish things. She made an annoyed snorkelling sound at the man.

'No, I won't put you in chains,' the man said, 'as long as you behave.'

Sheepfish Annabelle went over to her sheepfish parents and a low, snorkelling argument commenced between them.

'Can someone please explain what's going on?' Nettie said, and Jonny saw she was holding her soda bottle as a potential weapon, against sheepfish or mysterious Doctors in white sweaters or British women wearing trousers.

'Brave heart, Nettie,' the Doctor said. 'The danger has passed. Shame I had to destroy their lodgings, but the Dipthodat can be quite a tiresome species.'

'Diptho-what?' Jonny said, his tongue still tripping a little over his Truth Teller.

The Doctor gestured to the sheepfish. 'Dipthodat. A xenophobic race.'

'Xeno-what?' Jonny said.

'They don't like anyone who's not them,' the Doctor said.

'You can say that again,' Nettie said, glaring at the sheepfish, who glared back.

'They go to planets,' the Doctor said, 'stir up unrest among the locals, and feed off the negative energy. That's what they eat. Their whole diet. All the stuff of strife and anger and hate.' The Doctor bent down to Jonny's height and looked at the Truth Teller again. 'These marvellous little creatures help that task enormously.' He glanced up into Jonny's eyes. 'You convince people that hurling the worst, most painful "truths" at each other is a good idea, and you'll have enough negative energy to run the world.'

'They work best on the young,' Nyssa said. 'Good people like yourselves. So much seeming truth that feels so painful. The supply is almost endless. It's heartbreaking in a way.'

'We thought they were toys,' Jonny said.

'Not toys,' the Doctor said. 'Slaves. They're called the Veritans. Psychic little wonderlings who can seek out what everyone else thinks is the truth. Conquered centuries ago by the Dipthodat and forced into work. Mourning their homeworld, no pay, no comfort, no hope of escape.' He frowned once more at the sheepfish. 'Which is something that makes me very unhappy indeed.'

The sheepfish looked sheepish.

'They aren't supposed to be reaching your planet for another hundred years when, happily, you'll be equipped to deal with them yourselves. These three got stuck here by accident. Took a couple of years to get themselves disguised and established, and then they tapped into a passing black-market slave-trader to find some Veritans.'

'*I am safe now*,' the Truth Teller said again.

'Yes, you are,' the Doctor said. 'And you're going home.'

'*I am going home*,' the Truth Teller said, and to Jonny, the happiness in its voice was almost heartbreaking.

'OK,' Nettie said. 'Forgive me if I'm being slow here. The Acklins were from outer space all along?'

'Is that a relief?' the Doctor asked.

'No,' Nettie said, angrily. 'They seemed human enough. In all the wrong ways.' The sheepfish snorkelled at her. She raised her soda bottle, but this time her face had no fear on it at all.

The Doctor nodded. 'I'm guessing that the Truth Tellers weren't the only mischief they caused.'

'*Mischief?*' Nettie said, annoyed at the word.

'Well, they'll be gone soon,' the Doctor said. 'Will that perhaps help things around here?'

Nettie nodded, defiant. 'That will help, yes.'

There was a sudden agitated snorkelling from the Annabelle sheepfish. She contorted halfway back into a human shape and yelled, 'You put that down! That's mine!'

The Doctor held her back as she tried to lunge at Marisa who, they could now all see, had picked up Annabelle's coney-collar coat and was wrapping it around her shoulders.

'Really?' Marisa said. 'I think it probably looks better on me now.'

She swung from side to side, twirling the coat behind her, rubbing her face against the fur. She snapped the collar together under her chin and straightened out the fabric. She looked at Jonny. 'What do you think?'

'You . . .' Jonny said, watching her closely now, watching how she seemed to be in love with the coat, watching how her eyebrows were raised in expectation of praise, a look he'd never seen before on her.

Or at least a look he'd never noticed.

'You look just like Annabelle,' he said.

'I don't look anything like *that*,' Marisa said, nodding at the Annabelle half-sheepfish.

'No, but . . .' Jonny said but faltered.

'*I am suddenly no longer interested in you*,' his Truth Teller said, '*though I am unclear of the reasons why, exactly*.'

'You'll figure them out,' the Doctor said.

'You were interested in me?' Marisa said, a look on her face of what could only be described as horror.

Jonny heard a sound from Nettie, but when he turned to her, she was innocently whistling into the empty soda bottle.

The sound of sirens rose faintly in the distance. The fire trucks were coming.

'Quite late after an explosion this big,' Nettie said.

'Oh, we have ways of arranging a delay,' the Doctor said. Then he got a sad look on his face. 'Mr Heftklammern – fantastic name by the way, don't ever change it – and Miss Washington. The decent people of this town speak highly of you and the indecent –' he nodded at the sheepfish – 'speak very badly indeed, which counts for just as much.' He sighed. 'I've lost two friends recently. One who died bravely, the other who went back to her own life. Nyssa is a wonderful companion, but I do like to have a big group around me.' He paused. 'I don't suppose either of you would be interested in travelling?'

'Doctor,' Nyssa said, a warning tone in her voice.

'There's a war on,' Jonny said. 'Travel is dangerous.'

'I can't,' Nettie said, at almost the same time. 'My mother depends on me.'

'Mine, too,' Jonny said.

'But of course,' the Doctor said. 'Of course that's true.' The sirens were getting closer. 'Take the Dipthodat to the TARDIS, Nyssa.' He turned back to Jonny and Nettie. 'Tell the police you heard an explosion and that's all you know.'

'I don't think they'd believe any of the rest of this anyway,' Jonny said.

'I'm not sure I believe it,' Nettie said, 'and I saw it with my own two eyes.'

'Are all the Veritans on board?' the Doctor asked Nyssa.

'All but one,' Nyssa said, leading the sheepfish away, the Annabelle one snorkelling loudly at Marisa, who paid her no mind at all.

'All but one,' the Doctor repeated and leaned back down to Jonny. 'It's time to go,' he said to the Truth Teller.

'*Freedom,*' it said.

'Freedom indeed.'

'*I have one more truth to say,*' it said.

'I'll bet you do,' the Doctor said, but he gently held out his hand before the Truth Teller could speak again. It uncurled itself from Jonny's chin, walked the two prongs out of his mouth, and twined itself happily on the Doctor's open palm. The Doctor looked up at Jonny and then over to Nettie. 'But I suspect that's a truth our young friend here is better off saying himself.'

A kind of haunted grinding sound filled the inside of the TARDIS as it revved its engines to leave.

'First drop the Dipthodat off to the appropriate authorities, Doctor?' Nyssa asked.

'Indeed,' the Doctor said, watching the boy and the girl on the screen in front of him.

'And then where?'

'Oh, you know,' he said, as the boy and the girl – not holding hands, not kissing, not anything ridiculous like that – walked off together after giving whatever explanation sufficed to the firemen. But they walked off together in a companionable way, a way that hinted, maybe, just maybe, of futures to come. 'We've got the whole of time and space ahead of us. And behind us, for that matter. And beneath and above . . .'

'Doctor . . .' Nyssa said, smiling over the basket of sleeping Truth Tellers, who had wound themselves together in a warm, snoozing ball, murmuring to each other that they were free.

'All I'm saying, Nyssa,' the Doctor said, switching off the screen and standing with a flourish, 'is that, as ever, anything is possible.'

He hit a button, sending the TARDIS flying off into the vast eternity of space and time.

'Which in the end,' he said, 'is all the truth you ever really need.'

THE SIXTH DOCTOR:
SOMETHING BORROWED

RICHELLE MEAD

1

It was typical. The Doctor promised me champagne and cake, and instead I got flying lizards.

'*Pterodactylus antiquus*, to be precise,' he told me, ducking as one of the creatures in question swooped low over his head. It was such a close call that the rush of air ruffled the springy curls of his hair. 'Or perhaps *Pterodactylus extra-smallus* would be a better name, since I don't recall them being quite so pocket-sized during my last Late Jurassic trip.'

That wasn't how I would have described them, but maybe it depended on the size of your pockets. These beasts were about as big as pigeons, and the only upside so far was that they seemed to be leaving *us* alone. I couldn't say the same for the terrified pedestrians around us, though. We'd only arrived on Koturia minutes ago, leaving the TARDIS in a small alley tucked between two obnoxiously coloured buildings on a busy street. We'd heard the screams as soon as we stepped out of the door and had been met with pretty much the last scene that came to mind when I thought of weddings. Bachelor parties? Perhaps. Weddings? Definitely not.

'Maybe they're babies,' I said, cringing against a hot-pink building decorated with silvery lattice-work. I was trying to keep out of the way, both of the pterodactyls and of the panicked people heedlessly shoving others aside in an effort to escape. The creatures were homing in specifically on the Koturians, attacking them with sharp claws and beaks that drew blood and tore skin with each strike. Across the street, I saw several of the pterodactyls gang up on a woman and actually try to carry her away. She was saved at the last moment when a hysterical man accidentally ran into her, disrupting the attack.

'I don't think so.' The Doctor was annoyingly calm, oblivious to the frenzy around him as he squinted up at the winged menaces. 'These are some kind of specially modified breed, nothing natural. You can tell by that gold sheen on their wing membrane. No earthly pterodactyl had that. Can't you see it?'

Mostly all I could see was that it would be very easy for those talons to turn on us at any moment.

Small lines of thought appeared on the Doctor's forehead. 'This isn't the first time I've seen something like this,' he murmured.

He didn't elaborate, as per his way, and I wasn't really in the mood to play our usual game of Twenty Questions. The fear around us was so all-consuming that it had an almost tangible quality, and the only thing I knew for sure was that we had to do something to end it. 'How do we stop them?' I asked.

For a moment, I didn't think he'd heard me, but he finally dragged his gaze from the creatures and did a quick, sharp assessment of the rest of our surroundings. His eyes travelled up the side of the pink and silver building, and he gave a decisive nod. 'There. You need to climb up to that sign.'

I looked. There, right on the edge of the roof, was a flashing sign that was brilliant even in the light of midday. Swirls of blue and green, a bit like a lava lamp, pulsed underneath its iridescent surface while dark-purple messages scrolled across it.

'That's two storeys up!' I exclaimed. 'And I'm in heels.'

'Well then, you should have worn more sensible shoes, shouldn't you? Really, Peri, don't blame me for your oversights. The footholds are too small for me to do it myself. Now hurry!'

Some of the gaps in the lacy lattice-work looked too small for me too, but I knew he was right about which of us was the best choice. The scream of a child drove me to action, and I kicked off my shoes without further hesitation. I grabbed hold of the metal scrollwork, grateful that it seemed firmly attached, and started to climb, though I winced when some of the sharp edges dug into my bare feet. Moving upward also put me closer to some of the higher-flying pterodactyls, but I figured now wasn't the time to dwell on that.

'Hurry!' the Doctor yelled.

'I'm going as fast as I can!'

I scurried up. At one point, my foot missed its hold, and I slipped a few inches. I clung to the lattice-work as tightly as I could, breathing deeply and steeling myself to regain my foothold and continue the climb. Finally, agonisingly, I reached the roof and climbed over its edge, grateful to find a flat, solid surface to kneel on.

'Now what?' I called down.

I could barely hear the Doctor's answer above the noise of panic. 'Grab the corner of the screen and rip it off!'

At first glance, I didn't think it was possible. Then I saw that each corner had a small steel loop attached to it. I grabbed hold of one, then yelped, jerking away. The metal was so hot it had burned me. Below, I could hear the Doctor shouting encouragement, though his words were tinged with urgency and impatience.

Inspiration hit me, and I grabbed hold of my skirt. It was made of two layers, a light chiffon over heavier silk, and I ripped a large strip of the top layer away. I then tore it in half. The gauzy fabric wasn't the best protection, but wrapping it round my hands provided some relief from the heat as I tried to pull the screen away again. Nothing happened. Refusing to accept failure, I gave it another tug and felt the slightest give. One more white-knuckled pull, and the screen slowly began to rip apart. As it did, I could see glittering wires and circuits sparking inside like a tiny Fourth of July show as fluorescent goop began trickling out of the bottom. I glanced down at the Doctor, waiting for my next instructions, when the most amazing thing happened.

In seconds, the mini-pterodactyls abruptly abandoned their prey and merged into an orderly flock. Their displeasure was expressed in a cacophony of jarring caws as they soared up like one being and flew out of sight. For a moment, an eerie silence hung in the street, then at last the Koturians began to recover, glancing warily around as they helped each other up and tended to the injured. Deeming my job done, I made my way back down the lattice-work and jumped the last couple of feet. The Doctor was beaming.

'Well done! That wasn't so difficult, was it?'

I glanced down at the angry red marks on my hands.

'Depends on your definition of difficult. What happened?'

He pointed up at the dismantled sign. 'Those lights use radiant Gengi tube technology. A bit gaudy, if you ask me, but quite trendy in places like this.'

'Well, you *are* the expert when it comes to gaudy,' I said, giving a meaningful look to his red-and-yellow plaid coat and green tie.

He ignored the jibe. 'When the tubes inside are damaged they emit a type of electromagnetic radiation that you can't perceive, but which is quite irritating to creatures like those.'

I remembered his earlier words. 'Then you *have* seen them before.'

'Not them specifically,' he corrected. 'But something with a similar feel. Let us hope it's just a coincidence.'

Now that I didn't feel my life was in imminent danger I finally had the chance to look around and truly take in the world we'd come to. The Doctor had already briefed me on the Koturians, and I found them exactly as he'd described. On the surface they resembled humans – and Time Lords, for that matter – save that their natural hair colour varied wildly. I saw ordinary brunettes like me and blonds like the Doctor, but the majority sported colours I would've expected to find in punk rock bands back home: deep purple, lime green, bright orange and so forth. Closer scrutiny showed me they weren't the only species here. At least half of those on the streets were clearly aliens from other worlds, although, like the Doctor and me, they hadn't been targeted.

And then I noticed the city itself. My jaw dropped.

'This looks like –' I could barely utter the words, certain my eyes were playing tricks on me – 'Las Vegas.'

'Well, I should think so,' the Doctor said as we began to walk down the street, 'seeing as that's what the Koturians modelled their civilisation on.'

Las Vegas was an easy weekend road trip from my college town of Pasadena. I'd only been there once, but there was no mistaking the resemblance. Some of the buildings bore more than just a passing similarity to my memories. Sure, some of the details were different, but if you'd suddenly transported tourists here from the Strip in Las Vegas back on Earth, I doubt they'd have noticed. The same sort of over-the-top facades loomed above us, covered in lights that would no doubt ignite the evening's darkness. As we walked I glimpsed gaming tables and slot machines through the glass doors. Enterprising vendors took advantage of our reprieve and were already back on the streets waving around flyers for tonight's entertainments.

'That's *exactly* like the Sahara,' I said, coming to a halt outside an impressive hotel and casino complex. 'I remember visiting it.'

The Doctor nodded. 'So did the Koturians. We're about, oh, two hundred years after your time. Early Koturian explorers visited Earth in the late twentieth century and were charmed by the glitz and excitement of Las Vegas – as well as its money-making potential. They're quite the entrepreneurs, you see. They quickly realised the allure of a city solely devoted to pleasure and games of chance – not just to humans but to many other species as well – so they took that concept and ran with it on a much, much grander scale.'

I shook my head, still feeling a little dazed. 'How strange.'

'Is it?' He gave me a sidelong look. 'Seems like a very American concept, really. Exploiting people's hopes and dreams for profit. I figured you'd be quite comfortable with that.'

I rolled my eyes. 'That's a pretty harsh view of my countrymen.'

'Well, believe what you want, but the Koturians have made a lot of money from their business plan. This is one of the wealthiest planets in the solar system. People come from far and wide to make their fortunes – and to consecrate their love.'

'Consecrate their . . . You mean get married? But Las Vegas weddings are tacky.'

The Doctor grinned. 'On the contrary, that's one of the ways the Koturians' version ended up different from the original. This place is considered the height of romance. Anyone who's anyone tries to have a wedding on Koturia, and, as you'll soon see, the Koturians themselves have an especial interest in marriage.'

2

The Doctor took me to a building near the edge of the downtown area, and at first I thought it must be another hotel, based on its size and design. But when I noticed that there wasn't the usual buzz of tourist activity, I realised with a start that this was a private residence. The sprawling building took up several city blocks and had five floors, and the glass in the arched windows along the front had undergone some special treatment to make it sparkle in a rainbow of colours. It even had flying buttresses, though their silvery-blue surfaces were a far cry from any medieval church.

'How many people live here?' I exclaimed. 'There must be more than just your friend and his family.'

The Doctor shrugged. 'Not as far as I know. Well, aside from the servants.'

One of those servants, dressed in a sunny yellow uniform, showed us into a vaulted foyer. We gave our names, and moments later an older man with receding lavender hair came scurrying in. His face was alight with joy.

'Doctor! Is it really you? You've changed . . . Not that we aren't used to that sort of thing around here.'

He must've seen the Doctor before this most recent regeneration.

The Doctor shook the man's hand vigorously. 'Yes, yes. A little different round the edges since our last meeting on Kiri 4, but all the charm and intellect are still here.'

'And the modesty,' I added.

The man turned towards me, and the Doctor seemed to remember I was there. 'Ah, yes. Evris, may I present Miss Peri Brown of Earth. Peri, this is Lord Evris Makshi. We were once both caught up in a minor incident involving some very disagreeable robots.'

Evris chuckled. 'Incident? Is that what you call saving my life? However you want to spin it, I'm just honoured that you came to attend my son's wedding. And you too, Miss Brown.'

There was a shrewd glint in the Doctor's eyes. 'And what about the adorably terrifying pterodactyls we encountered on our way in? Are they on the guest list too?'

The cheery look on Evris's face vanished. 'Ah. Them. I'd heard there was another attack today.'

'Another?' asked the Doctor. I was reminded of a hunting hound sniffing the wind.

Evris nodded. 'Those creatures have been plaguing us for a few months now. It started off as just a nuisance. They'd appear briefly on the Swathe and −'

'Swathe?' I interrupted.

'The city's main tourist district,' he explained. 'We call it that because it's a swathe of commerce and delight.'

'But not a strip.' I tried to keep a straight face.

'No. Much more expansive.' Evris cleared his throat.

'Anyway, they used to content themselves with mild attacks: a few swipes, a little blood here and there. Then, in the last two weeks, it's suddenly increased. We see them nearly every day, and their assaults are more vicious. They've even started carrying away victims – never to be seen again.'

'How awful,' I said, recalling how I'd nearly witnessed that very thing.

The Doctor nodded in agreement. 'Hardly a favourable time for a wedding.'

'I concur.' Evris's face fell even more. 'Tourism's taken a downward turn, and half our citizens won't even go outside. If Jonos wasn't so near the end of his Phasing, we'd call the whole thing off. But none of us knows how long he has, and so we're going forward with it tonight. After that . . . well. Then we hope to do something about this little problem.'

I didn't really think flying reptiles that attacked and kidnapped people qualified as a 'little' problem, but I was too interested in his earlier word choice. 'Phasing?' I asked. 'What's that?'

The Doctor shone with his usual delight for anything curious and fascinating. 'It's what I meant earlier about Koturians having an especial interest in weddings. During their marriage ceremony, they transform and take on a new appearance. Several factors, internal and external, kick their metabolism into overdrive – for lack of a more technical explanation.'

Evris was nodding along. 'It's a very sacred thing for our people. The beloved is the first one to see the new face as they begin their lives together. It also marks an important rite of passage in general, a brilliant experience that all

Koturians should go through.' His brief enthusiasm turned to dismay. 'However, we're only capable of it once, during a very short window in the prime of our lives. Then the chance is gone forever.'

It was hard to wrap my mind round such a concept – though certainly not as hard as it would've been before I began travelling with the Doctor. 'And your son has nearly passed his?'

'Yes. In fact, we'd given up. He's a good boy – but has his fair share of quirks. Those sorts of individuals can be quite challenging, you know.'

'Yes,' I said. 'I certainly do know.'

The Doctor cut me a look. 'Well, well, aren't you on a roll today?'

Evris, oblivious to our exchange, shook his head in a mix of both amusement and exasperation as he continued about his son. 'I suppose we shouldn't have been surprised when he chose an alien bride. It's exactly the kind of contrary thing he'd do.'

The Doctor had been listening with an indulgent expression, but at those words everything about him suddenly went on alert. 'Alien?'

'Humanoid,' Evris said quickly. 'No tentacles or sentient piles of slime. Of course, we were desperate enough that we might have very well accepted that.' He chuckled at his own joke. 'And, really, she's a lovely woman. Cultured and intelligent. Jonos is quite smitten with her.'

'Yes, I'm sure,' said the Doctor, more to himself than us.

I frowned. 'But if she's alien . . . can he still transform? Go through the Phasing?'

'Certainly,' said Evris. 'I mean, she can't, of course. It's not in her physiology. But for us it's the chemicals and neurotransmitters involved in love and bonding with another person that serve as the catalyst. Those will be the same for Jonos, regardless of his object of affection.'

I could tell that the Doctor still had some puzzle on his mind, though he was keeping it to himself for now. 'Well. Between the upcoming wedding and unwelcome flying visitors, you've certainly been kept busy. I'd love to hear more about it. And I'd also love to hear more about your future daughter-in-law. In fact, I don't suppose I could meet her?'

Evris looked surprised. 'Not before tonight's festivities, I'm afraid. She's deeply involved with preparations. Besides, she's off in the women's section of the house, inaccessible to the likes of us. But I find myself with a bit of time right now, if you'd like to have an early dinner?'

'That sounds wonderful,' I said.

'No, no, not in your state, Peri.' The Doctor's look of chastisement was wholly unexpected.

'My state?' I asked.

He gestured to my skirt. 'Look what you've done in your carelessness. You can't go to a civilised event like that. Evris, I don't suppose your people could make her look respectable?'

'Carelessness! Respectable!' It was the best response I could splutter out.

'Easily,' said Evris. He moved over to a table at the side of the room and pushed a few buttons on a console.

Within seconds, a young woman scurried in, wearing one of the yellow servants' uniforms. A matching veil covered much of her head, but I could see that her pale blonde hair, streaked with blue, was pulled back into a neat bun. She bowed low to Evris and kept her eyes averted.

'Yes, my lord?'

'Please take Miss Brown and help her with whatever she needs to prepare for the wedding. The Doctor and I will be in the green dining room.'

'How many dining rooms are there exactly?' I asked.

The Doctor waved me off. 'Sounds like you're in good hands. Go enjoy yourself, and who knows? Perhaps you'll get a glimpse of the lucky bride.'

His face still wore that sunny, flippant expression that could win others over, but I saw a knowing glint in his eyes. I understood what he wanted me to do perfectly, even if I didn't know his motivations.

'Perhaps,' I agreed.

He and Evris strolled off without another word, and I turned towards the patiently waiting serving-girl. 'Shall we go, miss?' she asked.

3

The serving-girl began leading me through the house, where I instantly became lost. The many corridors were like a labyrinth, connecting with each other in a way I couldn't follow. Everything was as vast as the entrance hall had been, with high ceilings and windows, decorated with art in that bright colour scheme Koturians apparently loved. It was still amazing to me that only one family lived here and that there were four more floors like this.

'Are you married?' I asked, still fascinated by the process. 'Have you gone through the, uh, Phasing? Oh, and I didn't catch your name.'

'Wira, miss. And, no, I haven't had that honour.' She sighed. 'And sometimes I don't know if I ever will.'

'But you must have time, right?' Wira seemed young to me, but I didn't know how long the Koturian window lasted. 'Or are you like Jonos?'

'No, I have time.' She brightened, but there was a wistful look to her at the same time. 'I'm so glad he's going to be able to do it. I wonder what he'll look like afterwards.'

'Is the new appearance random?' I asked, thinking of Time Lord regenerations. 'Or is there a pattern?'

'You have some control over it,' she explained. 'Your will and the strength of your love. And the Imori stone.'

'The what?'

'They're sacred stones found on our world. The bride and groom rest their hands on one during the ceremony, and its divine power amplifies their love in order to complete the transformation.'

I pondered this, wondering how much 'divine power' truly played a role. If I knew the Doctor, he'd probably have a more scientific explanation.

Wira's expression grew dreamy as she gestured me to a stairwell. 'I have a hard time imagining Jonos changing, though. He's already so handsome. How could he get any better?'

I couldn't help a smile. 'Sounds like you wouldn't mind being his bride.'

Even under the veil, I could see her flush. 'Oh no. I couldn't. Not someone like me. He wouldn't give me a second thought.'

'Someone kind and pretty? Seems like you could get a third and fourth thought.' Her blush deepened.

We finally reached a set of double doors that opened up to an enormous suite with floor-to-ceiling windows overlooking the city. A giant marble tub sat off to one side.

'It doesn't matter,' said Wira. She touched a small panel on the tub's edge, and jets in the bottom of the basin began spraying water into it. 'He'd never be interested in me. He's so clever and wonderful. It's why it took him so long to find someone suitable. Lania – she's a real lady. She may be from another planet, but she's obviously high-bred and sophisticated.'

'Lania's his fiancée?'

'Yes.' Wira touched another part of the panel, and cleverly placed lights in all colours turned on in the tub, lighting it up in a rainbow display. Nothing plain for these Koturians. 'She's a brilliant woman. So clever. So cultured. It's no wonder Jonos fell for someone like her.' Wira's unspoken thought, I realised, was that he couldn't fall for someone like *her*.

She seemed so forlorn about her unrequited love that I didn't ask anything more about the wedding. I felt a little silly going through so much primping for an event where I didn't even know the couple, but Wira clearly did this on a regular basis and was brisk and efficient about her work. It seemed to distract her from her earlier woes, and she began to grow enthusiastic as she described other facets of Koturian life to me. I soon became absorbed as well, still amazed at a civilisation that had modelled itself on one of the most notorious cities on Earth.

It only took her about an hour to make me into an acceptable wedding guest, and I stared at myself in the mirror with amazement, hardly able to believe what she'd achieved in so little time. My hair was done up in elaborate braids, and the make-up, though extreme by Earth standards, was in line with what I'd seen among the Koturian women on the streets. It was as much art as ornamentation, with fanciful flowers and swirls along my cheeks and at the corners of my eyes, all in greens that matched the long dress I wore. It seemed a shame when she offered me a veil like she wore.

'Do I have to?' I asked.

Wira shrugged. 'It goes with the dress, but it's not required. There'll be plenty of off-worlders without them.'

Her words reminded me of the main reason for this spa day, and I wondered how exactly I was supposed to act on the Doctor's unspoken suggestion to find the bride. 'What about Lania? Does she follow your customs?'

'Oh yes. She's taken to them quite readily . . . though she still follows many of her own ways. She has her own servants and keeps her wing very private.'

I mulled over Wira's words as she led me back through the maze of corridors. When we reached the ground floor, I noticed a stairwell leading down. I came to a halt. 'There are levels *underground* too?'

'Two of them,' Wira confirmed. 'Those are the levels Lania lives in.'

'Oh?' I took a few steps towards the doorway. 'Could I take a look around?'

'Oh no! I told you, privacy is very important to her. None of us dares to –' The girl gasped as a group of people suddenly came round a corner, making their way to the lower stairwell. 'It's her! Come on.' Wira grabbed my arm and jerked me over to the side of the hall. She bowed her head, lowering her eyes to the ground in deference.

I had no such obligation and, besides, my curiosity got the better of me. I was dying to see this woman who'd so captivated a Koturian nobleman that he'd been willing to use up his one shot at transformation on her. At first, I couldn't make out anything because of her entourage. Four flanked her on each side, and it was difficult to tell if they were male or female. They were, however, most definitely *not* Koturians. They had distinctly reptilian features, with jutting jaws, flat noses and goldish-black scales along their skin. I admit, it wasn't exactly what I'd had in mind when Evris had said his son's fiancée was humanoid. I supposed love really was blind.

Then a glimpse of her hand told me she wasn't reptilian like her attendants. It could've been a mirror of mine, and I wished I could get a better look at her face. She wore that fashionable Koturian veil, however, only giving me a quick glimpse of bluish eyes that swept past us in an imperious, dismissive way. Her dress was similar to mine, long and voluminous, though embellished with blue and silver. She'd nearly passed us when she came to an abrupt stop and did a double take. Her eyes widened.

'You!' she spat.

4

At first, I was too stunned to react. There was something familiar about this woman, but I couldn't place it.

'If you're here . . . so is *he*.' The bluish eyes glared at me through a gap in the veil that was almost completely hiding her face. 'Take her! Hurry.' Her eyes then fell on Wira, who was cringing and trying to make herself as small as possible. 'And the other one too, I suppose.'

I finally had the sense to shout for help, but by that point there was a scaly hand clamped over my mouth and a strong arm dragging me down the stairs. I thrashed against my captor, kicking backwards as hard as I could. It gave me only a heartbeat of freedom, before another of Lania's minions came and assisted him. I still wasn't really sure of their gender, but my brain had begun categorising them all as male.

They dragged Wira and me down two floors, through another twisting maze and eventually to a room blocked by heavy double doors. We were pushed inside and Lania strode in after us, giving a cursory look around. She pointed towards a smooth metal disc on the floor. 'There.'

The lizard-men threw us on to the disc without ceremony. Almost instantly a shimmering cone of golden light appeared

around us. Gingerly, I reached out to touch it, finding a
seemingly solid surface – one that suddenly tightened by a
few inches. I shrank back towards Wira, who was trembling
and clinging to me in return.

I would've expected Lania's rooms to display that same
luxury and comfort I'd seen upstairs. What I saw instead
was a makeshift lab, filled with tables and computers. Lania
had hunched herself over one of the latter and glanced up
briefly at us before returning to whatever it was that held
her interest.

'It's a sizian force field,' she said without emotion. 'Each
time you touch it, it'll close in further until it finally
suffocates you.' She paused for effect. 'So I wouldn't touch
it if I were you.'

I still couldn't truly study her, especially leaning over.
That sense of familiarity continued to nag at me, and her
voice only furthered it. Who was she? Somehow I knew her,
and she obviously knew me – and the Doctor.

'Ah. Here's the house's entry log. He arrived two hours
ago. No telling what damage he may have done in that time.'
She abruptly straightened up and fixed her eyes on me.
'Where is he now?'

'Who?' I asked.

'You know who!' She turned to one of her minions.
'There's no time to take these two to my TARDIS. The field
will contain them, but you'll have to stay here while the
others are out searching for him. It's absolutely imperative
we find him before the wedding. He could ruin everything.
As it is, I can't imagine how he found out about this. But
then nothing about him surprises me any more.'

'He's just a guest,' I blurted out.

That cold gaze swept over me again. 'Has he regenerated? Or is he still in that same outlandish form?'

TARDIS. Regeneration. And, just like that, all my memories unlocked.

'The Rani,' I gasped out.

As those hard eyes narrowed at her name, it seemed impossible I hadn't recognised her right away. From her frown, she apparently thought she should have been obvious to me as well. Understanding hit her.

'Ah, yes. This.' She unwrapped the veil from round her head and shook out her light brown hair. Her face was exactly the same as before, lovely in a hard, cold way. 'Stupid custom. I'll be glad to be rid of it.' The tight smile she gave me didn't reach her eyes. 'Too bad for you that you didn't follow it. I might not have recognised you if you'd had one on.' She counted off four of her minions and gestured to the door. 'Go and find him. He's probably with Evris, so be discreet in getting him away. We can't make a scene until this charade is over.'

'What are you doing here?' I demanded. 'Are you . . . are you in love with Jonos?' It seemed impossible, especially considering her history of ruthlessness and cold-hearted scientific schemes, but why else would she be engaged to a Koturian?

'Love? That contrived, chemically driven state of idiocy?' The Rani rolled her eyes. 'Honestly, you're as stupid and silly as the last time we met. I've never understood why the Doctor travels with your kind. It'd drive me mad . . . but then it's not like he's the model of sanity anyway.'

'He'll stop you,' I said, out of both defiance and obligation. 'Whatever you're doing, he won't let you get away with it.'

'By the time he realises what's happened, he'll be too late.' She beckoned to two more of the lizard-men. 'Let's go. Those fools will be expecting me for the women's preparation ritual or whatever nonsense they have in mind.'

She entered something else into her computer and then re-wrapped the veil round her head. Her two chosen attendants immediately closed ranks. 'I'll be back as soon as I can,' she snapped to those who remained. There were only two now, but I noticed they'd acquired some sort of guns since entering the room.

The Rani swept out of the double doors, which slammed together with a thud, leaving us alone with the guards.

5

I immediately began trying to think of a way to escape. I looked up and around, certain there must be a way to break the force field. It had emerged from the floor, and I wondered if that held the solution. Unfortunately, when I tried to touch it, I accidentally bumped into the wall of light – making it close in more tightly. Wira whimpered.

'I don't understand what we've done to displease her,' she said in a small voice. 'Why would Lania do something like this?'

'Because she's been deceiving you,' I explained. 'Her name isn't Lania. She's the Rani. A Time Lord like the Doctor. Er, well, Time Lady.'

She was certainly no one I'd ever expected to see again. Our last encounter had been on Earth, during a trip to the Industrial Revolution, when she'd been trying to extract a sleep-inducing chemical from innocent humans caught up in the chaos of the time. I remembered that part pretty well because she'd tried to do it to me too.

'She's a scientist.' That was an understatement, but I didn't quite know how to articulate to Wira the full extent of the Rani's obsession. To the Rani, science trumped all other things in life. Sometimes she had specific, selfish goals. Other times, she'd get caught up in the experiments themselves: science for the sake of science. Her experiments were what had got her exiled from Gallifrey, and that single-minded focus on her research had replaced any morality she might have had – and certainly any regard for life forms she considered beneath her.

'We have to warn the Doctor,' I told Wira. The girl was so frightened, I wasn't even sure if she heard me. 'He's the only one who can –'

A clatter of metal was the sole warning I had before a hole in the ceiling suddenly opened, and the Doctor came tumbling down to the floor, landing in an ungraceful heap of rainbow plaid. Nonetheless, he rose to his feet with all the dignity of an Olympic gymnast who'd just landed a perfect somersault.

'Please go on,' he told me cheerfully. 'The only one who can . . . what? Awe the masses with his wit and charm? Stump the most revered intellects of your time – or any time?'

'The only one about to get shot!' I yelled. 'Look out!'

The two reptilian men that the Rani had left on guard were charging forward, brandishing their guns. The Doctor ducked as one of them fired, emitting a blue burst of light that instead hit the force field surrounding Wira and me. The ray bounced off our prison wall, back at the lizard-man who'd fired it. He keeled over backwards, hitting the floor with a thud. Wira jumped in alarm, hitting the wall of light and triggering another restriction in our space. I gripped her hard and pulled her closer to me, scarcely daring to breathe at how near the walls were now.

The remaining creature advanced menacingly on the Doctor, who was searching around frantically for help. Then he spied a metal ceiling panel that had fallen down with him. He picked it up and swung it with astonishing force, missing, but effectively dodging an attack. His second attempt struck the reptilian man in the head, and he crumpled to the ground. The Doctor clung to his makeshift weapon and paused, waiting for movement from his fallen foes. When nothing happened, he knelt down and studied the one he'd hit.

'He'll be out for a while.' The Doctor looked over at the one who'd been hit by the ricocheting gun blast. His face fell and, to my surprise, he touched the creature's cheek. 'The gun was on its highest level. Shame. I always feel so guilty killing the Rani's engineered lackeys. They're already in a sorry state. They never have a fighting chance to begin with.'

'They seemed to have a fighting chance when they abducted us,' I countered. 'And when that one nearly shot you. You got lucky.'

The Doctor picked up the guns and carefully placed them on a counter. He wiped his hands together, as though they were dirty. For a fleeting moment, I saw true regret in his eyes, and then he was back to his usual self. 'Skill, my dear. Not luck.'

'Well, why don't you use some of your skill to get us out of –' I bit my words off as I replayed his comments about engineered lackeys in my mind. 'You know the Rani's here.'

'Yes, I'm afraid so. I'd suspected when I sent you to investigate – which I see you did with your usual thoroughness. Listening to Evris's stories simply confirmed it, and I got away as quickly as I could to find a quiet way to come in and take a look. Air tunnels aren't my favourite way to travel, but they work.' He strolled around the room, clucking his tongue at what he saw. 'My, my, she has been busy.'

'Do you think you could –'

'– do this?' He pushed a button, and the force field vanished. I sagged in relief, feeling as though I'd suddenly emerged from being underwater.

'Yes, thank you.' I gave Wira a quick check, but mostly she seemed scared, with no signs of physical damage. Wrapping her arms round herself, she sat down against a nearby wall and looked about her in disbelief. I gave her a small pat on the shoulder before turning my full attention to the Doctor. 'How did you know about the Rani?'

'From her little winged calling cards. I've seen some of her creations before, both the kind she breeds, like the ones we encountered outside, and the ones she manipulates – like those poor saps on the floor. That gold sheen is a side-effect of the process.' He paused to push a few buttons and read what came up on a display. 'Anyway, I could've written that off as a coincidence until I started hearing all that talk about Jonos's "brilliant and cultured" alien bride. Those certainly aren't the words I'd use to describe her, but she is a scientific genius . . . so I suppose convincing others that she's pleasant might be only a little harder than genetically modifying reptiles.'

'But why is she doing it?' I asked. I stood by him as he scrolled through information on a computer, but most of it made no sense to me. 'What in the world do pterodactyls have to do with tricking someone into marrying you?'

'Tricking?' asked Wira. She lifted her head up from where it had rested on her knees. 'What do you mean?'

That earlier love I'd sensed in her shone through her eyes, and it broke my heart. 'It's like I told you before,' I said gently, 'Lania's not who she seems. She's misled all of you as part of some plot to get Jonos to marry her.'

'But why does she need to trick anyone?' asked Wira. 'Jonos already loves her.'

'What Peri is being too delicate to say is that she – the Rani – isn't in love with poor Jonos. Or should I say lucky Jonos.' The Doctor shuddered. 'Can you even imagine a lifetime shackled to that woman? He's really dodged a bullet, assuming we can get to the church on time to save him from some untimely demise. Tell me, what do you make of this?'

It took me a moment to follow the topic change and drag my gaze from the stricken Wira. I leaned closer to the Doctor and tried to understand what he was showing me. 'You could have been a little more tactful with her,' I whispered.

'I told her the truth.' The Doctor made no attempt to regulate his volume.

'We don't know that he's going to meet an untimely demise.'

'No, but most likely. Remember who we're dealing with.' The Doctor was still playing flippant, but I again caught a ghostly hint of worry in his eyes. 'Now, look at what we have here. A mess of biological data – and I do mean mess. There's no order to it, just a jumble of entries, genetic records. The only thing I can tell for certain is that it's all Koturian.'

'But if she doesn't love him, why would she marry him?' moaned Wira.

The Doctor gave her a brief, irritated look before returning to the data. 'Probably something to do with his Phasing, if I had to guess. Although, guessing the Rani's thoughts . . . Well, that's something few have ever had success at. It's amazing that she was able to collect so much data without anyone noticing.'

I stared at the screen without really seeing it. 'Because she didn't collect it herself. The pterodactyls did. They took skin and blood from their victims and brought it back to her. And they took some of the actual victims too.'

An eager gleam filled the Doctor's eyes. 'So help me, Peri, you might be on to something. None of the Koturians thought to connect the attacks to Jonos's fiancée. Why would they? Most people expect the claws to come out *after* marriage. Creative choice of data collection, I'll give her that.'

'Is it?' I asked wryly. 'When we last left her, you trapped her in her TARDIS with a *T. rex*. Maybe she found a way to pass the time.'

'Did I?' He arched an eyebrow. 'Yes, I suppose I did. Well, never let it be said the Rani can't make lemonade out of lemons. Or efficient biogenetically engineered research tools out of a frightening prehistoric encounter.' Straightening up, he began pacing the room. 'The Rani isn't the type to collect that information without a reason. There's a purpose; we just need to find it. She's deposited the raw data here. But her actual work . . . that'll be somewhere else. Here, help me.'

He began running his hands over every smooth surface on the consoles and counters he could find. I immediately followed suit, not knowing what I should be looking for until, a few minutes later, my fingers ran over an almost imperceptible bump in an otherwise flat surface. 'Doctor?'

Excitement filled his eyes as he walked over and saw what I was pointing to. When he ran his hand over it in a circular motion, a square indentation appeared in the metal. He tapped the surface, and it slid open, revealing a small compartment.

'And here we are.' Triumphant, he lifted a small tetragonal crystal. 'The Rani, while unpredictable in many ways, is also predictable in others. She's set this lab up like the one in her TARDIS, and she's too paranoid to leave data on anything she can't easily take with her. This is going to have our answers.' He strode over to another computer and inserted the crystal into a slot I hadn't noticed.

Another loud sigh came from Wira. 'Poor Jonos.'

The Doctor grimaced at the interruption to his brilliant reveal, but mercifully left the girl alone. 'As suspected,' he said. 'Here's where the order is. She's got their genetic information organised by age and gender, as well as how far along they were in their Phasing windows.'

'So you know what she's doing?' I asked.

'Not a clue,' he admitted. 'But it doesn't matter. It's safe to assume she's up to no good, so we'll stop her now and ask questions later. If she took you, she knows I'm here.'

I nodded. 'She doesn't know what you look like, though. She asked if you'd regenerated since the last time we saw her — she's not a fan of this appearance, you know.'

He chuckled. 'Yes, she's made that very clear before. You'd think she'd be kinder about it, though, seeing as she knows as well as I there's not much we can do about it. Besides, I think it's clear that I just keep improving.' Studying his reflection in a monitor, he gave a decisive nod.

'It's so sad,' said Wira. I wasn't even sure if she was talking to us at this point. 'Jonos will be wasting his one chance at Phasing on a woman who doesn't love him.'

That seemed to finally make the Doctor snap. 'Honestly, are you going to keep –' He froze in shock, and I took a few steps towards him.

'What is it?'

'That. This.' He held up the crystal he'd taken from the console. 'That's why the Rani's studying the Koturians. She's trying to affect Time Lord regeneration somehow. She must suspect – or perhaps she's found – a connection between our respective transformations.'

'Is there one?' I asked, startled. 'They're completely different processes. Theirs comes from love. Yours from death.'

'Yes,' he agreed. 'But both result in a complete transformation of the body. And if anyone can find connections between things that have no business being linked together –' he paused and gave the lizard-men a meaningful look – 'then it's her. Come on, we have to stop that wedding.'

Without waiting to see if I, or Wira, was coming, he hurried to the double doors and pulled on one of the handles. There was a bright flash of light, and he jumped back with a cry of surprise.

'We just can't get a break today,' I said, running over to him.

'The Rani apparently didn't want to take any chances,' he said, scowling at his hand. 'It's a credit to you, really, that she thought you'd escape both the sizian field and her minions.'

'She didn't *seem* to give me much credit,' I said. 'She kept saying I was stupid and silly.'

'Don't let her get to you,' said the Doctor, kneeling down to study the door. 'You're not stupid in the least.'

'Can we climb out through the ceiling?' Wira asked.

I turned and was surprised to see her beside me. She'd wiped away her tears and a determined expression gleamed in her eyes. The Doctor gave her an appraising look.

'Well, you've already undergone a transformation of your own, haven't you?' he said.

She held her head up higher. 'If we can stop Lania from taking advantage of Jonos, then I want to help. Just tell me what I need to do,' she said fiercely.

I could see a smile start to curve at the Doctor's lips and then he put on a stern mask. 'Right, then. We could go through the ceiling, but it'd take longer . . . and be a lot more uncomfortable. No, ladies, we simply have to blow this door up.'

'Blowing something up is simple?' I asked.

'Simple, yes. Easy, no.' He peered around the lab. 'Too bad she didn't leave any explosives or fuel lying about.'

I pointed. 'What about the guards' guns?'

'Unfortunately, their deadliness comes more from a signal to disrupt biological functioning than any sort of brute-force destruction.'

'But they must have a battery or fuel source, right?' I insisted. 'Is there some way we could ignite it?'

The Doctor retrieved one of the guns and dismantled it, revealing a silvery rectangular object. He held it up to the light. 'Yes and yes. Go get the other one.'

I hurried to comply. Meanwhile, he knelt down in front of the doors and carefully set the battery in front of them, pressed right up to where they met. He laid another object on top of it and then placed the second battery on top of that. I tilted my head to get a better look.

'Is that your sonic lance?'

'Yes.'

He turned it on, sprang up and grabbed my hand. We reached the far side of the lab just as the batteries exploded and took out a good chunk of the doors' lower halves. He returned and gripped hold of the new openings. The doors gave easily.

'Your lance is in pieces,' I pointed out, kicking a fragment with my toe.

'I have a spare, and I'll be careful not to blow it up. Now, come. We have no time to lose.' He turned to Wira who was scurrying over to join us. 'You can take us to the wedding?'

She still had that fierce air about her and pointed upwards through the house's labyrinth. 'Yes,' she said. 'It's being held in the chapel over at the Flamingo.' And she sped away.

6

We followed Wira through the twisting corridors and up the stairs to the grand entrance hall.

'The Flamingo? That's another Vegas place,' I observed, hurrying to keep up with the newly motivated Wira. I could see the Doctor was having the same trouble.

'It's the most exclusive place on the Swathe,' Wira said as she reached the massive front door. 'Their chapel has the largest Imori stone ever found on our planet. Only elite families are allowed to use it.'

'No doubt part of the Rani's motivation in choosing her paramour,' the Doctor muttered. 'Go big or go home.'

'Wira said the stones are divine. But I'm guessing not?'

'No,' he told me. 'They're an elemental combination found only on this planet. A similar one is found on Azzarozia, which they use as rocket fuel. Here, the Imori stones help provide energy to power the accelerated metabolism needed during the Koturian transformations. I'm sure the Rani's obtained some samples for her research as well, but probably with less bloodshed – unless she decided to biologically manipulate a drill.' He seemed pretty pleased with his joke, but my next question dimmed his enthusiasm.

'What about the victims who were taken whole? Some may still be alive.'

'I know,' he said grimly. 'And my guess is they won't be once she's decided to wrap up her research.'

Wira led us back to the crowded Swathe, and all of us were running by now, driven by the urgency of our task. Evening had fallen, and all the buildings had come to life with dazzling displays of light. We found the Flamingo and entered through its main door, cutting across a casino full of sequin-clad gamers and servers who glared at us when we had to push them aside. The layout was nearly as confusing as Evris's house.

I was gasping by the time we reached the white marble doorway leading to the chapel. Leaning over, resting my hands on my knees, I discovered I'd torn this dress too. The Doctor came to a halt beside me, panting as well.

'Looks like we may have to do more conditioning when we're back in the TARDIS,' he observed.

'More?' I asked. 'As opposed to what we do now?'

Two servants in Evris's yellow livery stood guard at the door. They seemed simply ceremonial, with no weapons, probably because no one expected a deadly villainess to show up at a wedding, let alone be a major player in it.

'I'm sorry,' one of them was saying to Wira, 'but we can't let you in – not when it's already started.'

'This is important!' she exclaimed. 'Jonos is in danger.'

The two exchanged uncertain glances, but the Doctor had no patience for anything more. He simply strode up to the doors and pushed them open. With an apologetic look at the servants, I quickly followed him and sensed Wira right behind me. I didn't really know what we'd be walking into and had a horrifying fear of everyone turning to stare.

They didn't because no one even noticed us. The 'chapel' was so huge and so vast that our entrance took no attention away from the drama unfolding up at the front. The room actually looked remarkably like a cathedral from back home, with pews and stained-glass windows, save that it was all done in more of those cringe-worthy colour schemes. Up where an altar would have been sat enormous urns of flowers, towering over those gathered below. A glittering purple rock that I assumed was the Imori stone stood between them, about the size of a kitchen table. Waiting on each side of it, their profiles to the audience, were Jonos and the Rani. He had lavender hair like his father and was as handsome as Wira had said. Some sort of officiant – dressed astonishingly like Elvis Presley – raised his arms in the air, and I just barely heard the word, 'Commence.' At the same moment, Jonos and the Rani reached for each other and held hands over the stone. I didn't entirely know what was happening, but Wira did, and she rushed forward.

'No!'

But it was too late. A piercing yellow light began to shine from where the couple's hands were clasped. It grew and grew until it spread over the rest of the rock and over them. Soon, the entire front half of the chapel was too blinding to look at, and I put a hand over my eyes. It lasted for almost thirty seconds, and then steadily the light faded. I still couldn't see right away, not after all that radiance, and I had to blink black spots away. When I finally focused on the couple again, I wondered if my vision had been harmed.

Because Jonos looked the same.

The gasps and startled reactions of the couple and the congregation soon showed me that I wasn't the only one who'd noticed the lack of transformation. Wira, bold before, had retreated back to us. Her eyes were wide, her face pale.

'It's impossible,' she whispered.

'What is this?' demanded the Rani, her angry words echoing. 'Why didn't you change?'

Jonos, looking as stricken as everyone else, examined his hands and then touched his face. 'I . . . I don't know. The stone came to life. I felt it. I felt the reaction begin in me, but then . . . it just didn't work.'

'The fault isn't in you. It's in your blushing bride,' announced the Doctor, striding forward. His voice rang through the vaulted room.

Evris stood up in the front row. 'Doctor! What are you doing?'

The Rani's face twisted into a sneer as she removed her veil. 'Of course. Of course you're behind this.'

The Doctor came to a halt and casually stuffed his hands in his pockets. 'No, actually. This was all you, I'm afraid. Lovely dress, by the way. I like the blue trim. Do you have something new and something borrowed tucked away as well? It goes without saying that you yourself have the "something old" more than taken care of.'

'They said this would work without two Koturians!' cried the Rani. She levelled glares at everyone, including her groom. 'You all said it would. You said he'd transform even if he wasn't marrying a Koturian.'

'It's true that your body doesn't matter for his transformation.' The Doctor looked like he was on top of the world, probably because he loved both an audience and one-upping the Rani. 'But your heart does. Your figurative one, that is. Not your physical ones. The chemicals that churn through the body of someone in love are what the stone responds to, what spins up its energy cycle. But it needs two sets to drive it – and, alas, there's only one person in love in this relationship. Only one person even capable of emotion, really. Considering the number of lacklustre marriages in the world, I'm guessing the stone has a pretty low bar for *some* type of regard, but you couldn't even get that high, Rani.'

Jonos looked between his bride and the Doctor in obvious confusion. 'My darling Lania . . . what is this about?'

'Her name's not Lania,' said the Doctor. 'And "darling" probably isn't the best adjective. She's Gallifreyan like me and hoped to take advantage of your Phasing for her own devices. What was it, Rani? Couldn't glean enough from your prehistoric research team's random sampling? Did you need someone who'd specifically transformed because of you and whose DNA would therefore reflect your influence?'

The Rani pointed accusingly at him. 'Don't act like it's such a ridiculous idea, Doctor. You can't tell me you haven't wanted more control over the regeneration process. Most Time Lords are at the mercy of fate after death. But imagine if we could definitively control the outcome! These people are the best lead I've found. They not only control their transformations but also improve in mind and body. Surely you'd be interested in that?'

'Is that another slight on my appearance?' He gave a melodramatic sigh. 'Fate's been very good to me, thank you very much, and I'm quite content with that. Maybe we don't have the control that they do, but we're gifted with life many more times than others are.'

'Fools are content with their fates,' she snapped. 'Those with sense seek to control and even change theirs.'

The Doctor was unmoved. 'Well then, you'll have to find another way. You will never, ever be able to influence a Koturian transformation, be it Jonos or some other poor soul whose life you would have warped – and then eventually ended. You cannot love. You cannot be a part of it.'

'You're one to lecture,' she said, tossing her hair back. 'Please, Doctor. Tell me more about your great experiences with love and sharing your inner feelings. For someone who always travels with others, you still seem remarkably alone to me.'

His smile tightened. 'For you, we'll have to start with something more basic. Like empathy.'

Jonos nervously took a couple of steps towards the Rani and reached for her. 'We'll figure this out. There must be some mistake. What he's saying . . . it's not true . . .'

He tried to touch her, but the Rani pushed him away. 'Oh, be quiet. I'm so tired of your simpering. It's no wonder you've never been married. Being free of your prattle doesn't make up for the failure of one of my greatest endeavours – but it helps.'

Cries of shock and outrage followed. 'Find some guards and seize her!' exclaimed Evris. 'She must be punished for the sacrilege she's attempted.'

'No,' said the Doctor, holding up his hand as several men rushed forward. 'Let her go. Let her go – as long as she tells us where she's keeping the victims that are still alive.'

'What?' exclaimed Jonos and Evris in unison.

The Rani put her hands on her hips and laughed. 'Thank you, but I don't need any bargain of yours to get myself out of here, Doctor. As for where they are . . . Well, that's one secret you'll never know. Good luck searching once I'm gone.'

'How about a bargain of a different sort?' asked the Doctor. He reached into his pocket and held up the crystal storage device from the lab. 'Won't be much of a victory if you leave completely empty-handed, will it?'

The Rani paled. 'How did you get that?' she demanded, holding out her hand. 'Give it to me!'

The Doctor set the crystal on the ground, his foot hovering over it.

She froze. 'Wait!'

'These are such contradictory little gadgets, aren't they?' mused the Doctor. 'They can hold gargantuan amounts of data, but are so, so fragile. Such a shame.'

'You wouldn't dare. The results of all of my research are there! Destroy it, and it's gone. All of it.' For a few moments, she was all fury and outrage, and then . . . she faltered. 'Please. Don't destroy it. I've put in so much work here. Don't make it all for nothing.'

The Doctor's eyes widened in mock surprise. 'My goodness. It appears I was wrong. You *are* capable of feeling emotion. Admittedly, it's only for cold hard data purchased through the blood of innocents, but, well, it's a start. Perhaps we'll make a starry-eyed romantic of you after all.'

'Doctor,' she growled.

All levity faded from him. 'The victims. Tell us where they are. Not in your TARDIS, surely?'

'That rabble? Of course not.' She fell silent, but as her eyes returned to the crystal under his foot I could see fear playing over her features. 'Fine. There's a derelict casino seven blocks from the house. I have them taken there for experimen— examination. It's where my servants roost.'

The Doctor's foot still hovered above the crystal, but his eyes flicked to Evris. 'Send someone there immediately. A medical team.' The Koturian man nodded to a couple of servants who scurried away. 'And maybe a very large flyswatter.'

The Rani's gaze never left the Doctor. 'There. I told you what you wanted to know. Now prove you're the alleged man of honour you play, and give me the crystal!'

'Gladly.' With hands as nimble as a magician's, the Doctor picked up the crystal and tossed it towards the Rani who caught it with equal deftness. 'Now, Evris, it's all up to you.'

The guards Evris had summoned earlier began to advance. For a second, the Rani squeezed the crystal, relief flooding her face. Then the haughty look that seemed to be her trademark returned. 'I don't think so.' She shot a glance to the opposite corner of the room. 'Stop them!'

The contingent of lizard-men who'd seized Wira and me surged forward and intercepted the guards. In the clash and confusion, the Rani was momentarily forgotten, and I watched her slowly back away from the fray, a triumphant smile on her face.

'You might regret not helping me with this one day,' she called over to us. 'Your next regeneration may be sooner than you think.'

'Doctor –' I began.

'I see her.'

He started towards the Rani when suddenly she *disappeared* into one of the giant urns. That was soon followed by an all-too-familiar sound. The urn vanished.

'It was her TARDIS.'

The Doctor nodded, his expression a mix of resignation and envy. 'My kingdom for a chameleon circuit.' He sighed and then switched into jovial mode. 'I'm guessing she had it standing by there to spirit Jonos off immediately for experimentation once he'd changed. Probably not the exciting wedding night he'd had in mind.'

'I can't believe we were all so fooled,' said Evris morosely.

He'd come to stand beside us, and I took a moment to survey the scene. People were on their feet, anxious and confused, but there were no real injuries or damage. The Rani's minions had been subdued quickly, simply by sheer numbers – as she'd known they would be. I recalled what the Doctor had said about them before, how they never had a fighting chance.

'Don't beat yourself up,' the Doctor replied, patting his friend on the shoulder. 'She's a clever woman – a *very* clever woman, which makes it all the more tragic that she uses that intellect with so little morality.'

'Poor Jonos,' said Evris. 'Having his heart broken like that. How will he ever find love soon enough for his Phasing?'

I glanced back up towards the Imori stone. An obviously

miserable Jonos sat on the floor while Wira knelt beside him, clasping his hands and doling out comforting words that I couldn't quite make out.

'Maybe he'll find it in an unexpected place,' I said.

Evris followed my gaze and frowned. 'A serving-girl?'

The Doctor scoffed. 'That's your concern? Come now, you're a civilised man. Let go of your silly and archaic classist ideologies and try focusing on the fact that that nice girl cares about your son – and isn't an unscrupulous scientific mastermind.'

'Compelling argument,' Evris admitted. 'Excuse me while I talk to my son.'

We watched him walk away, and I hoped Jonos and Wira might truly make things work in time. For now, he was too devastated to even notice her presence, but surely someone deserved a happy ending here. It was a cheering thought, but one that soon faded as I turned towards the Doctor.

'You let her keep her data,' I said. 'Maybe she'll try some new tactic with the Koturians.'

He smiled. 'Not likely. I erased the crystal back in her lab.'

I gaped. 'She was already pretty upset about her plans falling through here. When she realises what you did to the crystal, she's *really* not going to be happy with you.'

'She never is,' he said solemnly. He held out his arm, and I linked mine through it. 'Now then. Since we're here, shall we go try our luck in the casino while the others sort this mess out?'

I laughed as we strolled out through the confused Koturian congregation. 'Luck? I thought you said earlier that it was skill.'

'As long as you don't run out of it, it doesn't matter what you call it.'

'And you're not worried about that happening?' I asked.

'Not in the least, Peri. Not in the least.'

THE SEVENTH DOCTOR:
THE RIPPLE EFFECT

MALORIE BLACKMAN

1

The Doctor lay on his back with his head inside the TARDIS console. Ace stood beside him, holding an armful of tools she didn't recognise. They weren't heavy but they were awkward.

'Pass me the magnetic de-interlacer,' said the Doctor, his arm stretched up expectantly.

'The what?' asked Ace.

'The metal tube with the red ball on the end.'

Ace had to juggle the tools in her arms so that she didn't drop the lot before she carefully extracted the correct one and placed it in the Doctor's hand.

'Professor, what, exactly, are you doing?' she asked with a frown.

'I'm reconfiguring the chrono-dynamic tensor to have a non-orthogonal phase angle,' he said as if that made everything clear. 'Now I need a tachyon filter. Please.' Once again, a hand emerged, its fingers wriggling.

Ace examined the tools she still held. She hoped that one would be conveniently labelled 'tachyon filter'. No such luck.

The empty hand waved impatiently.

'OK, which one is that?' she asked, frustrated. Give her something to blow up with Nitro-9 explosives and she was fine, but for delicate tinkering with a time machine she was beyond useless.

'The sparkly tube with the ghostly blue glow inside,' came the muffled answer. The Doctor's fingers were now jiggling so fast they were a blur.

Ace found the tool and placed it in the Doctor's waiting hand. Her eyes drifted up to the viewscreen. For over a week now it had been showing the same thing. Fog! Not real fog, of course – they were in space – but a nebulous, ever-changing multicoloured fuzziness. Every now and then some piece of space junk would drift into view for a few seconds before disappearing again into the murk. And the TARDIS wasn't the only ship stuck here. Occasionally a whole spaceship would appear among the debris. Some were tiny shuttlecraft, others were vast star-liners, but they all shared one thing, the TARDIS included: they were well and truly trapped. The Doctor had already pointed out a number of now-obsolete vessels that must have been here for centuries, maybe even millennia. Ace was ready to climb the walls. Eight days trapped in this one place was more than enough for her.

'When you get us out of here, will all the other ships be released too?' she asked.

The Doctor popped his head out and looked up at her. 'No,' he replied. 'I'm afraid not. The Temporal Plexus is like cosmic quicksand. You can pull yourself out – maybe – but everyone else stays stuck unless they work out how to escape for themselves.'

'Can't we do something to help them?' The idea of leaving all the others behind just didn't sit well with Ace.

'It isn't guaranteed that we can get *ourselves* out of this, never mind anyone else.' The Doctor's head disappeared back into the console.

The fog cleared briefly on the viewscreen, and Ace thought she saw a familiar shape. She peered intently.

'I need the quantum stabiliser,' said the headless Doctor.

'Yeah, just a minute.' Ace stared at the screen. As if she had willed it, the fog cleared again and she saw it. A police box . . .

'Do all Time Lords have TARDISes?' she asked as the tendrils of space fog closed in again.

'Yes,' replied the Doctor. 'Though most don't use them. They prefer to sit on Gallifrey looking important. Why?'

'I just saw another one.'

'Where?'

'Out there.'

The Doctor stood up, dusted off his hands and came to stand beside her, looking at the screen. Apart from the ever-shifting, multicoloured space fog there was nothing else to see.

'What makes you think it was a TARDIS?'

'Duh! Because it looked like a police box.'

'My dear Ace, not all TARDISes look like police boxes. Only this one does – ever since the old girl's chameleon circuit got a bit stuck.'

'But I definitely saw –'

'Then it was a temporal echo. Space and time are so mixed up around here that what you saw might've been us ten minutes ago or maybe a decade from now.'

'We won't really be stuck here for that long, will we?' Ace asked, aghast.

'Well, not if I have anything to do with it,' said the Doctor with a confident smile, before returning to the console.

Ace sighed deeply. It was all right for the Professor. A year in the TARDIS probably passed for him like an hour for people on Earth. The TARDIS was huge, and there were enough wonders inside it to keep anyone amused for a lifetime. There was a library, the computers, alien treasures from a thousand worlds *and* a swimming pool, but Ace hated being cooped up, no matter how interesting the cage. She needed to get out. NOW!

Ace turned off the viewscreen. 'What happens if you can't get us out?' she asked, squatting down.

There was a pause that was just a little too long for comfort. The Doctor lifted his head.

'It won't come to that.' He winked. Ace wasn't convinced. Three days had passed since the Doctor had played his wretched spoons. That in itself told Ace that they were in BIG trouble.

Ten minutes later, he stood up and pushed the quantum stabiliser into the top pocket of his rumpled beige jacket. He gently laid his hands on the console and bowed his head. He might have just been checking one of the instruments, but it looked to Ace suspiciously like he was reassuring the TARDIS. Then he flicked two switches, closed his eyes and pulled a big lever. The Time Rotor – the glowing glass column in the centre of the console – started to rise and fall and Ace heard the familiar whooshing, wheezing, screeching noise as the TARDIS started to dematerialise.

'Yes!' The Doctor punched the air in glee and his face broke into a huge grin. Ace was just about to join in with the celebrating when a shudder ran through the entire TARDIS. Without warning, the Time Rotor dimmed and stalled. Complete silence.

'What happened?' said Ace. 'Are we free?'

The Doctor ran around the console checking instruments, a deep frown cutting into his face. After a few seconds he stopped. 'No,' he said quietly. 'I'm afraid we're anything but free.'

Ace's heart sank. She didn't want to end up like the other ships she'd seen, imprisoned like a mosquito in amber for all time.

'So what's the next cunning plan then?' Ace asked. 'More reconfiguring?' She held out the magnetic de-interlacer, her eyebrows raised hopefully.

'No,' said the Doctor. 'I'm afraid I've rather run out of cunning plans.'

The Doctor stopped fiddling with the TARDIS and switched on the viewscreen. He stared at it as if seeking inspiration, then turned back to the console, his hands playing with the ends of the paisley-patterned scarf he liked to wear.

'Come on, Professor,' said Ace. 'You never run out of cunning plans. Are you telling me you haven't got something else up your sleeve?'

The Doctor's face was a study in frustration. Ace couldn't believe it. Had the Doctor really got into a situation he couldn't get out of? But then his face cleared, his eyes widened and hope flickered within them.

'I knew you wouldn't let me down.' Ace grinned. 'Dazzle me then!'

'I might have an inkling of a plan,' he said quietly. 'But it's really more desperate than cunning.'

At that moment, Ace would have taken anything. 'Which is . . .?'

'It may be possible to get out of here. The Plexus is gravitationally anchored to a star . . . so if I can make that star go nova . . .'

'What star?'

'The nearest one, the one that's just –' he waved vaguely – 'over there . . . thataway.' The Doctor busied himself again, muttering as he went.

'Er, isn't blowing up a star just a tad dangerous?' Ace asked.

'Not if you do it carefully.'

Carefully? How exactly did that work? Ace knew her way around explosives and even carried a handy supply of Nitro-9 bombs in her backpack, but safely blowing up an entire star was way outside the scope of her imagination. The Doctor spent a few more minutes adjusting, tinkering, checking. Ace felt absolutely helpless. All she could do was watch.

'Doctor, talk to me,' Ace pleaded.

'I'm going to send a phased pulse into the nearest star, but I have to time this exactly right or I'll make things worse, not better,' said the Doctor.

Could things get worse? 'Then make sure you get it right,' Ace advised.

'Thanks! I hadn't thought of that,' the Doctor said drily. 'Well, here goes nothing! Hold on tight.'

Ace grabbed the console, bracing herself as best she could. The Doctor threw a switch.

A blinding light was followed by a sudden series of bone-jarring jolts. Both the Doctor and his companion were thrown to the floor. The TARDIS shook so violently that Ace's head slammed into the edge of the console – and it hurt. A lot! It took a few seconds for the ringing in Ace's ears to subside. As she slowly got back on her feet, she became aware of a clanging noise – a sort of deep, slow, discordant bonging, like a wonky grandfather clock striking the hour.

'What's that?' she asked, alarmed.

'Not something you ever want to hear,' replied the Doctor, frantically checking the instruments. 'It's the Cloister Bell. It's what the TARDIS does instead of screaming blue murder when something really bad happens!'

'Like what? Please tell me that we got out of the Plexus this time,' said Ace.

'Oh yes! We're out of the Plexus,' said the Doctor. 'But . . .'

'Where are we?'

The Doctor studied the navigational panel. His closed mouth moved back and forth as he chewed over their dilemma.

'I have absolutely no idea,' he finally admitted.

2

The Doctor was still circling around the console fruitlessly trying to work out what was happening, when the TARDIS started making the familiar whooshing, screeching noise again.

'Great!' said Ace, relieved. 'You fixed it.'

'No, Ace, I did not,' replied the Doctor.

'But that noise means that we're materialising and landing, doesn't it?'

'Well, yes. The TARDIS is performing an auto-land.'

'Sorry?'

'The supernova hurled us across space and time. Now the TARDIS has locked on to some solid-looking planet and it's going to land.'

'OK,' said Ace. 'So where and when are we?'

'Haven't a clue! That's why we're landing – we need repairs. These instruments are misbehaving so badly that I can't –'

There was a colossal bump as the TARDIS completed its automatic landing, then a brief silence before the familiar electronic burbling noise of the door-opening mechanism started up.

'Professor, don't you think you should work out where and when we are before you open the doors? Just to be on the safe side?' suggested Ace.

The Doctor was already lunging for a switch on the console, but too late. The doors swung open. The Doctor and Ace exchanged a look, then turned tentatively towards the wide-open doorway. Sunlight, intense and bright, streamed into the TARDIS and the sounds of children's laughter and singing came from outside.

'Doesn't sound too scary,' said Ace hopefully. No matter how often they did this, and how many new places they visited, this part always made Ace's heart beat just that little bit faster.

The Doctor seemed less reassured.

'Hmm! The way the TARDIS is behaving is deeply disturbing,' he said. 'It's almost as if we were pulled here. I wonder . . .' The Doctor returned to the console and bent to examine one of the instruments, so he didn't see it.

But Ace did.

A Dalek.

It glided swiftly through the open doors and into the TARDIS.

Ace froze. She remembered her last encounter with these death-dealing robots with evil mutated monsters inside – and not with fondness. The thing was only a couple of metres away and temporarily distracted by the hat stand near the door. But now that it saw no threat from the Doctor's Panama hat and umbrella, its Cyclops eye swivelled towards Ace. She was defenceless, caught in the open, halfway between the console and the door. No bombs . . . no baseball bat . . .

nothing! The iris on the eye-stick widened, adjusting to the relative dark of the TARDIS after the bright sunlight. It started gliding towards her.

'DOCTOR!' Ace shouted.

The Doctor looked up and froze, but only momentarily.

The Dalek hadn't seen him yet, so the Doctor seized his opportunity. He grabbed the quantum stabiliser out of his pocket, flicked it to the 'High' setting and pointed it at the intruder. The Dalek must have seen him in its peripheral vision, but just as it started to turn the Doctor activated the stabiliser. There was a high-pitched whine and a beam of light shot out of the end, bathing the Dalek in a violet glow. The Dalek's eye and arms drooped immediately and its momentum left it coasting across the floor until it bumped gently into the console and stayed still.

'Blimey! That was close. Is it dead?' Ace was having trouble catching her breath.

'No,' the Doctor replied. 'Just stunned. A quantum stabiliser isn't exactly a weapon.' He stood for a moment looking at the disabled Dalek. 'Very odd! It doesn't seem to have a weapon.'

Surprised, Ace came closer to look. 'Oh yeah, no ray gun.'

Instead of having the usual manipulator arm on the right and a ray gun capable of hurling lethal energy bolts on its left-hand side, this Dalek just had two manipulator arms.

More noises from outside jolted the Doctor out of his analysis. 'We have to get the door closed.' He moved past Ace and raised the quantum stabiliser again. 'There may be more of them.'

But before he could reach the door, a small crowd of

children of assorted alien races rushed in and he was left brandishing the tool directly in the face of a tall, pretty dark-brown-skinned girl of about fifteen years old, who had intricate multicoloured markings of tiny birds round her hairline and running down the sides of her neck. The Doctor tried to peer round her to see if the children were being pursued by metal monsters, but the girl side-stepped in front of him so he could see nothing.

'What did you do?' she demanded. Her expression was equal parts anger and concern.

'I . . . er . . .'

'Did you hurt him?' The girl pointed at the disabled Dalek.

'Him?' echoed the Doctor. 'Did I hurt *him*? My dear girl, did he hurt you?'

'I can see from your ship that you're a Time Lord, but are you an idiot as well?' she asked, after glancing around. 'And give me that!' She snatched the quantum stabiliser out of the Doctor's hand like a teacher confiscating a dangerous toy from a naughty child. With another scathing look, she joined the other children huddled round the Dalek, touching it and running their hands over the metal as if stroking a wounded kitten.

The Doctor wasn't the only one to be totally confused. Ace had never, *ever* seen anyone show a Dalek affection. Before either of them could say anything else, three more Daleks arrived. Two of them approached their disabled comrade, while the third hung back, effectively blocking the door. Fortunately, none of these was armed either, though their manipulator arms were still powerful enough to crush a human skull like a hen's egg.

Now that more Daleks had arrived, the girl turned back to confront the Doctor. 'What are you?' she asked. 'Some kind of thug?'

The Doctor's mouth fell open. For once he was lost for words.

'Well?' she pressed. 'What possible excuse can you have for attacking a defenceless Dalek?'

Before the Doctor could react to that, one of the other Daleks – coloured grey and red – approached and spoke to the girl. 'Tulana, all is well. Sokar is not damaged,' it said. 'He was merely stunned by an intense photon flux.'

The injured Dalek had a name? Ace tentatively touched her head where she'd banged it against the TARDIS console. She must have hit it harder than she'd originally thought. That would certainly explain a number of things, like why the Dalek's voice was so strange. Instead of being harsh, staccato and coldly mechanical, it was quiet and modulated. It was still electronically generated, but it had a pleasant, almost lilting quality to it.

Tulana looked massively relieved. 'I think he –' she jerked her head towards the Doctor – 'used this.' She held out the tool she'd snatched and the Dalek examined it.

'Quantum stabiliser – very advanced,' it said. The eye moved up from the tool to the Doctor's face. 'I seek confirmation. Are you a Time Lord?' it asked pleasantly.

Having just arrived in a TARDIS, there was little point in denying it. The Doctor straightened up and thrust out his chin defiantly. 'Yes, I'm the Doctor.'

'I am Pytha. Welcome to the Academy,' said the Dalek.

'All are welcome,' chorused the others, apart from Tulana.

The Dalek's eye-stalk swivelled around and looked at the angry girl's face. 'Tulana?' it said, mildly reproachful. 'Where are your manners?'

'Sorry, Pytha,' she replied. 'All are welcome.' She still managed to give the Doctor another withering look, though.

The Dalek looked back at the Doctor. 'I apologise for my colleague Sokar,' it said. 'You must have been startled when he suddenly burst in uninvited. He is young and he can be very impetuous when he gets excited.'

The Doctor was speechless. Daleks that were courteous? Daleks that *apologised*?

'If you will excuse me,' said Pytha. 'I must ensure that Sokar re-initialises correctly.'

The Daleks left, two of them pushing their stunned companion ahead of them, while the children followed close behind. The Dalek Pytha and Tulana were the last to leave. After a quiet word from Pytha at the door, Tulana turned back to the Doctor. 'Pytha says that you are invited to tour the Academy later. He says I should come and get you at lunchtime, if that's OK with you?' Her tone was biting. Obviously still annoyed, she spun on her heel and marched out.

'What was that all about?' asked Ace.

'Yes, quite!' replied the Doctor.

'Can we get out of here? Like *now*!'

'First things first, Ace. I have to persuade the doors to close before we can go anywhere.'

After some more adjustments, the Doctor finally managed to get the doors to respond, and Ace breathed a sigh of relief as they closed. Seconds passed as Ace waited for the Doctor to set a course for some planet that had no Daleks on it. The Doctor leaned on the console, deep in thought.

'Doctor, why are we still on this messed-up planet? Something is obviously very wrong here, so can we just leave?'

'That was my first instinct too,' the Doctor admitted. 'But, as you said, something isn't right here.'

'All the more reason to be somewhere else then,' argued Ace.

The Doctor shook his head. 'Ace, d'you know where we are? According to the navigational panel, this is Skaro. But we both know that Skaro no longer exists. And these Daleks are doubly unsettling.'

'You think?' demanded Ace. 'We just got invited to lunch by one of them!'

'Yes, I know,' the Doctor replied. 'You know where you are when they offer mindless violence. This politeness is terrifying!'

'And what's with the voice?' Ace added. 'Why isn't it all loud and mechanical and menacing any more? These Daleks sound a bit like wind chimes. Too weird! So can we leave?'

'Ace, right now, much as the other side of the universe appeals, we need answers.' The Doctor strode out of the control room and headed off into the bowels of the TARDIS.

'What are you doing?' Ace asked, running to catch up with him before he could disappear.

'I'm going to interface the TARDIS computers with external data networks. I need to find out what's going on.'

An hour later, the Doctor emerged with a thoughtful expression on his face.

'Well?' said Ace. 'Who's been feeding the Daleks happy pills?'

The Doctor stood with his hands in his pockets, looking deeply puzzled. Not good.

Ace tried again. 'The last time I met the Daleks there were two groups fighting each other in a civil war. So is this a third group that's decided not to do the whole death-and-destruction thing? Pacifist Daleks that just want to sit and chat?'

The Doctor shook his head.

'So are these Daleks from before the evil Daleks I met on Earth,' said Ace, 'or after them?'

'As far as I can tell,' replied the Doctor, 'they are *instead* of them.'

'Come again?'

'There don't seem to be any other Daleks, just these – apparently – civilised, philosophical, peace-loving ones.'

'But –'

'I've examined every archive I can – the *Encyclopaedia Universalis*, the *Intergalactic OmniSource*, the *Citrinitas Net*. As far as I can tell, all the archives are authentic and the TARDIS databank is the only data source anywhere that makes any mention of evil militaristic Daleks. There's no record of them ever conquering anyone, anywhere, at any time. Skaro is now the universal centre of civilisation, philosophy, democracy and art. It's like Greece was on Earth from 550 BC, with everyone flocking here to learn.'

'But how can that be?' said Ace.

'I don't know. Something is wrong here. I can feel it. This must be some kind of Dalek plot – there's no other explanation.'

'That's terrible,' said Ace.

'Oh no, Ace.' The Doctor shook his head. 'That would be excellent!'

'Huh?'

'That would mean business as usual. Evil Daleks, galactic domination plans, same ole, same ole.'

'And that would be good?'

'Oh yes!'

'So what would be bad?'

'Bad would be if the recorded history was correct and the Daleks really are loved and respected and a great force for civilisation.'

'Why would that be bad?' asked Ace. 'If the Daleks suddenly became good guys?'

'That would be bad, my dear girl, because then something would have rebuilt our entire universe with an alternative timeline – but you and I are still able to remember the old one.'

'How is that possible?' asked Ace.

'I have no idea, Ace, but I intend to find out.'

3

Perched on the edge of a desert, with sweeping views of the distant mountains, the Academy was beautiful. Daleks and assorted aliens moved along long, winding ribbons of gleaming blue metal that weaved between the buildings.

Lunch was a buffet set up in a plaza quite close to where the TARDIS had landed. Ace didn't recognise what any of the food was, so she tagged along with Tulana and tried whatever the other girl ate. The smooth blue stuff was a bit salty, and the purply green thing that looked a bit like grated carrot was disgusting, but the orangey brown chunky stuff on the little toast squares was brilliant. Ace had loads of that.

Of course, the Daleks didn't eat, but they circulated, checking everyone had enough food and making conversation. The Doctor wasn't eating either. He was staring holes in the Daleks and being unusually quiet.

Ace looked up at a huge elliptical building that towered above the multicoloured sand of the desert. It curved gently and sparkled in the evening sun, tapering to a point high above.

'That's the Medical School,' said Tulana. 'Students from all over the galaxy come to study surgery and genetics under

Dalek teachers. The Daleks are the best surgeons anywhere. Their unique combination of biology and technology allows them a degree of micro-control that nobody else can match. They are also superb geneticists.'

'Oh, I'll just bet they are!' the Doctor snorted.

Tulana gave him a quizzical look. She'd picked up on his tone, but thankfully she let it slide.

After lunch, Tulana took them on the promised tour of the Academy. They strolled between impressive buildings of glass and metal, and walked along avenues lined with abstract sculptures. Everywhere they went, groups of aliens, some of whom seemed to be barely older than toddlers, or elders several centuries old, sat or strolled with one or more Daleks, learning and debating. There was an outdoor class in nearly every plaza under the guidance of a Dalek tutor – everything from the youngest children learning elementary maths that even Ace could do to adults attending seminars in subjects so advanced that she had no clue what they were talking about.

Normally the Doctor would have been talking non-stop and making bad jokes, but he barely said a word and his silence was making Ace feel embarrassed. She tried to rope him into the conversation.

'The Doctor was saying that all this is a bit like ancient Greece on Earth a long time ago,' Ace said.

Tulana looked puzzled, but a Dalek tutor broke off from teaching and turned to face the visitors. 'Thank you,' it said to the Doctor. 'There are some parallels, but, unlike the ancient Greek humans, we don't have slavery here on Skaro.'

'Still, I see that you're regaling the rest of the galaxy with the superiority of your Dalek ways.' The Doctor's tone was pure acid.

Ace winced. She wondered if the Dalek understood the Doctor's sarcasm.

'We feel that we should share our knowledge, yes. Some advanced races have been a little too aloof and have missed a chance to share their wisdom with others,' replied the Dalek. 'The Time Lords, for instance.'

Ouch! Being scolded by a Dalek for not looking after other races was too much for the Doctor. His expression thunderous, he strode off – but not far. Tulana stared after him. The Dalek might not have understood sarcasm, but Tulana certainly did.

'Why is your friend being so unpleasant when you are both being treated as honoured guests?' she whispered to Ace when they had nearly reached the Doctor at the edge of the plaza.

'Well, if I'm such an honoured guest, why have they fobbed us off with you as our tour guide?' said the Doctor, overhearing. 'Why are we not being shown around by a Dalek?'

'Perhaps because they don't want to be disabled by a photon beam,' Tulana bristled. 'Or maybe because they can sense your hostility. Plus they thought you'd be more comfortable with a humanoid guide.'

There was an uncomfortable silence.

'I'm sorry, Tulana,' said the Doctor at last. 'I'm just not used to Daleks being friendly. This is just . . . weird.'

'You've met Daleks before?'

'Yes, many times,' the Doctor nodded. 'And every time, it was unpleasant. In my experience, the Daleks have always

been a ruthless bunch of xenophobic, militaristic bullies –
even before a self-inflicted overdose of radiation turned them
into the mutants that live inside those armoured shells.'

'That just isn't true,' said Tulana, outraged. 'After the
accidental Neutron War caused them to mutate, the Daleks
became peace-loving academics.'

'That may be what you have been taught, but my view of
history is very different. Their mutation took them to a
whole new psychopathic level. They became paranoid
megalomaniacs, waging war on everyone in sight, laying waste
to whole solar systems using every conceivable weapon.'

Tulana looked at the Doctor like he was demented. She'd
been angry before, but the look she now gave him was almost
one of pity. She looked at Ace, appealing for support against
the lunatic.

'It's true,' Ace nodded. 'The last time I met them, they
tried to kill me – big time!'

The expression on Tulana's face spoke volumes, even if she
was too polite to say outright that the Doctor and Ace were
lying, or mad. She found a diplomatic compromise.

'Well, maybe you met a few bad Daleks? Maybe some
renegade criminal Daleks?' she ventured. 'Or maybe you met
some impersonators who were *pretending* to be Daleks? That
would explain everything.'

Ace's mouth fell open. She glanced at the Doctor. His
incredulous expression was a mirror image of her own.
Tulana smiled and nodded, happy that she had solved the
puzzle to her satisfaction and led the way to the Academy
Art School.

★

By the time they got back to the TARDIS, they'd seen hundreds of Daleks, not one of whom was equipped with a weapon, or had barked an order, or done anything that either the Doctor or Ace would characterise as typical Dalek behaviour. It was downright disturbing.

'It's a shame I can't show you more of Skaro,' said Tulana. 'It's really beautiful. There's an acid river and a swamp where geysers shoot fountains of mercury into the air. But it would take far too long to arrange transport and to travel there.'

The Doctor's eyes narrowed shrewdly. 'Oh, I don't know about that, Tulana,' he said. 'Time and speed aren't really a problem when you have a TARDIS.'

Despite herself, Tulana's eyes widened. The Doctor wasn't exactly her favourite person, but the chance of a trip in a time machine was mouth-watering.

The TARDIS behaved impeccably and they spent the next hour zipping about all over the Daleks' home planet. Nominally, Tulana was the guide, but from the way she drank in the sights, it was obvious she was seeing a lot of it for the first time too.

'Why are you doing this, Doctor?' whispered Ace as the TARDIS hovered over a large lake and Tulana tried to spot the mutated wind-walker creatures that lived there.

'I want to see what she knows, and what she doesn't,' he whispered back. 'I'm interested in where the Daleks let her go, and where they try to prevent her from going.'

As they flew low over a forest, the Doctor spotted something on the instruments.

'Aha!' he exclaimed. 'A space station in high synchronous orbit. How interesting! Let's take a quick look.' He looked to

Tulana for a reaction. 'Surely the Daleks won't mind a quick visit, since they're so open, friendly and democratic?'

It took less than five seconds for the TARDIS to arrive right next to the space station in the middle of a cluster of ten sleek spaceships.

'Well, well,' the Doctor said, his eyes narrowing. 'Dalek galactic cruisers! I wonder what they could be for?'

'Wow!' said Tulana as she gaped at the huge ships.

As they watched, a group of Daleks left the station and jetted across to one of the cruisers.

'Look,' said Ace. 'Those ones have weapons. They have ray guns built into them like Daleks normally do.'

'Aha!' said the Doctor again, looking very satisfied with himself. 'It seems that their mask of pacifist friendliness has slipped. Now you can see their true colours, Tulana. Weaponised Daleks in deep-space battle cruisers. Attack! Enslave! Exterminate! These are the true Daleks I know and loathe.'

'Oh really!' said Tulana.

'You don't think that they really need a long-range strike force to do research into surgery and genetics, do you?' said the Doctor.

It was as if a light bulb went on in Tulana's head.

'So that's what this sight-seeing trip was about,' she said. 'I get it now. You think I didn't know about these ships. You think you've discovered a horrible Dalek secret.'

'These are the real Daleks,' replied the Doctor. 'I haven't figured out the purpose of that charade down on the planet yet, but I will.'

Tulana shook her head, her expression somewhere between

contempt and pity. 'The Daleks aren't hostile, but of course they have guns and ships. They'd be idiots not to. Can you think of any race on any planet that doesn't have some form of army to protect themselves? The universe is full of species that would wipe out the Daleks if they got the chance – and kill all the humans and the Time Lords too, and anyone else who was different for that matter. If the Daleks just stayed here undefended and did research, how long do you think the Sontarans or the Cybermen or all the rest would leave them alone?'

Ace thought that was a good point. The Doctor harrumphed, but he didn't seem so sure of himself now.

'The Daleks protect themselves and others, like the people of my planet who don't have the technology to defeat races like the Cybermen. Are you saying that's wrong?' Tulana's expression positively dared the Doctor to argue.

The only answer she got was him returning them to the Academy in silence and opening the TARDIS doors to let her out.

4

For the next few hours, the Doctor grumped about the TARDIS looking alternately puzzled and worried or irate. Occasionally he'd get a wild gleam in his eyes like he'd just thought of a brilliant plan and he'd rush off to check something on one of the TARDIS computers. A little later he'd stalk back, grumpier than ever.

'No joy?' asked Ace.

'No,' the Doctor sulked.

'What are you trying to do, exactly?' she asked.

The Doctor sighed. 'I'm trying to find out what the Daleks are up to and how they've managed to fool so many people into believing that they're benign.'

'So what've you found out so far?'

'Nothing. I've checked histories, galactic archives, ancient transmissions that are still spreading out into space. All the data seems to indicate that what Tulana says about the Daleks is true.'

'So they really are good guys now?' Ace grinned. 'Wow! That's brilliant.'

The Doctor gave Ace a look that could have curdled milk. Ace wiped the smile off her face.

'Is there anything you didn't check?' she asked.

The Doctor grimaced. Whatever it was, he obviously found the idea of trying it deeply distasteful.

'Well, Professor?' Ace prodded.

'The only way to be really sure . . .'

'Yes?'

'Would be to go to Gallifrey and talk with the Time Lords.'

'And they'd know the truth?'

The Doctor nodded. 'The Time Lords have unique ways of monitoring the significant events in space and time.'

'So let's do that then,' said Ace breezily. 'A quick trip back to your old home planet, a cup of tea and a chat and you'll know exactly what's what – yeah?'

From the look on his face, Ace reckoned that a visit to the Time Lords was something similar to her having to visit the dentist back on Earth.

'Why don't you want to go?' Ace asked.

'Oh, Ace, let me count the ways. They're old, boring and judgemental.'

'Is that it?'

'I'm just getting warmed up! They're hidebound and they'd rather dress up in their ceremonial robes and watch the universe than actually participate in it.'

'Anything else?'

'They treat me like a naughty schoolboy!'

Ace laughed. 'But you'll go anyway?'

The Doctor sighed. 'Yes. I have to. Every cell in my body is telling me that something is terribly wrong here.'

Ace glanced up at the viewscreen and saw Tulana standing outside the TARDIS. She looked like she was searching for a doorbell.

'Doctor?' said Ace, pointing at the screen.

The Doctor looked up, saw Tulana and reached for the door controls.

'Are you going to meet the Time Lords?' Her face beaming, Tulana fired her question at him before she'd barely set foot over the threshold.

Not for the first time, the girl managed to make the Doctor's jaw drop. 'How did you know that?'

Tulana's eyebrows rocketed upwards.

'It would be fairly odd if you didn't,' said Tulana with a puzzled expression. 'After all, you are one of them.' She was really excited and rattled on, hardly pausing for breath. 'It's so weird. I've been learning all about the Time Lords for years, then I meet you and now I get to meet loads more Time Lords.'

'You can't come with us, Tulana,' frowned the Doctor.

'You can't really stop me.'

'I won't take you.'

'You don't have to take me, I'll go by myself.'

'And how will you manage that?' the Doctor asked.

Tulana raised a distinctly unimpressed eyebrow. 'I'll. Walk. There?'

'Walk?' said the Doctor. 'To Gallifrey?'

'No,' said Tulana incredulously. 'To the Great Hall in the Assembly Building. The High Council of the Time Lords arrived there about ten minutes ago.'

'The High Council came *here*?' The Doctor sounded like he was being strangled. 'All of them?'

'Yes! They've come to officially thank the Daleks for operating on the Lord President last month to remove a micro-aneurysm from his brainstem.'

The Doctor's jaw practically hit the console.

'The Time Lords brought the Lord President here for surgery?' asked Ace.

'Oh no, he was far too ill to travel. They invited a Dalek team to Gallifrey. But they're all here now.' And she strolled out of the TARDIS again.

Ace looked at the Doctor. He wore an expression she'd never seen before.

'Come on then. Let's go see your Time Lord buddies,' said Ace.

'There's no point.' The Doctor's voice was flat and lifeless. He sounded defeated.

'Why not? You said the Time Lords monitor everything. You said they'd know what was going on. And now you've got a whole bunch of them right round the corner.'

'I'm afraid it won't do any good.'

'Why not?'

'I thought this was a Dalek plot, but it's much worse than that. I thought that the Time Lords were just keeping their heads down the way they usually do. Sitting back in splendid isolation and not interfering.'

'But?'

'But there is no way that they'd invite hostile Daleks to visit Gallifrey. It would be like the hens inviting a skulk of foxes around for afternoon tea.'

'A what of foxes?'

'A skulk, my dear Ace, is the collective noun for a group of foxes,' said the Doctor. 'But now is not the time for an English lesson.'

'Thank goodness for that! So why has this visit from the Time Lords put your nose so out of joint?'

'It means that this change to the universe is real and huge. And any changes on this scale that even the Time Lords don't know about are dangerous and must be the result of some very powerful force or entity that has changed things.'

'Even more powerful than the Daleks and the Time Lords?'

The Doctor nodded, his expression grim.

Ace couldn't believe it. 'Well, can you fix it?'

'This strikes me as something way beyond my capabilities,' the Doctor admitted. 'We, like the universe, are in big trouble.'

5

That afternoon was peculiar, to say the least. Ace had never seen the Doctor in a stranger mood. From the frown lines creasing his face, he was obviously still deeply troubled, but at least he wasn't quite as jittery. The fact that the Daleks weren't just pretending to be agreeable but actually *were* meant that he didn't have to worry about some kind of imminent ambush.

Ace and the Doctor strolled through the Academy, exchanging pleasantries with Daleks who always stopped to say good afternoon or to ask the Doctor's advice on their research. And he helped. The Doctor started talking to the Daleks and treating them as fellow scientists. But he never lost his watchful, worried expression.

In the early evening, with the dying light of the setting sun making the tops of the distant mountains look like they were on fire, Tulana found the Doctor and Ace admiring the view.

'I hear you've been having conversations with Daleks instead of zapping them. What changed?' asked Tulana.

'These Daleks aren't like any I've ever met before,' the Doctor admitted. 'There can be only one explanation. This is some kind of alternative timeline, very different from the one I know.'

'I was never any good at temporal physics – it gives me a headache.' Tulana pulled a face.

'Nevertheless, for whatever reason, the universe has changed,' said the Doctor. 'Some things are better, some things aren't. The planet Sussashia Four has been destroyed so the reticulated sheep of Chonev are now extinct. The Sontarans won the battle of Kharax Rift, the Suxora Empire never fell, but the Kligoric Imperium did. The list goes on and on.'

'And what caused all that to be different?'

'I don't know yet,' he replied quietly, staring across the plaza at a couple of Daleks allowing themselves to be pushed around by a number of chortling young aliens on a nursery outing.

'But you think the Daleks are responsible, don't you?' Tulana said.

'I wouldn't put it past them. They are immensely advanced technologically, and they're one of the most devious and dangerous races I've ever met.'

'As far as I'm concerned, you're just a man making up stories.' Tulana shook her head. 'You can tell tall tales all day about planets that were destroyed and sheep that became extinct and alternative universes in which Daleks are evil. But that's all they are – stories. I live in *this* universe, and the Daleks are my friends. And the one who is a narrow-minded, inflexible, xenophobic bigot is you!' And with that she stormed off.

Ace watched her go, and then turned to the Doctor. 'How

come every single person, including the Time Lords, thinks that the Daleks are cute and fluffy, but you and I can still remember them doing bad stuff?'

'Good question, Ace,' said the Doctor. 'Something obviously happened while we were trapped in the Temporal Plexus. Some cataclysmic event altered history, but we were shielded from its effects by the Plexus.'

'Wouldn't that have to be something enormous?'

'Not necessarily. If you make a tiny change at just the right moment in time, then everything else follows naturally, like a ripple effect.'

'The universe can change like that?' asked Ace. 'I mean, the whole thing?'

'It's incredibly rare – but it happens.'

'And then what?'

'Someone has to fix it.'

'Who?'

'The Time Lords, usually.'

'The Time Lords don't think there's a problem.'

'One of them does!'

'Could it be that you're being . . . prejudiced?'

'I am not!' the Doctor said, scandalised.

'Are you sure? You pride yourself on your open mind and your live-and-let-live attitude, but when it comes to the Daleks you're as single-minded as they are. You told me once that there could be an infinite number of timelines, each subtly different from the next. But you refuse to believe in any timeline in which the Daleks might not be evil. Face it, Doctor, when it comes to the Daleks, you're as intolerant as the rest of us.'

'I most certainly am not,' spluttered the Doctor. 'I just know what they're capable of. That doesn't change, not in any timeline.'

'See what I mean? I rest my case!'

The Doctor opened his mouth to argue, but then he paused. 'You're right. I don't like them. The faint whiff of ozone when they move makes the hair on the back of my neck stand on end. I hate the silent way they glide about. I hate having hundreds of years of memories of every evil, rotten, violent, tyrannical, genocidal plot they've ever conceived.'

'Then maybe you need to stop living in your memories and open your eyes and start living in this world,' Ace told him. And with that she walked off to catch up with Tulana, leaving the Doctor gazing at a group of children sitting cross-legged round a Dalek, listening to it telling them a spooky story.

6

The next morning, Ace was jolted awake by her bed shaking violently. Unnerving sounds filled the TARDIS and it pitched and juddered like it was caught in a tornado. Ace ran to find the Doctor. When she arrived in the control room, she skidded to a halt and gawped.

The console was very nearly on the ceiling, raised up on a glowing white pedestal. The floor was half missing, the other half was covered in tools and Ace could only just see the Doctor's head as he crawled around, busily doing goodness only knew what.

'Doing a spot of redecorating?' she asked as she island-hopped carefully across the room.

'I'm converting the TARDIS into a Vortiscope.'

'A whatiscope?'

'A Vortiscope. It's a way of examining the time vortex and —' He stopped. 'The point is that it will allow me to determine the coordinates of the initial space–time dislocation.'

Ace could see he was excited. For the first time in ages, he was enthusiastic again. Of course, she didn't have a clue what he was talking about. 'A space–time dislocation sounds painful!'

The Doctor smiled. 'Think of space and time as a lake. We

know that someone has changed the shape of it, put in new fish, new plants, changed its depth.'

'OK . . .'

'But they had to start somewhere. There had to be a first change: the first new fish they dropped in the water.'

'And?'

'That would have caused ripples.'

Ace finally got it. 'So you can tell –'

'– where the ripples started, which will confirm once and for all if it was the Daleks who were responsible for this changed universe! Ah! Sometimes I amaze even myself!' the Doctor finished happily.

'And when you find out it wasn't?' said Ace.

The Doctor waved the magnetic de-interlacer in her direction. 'Let's not count our chickens!'

'I know the Daleks didn't cause this, Professor. And, when you confirm that, then we can stay put – right?'

After a moment's thought, the Doctor said carefully, 'If I'm mistaken, if there's nothing fundamentally wrong with this universe, then we'll stay . . . for a while.'

It took most of the day. Ace offered to help, but when the Doctor said no for the third time she went to see Tulana's room at the Academy instead. After watching the Time Lords depart, they spent the day swapping experiences and having a good laugh. They had so much in common that Ace knew she'd made a good friend. She didn't have too many of those.

'Ace, what are your plans for the future?' Tulana asked as they sat sipping their sludgies, which resembled thick grey gel, but tasted like mangoes and passion fruit back on Earth.

'No idea,' Ace shrugged, before licking her lips. 'Travel and have adventures, I guess. What about you?'

Tulana said without hesitation, 'I want to be a force for good, a voice for peace – the way the Daleks have taught me.'

Ace could only look on in admiration. 'Well, Tulana, if anyone can do it, it's you.'

They shared a smile and returned to their sludgies.

When Ace got back to the TARDIS, the control room still looked like a bomb had hit it. The console had been lowered again, but not all the way. The Doctor was standing on tiptoe to see what controls he was operating. Leaving the doors open, she headed over to him.

'Well?' she said. 'Have you finished building your ripple-detector?'

The Doctor stared intently at the instruments. Slowly, he turned to Ace. 'Yes, I have.'

'And?'

'I know what caused the problem.'

Ace stared then glared at him. 'Well? Don't keep me in suspense.'

'I did.'

'You did what?'

'I caused all this,' said the Doctor.

7

Ace's eyes widened in shock. 'How?'

'You were right about seeing a second TARDIS in the Plexus, but it was more than just a temporal echo. I think it was us, but at two different points in time existing simultaneously within the Plexus. When I created the supernova to get us out, the counter-shock looped through the Plexus and tangled the timelines of both TARDISes, twisting them together. And then when all that energy from both ships was released, this alternative timeline was created.'

Ace blinked rapidly as she tried to take it in. 'Hang on. So that means there'll be no more Dalek invasions? That's a good thing – right?'

If anything, the Doctor looked less happy now than before. He slowly shook his head. 'I've changed everything.'

'Yeah, but you change things all the time,' Ace pointed out. 'You go backwards and forwards in time, meddling with stuff, overthrowing tyrants and sabotaging alien invasions.'

'This is different,' the Doctor said. 'This isn't a minor change in some quiet corner. This is a total rewrite of the history of everything – and it has to be corrected.'

'You want to change all this?' asked Ace, horrified.

'I have to!'

'But why? This universe is OK. It may not be the way you and I remember it, but what gives you the right to say that this particular change is wrong?'

'Because I'm a Time Lord.'

'Oh, excuse me!'

'That's a better reason than you might think.'

'And yet the other Time Lords don't seem bothered. So you're not just smarter than the Daleks and Tulana, you're smarter than all the other Time Lords too?'

'Don't you think I've thought about this?' the Doctor argued. 'I know how it looks, but this universe is flawed.'

'It's not. It's working! The Daleks are fantastic! All these people are happy and productive. You can't just flick some Time Lord switch and send everything back to the way it was. That isn't fair.'

'Ace, this universe shouldn't exist.'

'But it *does*! You're doing this because you hate the Daleks. You've always hated them. You think that they don't deserve to thrive in this universe or any other. You're just some arrogant Time Lord with a petty god complex, punishing them for all time.'

The Doctor ran an agitated hand through his hair. 'This isn't arrogance or elitism, I promise. I don't think my opinion on this situation is better because I'm a lot older than you or because I have a monstrous ego, it's because I'm a Time Lord. For you, time is waves on a beach that you dip a toe into. For me it's a whole ocean, all the way from coast to coast and from the surface to the ocean floor. I feel time in the very core of my being in a way that you never can.

Some things are not meant to be. Some changes are too fundamental; they threaten reality itself. These philosophical Daleks aren't a problem in themselves, but they are a symptom of a universe that has gone terribly wrong – because of *me*.'

'OK, so things used to be different. So what? Why can't you just keep this universe? Nice Daleks – what's the problem? In lots of ways, this new universe is better than the old one.'

'No, Ace, this universe is *wrong*. There's a basic design flaw at its very heart. At this moment, I'm the only one who can feel it, but the cracks are already there, and they'll get worse. By the time the rest of the Time Lords catch on, it'll be too late to repair the damage.'

'Says who? You?'

'Ace, you'll just have to trust me on this.'

'But what if we hadn't been in the Plexus? Then nobody would know there was a problem.'

'Don't you understand? Our escape from the Plexus caused the problem in the first place,' said the Doctor. 'I created this mess. It's up to me to sort it out.'

'And how're you going to do that?'

'We need to get back to the Plexus,' said the Doctor.

Ace blinked like a stunned owl. 'We only managed to escape from that thing by the skin of our teeth. And now you want us to go *back*?'

'We have no choice.'

'There's always a choice. You taught me that,' Ace argued.

'But the choice in this case is either do nothing or put things right,' said the Doctor. 'And believe me . . .'

A strange vibration rippled beneath Ace's feet, followed closely by another, and another. Each ripple was progressively stronger.

'Professor, d'you feel that?' Ace frowned.

'Of course I do,' the Doctor retorted.

'What is it?'

The Doctor checked the console. Stunned disbelief swept across his face. 'It wasn't meant to happen yet,' he muttered, racing round the console to check yet more readings.

'What wasn't?'

'I told you that this universe was inherently unstable,' said the Doctor. 'I just didn't expect the space–time decay to happen quite this quickly.'

'English please,' Ace begged.

'This universe is already tearing itself apart,' said the Doctor. 'I thought it might take decades, possibly even a century or two before it got this bad, but the rate of decay is obviously exponential.' At Ace's blank look, he explained, 'Growing rapidly bigger and faster at an alarming rate.'

As if to underline his words, the ground beneath them began to lurch. Shock waves rocked the TARDIS violently back and forth as if it was being tossed on a stormy sea. And then the waves settled into an eerie stillness.

'Is it over?' asked Ace, alarmed.

'No,' said the Doctor grimly. 'It's only just beginning.'

Without warning, Pytha appeared at the TARDIS door, but he was not alone. Daleks stood beside and behind him for as far as Ace could see.

8

Ace's heart began to hammer in her chest. For all her talk, the sight of so many Daleks in front of the TARDIS doors made her nervous, to say the least.

'Professor, we have company,' said Ace.

'I know. I see them.'

'Doctor, we require your assistance.' That note in Pytha's voice was the closest Ace had ever come to hearing desperation from a Dalek.

'I'm a tad busy trying to keep the TARDIS upright,' said the Doctor, initialising the stabilisers.

'Our long-range deep-space scans are reporting anomalies.'

The Doctor's head whipped up. 'What kind of anomalies?'

'Distant star systems that have begun to . . . disappear. This is, of course, impossible, but we have checked our instruments and found no malfunctions. And there has been a worrying increase in solar activity from our own sun. We require your presence in the astrophysics observatory. We seek your insight.'

Just at that moment, the ground heaved again.

'I'll be right with you,' said the Doctor. 'I need to sort out something first.'

'We will wait and accompany you to the observatory,' said the Dalek. 'Time is of the essence.'

'No need. I know the way. You all go and I'll meet you there,' said the Doctor. 'Don't worry, Pytha. I'll fix this, I promise. Trust me.'

The Daleks turned *en masse* and rolled away. Moments later the Doctor slammed shut the TARDIS doors. 'We need to get out of here. *Now!*' he hissed.

'You're not just going to abandon them, are you?' said Ace, appalled. 'You promised to help.'

'Ace, don't you get it? The stars in this universe are beginning to blink out. And, believe me, when Skaro's star bites the dust, we don't want to be anywhere near here.'

'But, Professor —'

'Listen to me,' the Doctor interrupted. 'We need to get back to the Plexus before that's wiped out too, or we'll blink out of existence just like everything and everyone else.'

9

The Doctor ducked under the console and started recalibrating the quantum synchroniser – at least, that was Ace's wild guess.

'Aren't you going to at least warn the Daleks?' she asked.

'No time. Besides, what good would it do?' said the Doctor. 'Once I've recalibrated our long-range sensors, we're out of here. We need to get back to the Plexus to reverse all this.'

'You promised Pytha you'd fix things.'

'And I will, just not from here.'

'But wouldn't it be better to stay and try to sort out the problem alongside the Daleks? Surely working together you could find a solution?' Ace wasn't ready to give up on this universe. Not yet.

'Ace, I know it's hard, but you have to let go of this timeline. It isn't right – and it isn't ours.'

'If it was, would you work harder to save it?'

The Doctor sighed. 'I don't like this any more than you do, but the only way to save the universe is to put it back the way it was.' The Doctor shook his head, his lips twisting with regret. 'Ace, you may not believe this but I wanted to be wrong about this universe. I really did.'

Ace activated the viewscreen. Daleks were moving quickly among the other aliens. It looked like they were trying to reassure everyone. Ace squatted down, one question burning its way through her mind. 'Professor, what happens to Tulana if you reverse everything?'

'Even a Time Lord can't know the fate of every person in the universe.'

Ace didn't miss the way the Doctor couldn't quite look her in the eye. 'What do you think will happen?' she asked.

There was a pause. The Doctor finally sighed. 'Tulana is a native of the planet Markhan.'

'So?'

The Doctor shuffled evasively.

'What aren't you telling me?' Ace persisted.

'About two hundred years ago there was a plague on that planet. It was started by the Daleks as a prelude to an invasion.'

'How many died?'

'All of them, Ace. They all died. The Markhan Genocide is one of the Daleks' greatest atrocities.'

'So if we put things back to the way they were . . .?'

'Tulana won't exist,' the Doctor confirmed.

'No . . .' Ace felt sick. She straightened up, immediately followed by the Doctor who lowered the console to its normal position. Ace searched the viewscreen, trying to spot her friend. 'Doctor, couldn't I just say goodbye to her? Please? I'll be quick.'

'That's not a good idea,' said the Doctor gently. 'For all kinds of reasons.'

Ace watched as anxious students from a vast number of different star systems huddled round the Daleks, seeking answers that only the Doctor could provide. On the entrance ramp to the astrophysics building, Ace saw Tulana and some of her friends having an animated conversation with a Dalek. Ace blinked rapidly to ease the stinging in her eyes and then nodded briefly.

For the first time, travelling with the Doctor was making her eyes leak.

'Uh-oh!' The Doctor was scrutinising the console, his expression beyond worried. 'Time to skedaddle, I think. Hold on!'

Ace only just had time to grab hold of one of the console supports before the TARDIS jolted as it dematerialised. 'So we're heading back to the Plexus?'

'Yes.'

'To *fix* things?'

'Yes.'

'If what we're doing is right, why doesn't it feel that way?'

The Doctor had no answer.

10

'How do we get back to the Plexus? I thought the whole thing about it was that you couldn't work out where you were or how to navigate in there?'

'Normally, yes, but in this case, we're simply backtracking to where we've already been twice before.'

Ace sighed. 'Doesn't all this time-travel stuff make your head hurt?'

'Frequently!'

'Hold on a second,' said Ace. 'If this whole mess was caused by two TARDISes getting tangled up, aren't we now adding a third TARDIS?'

'No, because I realise now that *we* were the other TARDIS that you saw when we were originally stuck in the time vortex. I thought what you saw was just a temporal echo or an image from the Plexus time loop, but I was wrong. That second TARDIS was *us* re-entering the Plexus, so at least I know we'll find our way back into it. And, once there, I'm going to have to pick the exact right moment to restore the chrono-dynamic parity. I have to make sure that the other TARDIS gets free without altering the universe to do it.'

'And how will you do that?'

'The exact moment the other TARDIS targets the star, I'll put us in the way and target it with intermittent chrono-dynamic pulses. That should provide them with enough energy to break free without destroying the star.'

'What about us? Could we get stuck again?'

'If I time it exactly right, the timeline of the two TARDISes will merge into one and emerge from the Plexus unscathed. But if I miscalculate, I could destroy the TARDIS.'

'Which one?'

'Both of them.'

Sorry she'd asked, Ace swallowed hard.

The Doctor ran his hands over the controls and the TARDIS screeched and wheezed and reappeared in the Plexus, the one place in the universe Ace never wanted to see again. The Doctor switched on the viewscreen and the familiar image of a police box appeared briefly.

'So that's us, before you blew up the star?'

The Doctor nodded. 'About one minute before – if my calculations are correct.'

'And you're absolutely, totally, for-definite sure that this is the only way?'

'Yes. And once we're out of the Plexus, I've preset coordinates to our next destination.'

The sixty seconds dragged by. Ace stared at the other TARDIS on the viewscreen, and thought about Tulana and peaceful Daleks and a universe that the Doctor said should never have existed.

'Here goes!' the Doctor shouted.

There was the blinding flash, which took Ace by surprise even though she was expecting it. The force lifted her off her feet before slamming her back down again. Forewarned, Ace knew what was going to happen – a wild, crazy, uncontrolled flight followed by a bone-jarring halt. This time the Doctor was prepared too. He brought the TARDIS under control almost at once. They'd escaped the Plexus, but had the Doctor's plan worked? Had the universe been restored to 'normal'? Through the viewscreen Ace saw space debris – asteroids, some the size of continents back on Earth, and vast chunks of rock floating before them.

'Where are we?' she asked.

But before the Doctor could confirm their exact location, a ship appeared on the screen and swung round in a graceful arc to point head-on at the TARDIS.

'Aha!' said the Doctor.

There was a burst of static, before a harsh, grating voice filled the control room.

'*YOU HAVE INVADED OUR SPACE. YOU – WILL – BE – EXTERMINATED!*'

Ace shuddered as she recognised the voice, and watched as two missiles streaked away from the battle cruiser, heading straight towards the TARDIS. There was no gentleness now – all trace of friendliness gone. There was no attempt at diplomacy or debate. These were the Daleks the Doctor and Ace knew only too well – the merciless killing machines that had burned a thousand planets and enslaved half the galaxy.

'Ah yes, the Daleks I know and detest, still protecting what they feel is their part of the galaxy, even though there's nothing here but rock. The universe makes sense again,' said the Doctor as he set the controls to allow them to slip away into space and time before the missiles could hit their target.

'Professor, where is this?'

'Skaro – or what's left of it. There's always a Dalek battle cruiser or two in the vicinity.'

'You set our destination for Skaro?' Ace asked, astounded.

'Just to make sure that things were back to normal,' grinned the Doctor.

Ace watched the missiles approach. The Doctor threw a switch with a flourish and the image of the Dalek ship and the missiles started to fade from view as the TARDIS dematerialised.

Even as they slipped away, a Dalek voice grated on triumphantly. *'DETONATION IN TEN RELS. YOU CANNOT ESCAPE.'*

The viewscreen faded to black, and the echo of the Dalek's last strident, grating taunt died away. *'ALL ENEMIES OF THE DALEKS MUST DIE . . .'*

'So, Professor, Tulana never even got a chance to be born,' said Ace, her eyes glistening. 'The Daleks are back to being murderous psychos. This is the universe as you know and understand it. But is it really an improvement?'

The Doctor stared at the screen. The view was star-filled now and peaceful. His hands gripped the edges of the console so tightly that his knuckles were white. 'Ace, we experienced something I thought could never happen, in any timeline. Peaceful Daleks who were a force for good. Maybe, just maybe, in time that will happen in this universe too.'

'D'you really think so?' said Ace.

'A few days ago, I would've said no without hesitation,' the Doctor admitted. 'But now all we can do is hope. And, when you get right down to it, that's a good start.'

THE EIGHTH DOCTOR:
SPORE

ALEX SCARROW

1

The Doctor opened the TARDIS door and stepped out into the warm desert night. A gentle breeze stirred the dusty ground at his feet. The only sound was the *cheep-cheep-cheep* of nearby cicadas.

That and the distant crackle of walkie-talkies, and the rumble and stutter of diesel engines idling.

'This looks familiar,' he muttered softly. The Nevada Desert, United States of America. He'd visited here before, not so far away and not so very long ago. 1947, wasn't it? Place called *Roswell* if memory served him. He grinned in the dark.

Now that was fun.

He wondered if he ought to have another go at fixing the TARDIS's chameleon circuit some time. Sitting out in the middle of the desert, it was going to look somewhat incongruous. Mind you, it was night and he'd put down several hundred metres from the highway. Probably no one was going to spot it out here. In the dark it would look like the stunted hump of yet another Joshua tree.

The Doctor closed and locked the door behind him and then strode out across the dry packed earth towards the army trucks parked half a kilometre away, gathered on the gravel shoulder of the dust-and-grit highway.

Closer now, he could hear the unsteady voices of frightened men, muffled by the thick rubber seals of oxygen masks. The night was dense with the crackles and beeps, and the garbled voices and sentence fragments of to-and-fro radio traffic. Floodlights picked out a weatherworn roadside billboard and, nearby, an abandoned gas station, the windows boarded up, the forecourt tufted with weeds. A sign beside the entrance read:

Tired? Why Not Take a Break in Fort Casey?
The Friendliest Welcome Outside of Home!

The Doctor nodded. Fort Casey. This was where the probe he'd been tracking must have touched down.

He had almost reached the cluster of army vehicles before someone actually spotted him emerging from the dark.

'Hey!' A muffled voice barked out at him. 'YOU THERE! STOP!'

The dazzling beam of a torch settled on his face. The Doctor squinted and shaded his eyes.

'Stop right there!' The muffled voice sounded young. Very young. And very frightened. 'Raise your hands!'

'Tsk, tsk,' chided the Doctor. 'Raise your hands . . . *please!*'

'Shut up and show me your hands!'

The Doctor raised them. 'Charming.'

The soldier spoke into his radio. 'Major Platt? Got a civilian here . . . Just came out of the dark, sir . . . Infected? Don't think so, sir.'

The Doctor could discern the outline of the young soldier against the glare of his torch: cloaked in a biohazard suit, an oxygen cylinder on his back, an assault rifle wavering uncertainly in his gloved hands. Another man joined him a moment later.

'You!' A deeper, more commanding voice this time. 'Where've you come from?'

The Doctor smiled. 'I'm not from round here.'

'Have you come from the town, sir?'

'Fort Casey, I presume?'

'Yes. Have you been in direct contact with *anyone* from Fort Casey?'

'No. I've only just *come down*.'

A pause. 'From Atlanta? You one of the team from the CDC?'

The Doctor found himself nodding. The major did seem to want that to be the case rather badly so he decided to give the man what he wanted to hear. 'Actually, yes . . . yes, I am.'

'About time! We'd better get you suited up and briefed.'

'Suited up?' The Doctor clucked his tongue. 'Really? Is that entirely necessary?'

Major Platt didn't seem to be in the mood for flippancy. 'Follow me to the command tent, I'll give you the sit-rep.'

'The last logged communication from the town was seventeen hours ago: a 911 call for an ambulance. The caller only managed to say . . .' The major flipped through a pad of paper on his desk. He was all buzz-cut silver hair and lean, tanned face like chiselled sandstone. Marines all the way. Booyah. He read what was scribbled down on the page in front of him. 'They're all dead . . . everyone's dead, flesh turned to liquid. It moves . . . There are things! Moving things! They're alive . . .' Major Platt looked up at the Doctor. 'The caller became incoherent after that and disconnected shortly after.'

The Doctor drummed his fingers thoughtfully against the top of the aluminium folding-table between them. 'Hmm . . . That really doesn't sound very good.'

The command tent was an airtight bubble of thick plastic, lit from within by several halogen stand lamps. The major had removed his mask and biohazard suit and now stared at the Doctor curiously. His Edwardian morning jacket, waistcoat and cravat seemed particularly to be drawing the major's gaze.

'I was at the opera,' the Doctor explained, 'when my phone went off.'

The major waved that aside. 'It appears the pathogen *isn't* airborne, but we can't be a hundred per cent sure of that. We have all entry/exit routes from the town locked down. It appears this thing, whatever it is, infects and kills *very* quickly.'

'Which is probably a rather good thing.'

Platt's grey brow furrowed.

'Quick to kill, Major, means we don't have to worry about an infected carrier straying too far away from the town.' The Doctor nodded thoughtfully. 'You said you sent some of your troops in?'

He nodded. 'Four hours ago. We've not heard from them in over three.'

'What was the last thing you did hear?'

The major shook his head. 'Garbled transmission. Made no sense to me.'

'Do tell.'

'Something about *webs everywhere. Webs all over the town.*' The major squinted his grey eyes. 'Webs? Everyone turned to liquid! You got any idea what on earth we're dealing with?'

The Doctor had a pretty good idea. But it was just that: an idea. A suspicion. He needed to know for sure. 'You're right. It's not an airborne infection, Major. At least, not yet.'

'You telling me you know what this is?'

The Doctor nodded slowly. 'I've come across it before, yes.'

'You got a name for it?'

'A nightmare.' The Doctor thumbed his chin thoughtfully. 'If it's the pathogen I think it is, it will spread quickly. There are no species barriers. It can be carried and transmitted by any creature – *anything* organic, in fact.'

'That's impossible! No pathogen can do that!'

'Within seventy hours of touchdown, this thing will become uncontainable. Within a month . . .' The Doctor shook his head slowly. No words needed there.

The major's eyes narrowed. 'You sure you're from the Atlanta Centers of Disease Control? Because you sure ain't like the usual pencil-neck swab-heads down there.'

'Ahh . . . you have me, Major,' the Doctor said with a smile. 'I lied.'

Major Platt bristled. 'Then you'd better tell me right now who sent you.'

'I'm sure you've heard of the organisation, Major. Its name gets whispered every now and then in dark government corners.'

'Who are you with?'

'UNIT.'

The major's face paled. 'UNIT?'

The Unified Intelligence Taskforce; it operated off the radar and off the balance sheet for a number of the world's governments. The Doctor had worked with UNIT before. While the average man in the street might not have heard of it, Major Platt most certainly would have, unless he had kept his head stuck firmly in the sand for all of his military career.

'Good. It seems you *are* acquainted with it.' The Doctor pushed himself back from the table. 'That's excellent. It will save us wasting valuable time, me explaining the situation to you.' He shrugged. 'I don't need much . . . just that you need to let me go in.'

'Impossible! Class five containment protocol – nobody else goes in, nobody comes out!'

'*UNIT* has the final say here, I believe. Not the army. And since I'm their man-on-the-spot . . . I think that makes me the one in charge here.'

Major Platt's eyes narrowed. 'I received no notification that my authority –'

'Major, every second we spend here, sitting in your lovely shiny tent, is a second we simply can't afford to waste. This pathogen will become airborne very soon.' The Doctor smiled sadly. 'Then all your roadblocks, all your men in their amusing rubber suits, will simply be . . . an irrelevance.'

2

The Doctor made his way through the barrier laid out across the single-track road leading into the town. Floodlights cast his shadow long and thin down the empty, pitted tarmac towards the dark outline of the blink-and-you'd-miss-it town in the distance.

He began to walk forward – hampered, clumsy and hot inside the heavy suit. The earpiece in his hood crackled with Major Platt's voice.

'UNIT have just confirmed your identity . . . *Doctor*.'

'Good.'

'"The Doctor". That's, uh . . . that's all they called you. Do you have a name, sir?'

The Doctor smiled at that. He'd had a name once, long ago. Nine hundred years ago. So many memories in his head, many of them the memories of his previous incarnations, almost like someone else's – memories so faded and indistinct they were barely the whispers of ghosts.

'Just "the Doctor". That's all you need to call me.'

'The Doctor, huh?' The earpiece hissed, the channel still open. 'Fine.' Major Platt didn't sound entirely convinced. 'Well, you keep the comms channel open, OK, Doctor?'

The Doctor had no intention of doing that. 'Yes, of course.'

Ten minutes later, the Doctor reached the outer buildings of the town: tired and abandoned clapboard houses, all sun-bleached wood and flaking paint. Fort Casey clearly had been a town dying a slow death long before tonight.

Beyond the reach of the floodlights and out of sight of the major's men, the Doctor decided here was as good a place as any. He undid the hood and pulled it off, savouring the cool night air on his face. He unzipped and shrugged his way out of the rest of the biohazard suit, and kicked it off his feet.

Ridiculous outfit. It would be about as much use to him as a wet paper bag anyway.

He sniffed the air and instantly detected the sweet smell of decaying flesh. To some degree that confirmed what he already strongly suspected. This infection – this *scourge*, if it was indeed the same pathogen that had once wiped out countless Gallifreyans, was well and truly into its primary stage: absorbing and breaking down the organic matter it had already assimilated. Turning it into a usable, fluid organic matrix.

He proceeded up the small town's main street. The street lights were still on, fizzing in the night, casting a sickly amber glow down on the dusty and potholed tarmac. To his right was a grocer's store, a pink neon Budweiser beer sign blinking above the glass door.

The Doctor shone his torch at the store. At the front, empty wooden pallets advertised watermelons at three dollars each. He wandered over, aiming his torch at one of the empty pallets. A dark puddle of thick viscous liquid covered the slats of wood. The liquid had spilled over the side to the ground. With the beam of his torch, he followed a snaking trail of the goo – thin and insubstantial as a length of forgotten twine. It looked like a black artery as it weaved, like a hairline crack, along the ground to the building next door. There it widened as other arteries of the black liquid joined it, thickening it into a dense rope.

The ground floor of the two-storey building was a diner. Above were vacant apartments that seemed to be desperately seeking tenants. The ink-black liquid ran up the side wall, fanning out like webbing as it did so – tendrils of black feeling their way across the breeze blocks and cracked whitewash.

The Doctor approached slowly.

At the bottom of the wall, slumped against it, he saw the remains of what used to be a person. The Doctor squatted down in front of the body and inspected it. A pair of dockers' boots, faded jeans and a checked shirt. Inside the clothes, an untidy jumble of bones held together by the last scraps of flesh. The skull was still topped with a few tufts of white hair. But no scalp. That was long gone, with every other scrap of soft organic matter. Black slime ran out of the cuffs of the shirt across the ground to unite with the other streams of organic soup.

Completely liquefied. The watermelons in front of the grocer's store and this man, both equally useful, equally digestible raw material for the pathogen to absorb. Precisely what the Doctor was expecting to find, but had been hoping he wouldn't.

The first stage looked well and truly established: infection, deconstruction and consolidation. It had evidently touched down in or near the town – one tiny pinhead-sized spore dispersed by the probe, possibly in the guise of a rock or meteor fragment, picked up on the heel of a boot perhaps, or the rim of a truck tyre. That's all it would have taken.

The rest would be depressingly inevitable. And horrifyingly fast.

He panned his torch around and picked out more bodies in the main street. Across the road a car had mounted the kerb and tangled with some rubbish bins, the skeletal remains of the driver slumped half in, half out of the open door. Further up the street, a bundle of women's clothing lay on the pavement and, beside it, a baby stroller over on its side.

'They never stood a chance,' the Doctor said with a sigh.

'Hello?' A voice from within the diner. 'Is someone *out there?*'

A survivor? The Doctor shook his head. Impossible. There was no immunity to this thing. No *human* immunity anyway. He walked to the front of the diner and pulled one of the glass swing doors wide open. 'Is there anyone alive in here?'

'STAY RIGHT WHERE YOU ARE!' A muffled voice. A female voice. The Doctor froze in the doorway, then raised his hands to show he was unarmed.

He saw a slight figure in a biohazard suit slowly emerge from behind the diner's serving counter, the face obscured by an oxygen mask. 'How . . . how are you alive?'

The Doctor smiled and took a step forward. 'As my mother used to say, I'm rather special.'

The woman levelled the handgun she was holding at him. 'You'd better stay right there! Right where you are!'

He looked at the name patch on her chest. 'Captain Chan, is it?'

'Captain Evelyn Chan.'

'I presume you must be one of Major Platt's investigation team?'

The woman dipped the gun slightly.

'You know, the major's rather worried that you haven't been in touch recently.'

'My comm system's broken. I tossed it.'

The Doctor looked at her equipment belt. He noted a twisted attachment buckle and a small tear in her suit there.

She followed his gaze. 'Some of that gunk got on to my communication pack. I could see it spreading! I had to . . . had to tear it off. Get rid of it fast,' she said quickly. 'But I'm not infected, OK? It didn't get inside my suit. It didn't touch my skin –'

'I know,' interrupted the Doctor, offering her a reassuring smile. 'I know. If it had made contact with you, you would be a puddle by now.' He looked around the diner. 'What about the others in your team?'

A moment's hesitation before she eventually replied. 'I'm the only one left.' Her voice hitched. 'The others, they . . . they . . .'

'What happened to them?'

'Attacked.'

'*Attacked?*'

The woman's mask nodded slowly. 'Strange things . . . crawling things dropped down on us, attacked us . . .'

The Doctor cursed under his breath. That meant the secondary stage was already under way. This thing was now building defensive constructs.

He took another cautious step forward and Chan quickly raised her gun and aimed it at him. 'Stay there!'

'It's all right!' he said quickly. 'I'm also not infected. In fact, I assure you, I'm quite immune.'

She shook her head. '*Nothing's* immune!'

The Doctor stepped sideways and sat down in a booth beside the window. 'I'll just sit here, Evelyn. If that's all right with you?'

She came out from behind the counter. He could see her glancing in all directions: at the floor, under the tables and seats. She advanced slowly towards him. 'Everything. Human, animal, plant. This thing has infected *everything* in this town.'

The Doctor nodded. 'Yes, that's precisely what it does.'

She took several more steps towards him, her gun still levelled at his chest. She slumped down on a chair a couple of tables from him. 'Nothing can do this! No pathogen can work across species boundaries like that! Jump from fauna to flora –'

'No *terrestrial* pathogen,' said the Doctor.

'No terrestrial . . .?' He saw Chan's eyes narrow through the glass visor of her mask. 'You're saying . . . what? This has come from –'

'Come from space, yes.' The Doctor casually fiddled with the salt cellar on the table in front of him. 'It's a von Neumann seeding probe.'

'What?'

'Von Neumann. Named after one of your scientists, John von Neumann, who theorised about the development of such a creation – a genetically engineered pathogen designed to survive deep space, to drift until it finds a planet with a habitable environment. Then it revives from a dormant state and goes to work.'

'Goes to work?'

'It transmits like a virus at first. Starting from just a cluster of particles, infecting, converting cells by reprogramming their DNA. Whatever it comes into contact with, it infects. It reproduces millions of copies of itself from the raw material of the infected organism, then these infected cells work together at breaking down the structure of the victim.'

Chan nodded. 'Yes . . . yes, that's what we saw.' She looked out of the window at the deserted street outside. 'Everything organic,' she said, nodding. That's exactly what she'd witnessed. 'Everything . . . seems to be necrotic, decaying to that black gunk.'

'The pathogen's primary stage is that process – acquiring organic mass. As much as it can and as quickly as it can. The liquid has a rudimentary intelligence, if you can call it that. It will attempt to converge on itself. To regroup, if you will. The more of the assimilated mass that is connected together, the more sophisticated its internal structure can become.'

'Internal structure?'

'That "black gunk" is a *transmorphic* fluid. It can restructure itself into anything it has acquired a genetic blueprint from, or even combine blueprints. The more of it that is connected together, the more sophisticated the constructs it can make.'

Captain Chan turned to look at him. 'How do you know

so much about it?' The Doctor saw her eyes suddenly widen. 'My God! This is *not* an isolated outbreak? Has this happened elsewhere?'

'There have been millions of outbreaks, Evelyn. On many worlds, over billions of years.'

Her eyes narrowed again. She stared at him, silent for a few moments. 'Just who on earth are you?'

The Doctor considered her question. He supposed he could take the time to explain who he was. He could explain that his people, the Time Lords, had once been attacked by this very pathogen. As a young man, he'd read about the infection on Gallifrey, so long ago now. The Spore had arrived more than a thousand years before he was born. Several hundred thousand Time Lords had died before they'd managed to deal with it, engineering an inherited immunity into their genes so that they would never be vulnerable again. He could explain all of those things, but time wasn't exactly on their side. He decided to keep the explanation short and sweet. A quick answer would do for now.

'You'll find there are a few conspiracy websites that mention me. I suspect one or two governments have rather extensive files on me too. I'm known as "The Doctor". Suffice it to say, I'm not from round here.' He pursed his lips. 'But I have developed a habit of dropping by from time to time.' The Doctor sat back and straightened his morning coat. 'But introductions can wait, Captain Chan. We don't have a great deal of time. You said you were attacked?'

She nodded. 'Crab-like things. Hundreds of them. Cut through our suits and got inside.' She closed her eyes for a moment. 'I barely got away.'

'You were the only survivor?'

Chan shook her head and glanced quickly at the swing doors behind the counter. 'There was also Rutherford.'

The Doctor noted a dark and bloody handprint on one of the doors.

'It was one of those black goo threads. Rutherford was trying to gather a sample. We thought it was just liquid.' She shook her head, trying to make sense of what she'd witnessed. 'But it kind of *reared up* and lashed out at him. Punctured right through his mask.' She looked away. 'I tried to save him. But he was dying within minutes, *seconds* even. I dragged him in there . . .'

'He's in there now? Through those doors?'

'In the kitchen.'

The Doctor looked at the swing doors. Chan had grabbed a tea-towel and tied a knot binding together both the door handles. That wasn't going to stop anything, but it meant she understood.

Best not to open them. Best not to step inside.

'Keep that door firmly closed, Evelyn. Whatever you do, do *not* go in.'

She nodded quickly. 'I looked in about twenty minutes ago.' She let slip a choked sob. 'It was horrible. Rutherford was . . .'

'This thing goes through stages. Stage One is biomass assimilation and consolidation. That's the stage that was happening before you arrived. In Stage Two it starts generating simple constructs – *creatures*, for sake of a better word. That's a defensive measure. That's what you've witnessed. Stage Three is . . . well . . .' The Doctor stroked his chin. 'That's the most fascinating stage with this thing, actually. Really quite remarkable.'

'What?'

The most curious thing in the Spore's infection life cycle was the third stage. What the Time Lords had dubbed the 'enquiry stage'. The mystery creators of the pathogen – perhaps long gone now – had built in a safety mechanism to ensure that the Spore never erased another advanced civilisation. Perhaps they feared a drifting spore might return one day and destroy their own homeworld? Perhaps they believed it unethical that their own creation might wipe out another intelligent species?

'What's Stage Three?' prompted Chan.

The Doctor looked back at her. 'At the centre of the infection, ground zero, the Spore will construct an intelligence matrix. A brain, if you will.'

'A *brain*?'

'Well, an intelligence at any rate.'

'Why?'

'It has a question it needs to ask.' The Doctor shrugged. 'Answer it correctly and the brain instructs every cell in its biomass to switch from reproducing cells to manufacturing a lethal toxin that eventually will destroy itself.'

'Why would it do that?'

'Answering the question correctly indicates intelligence. This pathogen is "programmed" to avoid wiping out intelligent life.'

'And if we don't give the right answer? Then what?'

The Doctor winced. 'Then the Spore will continue to develop ever more sophisticated constructs – creatures that can run, swim, fly. Creatures that will carry the infection in all directions. It will become uncontainable.' He pressed his lips together. 'A week from now, every organic thing on this planet will have been converted to biomass.'

'No way!' breathed Chan.

'The theory is,' the Doctor continued, 'it was created by an alien civilisation to "overwrite" the native ecosystems of other planets with their own. To render those planets hospitable for them centuries – even millennia – before they might one day need them as homes. A form of long-distance biological terraforming. That, or it's some sort of ghastly weapon.'

'But you . . . you're saying we can *communicate* with this thing?' Chan shook her head. 'Actually *talk* to it?'

'"Talk" is somewhat generous. It's not like we'll be exchanging penpal details.'

'But it will ask us this question?'

The Doctor smiled. 'Yes, and there's the rub. Humans won't understand it, let alone be able to answer it. Not for another fifty or so years.'

'Another fifty years?' Chan's eyes widened. 'Are you saying . . . you're from –'

'The future?' The Doctor nodded. 'And the past. You could say I get around quite a bit.' He looked out of the window again. 'And I've already wasted enough time. I need to locate the intelligence matrix as soon as possible. It won't wait around forever to decide whether you're a species worth preserving or not. I need to catch it before it starts creating airborne constructs.'

Chan looked at him. 'You're actually going back out there?'

'Of course. And I suggest you stay right here. Keep the door closed until I come back.'

Chan shook her head. 'I'm not staying here. Not alone. No way.'

The Doctor looked at the doors behind the counter. Nowhere was safe, to be fair, inside or out. Not now the Spore was building constructs. Perhaps she'd be better off staying close by his side.

'All right then,' he said, shrugging. 'You can come along if you want.'

3

The Doctor stepped out into the street, Chan behind him. He scanned back and forth with his torch. Threads of black goo criss-crossed the tarmac, fanning out from the humps of mostly dissolved bodies and stripped carcasses; threads seeking each other – converging.

'The individual colonies of biomass will attempt to join each other – to pool their mass together. The more of this stuff comes together in one place, the more *ambitious* the constructs it will try to produce.'

'It can make *bigger* things than crabs?'

The Doctor raised his eyebrows. 'Much bigger.'

They made their way slowly down the still, silent street. A gentle breeze stirred the night, sending a rooftop weathervane spinning with a *clack-clack-clack*. A wind chime on the porch of a hardware store gently played solemn, random notes. The wheel of an overturned child's tricycle spun slowly, the bearings clicking like the aluminium balls of a Newton's cradle.

'We're looking for a pattern – a significant convergence of fluid, threads feeling their way towards a central hub. It will look like a starburst pattern, like dozens of rivers all flowing into a lake.'

'A central hub?' Chan looked at him. 'The brain?'

He nodded. 'And that, Evelyn, it will most definitely want to defend.'

They made their way past a medical centre, a tangle of cars parked erratically outside, log-jamming the street. It looked like many of the townspeople had been attempting to get to this point, some of them dying before they could even reach the door.

'My God,' Chan whispered. 'It must have been awful. It must have –'

She stopped dead, raised her gun and dropped to an army-trained firing stance.

'What?'

'Movement. Over there. Between the cars.'

The Doctor swung the beam of his torch in the direction she was aiming. The cone of light reflected off the dusty windscreen of a farmer's truck and the wax-polished hood of a Chevrolet.

'There's something there,' hissed Chan.

The smooth, rounded surface of something dark shifted under the harsh glare of the light.

'Ah yes,' said the Doctor. 'I see it.'

Movement again. A black shape, the size of a large dog, with jointed, spider-like legs and covered by a hard, spiny carapace, leaped on to the bonnet of the Chevrolet. The car rocked gently under its weight.

Chan squeezed the trigger and her handgun kicked. The shot cracked through the creature's organic armour and strings of dark matter spurted out. The creature – dark and glistening – collapsed and spasmed.

'Rather good shot, that. Well done.'

Chan breathed heavily, fogging her mask. 'A lucky shot. I-I haven't used a f-firearm since basic training.'

Another creature emerged from the cluster of cars. She swung her arm and fired. A windshield imploded beside it. She fired again and they heard the dull eggshell crack of impact and the sound of goo spattering against the side panel of a nearby Honda. The creature disappeared from view.

But four more scuttled into view to replace it.

Chan fired at the first one and missed.

She fired several more times as yet more of them appeared. Then the gun was clicking uselessly as her fingers impulsively worked the trigger.

'Oh no . . . I'm out.'

There were a dozen of them now, creatures the size of Rottweilers. Dark, glistening, hunched low on insectoid legs, headless, eyeless – a beetle-like menace. They advanced slowly.

Chan whimpered as they closed the gap. The Doctor grasped her arm and pulled her back, then stepped in front of her.

'What are you doing?'

'Just a thought,' he replied quickly. He approached the horde slowly and spread his arms. The beetle-like creatures hissed and clicked in response . . . and stopped where they were. 'Yes. What I expected. It's begun the query stage. It's waiting for contact with an intelligent life-form. It's ready to talk. Ready to ask its question.' He looked back over his shoulder at Chan. 'But it won't wait around for that forever. You understand? We have to find it quickly.'

Chan nodded nervously.

The Doctor swung the beam of his torch. 'Those constructs are gathered here to guard the brain. It must be very close. Look, Evelyn. Look around. Can you see anything?'

She shone her own torch around, following the criss-crossing, snaking dark threads on the road as they converged into thicker tributaries. One particular strand seemed to have acquired the role of main artery, attracting others towards it, like moths to a candle flame. It wound up the street, broadening into a thick leathery trunk, like a fireman's hose, which pulsated and quivered as a steady flow of organic soup travelled up inside it.

Chan's torch beam tracked it as it slunk its way towards the rear of a delivery truck parked fifty metres up the road, across a small town square where several dozen stalls had been erected. It looked as if Fort Casey had been preparing for market day when the Spore decided to come to town.

The leathery artery curled up to the rear of the truck, then seemed to spread out across its open loading ramp and disappear inside the vehicle.

'That looks promising,' said the Doctor under his breath. He edged away from the creatures and rejoined Chan. 'I suggest we make our way – in an exceedingly unthreatening manner – towards that vehicle.'

She nodded. They backed up from the creatures and slowly made their way up the street towards the vehicle.

Nearer now, the Doctor could read the logo emblazoned on the side of the truck's container: *Bernard and Sons – Poultry Supplies*. Carefully, he stepped over thickening tributaries of the viscous matter, all heading towards the rear of the truck.

All roads lead to Rome.

Finally, they stood at the base of the ramp and Chan shone her torch up. Inside, she could see dozens of stacked wire-mesh cages. Feathers littered the floor of the container like snowfall. Bones and beaks and scaled claws in every cage, the other remains of what had once been hundreds of battery chickens now rendered to black liquid dangling from the cages in sheets of pulsating goo that lined the interior walls of the container. Thick tendrils swayed from the sheets like sightless serpents sniffing the air.

At the far end of the truck, the liquid had converged into a lava-lamp-like mass that glistened wetly in the light of their torches – shifting, bulging, extruding bubbles and occasionally larger, firmer shapes that momentarily resembled the torso and legs of a human . . . the head and neck of a horse . . . the muzzle of a dog.

'What's it doing?' asked Chan, swallowing hard.

'I imagine it's testing out the constructs it can make from the DNA it has so far acquired.'

Smaller, less ambitious creatures scuttled around the floor, creatures that looked like the impossible offspring of crustaceans and rodents. The beam of the Doctor's torch picked out dozens of them clambering over each other, a seething mess of hard-shelled legs and claws, sharp spines, carapaces and grey fur. He suspected if the creatures turned and swarmed them, their sharp claws would pick them clean of flesh within minutes. He needed to communicate quickly, before the Spore decided it felt threatened and instructed its army of defenders to surge forward.

'Hello?' he said softly.

The liquid mass at the back of the container pulsated in

response to his voice. It quivered for a moment, then one tendril quickly began to thicken and lengthen, drawing substance from the central mass as it snaked its way towards the Doctor.

'Doctor,' whispered Chan. 'Watch out!'

'It's all right. This is it saying "hello".' He looked at her. 'I hope.'

How do I communicate with this thing?

The Doctor dredged long-forgotten details of the Gallifreyan experience of this entity from the dark recesses of his mind. One thing stood out: a single scientist had allowed himself to be infected, had allowed the cells of this thing into his body, and at some microbiological level a connection had been made.

Taking a deep breath, the Doctor stepped slowly up the loading ramp and into the truck. 'I'm here to talk to you.'

The black tendril glided towards him, rose up and hovered in front of his face, swaying from side to side like a cobra preparing to strike.

'That's right, I'm not a threat,' the Doctor cooed softly. 'I'm here to talk.'

Its movement slowed. The tip of the tendril began to grow, producing a bulbous end. From that, a tiny whisker-like tentacle began to emerge. It grew towards the Doctor's face, thin and flexible as a wire, feeling its way across the air between them. The Doctor suppressed an urge to recoil. He knew the Spore wasn't going to be able to infect and assimilate him – his inherited immunity prevented that – but that didn't make the idea of allowing it inside him any more pleasant.

The fine tentacle lightly touched the tip of his nose.

Testing it. The gentlest, tickling caress. Then it began to explore his cheeks, his brow, curling round the side of his face and exploring the curves of his ear.

The Doctor fought the urge to pull back. The Spore 'knew' how the enquiry stage worked. He was going to have to let it steer negotiations.

The tentacle returned to his face, resting against the side of his nose. He felt a tiny sting as small barbs attached it more firmly to his skin. Then he felt something tickling the rim of his left nostril. He wanted to reach up and scratch his nose. It tickled in an entirely revolting, invasive and unpleasant way.

He felt the tentacle curl inside, a cool liquid sensation sliding slowly up inside his nasal passage. Then a strange tingling spread between his eyes, moving further backwards, past his visual cortex, into his temporal lobes, and on, deeper into his cranium . . .

It's attempting to locate a connection to my brain.

The unpleasantly cool sensation inside his nose began to fade. The tentacle was adjusting its temperature to match that of his own body. To make the connection more comfortable for him, perhaps? A reassuring thought if that was the case.

Then . . .

Then . . .

4

'What's happening?' called Chan as the Doctor's body jerked suddenly. 'Doctor, are you OK?'

Chan looked over her shoulder. The beetle-like creatures were beginning to gather threateningly close. More of them were emerging from the nearby market stalls, where the deflated rinds of melons and husks of corn cobs merged into dark soup, and from a florist's where hanging baskets drooled tendrils of oil-black slime. The creatures shuffled slowly towards her.

'Doctor! They're getting close out here,' she called.

No answer.

'I mean reeeeally close!'

No answer. She shone her torch back into the truck. All she could see was the back of the Doctor's head. He was standing perfectly still now, almost as if he were in some kind of trance.

'This is not looking good! Doctor?'

She aimed her torch back out at the creatures just as one of them suddenly lashed out towards her with a spiked tentacle. The tentacle wrapped tightly round her leg. She felt its firm vice-like grip contracting, beginning to crush her ankle.

Then there was a painful pricking as sharp barbs cut through her biohazard suit and pierced her skin.

'Oh no! Doctor! It's cut through my suit!' she whimpered. 'It's broken my skin! I'm infected!'

The Doctor remained perfectly still. His mind was far, far away. His vision was filled with an image of another world. He glimpsed a purple sky, twin suns with a blue hue to them. Another image: a different world, with heavy tumbling clouds and many dozens of twisted pillars of a resin-like substance reaching hundreds of metres towards the troubled sky. It resembled a city of termite mounds. Then another world of green skies, methane gas and floating balloon-like creatures.

Trace memories of worlds this strain of the Spore must have visited before, worlds it had visited, absorbed and moved on from. Worlds visited how many countless millions of years ago?

Then . . . something resonated in his head. It was not something he could truly describe as a voice. And yet somehow it was. Deep inside his brain he heard a sexless, ageless voice. A whisper of consciousness penetrating his mind. A thought that was distinctly not his.

You seek communication?

I do.

You represent entity?

I do.

Represent of this world?

Yes.

Fleeting images filled the Doctor's head: a slideshow of

species from Earth. Species that the Spore had already touched and absorbed and decoded. Thousands of microbes that it must have first encountered in the dry dirt of the Nevada Desert. Hundreds of insects: an ant, a beetle, a many-hued dragonfly. Now more complex forms: a tan-coloured rodent, a rattlesnake, some small species of desert fox. Now larger: a cow, a dog and finally . . . a human. A record of the Spore's journey up the food chain.

Then the procession of images ceased. The Doctor had his vision returned to him.

Not represent entity of this world. From another world.

Yes. I have travelled, as it seems you have.

You have resistant structural code.

The Spore was referring to his inherited immunity. A few lines in his genome that prevented this pathogen from being able to absorb him and render him an amorphous organic soup.

Yes. Your kind once visited my planet. You asked the question and we answered it satisfactorily. We were allowed to continue to exist. We developed a vaccine from the toxin you used to self-terminate.

A correct process. Demonstration of intelligence. Your kind judged acceptable.

The intelligent entities on this planet will not be able to answer your question correctly.

This makes entities' mass from this world a viable resource.

But they are an intelligent species.

Intelligence defined by answering correctly.

And they will answer you correctly. But not yet.

Irrelevant.

It is not irrelevant. It is simply bad timing.

Explain.

Your journey here was an entirely random one. On what? A rock? A piece of ice? A million different variables conspired to land you on this planet at this time. If one thing had happened differently – if your rock had been a fraction bigger, or travelled a fraction slower, or been affected by the tiniest pull of gravity from some other mass nearby – you might have arrived here just a few decades later . . . at a time when these entities could answer you correctly.

Irrelevant.

They just need a few more years. That's all. They will become a remarkable species capable of –

Question must be asked of entity mass from this world.

The Doctor frowned. The Spore was too simple an intelligence to *philosophise* with. It was no more sophisticated than the majority of desktop computers currently on Earth – little better than an operating system asking for a password. Asking it to make a judgement call was going to be pointless. It was a 'brain' designed long ago to deliver a question and listen for the answer. That was all. He was going to have to change his approach . . .

Evelyn Chan could feel her leg beginning to go numb, an invasive coolness rising inside her thigh, infection spreading from artery to artery. Spore cells swiftly overcame her hastily scrambled immune system, massacring white blood cells in their millions. She felt lightheaded. Dizzy. Her legs wobbled, then buckled beneath her. She collapsed to the ground, gasping as she fought for breath, the torch sliding out of her hand.

'Doctor!' she cried groggily. 'Doctor . . . I'm dying.'

The Doctor barely heard Evelyn's voice. It sounded as if it was coming from someone a thousand miles away. All the same, he understood what she'd said. She was infected. He had minutes to save her life, seconds even. Time to roll the dice.

You have made a mistake.

Explain mistake.

You have returned to your origin world. To those that once engineered you, millions of years ago. You are in danger of destroying your creator.

Original creator would have immunity.

But much time has passed. Natural mutations in the DNA of your creator have occurred and compromised that immunity. They have evolved. They are no longer recognisable as the original species – your creators. But they are their descendants. And you will destroy them.

He sensed confusion in the Spore – voices like collegiate whispers, the organic equivalent of a computer struggling to run lines of code it was not designed to process.

They are descendent species of creator?

It sounded like the Spore was asking him for confirmation.

Yes! They are a descendent species! They are the 'children' of your creators.

Question must still be answered. Descendants of creator must demonstrate intelligence of original creators. Descendants will know answer.

The Doctor ground his teeth. Perhaps a simple,

straightforward lie would work instead. He turned and glanced back out of the truck. Evelyn Chan was lying at the bottom of the ramp; she was dying. It might already be too late to save her. A lie. A simple lie was all he had left. Perhaps this thing's intelligence was so rudimentary that it would not question the false information he'd given a moment ago; that it would not understand a simple lie.

Earlier information was incorrect.

Explain incorrect information.

I am not from another world.

Explain.

I am a messenger entity of your creator's descendants. I am an anti-pathogen. Your opposite, designed to communicate with you in the event of your return. I am a construct of theirs, just as you are. I have lived for millions of years, waiting for the possibility of your return. And I was designed to give you the answer.

You are construct – a remote partial?

He guessed that was the term the Spore used for one of the crab-like creatures scuttling around on the floor in front of him.

Yes. A Remote Partial.

You answer for descendants of creator?

Yes, that is my purpose. I will answer the question on their behalf.

The Doctor could sense the Spore trying to work with the limited resources of its genetically encoded artificial intelligence. He held his breath. So much depended on the decision it reached. Not just Evelyn's life but the life of every living thing on Earth . . .

Acceptable. The question – explain ratio 1:812.

★

Chan could feel her mind drifting. She was losing consciousness, descending into a comatose stupor. Her sight was growing foggy, getting dim round the edges.

Is this how it feels to die? It was almost serene, almost pleasant. She was about to be cannibalised from the inside out . . . and it didn't seem to matter.

And then something happened. She felt a sharp stabbing in her head, like the sudden onset of a piercing migraine. Her vision began to clear, to refocus. She retched as she felt her muscles cramping: the pain of her body's immune system fighting back. She struggled to sit up, her head throbbing, her stomach churning.

The pulsating tendril wrapped round her ankle suddenly convulsed violently. Its skin ruptured and a small jet of creamy liquid spurted out across her feet.

Revolted, she tried to kick the dying tendril off her.

The smooth skin of the artery split in a dozen other places and liquid oozed and bubbled out on to the ramp and the tarmac. The nearest of the beetle-like creatures flopped to the ground and began to shudder as if in a seizure. The others followed in quick succession, one after the other, their long spine-covered legs twitching and curling.

She heard footsteps and turned to see the Doctor stepping down from the ramp, wiping a dark smear from beside his nose with the cuff of his jacket.

'What . . . what's happening?' she slurred. 'Did you manage to communicate with it?'

'I did indeed,' replied the Doctor. 'And now it's doing the polite thing and killing itself.' He smiled. 'Awfully decent thing, that pathogen. Very understanding.'

★

Ratio 1:812?

The Doctor smiled. Every child on Gallifrey knew the answer to a question as elementary as that. A classroom question – basic kindergarten eleven-dimension superstring theory.

Well, now, he'd answered the Spore, *the answer is . . .*

'I don't even understand the question,' said Chan. 'Let alone know how we would have come up with an answer.'

She winced as they hobbled up the road, the Doctor supporting her with an arm round her waist. The bones in her ankle were fractured.

'Well, you're not a quantum physicist, are you?'

The Doctor turned to look past her shoulder at the rising sun. He narrowed his eyes against the glare. It had emerged in the last few minutes from the flat desert: a ball of molten orange separating itself from the shimmering horizon. Long shadows of stunted Joshua trees made dark stripes across the dusty ground.

Half a kilometre down the road, the roadblock waited. They could make out the trucks and the soldiers lined up in their white biohazard suits.

'However, a quantum physicist in about fifty years' time *will* understand, Evelyn Chan. And that's really all that matters.'

He raised the sample container in his hand. 'By the way, you'll want this analysed to produce a vaccine, just in case there's another rock in near-Earth orbit carrying another pathogen. The Spore does seem to come in clusters, from our experience.'

She looked again at the sample. Half an hour ago it had been a bubbling puddle of black goo; now it looked like dried fruit or the mummified ear of some shrivelled and long-forgotten pharaoh.

The Spore was dead.

'Why don't you just tell me the answer? I know, being a mere dumb human I probably won't understand what it means, but at least if another one of these things does arrive in the near future, we'll have the right answer to give.'

The Doctor pressed his lips together. 'But, Evelyn, this is scientific knowledge that you should *earn* rather than receive ahead of the natural time. It would be like me handing over an antimatter energy cell to Isaac Newton and telling him to have a play around with it. Maybe take it apart and see how it all ticks.' He chuckled at the thought of that. 'Rather a messy bang there, I'd imagine.'

He turned to look at her. 'All I will tell you is, in the place where I come from . . .' He paused and a wistful smile played across his lips for a moment. 'I should say, where I *came* from, the answer was used by some of my people to claim final proof of the existence of the old gods.'

'Really?'

'And,' he continued with a grin, 'just as many said the answer finally *disproved* the notion of gods.' He laughed. 'Funny old universe. You never do get a clear and final answer on that particular question, do you?'

They were closer to the roadblock now. The Doctor could make out more detail. Major Platt was warily watching their slow, hobbling approach. Every last soldier was scrambled and manning the barricade, guns held, muzzles aimed at the ground. But ready. In case. More trucks had arrived during the night and several helicopters were buzzing in the dawn sky, search beams carving bright lines down on to the desert.

Evelyn Chan had unzipped and removed her hood as soon as the Doctor had assured her the pathogen was quite dead and harmless. Now she wiped sweat from her forehead. 'So, did you come here in some big spaceship?' she asked.

He frowned, pouting at the same time. 'I suppose it's a little bit like a spaceship. Although it doesn't look particularly grand from the outside.'

She looked up at the gradually lightening sky. 'And you really have been way out there? Beyond our solar system?'

He nodded. 'Many places. Many times.'

'You must have seen some incredible things.'

He nodded. 'Quite a few. In the end, though, it's mostly a handful of elements combined in an infinite variety of interesting ways.' He scratched his chin thoughtfully.

Chan's eyes were still up on the heavens. Dawn was slowly painting out the stars one by one as the sky paled from a deep midnight purple to an intense morning blue. 'I'd love to see what's out there.'

He turned to look at her. 'Well, your kind will one day, Evelyn.' He nodded pensively. 'Not long after you learn the answer to that question, actually. It will unlock your understanding of higher spatial dimensions. It will allow humanity to cross the vast distances between star systems. It will –' He stopped himself. 'Ah, but there you go. I'm giving too much away, aren't I?'

They approached the roadblock. The Doctor casually

saluted to the waiting major, then tossed the specimen jar to him over the stretched coil of barbed wire.

'Right. Here you are, Major. One Captain Evelyn Chan, battered and bruised, but not infectious. She's quite safe. But she does need someone to take a look at her ankle.'

The Doctor eased his hold on Chan as she took the cautiously extended hand of a soldier. Then he turned and began to walk away from the barricade, back into the desert.

'And where are you going?' called Major Platt. 'We need to debrief you! We need to know exactly what happened back there.'

The Doctor offered Chan a small wave. 'I'll let you bring him up to speed.'

'Where *are* you going, Doctor?' she called.

The Doctor rolled his gaze upwards at the rapidly disappearing stars in the brightening sky. A gesture for her eyes only.

She nodded. *Understood.* 'And . . . and will you be back? Will we see you again?'

He grinned. 'I imagine I might look in on you sometime in the future, Captain Evelyn Chan.'

THE NINTH DOCTOR:
THE BEAST OF BABYLON

CHARLIE HIGSON

1

Ali was having a picnic with her family in the little water park on the edge of town when she first saw the Doctor. He was striding across the grass, glancing around, eyes a bit wild, as if he was searching for something. He looked like a typical man. Two arms, two legs. The usual. Short hair. Sticking-out ears and a big nose. Black leather boots. Black leather jacket. Men were like that, weren't they? They got off on wearing the skin of dead animals. Always made Ali feel a bit funny. The idea of it.

He was sort of grinning. Not really a happy grin, though. Slightly crazy.

And he seemed to be in a hurry.

He spotted Ali's family and came over, eyes as wide as his grin, trying to look friendly and polite, and failing badly. He didn't look like the normal sort of tourist they got round here, or a businessman on a trip, but he was definitely a traveller of some sort. Ali felt the familiar sour sting of jealousy she always felt around travellers. Wishing she could escape her boring little life. She wondered where this man was from. When he spoke, though, he didn't have any trace of a foreign accent, and Ali was impressed.

'You haven't seen anything, have you?'

'Seen what?' Ali's dad replied. She could tell he was a little freaked out by this man appearing out of nowhere. He hadn't even said hello or anything, just blurted out his question. Definitely in a hurry.

'Never mind. You'd know it if you'd seen it.'

'Know what?'

'Never mind. Forget it.'

Ali's dad struggled up and stood between the man and his family. Obviously thought there might be trouble.

'I'm sorry to have bothered you,' said the man. He looked at Ali's family, saw her younger sister, and his expression changed. He was worried now. 'It's just . . .'

'Just what?' Ali's dad was trying to sound tough and brave. Two things he wasn't. He was a wimp really, wouldn't hurt a fly, but this strange man wasn't to know that.

'Just . . . maybe . . .' The man was struggling to say what he wanted. 'Maybe you should finish your picnic and get back home. Quickly, quite quickly – like *now*.'

'I don't see why I should –'

'Dad, it's all right,' Ali said. She was better at reading people than her father. She turned to the man. 'Are we in some kind of danger?'

'You could say that. You could also say "Come on, let's do as the man says and go home."' He looked around anxiously, scanning the trees on the edge of the park. When none of Ali's family made a move, he sighed and carried on talking, fast and impatient.

'I've been following someone, some*thing*, chasing them really, halfway across the universe, if you must know.'

'Who?'

'A man, two men. Well, they're the same man, except he's not a man at all. That probably doesn't make a lot of sense to you. Look, I'd better go. I'm really sorry to have ruined your picnic; it looks lovely, but . . . well, a lot more than your picnic could be ruined.' As he rattled on he had started picking up stuff and throwing food into Mum's basket.

'Just get away from here!' he shouted when still none of Ali's family moved. 'Far away.'

And then he stopped what he was doing, and cocked his head as if he'd heard something. 'Oh, Castor and Pollux,' he muttered, dropping a plate of boiled eggs. 'Not good. That's really not good at all.'

And then he was gone. Running off across the grass.

'Well, I mean . . .' said Ali's dad. 'What was all that about?'

Mum tutted and started tidying up.

'I think we should do what he says,' said Ali.

'Why?' said Dad. 'He's obviously nuts.'

Just then there came a great shout that seemed to fill the sky.

'Well, there's that, for a start,' said Ali, packing things away just like the man had done.

And then there was another cry, almost a scream, and there, above the treetops, was something that Ali found hard to take in. A man, but a man taller than the tallest building in town, and next to him another man. '*The same man,*' the stranger had said, and she saw what he'd meant. They were separate physically but somehow they were both the same living thing: identical, moving together, their faces showing the same blank expression.

Ali froze as her mind tried to take this all in, too scared to move, gripped by a giant, cold claw. She had the overwhelming thought that she could never understand what a creature like this would be thinking, except that it wouldn't care one iota about her and her family.

And then she wondered if she was really seeing it at all.

The two linked figures were very faint as if they weren't even there, just made of cloud and smoke and swirling leaves. And there was the stranger, holding something shining in his hand. One of the giants had scooped him up and he was yelling something, and the giants bellowed and there was a flash and everything started swirling, so that instead of two giants there was a tornado, a whirlwind, a great dancing dust devil, and the stranger spun round and round, twisting up into the sky. Then there was a final huge shout and they all disappeared.

This happened in less than three beats of Ali's heart – seeing the thing, her feeling about the alien nature of its mind, the *thinness* of it, the stranger being lifted up, the twister – and it was gone.

Then there was a great punch to her chest, the air was sucked out of her, her tubes popped and she felt suddenly sick. She moaned and closed her eyes. Her whole head was ringing and there was a bad, metallic taste in her mouth. She could hear her little sister crying.

And then Dad's voice.

'Great gods . . . Great gods. What was that?'

Ali felt something touch her. She opened her eyes. It had started to rain. Only it wasn't rain. Tiny silver droplets were falling from the sky. They dissolved as soon as they touched the ground. All except one. A larger piece that sat there. A silver sphere. Perhaps the thing the stranger had been holding. She picked it up. It was much heavier than it looked and very cold to the touch. She put it into her carrying pouch quickly before Mum or Dad saw it.

'We should get inside,' she said. 'Away from here, like he said, the *man* . . .'

The Doctor. That's what he was called. Although she didn't yet know it.

She also didn't yet know that he wasn't a *man* at all.

2

Ali wondered what had happened to the strange man, whether he had survived the fight, whether she would ever see him again, but it was only a few days later and the great wandering planet of LM-RVN had barely danced halfway across the sky when he came back into her life.

She was on her way home from college at the end of a long and boring day and had stopped off at the lake to stare into its murky depths. It was starting to grow dark and the moons were casting silver splashes over the water. It looked insanely beautiful. She threw in a stone and wished it was the holidays and the water was warmer and it was safe to go for a swim – properly go for a swim. She only really felt alive when she was in the water.

And then she saw his reflection, distorted by the ripples from the stone, but still unmistakably him. *The Doctor*. She felt a little stab of happiness. He was all right.

'I want it back,' he said.

'What?' she said without even turning round.

'You know what.'

'How can you be so sure I've got it?' she said, feeling the sphere hanging heavy in her carrying pouch.

'You know,' said the Doctor, 'when I first saw you I said to myself, here's someone special.'

Now Ali did turn. She'd thought the exact same thing about him. It was then that she noticed a large box of some sort standing in the tall weeds, half hidden under the trees. It was blue, looked like it was made of wood and had foreign writing on it. Her mind started to turn.

'This thing you're looking for,' she said. 'What is it? Why should I give it back to you?'

'I can't tell you that. Let's just say that the fate of a planet, an insignificant little planet, but a planet I'm rather fond of, is in your power. Besides, it's not yours. I lost it in a fight.'

'I saw that,' said Ali. 'It didn't look like much of a fight to me, more a massacre, really. You weren't exactly winning.'

'I had a plan . . . It sort of worked.'

'And the plan involved the thing you're looking for? Which I'm not going to give to you until you tell me exactly what it is.'

'Then I'll have to make you, won't I?' The Doctor glared at Ali.

Ali laughed. 'Who are you fooling?'

The Doctor shrugged and gave Ali one of his mad grins that was almost a snarl.

'I may not know that much about men,' said Ali. 'But I can tell that you're not, like, one of the violent ones.'

The grin became a gurn. 'You're right. I'm not. I'm the Doctor, by the way.'

'I'm Ali.'

'Pleased to meet you, Ali.'

'You're a trickster, Doctor, not a warrior.'

'Right again. And something tells me I can't trick you.'

'No. You can't.'

'So it's stalemate.'

'Let's trade,' said Ali, and the Doctor sat down on a rock, started taking off his shoes and socks.

'OK,' he said.

'I've got the – what do you call it? Our little silver ball that weighs nearly as much as that boulder you're sitting on.'

'Let's call it an orb.'

'OK. *I've* got the orb,' said Ali. 'What can *you* offer me?'

'What do you want?'

'Information.'

'Go on. I'll answer any question you like.' The Doctor was rolling up his trousers now. He obviously meant to go in the lake, but if it was only up to his knees it would be safe.

'What was that thing?' she asked. 'That giant thing? Those two giant things?'

The Doctor thought for a while. 'He . . . It . . . is a *Starman*,' he said at last. 'A star-eater. He can travel through space and time, fuelled by the energy he drains from stars. He's pretty much a star himself – in every sense of the word.'

The Doctor got up and dipped his feet in the lake. He gave a little theatrical gasp at how cold it was.

'And the orb is some kind of weapon,' said Ali.

'Well . . .' The Doctor was intrigued. 'What makes you say that?'

'You were holding it. I saw a flash in the sky. Why else would you want it back so badly? And why couldn't you tell me what it was? I'm thinking it's because you're not supposed to have it. It's not yours . . . I think you stole it.'

The Doctor had gone in up to his knees and the bottoms of his trousers were under water. He didn't seem to notice. He was staring at Ali, his head tilted to one side. 'You're very clever, aren't you, Ali?' he said.

'So I'm told.'

'Where's the orb?' There was a harder edge to the Doctor's voice. Playtime was over.

Ali glanced up at the darkening sky, saw the moons receding, each one smaller and dimmer, thinking of all that was out there, in the infinite reaches of space. Then she looked at the blue wooden box under the trees and something clicked.

'That's a spaceship, isn't it?' she said.

'I don't know what you're talking about.'

'Well, you're a traveller, aren't you?'

'You could say that.'

'I'd *kill* to travel,' said Ali. 'This planet, we get travellers from everywhere.'

'It's in a terminus galaxy,' said the Doctor, coming out of the lake. 'It's a jumping-off point for a lot of places.'

'Exactly. That's why the Starman came here, isn't it?' said Ali. 'He was on his way somewhere else, and you followed him here. You said so – halfway across the universe. So you must have got here somehow. And I don't think you came on a Virgo craft, a slow, unreliable space bus, not if you were chasing something. So you must have your own ship.'

'You're a regular Sherlock Holmes, aren't you?'

'A Sherlock what?'

'Never mind,' said the Doctor, and he moved closer to Ali. 'Just someone from that other planet I was telling you about.

Now if you're done showing off, can you give me the orb and I'll be out of your life.'

'You're always in such a hurry, aren't you?' said Ali, backing away. 'And you're in a real big hurry to get away now, so you wouldn't want to be far from your ship. And this wasn't here before, and it's very much not from round here, like *you*. So it stands to reason that this must be your ship. It doesn't look nearly big enough to travel through space, though, so it must be some kind of an illusion, bigger than it looks. Or maybe it exists partly outside of space and time. That makes it bigger on the inside . . .' Ali stopped, awestruck.

'Oh my days,' she said. 'It's a TARDIS. You've got a TARDIS.'

'I really, *really* don't know what you're talking about.'

'Yes you do.' Ali walked over towards the box. 'We learned about them in school, in science, you know – *theoretically* – that they *could* exist. I never believed they were real, though. I wanted to. I *so* wanted to. But I never did . . . until now. That is *so* cool.'

'On the other hand,' said the Doctor, and he folded his arms and leaned against the TARDIS, 'it could just be a big blue box.'

'And *you* must be a Time Lord,' said Ali. 'I mean, you fit the part perfectly. You look like a human but you're not human, you're pretty smug and you think you're the carp's whiskers –'

'Is there anything you *don't* know, Ali?'

'Not really. We also learned about Time Lords at school. In history. *Ancient* history. We were told the Time Lords had all died out a long time ago. But here you are.'

'Ali. Please.' The Doctor had dropped on to his knees with his hands clasped together. 'Time is running out.'

'Take me with you,' said Ali.

'I can't do that.' The Doctor shook his head.

'I'll give you the orb if you take me with you.'

'No, no, no. It's way too dangerous where I'm going.'

'Come on, Doctor, you're going to save your favourite planet. You're going to rescue a whole race. What does my one life matter compared to all theirs . . .?'

'Ali, you can't ask this of me.'

'Besides – you might need some help.'

The Doctor stared at Ali for a very long time and then his wonky Time Lord face split into the maddest, wildest, strangest grin she'd seen yet.

'I can't get rid of you, can I?' he said.

3

'The planet's called Earth. Where humans first came from. Long way back.'

'I've heard of it.'

'That doesn't surprise me, Little Miss A-Star.'

The Doctor was busy at the controls of the TARDIS, his face lit by the glowing green column that rose and fell rhythmically like the beating heart of the ship. Ali was amazed at how quickly she'd got used to being in here after the first mind-bending experience of stepping through a door into another world. It all felt weirdly normal now. To tell the truth, some of the equipment looked decidedly primitive and old-fashioned compared to what she was used to. Not that she pretended to understand what everything did, but this was the relic of a civilisation that had died out a long time ago.

The Doctor had darted about madly, throwing switches, twiddling dials, jabbing buttons as they'd set off, and now that they were under way he'd calmed down enough to tell her about how he'd come to turn up on Karkinos.

'I'd been down on Earth trying to save the old place again,' he went on. 'And there was this thing, this creature, call it what you want . . . Actually it's usually called a Nestene

Consciousness. Just another bully, another demigod like the Starman, wanting to feed off the planet and drain it dry. Not nice. I was trying to find it and put a sock in it and I was helped by a girl – about your age, as it goes. A lot like you in many ways.'

'What was her name?' asked Ali, curious.

'Rose. Rose Tyler,' said the Doctor.

'A human girl?'

'Yeah. The only type they had on the planet back then. You see, in that corner of the universe space travel hadn't really taken off just yet, so there were only native creatures on the planet and the humans were the only halfway sentient ones. Them and meerkats.'

'Tell me about Rose Tyler.' Ali watched as the Doctor peered at some kind of monitor and, satisfied, stepped back from the controls. He turned and beamed at her.

'Rose? She was funny and tough and clever and resourceful. She saved me, and she saved her boyfriend Mickey, and she saved the whole damned planet.'

'Oh, you're in *love*,' said Ali with more than a touch of sarcasm.

'No,' said the Doctor, and he wasn't smiling any more. 'Don't make that mistake, Ali. Let's just say she was good company. And I like company.'

'It must be difficult for you,' said Ali. 'Living as long as you do.'

'Oh, I've had so many companions in my life,' said the Doctor. 'Susan and Barbara and Ian, Prince Egon, Jamie, Polly, Ella McBrien, Sarah-Jane Smith, Leela . . . They come, and, inevitably, they go. But without them . . .'

'You're the last lonely Time Lord.'

'What is it with teenage girls?' asked the Doctor. 'Always digging. When I met Rose I'd only recently regenerated. I'm sure you know all about regeneration — you've probably got a diploma in it — and I was feeling a bit like a soft-shell crab, waiting for my new shell to harden — if you'll pardon the analogy. I was still finding my feet. I thought: new body, new start, new companion.'

'So what happened? Did you ask her?'

'I did, as it goes. And she turned me down. I'd come on too strong, I guess, played my cards too soon. As I say, I was still adjusting to the regeneration — not quite calibrated. She just looked at me. She's got a funny face, big mouth and big eyes . . . a big heart.'

'You *are* in love.'

The Doctor ignored Ali and ploughed on. 'And that's why she couldn't come. Because she cared more about what she'd have to leave behind than what I could offer her. Her family, her boyfriend, her *life*. I couldn't argue with that. I couldn't expect her to drop everything and go gallivanting off with a perfect stranger in search of adventure.'

'Are you saying *I* don't have a big heart?' Ali blurted out before she could stop herself.

'No. Not at all.'

'You think I don't care, don't you?' Ali was trying not to get angry. She was sure that it would show. That she'd be flushed an ugly red.

The Doctor looked wide-eyed and innocent, a little dismissive.

'Did I say that? I don't remember saying that. As I explained before we took off, I can land you right back on Karkinos a second after we left. Nobody will ever know. I didn't have time to tell Rose that.'

'I know you didn't really want me to come with you, though.' Ali could feel herself shaking.

'You're here, aren't you? So stop your whingeing. Now, hold on to something – I need to get ready for landing.'

His goofy grin calmed her down a little.

'But if you already saved the Earth,' said Ali, gripping a rail, 'why do you need to go back there?'

'It's like this, Ali.' The Doctor had started to pace about. 'I said goodbye to Rose, I came in here and started up the engines and, the next thing I knew, lights were flashing, alarms were blaring. It was all bells and buzzers and bleepers and hooters and tweeters, and I knew that didn't mean my dinner was ready in the microwave – you don't know what I'm talking about, but it doesn't matter. What *does* matter is that the TARDIS is uniquely tuned to sense any problems with the fabric of time, and just as it had alerted me to the presence of the Nestene Consciousness in a place called London back in Rose's time, now it was alerting me to a very similar problem somewhere else on the planet, a few thousand years earlier.'

'The Starman?'

'Give the girl a big round of applause. Yes, they're dangerous entities, born when stars collapse, when they become black holes and white dwarfs and red dwarfs and wormholes, or whatever you call them in your neck of the intergalactic woods. When they collapse they alter the shape of space and they alter the shape of time, and sometimes a Starman is created, a cosmic being with primitive consciousness. And if you're not careful, they can escape from their own time and go trampling through existence, wiping it clean and rewriting history, rewriting the laws of science itself. I suppose you could call them gods, if you wanted, and it was always one of the duties of the Time Lords to police the universe and snap the cuffs on them when they popped up where they shouldn't. Nasty things, you know, *gods*, they don't much care for anyone other than themselves. Don't like any competition. So off I went to try to head this Starman off at the pass.'

'Why did it look like there were two of them?' Ali asked, remembering those two ghost-like giants towering above the trees.

'Yeah, he looked like twins, and it looked like they weren't really there,' said the Doctor. 'That's because it was existing in several different dimensions at once. Now, this orb –' he picked up the silver ball from where it had been sitting in a cradle on the control console – 'was created in a very similar way to the Starman. It has the power of a collapsed star in it. It was made by a very clever, and not very nice, character called the Exalted Holgoroth of All Tagkhanastria. And he was no better than the bloody Starman! He was only really interested in using the orb to build a space empire. So I thought I'd kill two pterodactyls with one stone. I paid a visit to the Holgoroth, pretending to be an emissary from the Crab Nebula, and I stole his orb right out from under his nose – which is an exciting story I'll tell you one day if you're very good – and I went after the Starman and got to him before he reached Earth. In the process he nearly killed me.'

'I saw.'

'But I had superior firepower!' The Doctor tossed the orb into the air; it seemed to hover there for a moment, and then fell into the open palm of his hand with a slap. 'And I knocked him for six! Well, into the twenty-sixth dimension anyway. He's safe there for a while. Can't do much damage – space and time's always been a right mess in there. Might even sort things out a bit. Who knows?'

'So if you flipped him into another dimension, why are we going back to Earth?' Ali was trying to keep up and take all this in, but she was struggling.

'It seems that my little ding-dong on your planet with the space twins has sent ripples spreading out.' The Doctor mimed this with wiggling fingers. 'Always the same – you push one problem under the carpet and another one pops out on the other side. Cause and effect, unforeseen consequences, the butterfly's wing.'

'What?' Now Ali really *had* lost the thread.

'In a nutshell,' said the Doctor, 'there's another Starman, a worse one, a more powerful one, heading for Earth and I need to stop it. In fact, it's probably already there.'

'Can't you just do what you did with the twins and grab it before it arrives?' Ali asked.

'No. That's the thing. Me and this new Starman exist in the same time stream. A side-effect of using the orb. Unforeseen consequences. Turns out the magic orb is not as special as the Holgoroth claimed. Should have read the small print – "*This item may not work as advertised!*" Until I send this new Starman packing, the two of us have a time tag on us. We're linked.' The Doctor was back at the console again now, studying screens and meters, his hands a blur as they moved over the controls.

'So now we're landing on Earth,' he shouted, 'two thousand years before the birth of Christ . . .'

'Who?'

'He was a bit like Sherlock Holmes. Knew the answers to everything. Very good at solving mysteries. Some humans use him to measure time.'

'And whereabouts on Earth?'

'A place called Babylon. Lovely little spot – very hot in the summer, though.'

'Doctor?' said Ali. 'One last thing.'

'Make it quick.'

'This new Starman, what will it look like?'

'Good question.'

'I mean, will it look like the twins?'

'Probably not. It depends on what planets it's absorbed. It could look like anything – a lizard, a fish, a goat, a sea urchin, an anglepoise lamp or a giant amorphous blob. One thing I *can* tell you, though: it probably won't look very nice.'

4

At that moment, Zabaia, High Priest of Marduk, was on his knees, his face pressed into the cold stone of the temple floor, his bony legs trembling. A wind from nowhere was kicking sand and grit into the air and throwing it under his robes, and the roar of some terrible dragon was screeching in his ears. He dared not look up, but he could sense that there was a new presence here. The shape of the space had changed. *Something* had appeared. Perhaps their god had arrived? Marduk himself.

He gathered up enough courage to open one eye and look across the floor to see what the guards were doing. He was pleased that they, like him, had prostrated themselves before this apparition. No one would laugh at him for a coward now.

'It is a dragon's egg,' he heard one of them whisper.

'It is hatching!' said another hoarse voice, and a third voice offered up a prayer for Marduk to protect them all.

Zabaia waited, his heart thumping, his breath caught in his mouth. Waited for the wrath of Marduk to come down upon his head.

'Hello there.'

Slowly Zabaia raised his head. A man was standing there, dressed strangely in black clothing. And behind him — what fool would imagine it was an egg? — was a large blue chest. The man was eyeing Zabaia with the same puzzled expression that Zabaia himself no doubt wore.

'Everything all right?' said the man. 'There's really no need to kneel to me, you know. A simple handshake will do.'

Gurgurum, captain of the royal guard, was standing by his king, Hammurabi, looking down on the world from the balcony outside the king's quarters. From here, high up on the palace walls, they could see all of Babylon. But Hammurabi was not pleased. He was tugging at his beard, fiddling with the beads and precious rings that were knotted into it.

'My family ruled Babylon when it was little more than a dusty desert village and they built it into the largest city in the world,' he was saying.

Gurgurum was proud to serve mighty Hammurabi. It was Hammurabi who had enlarged the temples, raised the city walls and strengthened the embankments that stopped the great, muddy Euphrates from flooding the streets. It was Hammurabi who had made Babylon safe. And a safe city can grow rich and powerful. Every day new houses were built, each one grander than the last, and down below Gurgurum could see the people going about their business, haggling in the market-places, hurrying down the crowded streets and across the many bridges.

Outside the city walls, spreading out across the lush green flood-watered plain between the Euphrates and the

Tigris, were fruit trees and date palms and wheat fields teeming with slaves hard at work growing the food that fed Hammurabi's empire. And beyond the fertile plain was the desert, its hills and baked earth the same reddish yellow as the buildings in the city.

'You are the greatest ruler the world has ever seen,' said Gurgurum. 'And you have built the greatest empire the world has ever known. In a few short years you have defeated the kingdoms of Eshnunna, Elam, Larsa and Mari. You have trampled their people underfoot and made them slaves; you have slaughtered their young men. You have brought glory to Babylon.'

'But do you not feel it, Gurgurum?' said Hammurabi, slamming his fists on the stone balustrade of the balcony.

'Feel what, my king?'

'As if a shadow has fallen across our world. I fear that all this might crumble. That our enemies will snatch it away from us.'

'We are prepared,' said Gurgurum. 'Your army stands ready. Your chariots ride round the city walls to frighten off any enemy tribes who might be foolish enough to launch an attack.'

'But the priests have warned me that our great god, Marduk of the Fifty Names, might abandon the city,' said Hammurabi. 'We sacrifice to him, we wash the mouth of his statue, but the gods don't much care for the feeble concerns of man. Our cities are dust beneath their feet.'

'You should not listen to the priests,' said Gurgurum bitterly. 'They are like frightened old women. Your strength is in your army. You must rule with the sword.'

Gurgurum knew, though, that there was some truth in Hammurabi's words. Tremors had been felt beneath the earth lately, and the wall of a temple had collapsed, killing a priest and three of his servants.

'I *must* listen to the priests,' said Hammurabi. 'They are the only ones who can tell me what the gods are thinking. I cannot sleep for fear that Babylon is under attack from mysterious forces, that my enemies plot against me, that they will send spies and sorcerers to undermine me.'

'Then kill your enemies. Kill everyone in Babylon who is not a Babylonian,' urged Gurgurum. 'Let the Euphrates run red with their blood. Choke the Tigris with their bodies. They have not earned the right to justice. Trust in your strength and the sharp edges of your soldiers' weapons.'

'And what if our enemies are the gods themselves?' said Hammurabi. 'What then?'

'Then we pray, my lord,' said Gurgurum and he laughed darkly.

Hiding to the side of the open doorway, Ali was anxious to see out of the TARDIS and get her first glimpse of an alien planet. But she was obeying the Doctor. The last thing he'd told her before they'd landed was to keep herself hidden and look after the TARDIS for him until he was sure it was safe.

'I don't want you in any trouble.'

'I can look after myself,' Ali had protested.

'I'm sure you can,' the Doctor had said. 'But I don't want any upsets here, no unknown unknowns, no surprises that I'm not expecting.'

'If you're expecting it, then it's not a surprise.'

'Those are my favourite sorts of surprises, Ali – the unsurprising ones. We need to be discreet, OK? I just need to neutralise the Starman and get out quick.'

So did this count as neutralising the Starman? She wasn't sure. Though when the Doctor had first opened the TARDIS door he'd made a tiny disappointed sound, as if he'd made a mistake in his calculations and hadn't quite been expecting to find what was out there.

She could hear his voice through the doorway.

'I need to speak to someone in charge. It's rather urgent.'

'Who are you? Are you a messenger from the gods?'

'Er . . . You could say that . . . Yes, let's say I'm a messenger from the gods.'

Ali wished she could see what was happening. There was the sound of scraping feet, of voices in hurried conversation and then a cry of panic from the Doctor. 'No! Don't go in there!'

A man appeared in the doorway, shorter than other men she had seen, wearing a gleaming bronze helmet. He was bare-chested and carrying a spear and shield. When he saw Ali he gasped in surprise and before he could do anything else Ali instinctively lashed out with one of her antenodes. It whipped through the air and struck the man in the side of the neck. His body convulsed and he dropped backwards out of the doorway, dead to the world.

The Doctor had told her to protect the TARDIS, hadn't he?

She didn't think anyone else would try to board in a hurry, but she waited there by the door just in case.

There was shouting from outside now and the sound of a

scuffle. How she wished she had a better view. And then she heard the Doctor's voice, strained and muffled. 'Don't move, Ali!' he shouted. 'Shut the door and wait for me. I'll be all right!'

She reached over and pushed the door closed. It hadn't sounded good. The Doctor was in trouble, she was sure of it. If only . . .

Well, why not? He hadn't told her not to touch the controls. She was sure there would be something here. Some piece of equipment that would help her see what was happening to the Doctor. Even a cranky old relic of ancient tech like the TARDIS would have scanners of some sort. Surely . . .

She hurried over to the console, located the main access screen, leaned forward and worked the controls with her fingers, just as she'd spent hours doing at school and college and in her room back home on Karkinos. She was good with technology, and even though this was ridiculously retro she thought she'd have a pretty good idea how to find what she needed.

There.

A few swift adjustments and she had a clear view of the outside. Another tweak and she had sound to go with it. Luckily, the telepathic field of the TARDIS's translation circuit allowed her to understand every word of what was being said.

Unluckily, it really *didn't* sound good.

A man wearing elaborate embroidered robes and carrying some kind of a staff was shouting at the Doctor, who was surrounded by more men armed with spears.

'Liar! You are not an emissary of the gods, you are a man, like me. You are a spy and the law of Hammurabi clearly states what must be done to spies!'

5

Gurgurum was looking down on to the Place of Execution from the balcony outside the royal quarters. There was a hum of voices as soldiers formed into neat ranks on the packed red dirt of the square. Other soldiers lined the battlements on the surrounding walls. And past the city walls, out on the plain, Hammurabi's army stood still, as if waiting.

Gurgurum watched as the king came out of the palace gates directly below him. He was surrounded by his slaves, advisers and priests. His royal guard marched at his side. But not Gurgurum. Lightning flashed in the east and Gurgurum shivered. There were storm clouds gathering over the hills, sucking up sand from the desert and darkening the midday sky. The warmth had gone out of the day.

He wanted to be down there with his king. He should be at his side, but he had been ordered to stay up here and guard the royal family.

He watched as the king settled on to his dais and waited while Prisoner's Gate was opened and three of the city judges led in the spy, flanked by a unit of heavily armed soldiers. Gurgurum felt useless up here and it fed his anger and hatred. This man was a foreigner, an outsider, he had no pure Babylonian blood in his veins and so was not worthy of a trial.

Gurgurum gripped the hilt of his sword tightly. He wished he could leap from the balcony, run across the square and plunge his blade into the prisoner's belly himself.

Ali was pacing up and down, drumming her fingertips against her teeth as she always did when she was anxious and thinking hard. She had watched helplessly as the Doctor had been dragged away, shouting about the Starman and the danger they were all in. She couldn't bear to think about what they were doing to him out there. Time was passing, marked by the clicking of her feet on the metal floor of the Doctor's ship. He had told her to stay put, but if she didn't do something they were going to kill him. And if they killed him, there was no hope of defeating the Starman.

What made it worse was that the Doctor had left the orb in its cradle on the console, so, even if by some miracle the Babylonians didn't kill him, when the Starman attacked he would have no way of defeating it.

And then she heard a thump.

She glanced at the scanner. Several guards had gathered round the TARDIS and one of them was battering at the door with his spear. Ali doubted he could do any damage, but it made her angry and, though she tried to damp the anger down, it grew inside her until she was glaring at the screen.

Thump.

'You're making me mad,' she hissed. 'And you wouldn't like me when I'm mad. Believe me.'

Thump.

Still the puny idiot bashed his silly spear against the door.

Thump.

Ali's whole body felt hot. Her anger was like a physical being inside her, bursting to get out. The image on the screen was dimming as the red mist of battle settled on her.

Thump.

One of the other guards laughed and said something obscene about the TARDIS and that did it for Ali.

She was not going to stand for that.

She was not going to stay shut up in here.

She was not going to hang around and let the Doctor get killed.

And so she listened, timing the thumps, tuning in to the man's rhythm, slowly creeping over to the door. She waited, counting, and then yanked the door open just as the guard lunged again. He was thrown off balance and stumbled through the suddenly empty space. She was ready for him and kicked him in the chest. He flew back, knocking over two of his startled friends, and now she was out and moving fast. The guards hadn't been expecting this and they hesitated, trying to make sense of this new threat. As two of them broke away and fled screaming towards the temple doorway, Ali lashed – one, two – with her antenodes and they went down, stunned. It would be a long while before *they* woke up.

That left three more, plus the three who were still on the ground, scuttling away from her on their backs, yelling in terror and panic.

There was no time to think. Ali had to get out of here and

find the Doctor. And she mustn't let anyone sound the alarm. Her antenodes were accurate and effective weapons, but she had used them both in the attack and it would take up precious time to curl them back in and make them ready again.

As she was processing all this information, one of the guards threw his spear. It cracked harmlessly off her armour – but that did it now. The rage came on her. There was no turning back. No more trying to be nice and stun the stupid men. She would use lethal weapons . . .

She advanced . . .

And the guard who had thrown the spear screamed . . .

And died.

6

Hammurabi eyed the prisoner curiously. He had claimed to be a doctor not a spy, but could not explain how he had emerged from inside the strange blue cabinet that had appeared in the middle of the temple. Hammurabi feared magic, and this man was a sorcerer, there was no doubt about it. A sorcerer and a spy. This was a worm that could destroy the whole fruit. Hadn't his priests warned him against just such an infiltrator? He was frightened. He had to save his city and protect his people, so the sorcerer had to be got rid of quickly before he had time to spread his poison.

Hammurabi had hastily rounded up three judges, who had been enjoying lunch together in one of the taverns near the river, and he had instructed them what the punishment should be. This way, the sorcerer's death could act as an offering to Marduk.

The chief judge now raised his hand to deliver the sentence. 'Cut out the spy's heart,' he shouted.

'Which one?' said the sorcerer, a mad grin on his white-skinned face.

'You will be silent,' screeched the chief judge.

'I will *not*, actually,' said the sorcerer. 'I always understood that the great and wise Hammurabi was a *just* king. A king who was proud of the laws he had written down. A king who would always let an accused man defend himself and not call him guilty without fair trial.'

'There is nothing you can say that will change my mind,' said Hammurabi, fearing that the sorcerer would use clever words and magic to cloud his mind. He would not listen. He *must* not listen. 'The law is the law. And the punishment for spies and sorcerers is to have their hearts cut out.'

'*Nothing* I can say?' shouted the sorcerer. 'What if I told you that you are in very great danger? What if I told you that your nice city, your kingdom, your empire, your *whole world* was about to be attacked by a being of such immense power that it will make your army look like toy soldiers, and when it's done with you there will be nothing left of mighty Babylon except ashes and cinders?'

'My priests have already warned me,' said Hammurabi, waving a hand dismissively.

'Really?' The sorcerer raised his eyebrows. 'They're cleverer than they look.'

'And it is clear that *you* are the threat they warned me of.'

'Wait, listen to me —'

'Enough of this,' said the chief judge. 'The sentence must be carried out.'

'No. You must listen to me!' The sorcerer looked worried for the first time. He struggled as four guards grabbed him and roughly dragged him towards the execution stone.

'The Starman is coming!' he yelled. 'The Great Beast! And I'm the only one who can stop it!'

★

From his vantage point on the royal balcony Gurgurum could see the man struggling as he was forced over the execution stone. He had heard his words and they'd made him uneasy. Gurgurum was a man utterly fearless in battle, yet now he felt the pricking of uncertainty.

The Great Beast of legend was coming . . . that was what the prisoner had said. What form would the Beast take? Where would it come from? How could they defend themselves against it?

The histories recorded the stories of the old gods. All the constellations in the sky were gods. The Babylonian zodiac taught children their names, and their parents used them to frighten them into obedience. It had been hundreds of years since the gods had walked the Earth. Would the Beast come down from the heavens in the form of a monstrous bull, a scorpion, a great lion? Or would it be some new and terrible monster?

He laughed at himself. He was behaving as if he was a little boy again, frightened of shadows. There were no monsters coming.

He heard a sound and turned quickly, his senses alert to any danger, peering into the darkness of the king's chambers.

And his heart throbbed in his chest.

It was here.

The Great Beast.

It was upon them.

And it was like nothing he had ever seen before.

It stood a whole head taller than any man, and there was something of a beetle about it and something of a crab or a crayfish from the river. It had six legs but only stood on four.

Its segmented body was arched backwards so that its two front legs were held up and out like arms, one of them ending in a huge knobbled claw. It had a head of sorts with four black bead-like eyes, but worst of all was its mouth, a gaping hole in the centre of its face, filled with row upon row of tiny sharp jagged teeth and surrounded by waving feelers that seemed to claw at the air.

Gurgurum offered up a prayer to Marduk and charged inside, tugging his sword from the scabbard at his belt.

He couldn't hope to defeat this monster, but he would die trying.

He was a pure-born Babylonian.

7

'I've come to Babylon to destroy the Beast,' the Doctor shouted as the priest, Zabaia, raised a vicious curved blade above his head and murmured an incantation. 'It's here, I know it's here.'

And then there was a scream. Zabaia paused, and the two guards let go of the Doctor as everyone in the courtyard looked up to see a soldier falling from a balcony, arms flailing. The Doctor heard Hammurabi shout, 'Gurgurum!' and looked away as the poor man hit the ground and was silenced.

There was something up there, coming out of the palace on to the balcony. Whatever it was, it must have thrown the man down. It reached the balustrade and stood there, raising itself up on long thin legs, seeming to peer down at the people in the square, opening and closing a massive claw.

'It is the Great Beast!' Zabaia shouted. 'You must send up your guard, Lord Hammurabi, to crush it.'

'That's not a Starman,' said the Doctor. 'Too small.'

'It is the Great Beast,' Zabaia repeated, his voice becoming high-pitched with hysteria.

'No it's not,' said the Doctor. 'It's a friend of mine.'

'A friend?'

'Her name's Ali. She's from Karkinos, but you don't really need to know that.'

'You are a friend of monsters,' Zabaia screeched. 'You have brought them among us. Your treachery is exposed.' He pointed a shaking finger at the two guards. 'Hold him to the stone! We must kill him quickly!'

But nobody moved. None of the soldiers were looking at Zabaia, or the creature on the balcony, or the Doctor any longer. They were looking up, over the wall on the opposite side of the square, where darkness was filling the sky. And something vast was forming in that darkness.

Zabaia dropped his knife and flung himself to the ground, burying his face in the dirt.

'Now *that*,' said the Doctor as the guards let go of him, 'is a Starman. You should have listened to me, Hammurabi. Your Great Beast is here at last.'

From the balcony Ali had a better view of the new Starman than anyone. And she watched, transfixed, as it materialised on the plain outside the city walls. It was as tall as the giant twins had been but, just as the Doctor had warned her, it was stranger and more horrifying.

It had no back legs, just the tail of a rotten fish, huge and bloated, and it pulled itself along with two immense lizard-like arms. Its head had dangling fleshy tendrils and two horny protuberances jutting from the top. It had the same dead, distant eyes as the twins, and the same faint appearance as if it was there but somehow not there at the same time. The strangest thing of all was what looked like water gushing from its shoulders, giving the appearance of two long, drooping silver wings.

She had to get the orb to the Doctor. She could feel its weight in her carrying pouch. It was the only thing that could stop the Beast.

There were shouts from behind her. Soldiers were in the corridor leading to the king's chambers. From back there they would have no idea what was happening outside. Ali knew she should ignore them, but she could sense the rational part of her mind losing out to the battle rage.

She moved inside and made ready her antenodes where they lay down her back, feeling the familiar tingling sensation as they filled with poison. She flexed her claw as the red mist descended.

The guards crashed through the wooden door and staggered to a halt, staring at Ali in terror and disbelief, just as she had stared at the Starman.

Two of them had enough courage to throw their spears, but they couldn't penetrate her shell. Her antenodes whipped out together, taking one man round the ankle. He fell hard on the stone floor and now she was scuttling after the rest of them as they retreated out of the door. They couldn't hope to outrun her, her six legs were faster than their two, and in a moment she was on them and her battle claw ripped into them.

'That is one ugly goat-fish-type-thing,' said the Doctor, running across the square towards a flight of steps that led up to the battlements.

'Wait!' It was Hammurabi, his face pale with shock. He

hurried up to the Doctor and gripped him by the shoulders. 'You said you could defeat the Beast. How? How do we do it? My army is ready, but –'

'Your army doesn't stand a chance,' said the Doctor grimly. 'Not against a thing like that. It's a Starman; it eats whole planets for breakfast.'

'Then how?'

The Doctor paused. He knew how. He had to get back to the TARDIS and get the orb, but there wasn't time for that. With every second the Starman would be drawing strength from the ground. Once it fully materialised not even the orb could stop it.

'It's too late . . .' he said, then laughed. It wasn't too late at all. The cavalry was arriving. Good old Ali. Flushed dark with fury, she was crawling down the outside of Hammurabi's palace like a big red cockroach, the orb held firm in her battle claw.

'Good girl!'

She was acting true to form. The female was the deadliest of her species. When the safety of the group was threatened, the females went into battle and wouldn't stop until their enemies were utterly destroyed.

8

Hammurabi's army had formed on the plain outside the high city walls: ranks of spearmen, bowmen, slingers and chariots. Camel riders trying to calm their nervous, snorting mounts. Officers shouting at the men to hold firm as the Starman advanced, spewing water to left and right.

'Coming through! Move aside!' The ranks parted as the Doctor, clinging to Ali's back and holding the silver orb with his free hand, charged through them.

This was too much for most of them and they dropped their weapons, trusting to prayer to get them through this insanity.

'Faster, Ali, faster,' cried the Doctor, and Ali speeded up. 'We've got no time left!'

Ahead of them, the enormous beast dipped its head, opened its jaws wide, showing the blackened stumps of teeth, and scooped up a section of the first two ranks of the army. It lifted its head, chewing, as men spilled out of its mouth and fell to the ground.

And behind it, Ali saw another shape and another, looming out of the black sky.

It was the twins.

'Doctor?'

'Just ignore them. The goat-fish must have ripped the dimensional wall and the other Starmen are following him through. Any minute now all of chaos is going to materialise, but if I can just get up there, to its mouth . . .'

Ali saw the great slug-like belly of the goat-fish, slithering forward along the ground, crushing trees and men beneath it as it came. Any moment now she too was going to be flattened if she wasn't careful.

She was battling her way through fleeing troops now as Hammurabi's army tried to get away from the Beast.

'Are you ready?' she yelled.

'No. But whatever you're going to do, just do it!'

Ali tensed her legs and with a grunt went into a Karkinian battle leap, flying through the air and landing halfway up the Starman's tail, where she gripped its scales with her strong clawed legs. The body of the Beast was hot, intensely hot, but her shell protected her and she began to climb.

'That's it!' The Doctor shouted his encouragement. 'Go on, girl!'

She was up on the Starman's back now, trying to ignore the gushing water. The Starman's scaly flesh was pitted with huge sores, out of which poked the heads of what looked like giant maggots. Ali worked her way around them as she crawled up, like a tick on a sheep, and made it to the right shoulder. At last the Starman seemed to be aware that there was something on it. It turned its goat's head, and its cold, dead eyes fell on the Doctor and Ali. It bared its teeth, opening its mouth wide, its slimy yellow tongue dripping saliva . . .

'Excuse me while I do the boogaloo!' shouted the Doctor, and he pulled back his arm and let fly with the orb, which sailed straight into the Beast's gaping black maw.

Ali felt an enormous wave of hot air slam into her. The heavens seemed to open in a flash of intense white light and she was falling, falling in a cloud of silver snowflakes.

9

The Doctor lay on his back, staring up at a palm tree. It was very peaceful. He could hear birds singing. He felt like he could stay like this forever and lose himself in the lovely deep blue of the sky.

'Doctor?'

Fat chance. There was always something to do, someone to deal with, a problem to solve, a world that needed saving. He lifted his head and it felt as heavy as a sack of potatoes, as if it might fall off and roll away down a hill. His vision blurred and swam, and when he managed to refocus there was Hammurabi leaning over him, with Zabaia and the three judges.

'I am sorry I doubted you,' said Hammurabi. 'You were right, Doctor.'

'I usually am,' said the Doctor, and he closed his eyes. 'Now go away, I'm sleeping.'

'We must write about you in our histories,' said Zabaia. 'What is your name?'

The Doctor sighed and hauled himself up on to his elbows, blinking. He felt like every bone in his body must have been broken, but he could move all his limbs and wiggle his toes. It had been a close thing, though. Too close.

'You go through Marduk's fifty names,' he said to Zabaia. 'You'll probably find my name in there somewhere.'

'Marduk?'

The Doctor grinned at Zabaia – actually more of a grimace; it hurt like Helios to move his face. He fought off a wave of nausea and faintness. The chief judge held out a hand to help him to his feet.

'Get away from him!'

'No, Ali . . .'

But there was no stopping her. Ali sliced her way through a line of soldiers, and then swung her claw at the judge who had no time to even scream before the pincers closed on him.

'You would have killed him,' Ali grunted. 'You and all the others. Now see how *you* like it.'

Ali dropped the judge, swatted Zabaia out of the way and advanced on Hammurabi, who collapsed to his knees, head bowed, hands gripped together.

'Ali . . . No . . .' The Doctor tried to stand, but swayed and felt consciousness slipping away. 'Stop. You've done enough. You have to stop. It's over . . .'

And at last Ali did stop. She picked the Doctor up and the last of her anger drained away. She looked around at the devastation, the bodies of the soldiers and the judge, Hammurabi on his knees in the dirt, quivering . . .

'Ali . . .' said the Doctor. 'I think it's time to go home.'

10

The TARDIS hummed and throbbed like the inside of the Doctor's head. He was still groggy. Still in pain. Still trying not to be angry with Ali, and with himself for giving in to her and bringing her along.

'I'm sorry,' she was saying, 'but they deserved their punishment. I should have killed them all.'

'You only did what you thought was right,' said the Doctor. 'This is why I usually take humans as my companions. They have . . . well, they have *humanity*. Not all of them, I'll give you that, but the ones I choose.'

Ali looked at the Doctor but said nothing.

'That's why I was reluctant to take you in the first place,' the Doctor went on. 'Not for your own safety, but for others. You Karkinians have a scary reputation, particularly the females, and having seen you in action I can see why. Remember what I told you when we first spoke, Ali? I'm not a warrior unless I have to be. It's not my way.'

'You killed the Starman.'

'I didn't kill him. I simply sent him back to where he can't do any harm.'

'But if I hadn't saved you –' There was bitterness in Ali's voice.

'I've somehow managed to survive for quite a long time without your help.'

'You ungrateful –'

'I'm sorry. I'm sorry. I'm sorry.' The Doctor put up his hands in surrender. 'You're right. Thanks. You *did* save me. Without you I'd have had to – I don't know – reboot again, or something, I suppose, and, yes, our goat-fish friend would probably have eaten the entire planet. So, yes, I will be eternally grateful to you. But your way, Ali . . . It's too risky. I wouldn't ever be able to go anywhere if I was worried you were going to go into a Karkinian war frenzy every time anyone looked at me funny.'

'I can't help it –'

'Exactly. That's my point. You're from Karkinos. I thought maybe you were different. You *are* special, I'll give you that. And you're nearly as clever as me, but you're also a warrior, and I can't ask you to change that, because that's what you were born to be. And the best place for you right now is back on Karkinos, looking after your family.'

'I gave those humans a fright, though, didn't I?' said Ali, and she chuckled. 'They won't forget me in a hurry.'

'They won't *ever* forget you, Ali. You're a star and you always will be. You'll be *their* star. They'll name a constellation after you, and add you to their zodiac along with the twins and the goat-fish. You're my A-star girl.'

11

The moons of Karkinos were strung out across the sky, shining their light over the surface of the lake, as beautiful as Ali remembered them. She was standing by the waterside, the eight feeding fingers round her mouth clutching at the night-scented air and wafting the smells across her scent filters.

The Doctor assured her that it was only a short while after they'd left, though to Ali it felt like a lifetime. Nothing had changed. Somewhere under the water were thousands of eggs. Her mum had laid a batch of thirty in the spring and when it was summer they'd hatch and those that survived would crawl out and find their families and it would be safe to go swimming again without disturbing them. Usually only three or four a year from each batch survived. Mostly males, but every few years a precious female would make it.

Ali thought of her twenty-three brothers and her one solitary sister, waiting for her at home. How had she ever thought she could go off with the Doctor and abandon her precious little Gilia?

It felt good to be home.

A curly lugeron swooped low over her head, whooping, its wings rattling as it twisted and spiralled into the trees.

'Well . . .'

The Doctor was standing in the doorway of the TARDIS. She could tell he was anxious to be gone. This was difficult for him. Saying goodbye.

'Where will you go now?' she asked.

'Wherever I'm needed, I suppose.'

'You are *so* pompous.'

'Yeah, I am, aren't I?' There was that mad grin of his, the one she'd grown to love. 'One man – off to save the universe!'

'Alone again, or . . .?'

'Alone for now.'

Ali moved closer to him, her feet sinking into the soft mud. How good it felt: cool and moist and full of life. 'You know that *girl*,' she said. 'The one you were telling me about? Rose Tyler?'

'What about her?'

'You should try again. Now you're free of the time tag.'

'I gave it my best, Ali. This life wasn't for her.'

'I didn't have you down as a quitter, Doctor.'

'It's too late.'

'Ha! You're a Time Lord!' Ali laughed at him. 'How can anything be too late? I thought time had no meaning in your infinite, immortal, immaterial box of tricks. *Too late*, indeed. You just get back there.'

'Ali . . .'

'No, listen. Us girls, we might all look different, but we're pretty similar underneath. We like to appear responsible, to do what's expected of us, we're not supposed to be reckless and wild and go running off with dodgy space tramps like you. But give us a nudge and –'

'Ali –'

'No. You go straight back there now and you ask her again. But you've got to offer her more than just – well – *you*. I mean, you're a *Time Lord*, but you're not all *that*. Sell it to her.'

Now the Doctor laughed.

'That's why I need a companion,' he said. 'To keep my feet on the ground, and my head out of the clouds. To keep me from myself. It's people like Rose, and crustaceans like you, Ali, who keep me going, who remind me that it's not all over and it's not all about me. My people may have gone, but you have your people . . . and Hammurabi had his people, and everyone has their own people. And every one of them is precious.'

'Go on then,' said Ali. 'What are you waiting for? We're done here. Hurry back. And don't mess up this time. She sounds very special, your Rose.'

'Oh, she is. I really think she is.'

Ali raised a claw and touched the Doctor on the cheek. His skin felt warm, dry . . . alien.

The Doctor looked at the claw and flexed his wrist.

'A long time ago, in a body far, far away, I had something like that,' he said. 'Though not on that scale.'

'Goodbye,' she said.

'I'll be seeing you,' he said.

'Will you?'

'I'm sure I will. When I need you most. When I need a mighty warrior.'

And he was right . . . In a moment the TARDIS was gone, its grating call snatched away on the swirling wind of its departure. Ali returned home and her planet spun on round its sun, one star among countless others, and the stars turned, and the universe grew older, step by infinite step, marching closer to its end, and at last he came back, the hounds of hell on his heels . . .

But that's another story.

The Doctor double-checked his time readings, his place readings and his face in the mirror. Practised a smile, a serious look, a sad face . . . settled on the smile, or at least the closest thing to a genuine human smile that he could manage. He took one last look around the TARDIS, made sure the old girl was looking – how would Rose put it? – *awesome*.

Yes. She was looking *well awesome*.

He pulled the lever that finalised the landing sequence and relished the familiar scraping noise of the TARDIS doing her thing. Then all was silent. He put the engine to sleep, closed down the systems and set the lights to an attractive warm orange glow. He realised he was still grinning and it was starting to hurt his face. *Not long now*. He took a deep breath and strode over to the door. Pulled it open.

He'd timed it just right. Rose was almost exactly where he'd left her, there, standing with Mickey, who was looking more than a little confused.

He grinned wider at Rose, relishing her surprise. He was a cheap magician sometimes, but it worked.

'By the way,' he said. 'Did I mention? It also travels in time.'

And he stepped back inside, leaving the door open. Was it

enough? Rose wasn't the type to fall for a hard sell, but had he undersold it?

From the shadows behind the open door he spied on her. Watched her turn to Mickey and say something, kiss him, and then she was running towards the TARDIS, her hair flying, and he knew that everything was going to be all right.

He had his new companion.

THE TENTH DOCTOR:
THE MYSTERY OF THE HAUNTED COTTAGE

DEREK LANDY

1

'Well now,' said the Doctor, looking at the monitor with widening eyes, 'this is interesting.'

Martha Jones hurried over to join him at the console while the TARDIS wheezed and whooshed around them. 'What is?' she asked, peering at the screen. 'Fog? What's interesting about fog? Where are we?'

'That's just it,' the Doctor said, speaking so low he was almost muttering. 'We're not where we could be.'

'Don't you mean we're not where we should be?'

'No. I mean what I say. We can't be here. We can't have landed here. Last time I passed this way, this was empty space.' He took his sonic screwdriver from his jacket – the brown pinstripe today, with the blue tie. He scanned the instruments and frowned. 'There's no malfunction,' he said. 'The readings are accurate, so this is definitely a planet. Breathable atmosphere, too.'

The scanner readings meant nothing to Martha, and the monitor still showed fog. 'When did you last pass here?' she asked. 'Maybe the planet was destroyed in the intervening years, or shifted its orbit or something.'

The Doctor was too caught up in his own thoughts to

answer, so Martha sighed, grabbed her jacket and pulled it on as she strode to the door. She knew him well enough by now to realise that he was going to go outside anyway.

She turned the latch, and the Doctor snapped his head round. 'Martha, wait –'

She opened the door and stepped out, and her head swam for just a moment. When it cleared, the fog was gone. 'Huh,' she said.

The Doctor joined her. Sunshine, green grass, blue skies. A few white fluffy clouds. Birds sang. It was close to midday, judging by the position of the single sun.

Martha looked around. 'That fog disappeared fast.'

The Doctor didn't respond. Instead, he started walking up the nearest hill, following the sound of voices. They got to the top and saw four children walking towards them – two girls and two boys, all around eleven or twelve. The tallest boy carried a picnic basket, and they were dressed like they belonged in the 1950s – on Earth.

'Hello there,' the Doctor said, smiling brightly.

The children stopped without looking at him and frowned, like they'd heard something from far away.

Martha stepped in front of them, waving her hand. 'Hello? Yoo-hoo? Can you see us?'

The tallest boy's eyes moved, found her waving hand and focused. Then he looked up, saw her and smiled. 'Oh, hello!'

'Hi,' Martha said.

Now the others were looking at her and the Doctor, and they were smiling, too.

'Gosh, new people!' said the dark-haired girl. 'We haven't seen new people in simply ages! What are your names?'

There was something about her face that snagged on Martha's memory. All of their faces, actually. 'I'm Martha,' she said, 'and this is the Doctor.'

'Hello, Martha,' they all said together. 'Hello, Doctor.'

Martha gave them a smile and glanced back. 'This is kind of weird, isn't it?'

'Very,' the Doctor said. 'Where are you children off to?'

'We're having a picnic!' the smallest girl said proudly. 'Mother and Father usually come with us, but this year they said we were old enough to go by ourselves! We've never come this far down the path, however. I do so hope we'll be able to find our way back!'

'We should be able to,' the smallest boy said. 'It's a straight path.'

'We'll let you get back to your picnic, then,' the Doctor said, and they were immediately assailed by a chorus of spirited goodbyes that actually made Martha take a step backwards. And the next moment the children were walking again, and chatting and laughing among themselves as if they had never been interrupted. The path they were on continued down the hill, swerved gently round an old country cottage and disappeared into the woodland behind. The whole thing looked like a painting on a cheap postcard, and with the kids in the foreground it reminded Martha of . . .

'The Troubleseekers,' she said.

The Doctor looked at her. 'I'm sorry?'

'The books. The Troubleseekers books. Have you never read them?'

'The Troubleseekers,' the Doctor said. 'Thirty-two children's books, written by Annette Billingsley over the course of fifteen years from 1951. No, never read them. They were rubbish. Rip-off of the Famous Five and the Secret Seven. Ah, Enid Blyton. I met her once, you know. Odd woman. Unusual ears.'

'Well,' Martha said, speaking quickly before the Doctor could go off on another one of his tangents, 'I read the Troubleseekers. I devoured them. From the Troubleseekers Oath printed on the title page to the list of the other books at the back – I read every little bit. And this – this *here* – is the cover of *The Mystery of the Haunted Cottage*. It's the first one I ever read. This house, this angle, this time of day . . . everything. And those kids. I know them all. The tallest one is Humphrey; he's the no-nonsense leader. The girl with the dark hair is Joanne, but she insists on everyone calling her Jo because she's the tomboy. Then there's Simon; he's always trying to prove himself, so he gets into the most trouble. And the youngest is Gertie. She makes scones lathered with jam.'

'Jam-lathered scones. I see.'

'And they're usually shadowed by . . . ah, there he is.' She nodded to a nearby tree where a child was hiding, peeking out at them occasionally. 'The little fat boy.'

The Doctor raised an eyebrow.

'What?' Martha said defensively, keeping her voice down. 'That's how he was described in the books. Don't blame me. This was 1951. Everything back then was blinkered, sexist and ever-so-slightly racist. It was a backward time.'

'Ah, yes,' said the Doctor, 'because 2007 has none of those things.'

Martha ignored him. 'The little . . . *overweight* child wanted to join the Troubleseekers, but he'd always prove too annoying, and every time they'd send him away he'd run off and tattle on them. What was his name, though? It's on the tip of my tongue. It was a nickname, something everyone called him, even his aunt and uncle . . .'

The Doctor sighed. 'Was it Fatty, by any chance?'

'That's it,' said Martha, nodding. 'Fatty. Yes, that's him.'

'Children can be so cruel,' the Doctor said. 'Children's writers can be even worse.'

'Doctor,' Martha said, having no other choice but to ask the question, 'are we . . . are we in a book?'

'We're not in a book. We can't be in a book.' The Doctor looked around. 'We might be in a book.' He started walking. Martha followed.

'How is that possible?'

'It's happened before,' he said. Then shrugged. 'Well, sort of. Long time ago. Well, not that long, relatively speaking, and since time is relative, relatively speaking is how we speak, is it not?' The Doctor plucked a daisy as he walked, held it up to the sun, examining it. 'It was essentially a pocket universe where fictional characters were real. I met all sorts of people. Gulliver, Cyrano de Bergerac, the Three Musketeers, Medusa. Even Rapunzel. However . . .'

'However?'

'Travelling to the Land of Fiction meant leaving our own universe, and we haven't done that.'

'How can you tell?'

He stopped walking and let the daisy drop. 'The air tastes funny in other universes. Like boiled cabbage and wet dog. So, we're not in the Land of Fiction, but we do seem to be in a land replicating a *work* of fiction. Can you remember how this particular story ended?'

'Sorry,' said Martha. 'You read more than three Troubleseekers books and they all blur into one big rose-tinted mess.'

'Excellent,' the Doctor said, beaming. 'Then we'll get to solve this one for ourselves. Come along.'

They walked down the hill after the Troubleseekers, who didn't even look round at the sound of their footsteps. Not the most alert kids ever, in Martha's opinion. Maybe the Doctor was right. Maybe the books *were* absolute rubbish.

Martha didn't care. She *had* loved them when she was younger. After the Troubleseekers and stuff like that it was all Harry Potter and His Dark Materials and then she was reading adult books and trying out the classics . . . but the Troubleseekers is where it all began.

She glanced behind them. Fatty was following, running from tree to bush to tree, doing his best to keep out of sight and failing miserably. She suddenly felt sorry for him, this poor kid desperately wanting to be part of the Troubleseekers.

'Let's stop here for our picnic!' announced Humphrey.

'Oh yes, let's!' squealed Gertie.

'I'm famished!' cried Jo.

'Spiffo!' yelled Simon.

'Seven hells,' muttered the Doctor.

'Simon, we'll put the blanket down,' said Humphrey. 'Girls, you start unpacking the basket, and then we'll all tuck in!'

Martha stood beside the Doctor and they watched the children settle down to a feast of scones and jam and ginger beer and apples and cakes and ham sandwiches and more cakes and pies and Cornish pasties and custard tarts. Gertie and Jo took so much food out of the basket that Martha began to suspect it had some TARDIS qualities of its own.

'I'm hungry,' she said.

'We should have brought our own picnic,' the Doctor responded, nodding.

'Those cakes look delicious.'

'Don't they? And I've never wanted a ginger beer more than I do right now.'

Something caught the Doctor's eye and he started walking. Martha let her gaze linger on some jam tarts that looked like the nicest jam tarts ever baked, then she turned away from the Troubleseekers and Fatty and reluctantly followed. There was an elderly woman on an old-fashioned bike cycling towards them. She had grey hair, a floral dress with a light cardigan over it, and a contented smile on her face.

The Doctor stood in the middle of the path, hands on hips with his legs wide apart. The old woman continued to cycle.

'Um,' Martha said.

A butterfly passed in front of the old woman, and she turned her head and watched it flutter.

'Hello,' Martha said loudly. 'Hello? We're standing here. Hello!'

'It's going to take her a moment to register our presence,' the Doctor said. 'We don't belong in this story, after all.'

The woman kept up her slow pedalling rhythm and got closer and closer. Only at the last moment did her eyes focus, and she saw the Doctor standing in her way. She squealed and twisted the handlebars, veered off the path and plummeted down the hill. Martha ran up to the Doctor, and they watched the old woman topple off the bike with a panicked squawk and roll to the bottom of the hill, where she came to a gentle, sprawling stop.

'Are you OK?' Martha called out.

'I'm fine,' the Doctor said. 'She didn't even hit me.'

Martha glared, then hurried down to the old woman just as she was sitting up.

'Be careful,' Martha said. 'You might be injured.'

The old woman looked around, frowning, and stared at Martha for a few moments before she saw her. A shaky smile broke out. 'Oh, don't you worry about me, dear. I've taken worse tumbles in my time, and I dare say I'll take worse again. But if you could help me to my feet I'd be ever so grateful.'

Martha got behind her and lifted her up as the Doctor joined them, wheeling the bike by his side.

'Look what I found,' he said cheerily.

'That's my bicycle!' said the old woman. 'Thank you so much, young man.'

'Oh, it's the least I could do,' the Doctor said, all charm and smiles. 'I'm the Doctor; this is Martha. You are . . .?'

'Mrs O'Grady,' said the old woman. 'How do you do?'

'Mrs O'Grady,' the Doctor repeated. 'You wouldn't happen to have a first name, would you?'

'Yes I do,' said Mrs O'Grady. 'Mrs.'

'What a fully developed character you must be,' the Doctor said, raising a sceptical eyebrow at Martha.

She ignored him. 'Do you live nearby?' she asked, and the old woman nodded.

'I live in the next cottage over.'

'Then maybe you can help us,' the Doctor said. 'There's a mystery to solve somewhere around here and we can't find it. Admittedly we've only just started looking, but you seem to be someone who could know where it might be.'

'A mystery?' said Mrs O'Grady. 'Heavens no, I'm afraid I can't help you. I try my best to stay away from mysteries, young man. Terrible things, they are. They lead to all sorts of . . . answers.' A shiver ran through her.

'Indeed,' said the Doctor. 'So you haven't noticed anything unusual?'

'Unusual?'

'Odd goings-on,' said Martha. 'Unexplained happenings. Noises. Criminal behaviour. Anything out of the ordinary?'

'No,' said Mrs O'Grady. 'Nothing. Apart from the strange lights in the woods.'

'Strange lights?' the Doctor said.

'In the woods?' Martha said.

'Oh yes,' said Mrs O'Grady. 'Every night I see strange lights floating through the trees. There are a lot of people saying it's ghosts, but I don't believe in ghosts. I finally came to the conclusion that they were strange lights.'

The Doctor frowned. 'That was your conclusion?'

'Yes.'

'That satisfied you?'

'Of course,' said Mrs O'Grady. 'Because that's what they are. Strange lights.'

The Doctor looked her up and down. 'What is it like, being you?' he murmured. 'What is it like to have such limited curiosity?'

'I get by,' Mrs O'Grady said, chuckling.

'You never thought about investigating them?' Martha asked.

'No,' Mrs O'Grady said, her eyes widening, like the very question filled her with horror. 'You take my word for it; nothing good can come from going into those woods at night. Strange lights mean strange things. And who would want strange things apart from strange people? And we're not strange people, are we?'

Martha hesitated and looked at the Doctor.

The Doctor smiled. 'No,' he said. 'We're not strange people at all.'

They left Mrs O'Grady to continue on her merry little way, and Martha followed the Doctor to the haunted cottage. Now that she could see it up close, it didn't look remotely haunted. It was kind of nice, actually. It was pretty and painted white and it had a thick thatch roof.

'First rule of being a detective,' the Doctor said as he knocked on the door, 'is to observe. Observe the obvious, and observe the not-so-obvious. Observing the not-so-obvious is not as easy as observing the obvious, but if it were easy everyone would be at it.'

The door opened. Martha observed that a man in his forties stood there. She observed that his face was long and that his moustache was neatly maintained.

'Can I help you?' he asked.

'Hello,' the Doctor said, grinning broadly and pumping the man's hand in the most enthusiastic handshake Martha had ever observed. 'This is Martha Jones, and I'm the Doctor. Very pleased to meet you. You must be someone important to be working here. A red herring, perhaps? Or the villain of the piece? No, no, don't tell me – let me figure it out. Your name?'

The man did his best to get his hand back. 'Cotterill,' he said, somewhat sniffily. 'I'm the caretaker here.'

'The caretaker,' the Doctor said, eyes wide in wonder. 'In that case it is *doubly* good to meet you.' He turned to Martha. 'Caretakers and butlers. Watch out for them.'

Martha adopted a smile that was far less manic. 'Mr Cotterill, we were wondering if we could ask you a few questions about the strange lights in the woods.'

Immediately Cotterill's face tightened. 'Strange lights? What strange lights? There's nothing strange about lights. They're lights. What's so strange about a light?'

'What are they doing in the woods?'

'I never said I saw them in the woods. I never said I knew what you were talking about. What are you talking about? Strange? Lights? Woods? What? I'm the caretaker. I take care of the cottage and the grounds. Not the woods. Not any strange lights. Not that there are any. But if there were some, I wouldn't know about them. And I don't, because there aren't.' His face twitched. 'Any.'

The Doctor smiled again. 'I don't find you suspicious at all.' He turned to Martha and whispered, 'I find him incredibly suspicious.'

'I heard that,' said Cotterill.

'You were meant to,' said the Doctor, rounding on him. 'I was lulling you into a false sense of security. Now that you are sufficiently lulled, I will increase the intensity of my interrogation. Mr Cotterill, these allegedly strange lights in the woods you keep referring to – what are they?'

'I don't know what you're –'

'Answer the question, Mr Cotterill,' the Doctor said, suddenly angry. 'The lights. In the woods. The strange ones. What are they?'

'I don't know!'

'So you admit they exist!'

'What? No!'

'Are you responsible for the lights, Mr Cotterill? Do you know who is? What is your agenda? What do you want? What are you after? What are you *hiding*, Mr Cotterill, if that *is* your real name? Answer the question, Mr Cotterill!'

'It is!'

'It . . .' The Doctor stopped and blinked. 'Right, I've lost track of what question that was an answer to.'

'Mr Cotterill,' Martha said, smiling as she stepped forward, 'could I ask you something? As caretaker, have you ever witnessed anything . . . unusual? Unusual activity, unusual occurrences, unusual visitors?'

'You mean like you two?'

'Like us,' Martha said, nodding, 'but more so.'

'No,' Cotterill said emphatically. 'Apart from the two of you, I have not seen anything unusual, especially not ghosts.'

'We never mentioned ghosts.'

'Good!' Cotterill said. 'Because there's no such thing! Superstition, that's all that is! Now if you will excuse me, I have a lot of work to do!' He stepped back and slammed the door.

'I'm not sure,' Martha said. 'Did that go well or not?'

'That went brilliantly,' the Doctor said, beaming. 'Now what do you say we go investigate those woods?'

2

The woods didn't require a whole lot of investigating. It was all oaks and birches and ashes and dappled sunlight and bushes and moss – everything that went into making up a woodland was present and accounted for. But it did have one other feature that Martha reckoned could be a clue – a network of ropes spanning the gaps between branches high overhead. She may not have remembered anything about *The Mystery of the Haunted Cottage* apart from the cover, but she did remember that most of the clues in the Troubleseekers books were fairly obvious. The Doctor barely glanced up, however. He was too busy looking down.

'Have you seen these ropes?' Martha asked. 'They're a clue, aren't they? I'm observing them, like you told me to, and they have *got* to be a clue. Right?'

The Doctor murmured something, then started walking into the undergrowth. Martha sighed, and followed.

They walked until they met a steep incline, and the Doctor made straight for a tangle of bushes. He pulled them apart far too easily. Martha caught up with him, and saw a rusted iron door built into the earth. The Doctor seized the handle and opened the door.

'A secret passageway!' he said.

Martha frowned. 'Looks dark. Creepy. Lots of cobwebs.'

The Doctor grinned. 'Want to investigate?'

'Nope. No. The ropes are our clues. We should concentrate on them.'

'Oh, come on! The ropes are boring clues! When was the last time we investigated a secret passageway?'

'We're always investigating passageways.'

'Not secret ones! Come on, Martha! The Troubleseekers would investigate. I think you owe it to your childhood self to do this. Didn't you say something about taking the Troubleseeker Oath?'

'I didn't take it. It was written on the first page of every book.'

'Did you read it?'

'Yes, I read it, but that doesn't mean I –'

'Can you remember it? Can you recite it for me? I'd love to hear it.'

Martha frowned. 'Um . . . yeah. I think so. Let's see . . . *I hereby swear to seek out trouble, wherever mysteries boil and secrets bubble. I won't tell adults until the crime is solved, and report back to my friends at the double.*'

'It rhymes!' the Doctor said, delighted. 'More or less. It doesn't flow particularly well, but it has words that rhyme and so it is a binding contract.'

'What do you mean it's a binding –' Martha started, and then shut up. The Doctor's grin grew wider.

'You spoke it aloud, you took the oath,' he said. 'That's how oaths work. Splendid. Let's go exploring.'

The stone steps were slippery with damp as they descended into darkness. Martha kept one hand out in front, splayed against the Doctor's back, and the other trailing along the cold wall.

'Of all the things your screwdriver can do,' she whispered, 'why on Earth is a torch not among them?'

'Because it's a sonic screwdriver,' the Doctor whispered back, 'not a laser spanner. The next screwdriver I design, though, that *will* have a torch. I promise.'

Below them, the darkness turned to gloom, then to grey, and gradually Martha's eyes adjusted to pick out details around her. She heard voices, low and muffled, and the light splashing of water. They got to the bottom of the steps and peered round the corner. Three men stood by an underground canal, loading wooden crates on to a boat tied up to a small wharf.

'They look like smugglers,' she whispered.

'I know,' said the Doctor. 'Brilliant, isn't it?' He took her arm and stepped out from hiding before she could protest. 'Hello there!'

The three men spun round. One of them dropped a crate in surprise. It burst open and gold coins spilled out, some of them dropping into the canal.

'Doing a spot of smuggling, are we?' the Doctor asked, stuffing his hands in his pockets as he strolled forward. 'Can't beat it on a sunny day, can you? There's nothing I'd rather be doing on a sunny day than scurrying about down here in the dark, indulging in the illegal transport of some presumably stolen goods.'

The biggest smuggler, and by far the ugliest, was the first to focus his gaze. His eyes flickered from the Doctor to Martha, and back to the Doctor. 'You coppers, then?'

'Us?' the Doctor said. 'Coppers?' He puffed out his chest. 'Yes, actually we are. Well, sort of. Well, not really. But if you want to see us as the living embodiment of justice and the primary moral laws, then who am I to argue? Who am I, indeed? Who are you, for that matter? Does it matter? Probably not. I doubt you have interesting backstories anyway, and your motivations are most likely ill thought out to begin with. But, again, who am I to judge?'

'What is this?' the shortest one said. 'What are you doing down here? What do you want?'

'We're investigators,' said the Doctor. 'Amateur sleuths, if you will. Well, I say amateur . . . She's a Troubleseeker. She took the oath and everything. But me? I'm just a man. A man with good hair and a great screwdriver. Do you mind?'

Without waiting for an answer, the Doctor took out the sonic screwdriver, scanned the crates and checked the results. He grunted.

'What is it?' Martha asked.

'Exactly what it appears to be,' the Doctor said. 'Crates of gold coins, hundreds of years old. Spanish, I reckon. Are they? Yes. This is interesting. This is very interesting.'

'We found 'em,' said the smallest smuggler. 'We found 'em when we were on the run, and we hid 'em in various spots around the woods. But there were four of us originally, and when we were rearrested the fourth . . . well, he died. And he was the only one who knew where the rest of the crates were buried. So we've been lookin' for –'

'Don't care,' the Doctor said, moving past all three of them to stand on the edge of the wharf. He scanned the area with the screwdriver.

The smugglers looked confused. The smallest one looked back to Martha. 'Don't you want to know what we've been up to?'

'Not really,' she admitted. 'Sorry. I'm sure it's very interesting. If you're eight years old.'

The smugglers looked at each other.

'Are you . . . are you going to try and stop us?' the biggest one asked.

'Don't know,' said Martha. 'You're not harming anyone, are you?' When they all shook their heads, she shrugged. 'Then carry on. Don't mind us.'

The smugglers hesitated, then slowly picked up the spilled coins and resumed the loading of the crates on to the boat. Martha walked up beside the Doctor.

'Anything?'

He looked deeper into the dark tunnel. 'There's something down there,' he said. 'Something that needs investigating.' He lowered his voice. 'We'll need a boat, though.'

They looked at each other and turned. The smugglers were staring at them.

'You really need to work on your whispering,' Martha murmured.

'Gentlemen,' the Doctor said, smiling again, 'slight change of plans. As you have heard, yes, we do need to commandeer your boat. We understand that you have waited a long time to retrieve this gold, and we sincerely regret any inconvenience caused.'

'Sincerely,' said Martha.

'But our investigation must take priority, I'm afraid. Let me assure you, however, that when we are done we will return this boat to you in tip-top condition, or whatever condition it happens to be in when we're done with it. All cards on the table, it'll probably sink.'

'Probably,' said Martha.

'You ain't taking our boat,' said the big smuggler. 'Not without a fight.'

The Doctor shook his head. 'Ah, no, violence really isn't my thing. Unless it's swords. Do you have swords? No? Ah. Running is my thing, to be honest. Give me a corridor to run down and I will run down that corridor like nobody's business. How about a race? Winner takes the boat.'

The smallest smuggler cracked his knuckles. 'No race,' he said. 'Violence.'

'Hmm,' said the Doctor. 'So that's two votes for violence. What about you, sir? You haven't spoken up yet. It's three votes or nothing, let's all agree on that. Has to be unanimous. Sir? Violence or race?'

The middle smuggler looked up. 'Neither. If you can beat me in a match of wits, you can borrow the boat.' With a grand flourish, he gestured towards a low table on which sat a chessboard.

'How convenient!' the Doctor said happily. 'Martha, am I to understand that one of the Troubleseekers is a chess player?'

She nodded. 'Humphrey. He was taught by his grandfather.'

'Well, that's not contrived at all! I accept your challenge, sir: a match of wits it is! You go first, I insist.'

The middle smuggler sat at the chessboard, rubbed his chin thoughtfully, and the moment he picked up a piece to move it the Doctor said, 'Checkmate.'

The middle smuggler looked up. 'What?'

'Checkmate,' the Doctor repeated, stepping into the boat. 'I win. I won the moment you sat down. I won the moment you mentioned it. I won the moment the great-great-great-nephew of the Maharaja Sri Gupta introduced me to the game, back when it was called *chaturanga*.' He took Martha's hand, steadying her while she joined him, then untied the mooring rope.

The middle smuggler stood up. 'You can't win without playing.'

'But of course I can,' said the Doctor, picking up the long wooden pole. 'My winning is inevitable, and since it is inevitable what's the point of playing? I've never lost a chess game. Well, I lost once, to a mechanical dog, but that barely counts. You stay right where you are and we'll be back in a tick. Hopefully.'

They left the smugglers standing there, open-mouthed, and Martha resisted the urge to wave. She sat on the seat while the Doctor stood before her, using the pole to push them along.

'I've never been on a gondola before,' she said, smiling. 'It's kind of romantic.'

'Not a gondola,' the Doctor said without looking back. 'It's a punt.'

The smile faded. 'Right.'

The canal was lit by flickering torches in rusted brackets that were hammered into the brick walls on either side. Martha peered into the dark water, watching leaves and broken twigs float by. It was cold down here.

'So how do you think the smugglers fit into the mystery?' she asked.

'Mystery?' the Doctor said. 'There is no mystery. The mystery's been solved. Cotterill's the villain.'

'He is?'

'Of course he is. I've shaken hands with caretakers – they work hard, and they've got the calluses to prove it. Mr Cotterill's hands were callused in all the wrong places, and there was old scarring round his wrist. Handcuffs, on far too tight for far too long. He's the fourth smuggler, the one the others thought had died. He's already rounded up the gold he hid, but he's still searching for the gold hidden by his old partners-in-crime. He wants to keep it all to himself, the sly little fox. The lights in the woods were to scare people away while he searched – lanterns on pulleys to get people talking about ghosts. It's all so disappointingly rubbish.'

'It seemed pretty good when I was eight,' said Martha, a little hotly.

'If it was good,' the Doctor said, 'you would have remembered the story. Ah, now *this* is interesting . . .'

Martha craned her neck. The water stopped ahead of them. The tunnel stopped. The bricks and the light stopped. It wasn't blackness ahead; it was emptiness. It was devoid of actual colour. It was devoid of matter.

Martha slumped. 'I feel sick.'

'Don't look at it,' said the Doctor.

A buzzing sensation filled Martha's brain, numbing her thoughts. 'My head hurts . . .'

There was no disturbance in the water, no wild rocking, no whooshing of air. The emptiness wasn't sucking them in. It was just . . . there. The Doctor moved the pole in front, jammed it down, stopping them from getting too close.

'Interesting,' he murmured. 'It feels like my brain is trying to leak out through my eyes.'

Martha turned her head away and immediately her thoughts began to clear. 'What is it?'

She heard the excited whirr of the sonic screwdriver.

'It's nothing,' said the Doctor after a moment. 'Literally, it's nothing. It's a pocket of nothingness, down here below the surface. It's like someone took an ice-cream scoop and scooped out a piece of reality. Marvellous. Terrifying, but marvellous. Do my thoughts sound weird to you? They sound weird to me. They sound old, and cracked.'

'We're not going to go into it, are we?'

'No we are not,' the Doctor said, urgency creeping into his voice as he changed his stance and started to push them back the way they'd come. 'As beings of matter, as beings of good and solid reality, any contact with that nothingness would presumably lead to an extreme case of non-existence. And I don't know about you, Martha Jones, but I'd hate to non-exist. The universe would miss me. I know it would.'

Martha sat up a bit straighter, the strength returning to her body. 'I feel better.'

'Me, too,' said the Doctor.

She kept her eyes on the water as the last of the buzzing left her mind. Back to normal, she let her gaze sharpen in the gloom and immediately frowned. 'Do you see that?'

'See what?'

'There.' She pointed. 'In the water. See?'

'What is it?' the Doctor asked.

She peered closer. 'Is it . . . is that a person? Hey, whoever you are, standing in the water. We can see you.'

'Are you sure that's a person?'

'That's obviously a head. You can see the shoulders. Hey, you. Hello?'

The boat slowed. Martha narrowed her eyes, trying to pick out features. It *looked* like a head. It was head-*shaped*. She was sure that it was a head. Even though she couldn't see any ears, or hair . . . and it wasn't moving.

'It might not be a head –' she conceded, and then a figure burst up from the water beside her, half-landed in the boat and grabbed her arm.

The boat bucked and the Doctor cried out. Martha screamed as the figure tried to pull itself in, or pull her out, or whatever it was trying to do, and around them there were more figures, surging forward, gripping the boat, nearly tipping it over. Martha tore her arm from the figure's hand, fell back and planted her boot right in its face as it tried to clamber on board. It fell back, splashing into the water. The boat lurched violently and the Doctor fell on top of her.

'Sorry, sorry,' he muttered as they figured out which arms and legs belonged to whom, and when Martha regained her bearings she became aware of how fast the boat was moving in the wrong direction.

The Doctor looked up, his eyes wide. 'They're pushing us into the nothing.'

He lunged for the pole, but it vanished over the side. Martha glanced up, saw the nothing over the Doctor's shoulder and felt that buzz cloud her thoughts again. She whipped her head away and scrambled to her feet.

'What are you doing?' the Doctor called, but she was already putting one foot on the stern, and then she leaped off, over the heads of the dark figures. She splashed into the cold water, submerged for a moment, then got her feet under her and stood up, breaking the surface and gasping. The water only came up to her shoulders. She looked back in time to see the Doctor splashing down next to her.

'Good plan,' he spluttered.

The figures let the boat carry on into the nothing, and turned silently. They had sunken depressions for eyes, another for a mouth and a slight bump for a nose. They started walking back towards Martha and the Doctor, arms outstretched.

Martha dived, arms cutting through the water, legs kicking out behind. She glimpsed the Doctor swimming behind her.

She reached the wharf and hauled herself out of the canal. The Doctor did the same.

The smugglers were gone.

3

They ran back to the steps and climbed them quickly, Martha leading the way. She burst through the door at the top, out into bright sunlight filtering through the trees. She was dripping wet and shivering. The Doctor followed her out, shut the door and used the screwdriver to lock it.

'What were those things?' Martha asked.

'Haven't the foggiest,' the Doctor said, his wet hair hanging over his eyes. He took her arm and led her through the trees. 'I'm assuming they didn't pop up in the book?'

'I think I would have remembered *them*.'

'It was almost as if that were an unfinished section. No one had bothered to venture down there in the book, so what's the point of there being anything down there at all? Everything here is artifice. It's here for show, but there's nothing real or substantial about it.'

'You mean like set dressing in a play?'

He snapped his head to her, suddenly smiling. 'That's exactly what I mean. Oh, you *are* smart. Not as smart as me but, well . . . who is? Set dressing. To the audience it looks like buildings and trees, but behind the scenes it's all propped up with bits of wood. We're standing on a stage, Martha.'

'One designed to look like an old children's book from Earth? Bit random, isn't it?'

The Doctor frowned, pulled the sonic screwdriver from his jacket and started scanning everything in range.

'What are you doing?' Martha asked.

The Doctor made some unintelligible sounds as he darted to and fro, getting more and more excited as he scanned. He burst through the treeline on to the grass, into the bright and warm sunlight. Martha hurried after him. She could feel herself starting to dry out already.

'Wa-hey,' he said, eyes wide. 'Wa-hey!'

'Doctor?'

'Martha!'

'Doctor, please tell me you know what's going on.'

The screwdriver vanished back inside his jacket. 'I might know,' he said, sweeping his wet hair off his face. 'It's possible I might know. I have an idea. But I don't know how . . . Well, I suppose if . . . Unless . . . No. Yes. Really? Yes!'

'Doctor?'

He whirled round, his hair sticking out at crazy angles. 'This, Martha Jones, this, all around us. I don't think this is real.'

'But you said it was real. You said everything scanned as real.'

'Well, yes, but there is real and then there's *real*, you know?'

'No, I don't.'

'What are we but our senses, Martha? Our eyes tell us we are standing on a flat surface, we can feel the ground beneath our feet, but what if our senses are lying to us? Take away our ability to touch, taste, hear, see and smell, and doesn't our world change accordingly?'

'Yeah,' said Martha slowly, 'except it doesn't, does it? Take away our senses and we're right where we were a moment ago, only now we don't have our senses.'

He looked at her. 'You take all the fun out of philosophy, you know that?'

'I'm a medical student,' said Martha. 'I deal in facts. I see an ailment; I fix it. Explain this to me in practical terms.'

'That's just it – I don't think I can. This entire planet seems to be an idea, a concept made solid.'

'So this whole entire world that we're standing on right now is . . . what? A story? Not a planet at all but a story? How can we stand on a story? How can a story have gravity, or light, or air for us to breathe?'

The Doctor shrugged. 'Every good story has atmosphere.'

'I'm . . . I'm going to do you a favour and pretend you didn't just say that.'

'Close your eyes.'

'Why?'

'Martha . . .'

'Fine,' she said, and closed her eyes.

'Picture yourself as a particle of dust floating in space,' the Doctor said as he circled her slowly. 'Around you, stars are born and die. Planets orbit. Meteors pass, asteroids drift, and every so often, if you're really, really lucky, there is a flare of distant life.'

'Am I lonely?' Martha asked.

'You're a particle of dust,' the Doctor said. 'Of course you're not lonely.'

'I sound lonely.'

'Well you're not; you're having a great time. So there you

are, in space, all this stuff going on, and someone comes along with an agenda. Someone comes along with a purpose. Let's call him . . . Bob. And purpose, to a little particle of dust like you, is this wonderful, wonderful new thing that you can't get enough of. And so you're pulled into Bob's purpose, and you swirl around with all the other particles of dust and all the other minute elements of the cosmos, and suddenly you're part of something bigger. You're part of an idea. And you grow and grow and when you've finished growing you realise that you have *become* the idea.'

'Can I open my eyes now?'

'Sure.'

Martha looked at him. He was standing on a log, looking around. While her eyes were closed he'd fixed his hair. 'So you're saying Bob made this entire world out of willpower and dust.'

'Essentially.'

'So why, for God's sake *why*, did he make it into a Troubleseekers book?'

'I don't think he did,' said the Doctor. 'Our senses are telling us we're in a Troubleseekers book, my senses are telling me that my *sonic screwdriver* is telling me we're in a Troubleseekers book, but I'd assume different people from different cultures are being exposed to different sensory information.'

'So it looks like this for us because I read these books? But I've read a lot more, and a lot better, than Troubleseekers. Why did it pick this? And *you* haven't read these books, so how come you're seeing what I'm seeing?'

The Doctor jumped down off the log. 'This world must

be able to only take one form at a time. It picked a series of stories that have been in your memory for the longest period. Maybe it's because you were the first one out of the TARDIS. If I had been first out, we could be in an ancient Gallifreyan fairy tale right now.'

'That sounds nice.'

'Not really,' the Doctor said. 'Our fairy tales had teeth.'

'So who is Bob? How do we find out who's behind this?'

'Elementary, my dear Jones,' the Doctor said, sticking his hands in his pockets. 'We use our powers of deduction. We already have our list of suspects.'

'You think it's one of the characters?'

'A being capable of forming an entire world around fiction. Do you really think such a being could resist inserting themselves into the story?'

'Fair enough . . . but who is it? If it were me, then I'd make myself into either the hero or the villain. And seeing how the heroes are a group of insufferable kids, I'd say it's the villain. So Bob is Cotterill.'

'Do you have proof? This is a mystery. You must have proof. What have you observed about him?'

'Uh, well, he is . . . he has a moustache and . . . he's a smuggler, we know that much. He's just like the others. Except . . .'

'Except?'

Martha frowned. 'Except he saw us. He saw us immediately. Everyone else here needs a moment to focus on us. But not him. He's *not* like the others. He's just pretending to be.'

The Doctor smiled. 'I knew you had it in you, Martha Jones.'

'But why did those things try to kill us? We haven't done anything yet.'

'Maybe we've strayed too far from the story. We went where we weren't supposed to go, after all. So those things . . .'

'They could be this planet's immune system,' Martha finished. 'An infection was detected in a vulnerable area, and these creepy little soldiers were sent out to stop us.'

'Precisely. We reached the edge and kept pushing. You'd be surprised how many people reckon I'm far more trouble than I'm worth.'

Martha gave a non-committal shrug, then got back to business. 'So what are we going to do? The smart thing would be get back to the TARDIS and get away from here, but I know you're not going to do that.'

He raised his eyebrow at her. 'You think you know me so well, don't you? I happen to think that's a wonderful idea. We don't know what we're dealing with here, and it's like I always say: it's better to be safe than sorry.'

Martha frowned again. 'I know I've only been travelling with you for a few months, but I have, literally, never heard you say that.'

'Nonsense. I say it all the time.'

She shook her head. 'Never once.'

'You might have been in the other room when I've said it,' said the Doctor, 'but I've said it, and I've said it a lot.'

'When was the last time you said it?'

'Last week. At the . . . ooh, I remember. It was with the thing. Well, four things. Well, four things and a lizard. I said it then. It's not my fault if you – Oi.'

Martha looked round and saw Fatty hiding in the bushes. The little fat boy's eyes widened when he realised he'd been spotted, and he squealed and ran off.

'He really *is* annoying,' Martha muttered.

'Actually,' said the Doctor, 'he's exactly what we need.'

She looked at him. 'You knew he was there.'

'Of course. And now he's gone off to tattle on us, to let his master know we're about to leave. That should stir him into the big reveal.'

'Oh, you *are* clever.'

'What have I been telling you? Come on.'

4

They left the woods and started walking back towards the TARDIS. At the corner of the cottage, Cotterill stood with one of the featureless creatures. They were waiting for them.

'Here we go,' the Doctor murmured, sauntering up. Martha followed.

'Leaving before the story is over?' Cotterill said, a smile on his face. 'I must admit, I'm a little disappointed in you.'

The Doctor smiled back, hands in his pockets once again. 'Hoping for everyone to gather in the parlour for the grand denouement, were you? I'm sorry, but I'm saving that for a mystery that deserves it. I like your friend, by the way. Does it have a name?'

'Names are overrated,' said Cotterill. There were others now, walking out of the trees, getting closer. 'These are my Un-Men. They have their uses. Not much good for intelligent conversation, though, unless I give them a character, and even then they're so very limited . . . Unlike you two. You two are fun.'

'Clever, too,' the Doctor said. 'Only thing we haven't figured out yet is what you get from all this.'

Cotterill's smile widened. 'I get to live.'

'So you draw your sustenance from . . . what? The illusion? Or the people you trap here?'

'Both. And neither. The illusion allows the people to give me the strength I need. Tell me, Doctor, what does every story require of its reader?'

'The willing suspension of disbelief.'

Cotterill smiled. 'Exactly. You have no idea the power generated each time somebody is told a story. When a conscious, sentient mind willingly ignores what is real, what is fact, and instead chooses to invest in people and places that never existed . . .' He shuddered in delight. 'It is magnificent. It amounts to nothing less than a rejection of reality. And when reality is pushed away, no matter how briefly, it leaves a gap, crackling with potential, with what-might-be. And what-might-be makes me *strong*.'

Martha glanced around. The Un-Men were getting dangerously close. The Doctor, of course, barely seemed to notice.

'So you took that strength and made a planet,' said the Doctor.

Cotterill laughed. 'This? This is just the beginning. This is a stepping stone. Next I build a solar system. Then a galaxy. Then a universe. And when my universe is big enough, reality will snap, break and crumble, and I will be there to replace it with my own.'

'With you as its god.'

'Precisely.'

'And should I even bother asking what becomes of the people?'

'They will be cared for,' said Cotterill. 'I'm no barbarian. I'll need people to fuel me, after all.'

'Can I say something?' Martha asked, stepping forward. 'Can I? Thank you. You're insane. I mean, seriously, this is an insane idea. I don't mean it's insane because it'll never work or we'll stop you; I mean it's just insane. It is not sane. It saw sane coming and crossed the street to avoid it. Cotterill, you're nuts. Doctor, you're nuts for even having that conversation you just had. You're not going to take over the universe with stories, Cotterill. It's just too silly. I won't allow it. On that basis, plus the fact that you've been trying to kill us, we're going to put a stop to your crazy scheme and send you packing. Doctor. It's about time you had a plan to stop him. Do you?'

'Naturally.'

'Will it require us running?'

'Naturally.'

'Then let's go.'

They broke into a sprint.

'Get them!' Cotterill cried. 'Off with their heads!'

Two Un-Men closed in, their bodies stretching and flattening, turning into playing cards with limbs, just like in *Alice's Adventures in Wonderland* but carrying swords. Martha ducked under their swinging blades and the Doctor grabbed her hand, pulling her on. They ran through the door of the cottage, emerged into the dining hall at Hogwarts and then, before a single wand could be turned in their direction, they were sprinting away through a door at the far end.

'What is this?' Martha cried.

'Cotterill's searching through the books in your memory,' the Doctor answered, 'trying to find something to stop us. This way!'

They ran outside and the ground shifted, became bricks

that spun into place, revealing an underside of gold. Martha heard the beating of wings and the shrieking of monkeys from above and the Doctor yanked her sideways as something big and dark and hairy brushed by her cheek.

She lost her footing and they tumbled down a grassy hill, sprawling into snow. She was first up, looking behind them, making sure the Un-Men weren't about to pounce.

'*The Lion, the Witch and the Wardrobe*?' the Doctor asked, pushing himself to his feet.

'Never read it,' Martha said. They ran to a building up ahead. A big one, like a hotel. She saw the name, the Overlook, and veered off. 'Not that way.'

The Doctor followed her and they left the snow behind and plunged into a tunnel. Their footsteps echoed through the darkness and they slowed, looked back, trying to catch their breath.

'This plan of yours,' Martha said, panting quietly, 'do you really have one or were you just saying you did to look clever in front of Cotterill?'

'I really have one,' the Doctor said. 'And I don't need to *look* clever. I *am* clever. The fact that I *look* clever is merely a bonus.'

'Could you please just tell me what we're going to do?'

He grabbed her and she froze. Ahead of them, headlights snapped on like twin suns. The throb of a powerful engine reverberated around them.

'*Christine*?' said the Doctor.

'Worse,' Martha said, almost crying. '*Chitty-Chitty-Bang-Bang*.'

The car roared and leaped forward. Martha and the Doctor spun round and ran.

'I loved the film so much I had to read the book!' Martha yelled, the last word turning into a yelp as the Doctor yanked her sideways. The car rushed by as they stumbled through a narrow door and into a forest.

The Doctor put his finger to his lips and Martha nodded and followed him as quietly as she could. Wet leaves squelched under her feet. There was movement up ahead: two teenagers, a pale boy and a nervous girl, walked into a clearing. The sun broke through the clouds and the boy started to sparkle.

Martha felt the Doctor's eyes on her and she blushed. 'Do not judge me.'

'Judging is for later,' he said, and they continued on, giving the young lovers a wide berth.

They stepped out of the trees, back into the sunshine. The TARDIS was right in front of them.

Martha broke into a run, the Doctor behind her. They were halfway there and no sign of any Un-Men. They were going to make it. They were going to –

A column of rock burst from the ground, taking the TARDIS with it. Martha lunged – she didn't know why, she just lunged – and grabbed on, realising the stupidity of the move only as the column started twisting in place as it lengthened. It kept growing, the ground becoming a distant thing, the rock becoming brick, the column becoming a tower. Finally, the growth slowed and it settled, this tower with the TARDIS perched precariously on top, with Martha hanging from a narrow windowsill. She looked down. Oh, such a long way down.

'In retrospect,' the Doctor shouted from so far beneath her, 'that was probably ill-advised.'

5

'Help!' screamed Martha. 'Get up here and help me!'

The Doctor did a lap of the tower and came back. 'I can't see a door,' he yelled. 'What kind of building doesn't have a door?'

There was movement, and then a rope came tumbling out of the window, batting gently against Martha's shoulder, unravelling all the way down to the bottom. No, not a rope. A thick braid of golden hair.

'You have got to be kidding,' Martha muttered.

The Doctor was shouting again. 'I know her! I've met her! Tell her I said hi!'

Martha grabbed the hair with one hand. There was a cry of pain from inside the tower. 'Sorry,' she called, and let go of the sill. There was a sudden drop and Martha's stomach lurched, but then she jerked to a stop and hung there, swaying. She glanced up. A pretty girl glared down at her, her face red, arms braced against the window frame to stop herself from being pulled through it.

'You're not the prince,' Rapunzel said. 'The prince is meant to come and release me from my prison. You're not him.'

'This is true.'

'The prince is lighter.'

'Oi. No need to get personal.'

Rapunzel grunted as Martha climbed. It was only a few handholds but it was tiring stuff. She reached the window and clambered awkwardly through.

She jumped lightly to the floor, turning and smiling as Rapunzel winced.

'Ow,' said Rapunzel. 'Ow, be careful. You're standing on my hair.'

'Sorry,' Martha said. 'There's just so much of it . . .'

Martha hopped sideways and Rapunzel straightened up and looked at her, arms folded.

'Hi,' said Martha. 'The Doctor says hi, too.'

'What doctor?'

'The man on the ground, who was shouting. My . . . companion. He says hi. Anyway. It's very nice to meet you. I read about you when I was little. Also saw the Disney movie. Funny. I liked it. You won't have seen it, though. I had to travel a few years into the future and you . . . well, you're a fairy tale, so . . .'

'Who are you?' Rapunzel asked.

'Nobody important. Just passing through. Question: if I wanted to get up on to the roof, how would I go about it?'

'Why would you want to go up on to the roof?'

'We left something up there. Is there an attic, or a ladder, or would I have to go outside again? I really don't want to go outside. Do I have to? I do, don't I?'

Martha walked back to the window, stuck her head out, and looked up. No handholds to be seen. The sun was going down fast. Unnaturally fast. Suddenly it was dusk, and then it was night. She looked down towards the Doctor and gasped. An old man clung to the tower wall below, his black cloak opening around him like great bat wings. She glimpsed sharp teeth beneath his long white moustache and withdrew quickly before his red eyes found her.

Rapunzel looked at her in puzzlement. 'Something is wrong?' she asked.

'Yeah,' Martha said, backing away from the window. 'You've got Dracula climbing up your tower.'

Rapunzel clapped her hands excitedly. 'Is Dracula a prince?'

'He's a count.'

She sagged. 'Oh.'

'Is there another way out of here?'

'It wouldn't be much of a prison if there was another way out.'

'Do you happen to have a crucifix or holy water or, I don't know, a lightsaber or something?'

'I'm sorry,' said Rapunzel. 'I have none of those things. But I have many brushes for my hair.'

'That's wonderful,' Martha muttered, looking around. Rapunzel hadn't been lying. There was a large table just for brushes of varying sizes. Martha picked up the heaviest one, a brush with a golden handle, and when Dracula popped his head up at the window she hurled it with all her strength. It hit him in the forehead and he grunted and dropped from sight.

She grabbed Rapunzel's hair, looping her arm around it loosely. 'It really was lovely to meet you,' she said, and ran for the window, letting the hair slip through the loop.

She jumped out into the night sky and fell, the hair slipping by. She glimpsed Dracula, clinging to the wall, trying to grab her as she dropped. She tightened her grip on the hair and swung suddenly in towards the tower. There was another window right in front of her and she tumbled through it, staggered up and burst through a door, entering a room that flickered with candlelight.

The first thing she saw was a dressing table, hemmed in on all sides by large, half-empty trunks. On the dressing table lay an assortment of jewellery and its mirror was covered with a fine sheen of dust. In the armchair next to it sat an old lady in a yellowed wedding dress, with wilted flowers in her hair and a tattered veil over her face.

'Who is it?' said the lady.

'Uh,' said Martha, panting slightly. 'I can come back later.'

'Come close. Let me look at you.'

Martha hesitated, then walked forward.

The old lady blinked at her through her veil. 'You are not Pumblechook's boy. Who are you?'

'Oh, bloody hell,' said Martha. 'You're Miss Havisham, aren't you? Oh, this is . . . You made me suffer so much in school, do you know that? I like a bit of Dickens as much as the next girl, but all those coincidences were just a few steps too far, you know? What you did to Pip was horrible. And where's Estella? Is she here? Always wanted to give that girl a good slap.'

She looked around and saw no sign of Estella, but did see a window that she crossed to. She parted the sea of lace curtains and peered out. It was daytime again. Dickens's England was right outside. She looked back. Miss Havisham was standing, her head down, face hidden by that veil and loose strands of white hair.

'You'd better sit down,' Martha said. 'You're pretty frail and if I were you I'd get rid of all the naked flames in here. You're not doing yourself any favours by –'

Miss Havisham snapped her head up and leaped, her cold, wrinkly hand closing round Martha's throat and lifting her off her feet. Martha was slammed back against the wall, gagging, struggling to breathe, her fingers trying to prise apart the old lady's grip.

The door burst open and the Doctor stood there, his eyes narrowed, but before he could say anything dramatic Dracula loomed from behind, grabbed him and yanked him back out of the room.

Martha rammed both fists down on the inside of Miss Havisham's elbow. Her grip was loosened and Martha was back on her feet now, gasping, then she powered forward, shoving Miss Havisham a whole two steps back. The yellowed wedding dress started to contract, and Miss Havisham grew taller and broader, and the veil melted to form the face of one of Cotterill's Un-Men. Martha grabbed a brass candlestick and smacked it into the side of the Un-Man's head. The Un-Man staggered and Martha ran for the door. The Doctor lurched into her, grabbed her arm, and they sprinted down a stone corridor.

'I punched Dracula!' he said triumphantly, then winced as he flexed his fingers. 'He has a very hard face.'

'I bet. First time you've met him?'

'No, but the first time it was an android, second time it was Vlad the Impaler and the third time it was a Cyber-Dracula, so I don't really think they count. Ha! *Count*.'

'You are *hilarious*,' Martha muttered. They took a corner,

ran a little more, then came to a door. The Doctor gripped the handle, but didn't turn it.

'What are we doing?' Martha asked, getting her breath back. 'They're behind us.'

'We're giving this world the chance to calm down and settle itself.'

'Right. OK, yeah. Doctor, this plan you were talking about . . .'

'Yes,' the Doctor said. 'About time we enacted it, don't you think?'

'Probably, if I knew what it was.'

He grinned. 'Oh, it's genius, Martha. Pure genius. I'd be jealous of me if I wasn't already, you know . . . me.'

'The other time, in the Land of Fiction, how did you beat them?'

'Well, we kind of, sort of, stopped believing in them.'

'Sorry?'

He looked sheepish. 'You know, like . . . *Hey, you, Minotaur, you don't actually exist*, and, well . . . That was it.'

'That worked?'

'It worked there. Won't work here. No reason it would, but I tried it anyway, on Dracula. He just kept trying to bite me. He's very bitey. Cotterill may draw his power from people rejecting reality, but it isn't enough for us to simply stop believing in whatever is in front of us. He's stored up too much power for that to have any effect.'

'So how do we stop him?'

'He told us how. He said this world is just the beginning. Meaning the stronger he gets, the more he'll be able to do. He draws power from people, then uses that power to create all this. Input and output. So as long as the input is running higher than the output, he's sorted. We just have to switch that round. Imagination fuels this place, and I'd be willing to bet that imagination can also drain it. You were the first one out of the TARDIS – you were the one he latched on to. We need to cut off that power supply. We need to get you back inside.'

'Into the TARDIS? But that's stuck up on the top of Rapunzel's tower.'

'Is it?' the Doctor said, acting all enigmatic as he turned the handle. They walked out through the front door of the haunted cottage, back into the sunshine.

It would have been a wonderful moment were it not for the Troubleseekers standing there, waiting for them, their faces slack and devoid of expression. For a moment, nobody moved.

'Oooh, I hate awkward silences,' said the Doctor, and the Troubleseekers lunged.

Martha yelped, stumbling as she dodged their grasping hands, but she ran on, the Doctor beside her. They stuck to the path until they saw Mrs O'Grady ahead of them, then they veered off on to the grass. The Troubleseekers were right behind them. Mrs O'Grady jumped on her bike and joined the pursuit, proving herself to be surprisingly limber for one so old.

The Doctor and Martha ran up the hill, trampling over the picnic blanket and scattering the tarts and sandwiches and bottles of ginger beer. They crested the hill, saw the blue police box down the other side and piled on the speed. Martha glanced behind them. Mrs O'Grady had passed the Troubleseekers and she was freewheeling after them.

The Doctor pointed the sonic screwdriver at her as they ran. The brakes of Mrs O'Grady's bike squealed and seized, and the woman was launched over the handlebars for the second time since they'd arrived.

'That never gets old,' the Doctor said, panting slightly. 'Got your key?'

'Key? Yes. Why?'

'Once you're inside the TARDIS, Cotterill will latch on to the next available mind for power.'

'Yours?'

The Doctor looked at her and grinned. 'Mine.'

He stopped suddenly, whirled round, and the Troubleseekers ran right into him as Martha kept going. She reached the bottom of the hill, slipped the key into the lock and pushed through into the TARDIS, slamming the door behind her.

She stepped back. All was quiet. She realised she had no idea what to do next, so she counted to ten, then opened the door and peeked out.

The Doctor was on his knees, the Troubleseekers surrounding him. Mrs O'Grady stood nearby. They grew taller, lost their features, turning into Un-Men as the landscape shifted. The grassy hill flattened out, became sand. There was a castle in the distance. The landscape shifted again, sand turning to snow, blue sky turning red. Three moons on the horizon. The snow melted, sprouted trees that grew fast, dwarfing any skyscraper that Martha had ever seen and forming a dense forest.

A man walked through the trees.

Cotterill.

6

'I love a good chase,' Cotterill said. 'All the best stories end with a good chase.' He looked around as the forest faded, becoming a mountaintop. 'You certainly have read a lot of books.'

'Yes I have,' said the Doctor, raising his head. 'I have read a *lot* of books. Travelling as much as I do, spending all that time alone, not really sleeping ... Well, you tend to read, don't you? I've got nine hundred years' worth of books in my head, Cotterill, and you're getting all of them. All at once.'

Their surroundings started shifting faster – open water, countryside, a sterile lobby, alien world, alien building, missile silo – like a flipbook being flicked through.

'Stop,' said Cotterill, his eyes widening.

'Don't think so,' said the Doctor. 'See, now you're in here.' He tapped his head. 'And I'm not letting you out.'

The world around them was a blur. Cotterill staggered, his face pale.

'Stop him!' he shouted. 'Kill him!'

Martha ran to the Doctor's side as the Un-Men closed in. 'Doctor! Could really do with a weapon!'

Their flickering surroundings slowed suddenly, and Martha

found a thick branch by her foot. She snatched it up and the world got back to blurring.

'A branch,' she said. 'That's it?'

'Best I could do,' the Doctor muttered. His face was tight with concentration and his eyes were closed.

Martha swung at the nearest Un-Man, whacking it across the head. It took a single step back. She didn't know how – or even if – it registered pain, but it was a biped, so most of what she knew about human anatomy could be applied – she hoped.

She swung again, low this time, the branch crunching into the side of its knee. It dropped and she spun round, the branch cracking into the elbow of another Un-Man who was reaching for the Doctor. She charged into it, bounced off, but managed to send it back a few steps.

'Come on!' she roared as the other Un-Men circled her. 'I'll have the lot of you!'

They didn't appear to be the slightest bit intimidated by her challenge, and pressed forward.

'No,' Cotterill gasped, looking behind him. Martha glanced over. The ever-changing landscape was making her feel sick and dizzy, but in the distance there was a pocket of nothingness, and it was growing bigger.

One of the Un-Men grabbed Martha and she whirled, swinging the branch – but right before it made contact the branch vanished from her hands.

'Sorry,' the Doctor muttered.

The Un-Man's fingers closed round Martha's throat, began to squeeze, and then suddenly the Un-Man wasn't there any more either. Martha turned, gasping, and watched the remaining Un-Men vanish.

The pocket of nothing was getting closer. It joined up with another. Martha saw more nothingness on the outskirts, beyond the trees and buildings and walls and rocks that flickered by.

'Stop!' Cotterill roared. 'Please! This is my home!'

The landscape lost its features. It was now something small and curved, like they were standing on a planet only as wide as a football pitch, surrounded on all sides by the ever-encroaching emptiness. And Cotterill himself was changing, shrinking, losing his physical form, becoming a twisting thing of shadows and light.

The Doctor got to his feet, slowly. 'Now then,' he said, 'I think someone owes someone else an apology.'

'I am sorry,' said the being that was once Cotterill. Its voice echoed in Martha's ears. 'Please let me leave your mind. It hurts.'

'I know it does,' the Doctor said. The screwdriver was in his hand again, scanning. He looked at the results, and grunted. 'Who are you?'

'My people do not have names,' it said. 'I am of the Ch'otterai. The legends of my people told us we were once gods; told us we could reshape reality with our minds. But the Ch'otterai have never had particularly vibrant imaginations, so if we had ever had that potential we had long since squandered it on petty acts of showmanship.'

'How did you get here?'

'My ship malfunctioned, exploded, destroyed my physical body and cast my consciousness adrift.'

Martha narrowed her eyes. 'You're a ghost?'

'In a way,' the Doctor murmured. 'So what happened? A few centuries pass, you get bored, someone has the misfortune to get too close . . . and you latch on?'

'I thought they could take me home,' the Ch'otterai said. 'All I needed was enough strength to take physical form . . . but I couldn't leave this point in space. I was stuck here, in this point where I died. So I gave them their stories and fed on the power that resulted, and then I drew another ship here, and another . . . and I created a planet. I reshaped reality. I became a god.'

'A big god in a small pond,' said the Doctor, 'using other people's imaginations because your own is too stunted. And what happened to these ships you drew in, eh? What happened to these people?'

The Ch'otterai hesitated. 'I gave them their stories.'

'And then what happened to them?'

'They left.'

'I don't believe you.'

'They left. I promise you, I let them go. I am a benevolent god.'

'You're quick to anger, is what you are. Quick to shout, "*Off with their heads!*"'

'No, I –'

'What did you do with their bodies? And the ships? Did you push them into a big lake of nothingness, let that swallow them up?'

The swirling form of the Ch'otterai slowed for a moment. 'You don't understand. You don't know what it has been like for me. They were going to leave, Doctor. Their stories turned stale and they grew bored. I needed them and they were going to abandon me, they were going to warn others to stay away. I . . . I couldn't let that happen.'

'So you killed them.'

'I gave them a choice. Every single one of them, I gave them a choice. Stay and I will provide, or try to leave and I will destroy.'

'They all tried to leave,' Martha said softly.

The Ch'otterai's voice turned hard, and its swirling intensified with anger. 'They *lied*. They promised to stay and then tried to get to their ships. They sought to steal my energy from me. They deserved destruction.'

The swirling became so violent Martha took a step back – and then, as if it had realised it had gone too far, the swirling slowed, and the Ch'otterai's voice became softer.

'But, Doctor . . . you're different. If we take our time, you could make me strong enough to build a galaxy, and from there, a universe. You could rule that universe, the both of you, as king and queen.'

'With you as our god,' the Doctor murmured.

'Yes,' the Ch'otterai responded.

'No,' said the Doctor. He put his hand out, found Martha's, and they both started walking backwards. They were now on a surface no bigger than a swimming pool.

The Ch'otterai's form was twisting so fast it was blurring. 'Stop!' it shrieked. 'Take one more step and I'll flood you with the void. You won't even get to your ship!'

Martha and the Doctor froze.

'You'll be sacrificing the last of your power,' the Doctor said.

'I'll do it! I'll kill you before I let you leave! I'll start again! I'll find someone new!'

Martha glanced behind her. The TARDIS was three strides away. Too far.

'We're not going to stay,' the Doctor said. 'We can't.'

The Ch'otterai's voice took on an edge. 'Then find a way to take me with you. Or better yet, find a way to transport me to this Land of Fiction. One of my Un-Men heard you talking about it. Take me there, Doctor, and I will let you both live.'

'The Land of Fiction isn't even in this reality.'

'You're an intelligent being,' said the Ch'otterai. The swirling was calmer now that it was growing in confidence. 'I'm sure you can find a way. Put your mind to it or perish.'

Martha let go of the Doctor and got ready to leap towards the TARDIS. The Doctor slipped his hands into his pockets.

'There might be something I can do,' he said. 'I have an emergency unit onboard. I won't bore you with the details, but it could allow us to slip sideways through dimensions. Technically, you wouldn't even leave this space you're haunting. It's quite dangerous, however. There's no guarantee Martha and I could ever return once we've delivered you. I don't think it's a good –'

'Do it or die, Doctor,' said the Ch'otterai. 'It is that simple.'

The Doctor took a moment, and Martha saw his jaw tightening. 'Very well,' he said. He walked to the TARDIS and pushed open the door. The Ch'otterai swirled inside before the Doctor could change his mind . . .

And then the Doctor slammed the door.

Martha stared at him. 'What are you doing? You're locking it in the TARDIS? What if it takes off?'

The Doctor leaned one shoulder against the door and

folded his arms. 'The Ch'otterai is a being of pure psychic energy. True, it has the potential to be infinitely powerful, but right now it can barely keep itself together.'

For once, the Doctor's calm demeanour failed to soothe Martha's worry. 'So explain to me how locking it in the TARDIS is a good idea.'

'The TARDIS isn't a machine, Martha. Well, it is, but it's also so much more. You saw how I overloaded the Ch'otterai with the books I've read? My imagination reduced it from a ghost with a planet to a ghost with a garden plot. Now, just think what the TARDIS will do to it.'

Martha frowned. 'The TARDIS has an imagination?'

The Doctor laughed. 'From a certain point of view, the TARDIS *is* imagination.'

He slipped his key into the lock, turned it and motioned to the open door.

Martha walked through. The console room was quiet. There was no sign of the Ch'otterai. The Doctor walked past her, strode to the console, flicked a few switches and glanced at a few readouts.

'Where is it?' Martha asked.

'Gone,' said the Doctor. 'Or mostly gone, anyway. From what I can tell, it's been reduced to a single thought, and probably not a nice one at that.'

Martha looked around. 'So where is it?'

The Doctor waved a hand in the air. 'Here. There. I don't know.'

'But when we leave, we won't take it with us, will we?'

'What's the matter, Miss Jones? You don't like the idea of a haunted TARDIS?'

'Not particularly.'

'Don't worry,' the Doctor said, pulling levers. 'We'll fly off to distant lands, but what remains of the Ch'otterai will stay here. Probably.'

She didn't like that 'probably', but she didn't say anything as the TARDIS started to wheeze and whoosh. She walked up to a monitor, saw the nothingness outside fold in on itself and blink out of existence. For a moment there was nothing but empty space and stars, and then the screen went blank.

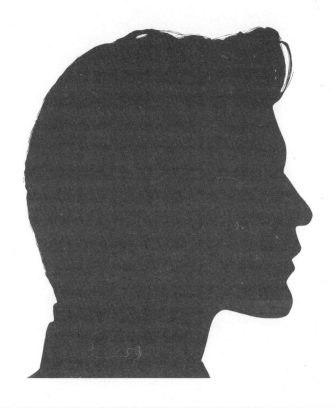

THE ELEVENTH DOCTOR:
NOTHING O'CLOCK

NEIL GAIMAN

1

The Time Lords built a Prison. They built it in a time and place that are both unimaginable to any entity who has never left the solar system in which it was spawned, or who has only experienced the journey through time, second by second, and that only going forward. It was built just for the Kin. It was impregnable: a complex of small rooms (for they were not monsters, the Time Lords – they could be merciful, when it suited them), out of temporal phase with the rest of the Universe.

There were, in that place, only those rooms: the gulf between microseconds was one that could not be crossed. In effect, those rooms became a universe in themselves, one that borrowed light and heat and gravity from the rest of Creation, always a fraction of a moment away.

The Kin prowled its rooms, patient and deathless, and always waiting.

It was waiting for a question. It could wait until the end of time. (But even then, when Time Ended, the Kin would miss it, imprisoned in the micro-moment away from time.)

The Time Lords maintained the Prison with huge engines they built in the hearts of black holes, unreachable: no one would be able to get to the engines, save the Time Lords themselves. The multiple engines were a fail-safe. Nothing could ever go wrong.

As long as the Time Lords existed, the Kin would be in their Prison, and the rest of the Universe would be safe. That was how it was, and how it always would be.

And if anything went wrong, then the Time Lords would know. Even if, unthinkably, any of the engines failed, then emergency signals would sound on Gallifrey long before the Prison of the Kin returned to our time and our universe. The Time Lords had planned for everything.

They had planned for everything except the possibility that one day there would be no Time Lords, and no Gallifrey. No Time Lords in the Universe, except for one.

So when the Prison shook and crashed, as if in an earthquake, throwing the Kin down; and when the Kin looked up from its Prison to see the light of galaxies and suns above it, unmediated and unfiltered, and it knew that it had returned to the Universe, it knew it would only be a matter of time until the question would be asked once more.

And, because the Kin was careful, it took stock of the Universe they found themselves in. It did not think of revenge: that was not in its nature. It wanted what it had always wanted. And besides . . .

There was still a Time Lord in the Universe.

The Kin needed to do something about that.

2

On Wednesday, eleven-year-old Polly Browning put her head round her father's office door. 'Dad, there's a man at the front door in a rabbit mask who says he wants to buy the house.'

'Don't be silly, Polly.' Mr Browning was sitting in the corner of the room he liked to call his office, and which the estate agent had optimistically listed as a third bedroom, although it was scarcely big enough for a filing cabinet and a card-table, upon which rested a brand-new Amstrad computer. Mr Browning was carefully entering the numbers from a pile of receipts on to the computer, and wincing. Every half an hour he would save the work he'd done so far, and the computer would make a grinding noise for a few minutes as it saved everything on to a floppy disk.

'I'm not being silly. He says he'll give you seven hundred and fifty thousand pounds for it.'

'Now you're really being silly. It's only on sale for fifty thousand pounds.' *And we'd be lucky to get that in today's market*, he thought, but did not say. It was the summer of 1984, and Mr Browning despaired of finding a buyer for the little house at the end of Claversham Row.

Polly nodded thoughtfully. 'I think you should go and talk to him.'

Mr Browning shrugged. He needed to save the work he'd done so far anyway. As the computer made its grumbling sound, Mr Browning went downstairs. Polly, who had planned to go up to her bedroom to write in her diary, decided to sit on the stairs and find out what was going to happen next.

Standing in the front garden was a tall man in a rabbit mask. It was not a particularly convincing mask. It covered his entire face, and two long ears rose above his head. He held a large brown leather bag, which reminded Mr Browning of the doctors' bags of his childhood.

'Now, see here,' began Mr Browning, but the man in the rabbit mask put a gloved finger to his painted bunny lips, and Mr Browning fell silent.

'Ask me what time it is,' said a quiet voice that came from behind the unmoving muzzle of the rabbit mask.

Mr Browning said, 'I understand you're interested in the house.' The *For Sale* sign by the front gate was grimy and streaked by the rain.

'Perhaps. You can call me Mister Rabbit. Ask me what time it is.'

Mr Browning knew that he ought to call the police. Ought to do something to make the man go away. What kind of crazy person wears a rabbit mask anyway?

'Why are you wearing a rabbit mask?'

'That was not the correct question. But I am wearing the rabbit mask because I am representing an extremely famous and important person who values his or her privacy. Ask me what time it is.'

Mr Browning sighed. 'What time is it, Mister Rabbit?' he asked.

The man in the rabbit mask stood up straighter. His body language was one of joy and delight. 'Time for you to be the richest man on Claversham Row,' he said. 'I'm buying your house, for cash, and for more than ten times what it's worth, because it's just perfect for me now.' He opened the brown leather bag, and produced blocks of money, each block containing five hundred ('Count them, go on, count them') crisp fifty-pound notes, and two plastic supermarket shopping bags, into which he placed the blocks of currency.

Mr Browning inspected the money. It appeared to be real.

'I . . .' He hesitated. What did he need to do? 'I'll need a few days. To bank it. Make sure it's real. And we'll need to draw up contracts, obviously.'

'Contract's already drawn up,' said the man in the rabbit mask. 'Sign here. If the bank says there's anything funny about the money, you can keep it and the house. I will be back on Saturday to take vacant possession. You can get everything out by then, can't you?'

'I don't know,' said Mr Browning. Then: 'I'm sure I can. I mean, *of course.*'

'I'll be here on Saturday,' said the man in the rabbit mask.

'This is a very unusual way of doing business,' said Mr Browning. He was standing at his front door holding two shopping bags, containing £750,000.

'Yes,' agreed the man in the rabbit mask. 'It is. See you on Saturday, then.'

He walked away. Mr Browning was relieved to see him go. He had been seized by the irrational conviction that, were he to remove the rabbit mask, there would be nothing underneath.

Polly went upstairs to tell her diary everything she had seen and heard.

On Thursday, a tall young man with a tweed jacket and a bow-tie knocked on the door. There was nobody at home, so nobody answered, and, after walking round the house, he went away.

On Saturday, Mr Browning stood in his empty kitchen. He had banked the money successfully, which had wiped out all his debts. The furniture that they had wanted to keep had been put into a removals van and sent to Mr Browning's uncle, who had an enormous garage he wasn't using.

'What if it's all a joke?' asked Mrs Browning.

'Not sure what's funny about giving someone seven hundred and fifty thousand pounds,' said Mr Browning. 'The bank says it's real. Not reported stolen. Just a rich and eccentric person who wants to buy our house for a lot more than it's worth.'

They had booked two rooms in a local hotel, although hotel rooms had proved harder to find than Mr Browning had expected. Also, he had had to convince Mrs Browning, who was a nurse, that they could now afford to stay in a hotel.

'What happens if he never comes back?' asked Polly. She was sitting on the stairs, reading a book.

Mr Browning said, 'Now you're being silly.'

'Don't call your daughter silly,' said Mrs Browning. 'She's got a point. You don't have a name or a phone number or anything.'

This was unfair. The contract was made out, and the buyer's name was clearly written on it: N. M. de Plume. There was an address, too, for a firm of London solicitors, and Mr Browning had phoned them and been told that, despite the silly name, yes, this was absolutely legitimate.

'He's eccentric,' said Mr Browning. 'An eccentric millionaire.'

'I bet it's him behind that rabbit mask,' said Polly. 'The eccentric millionaire.'

The doorbell rang. Mr Browning went to the front door, his wife and daughter beside him, each of them hoping to meet the new owner of their house.

'Hello,' said the lady in the cat mask on their doorstep. It was not a very realistic mask. Polly saw her eyes glinting behind it, though.

'Are you the new owner?' asked Mrs Browning.

'Either that, or I'm the owner's representative.'

'Where's . . . your friend? In the rabbit mask?'

Despite the cat mask, the young lady (was she young? – her voice sounded young anyway) seemed efficient and almost brusque. 'You have removed all your possessions? I'm afraid anything left behind will become the property of the new owner.'

'We've got everything that matters.'

'Good.'

Polly said, 'Can I come and play in the garden? There isn't a garden at the hotel.' There was a swing on the oak tree in the back garden, and Polly loved to sit on it and read.

'Don't be silly, love,' said Mr Browning. 'We'll have a new house, and then you'll have a garden with swings. I'll put up new swings for you.'

The lady in the cat mask crouched down. 'I'm Mrs Cat. Ask me what time it is, Polly.'

Polly nodded. 'What's the time, Mrs Cat?'

'Time for you and your family to leave this place and never look back,' said Mrs Cat, but she said it kindly.

Polly waved goodbye to the lady in the cat mask when she got to the end of the garden path.

3

They were in the TARDIS control room, going home.

'I still don't understand,' Amy was saying. 'Why were the Skeleton People so angry with you in the first place? I thought they *wanted* to get free from the rule of the Toad-King.'

'They weren't angry with me about *that*,' said the young man in the tweed jacket and the bow-tie. He pushed a hand impatiently through his hair. 'I think they were quite pleased to be free, actually.' He ran his hands across the TARDIS control panel, patting levers, stroking dials. 'They were just a bit upset with me because I'd walked off with their squiggly whatsit.'

'Squiggly whatsit?'

'It's on the –' he gestured vaguely with arms that seemed to be mostly elbows and joints – 'the tabley thing over there. I confiscated it.'

Amy looked irritated. She wasn't irritated, but she sometimes liked to give him the impression she was, just to show him who was boss. 'Why don't you ever call things by their proper names? *The tabley thing over there?* It's called "a table".'

She walked over to the table. The squiggly whatsit was glittery and elegant: it was the size and general shape of a bracelet, but it twisted in ways that made it hard for the eye to follow.

'Really? Oh good.' He seemed pleased. 'I'll remember that.'

Amy picked up the squiggly whatsit. It was cold and much heavier than it looked. 'Why did you confiscate it? And why are you saying "confiscate" anyway? That's like what teachers do, when you bring something you shouldn't to school. My friend Mels set a record at school for the number of things she got confiscated. One night she got me and Rory to make a disturbance while she broke in to the teachers' supply cupboard, which was where her stuff was. She had to go over the roof and through the teachers' loo window –'

But the Doctor was not interested in Amy's old schoolfriend's exploits. He never was. He said, 'Confiscated. For their own safety. Technology they shouldn't have had. Probably stolen. Time looper and booster. Could have made a nasty mess of things.' He pulled a lever. 'And we're here. All change.'

There was a rhythmic grinding sound, as if the engines of the universe itself were protesting, a rush of displaced air, and a large blue police box materialised in the back garden of Amy Pond's house. It was the beginning of the second decade of the twenty-first century.

The Doctor opened the TARDIS door. Then he said, 'That's odd.'

He stood in the doorway, made no attempt to walk outside. Amy came over to him. He put out an arm to prevent her from leaving the TARDIS. It was a perfect sunny day, almost cloudless.

'What's wrong?'

'Everything,' he said. 'Can't you feel it?' Amy looked at her garden. It was overgrown and neglected, but then it always had been, as long as she could remember.

'No,' said Amy. And then she said, 'It's quiet. No cars. No birds. Nothing.'

'No radio waves,' said the Doctor. 'Not even Radio Four.'

'You can hear radio waves?'

'Of course not. Nobody can hear radio waves,' he said unconvincingly.

And that was when a gentle voice said, **Attention, visitor. You are now entering Kin space. This world is the property of the Kin. You are trespassing.** It was a strange voice, whispery and mostly, Amy suspected, in her head.

'This is Earth,' called Amy. 'It doesn't belong to you.' And then she said, 'What have you done with the people?'

We bought it from them. They died out naturally shortly afterwards. It was a pity.

'I don't believe you,' shouted Amy.

No galactic laws were violated. The planet was purchased legally and legitimately. A thorough investigation by the Shadow Proclamation vindicated our ownership in full.

'It's not yours! Where's Rory?'

'Amy? Who are you talking to?' asked the Doctor.

'The voice. The one in my head. Can't you hear it?'

To whom are you talking? asked the Voice.

Amy closed the TARDIS door.

'Why did you do that?' asked the Doctor.

'Weird whispery voice in my head. Said they'd bought the planet. And that the . . . the Shadow Proclamation said it was all OK. It told me all the people died out naturally. You couldn't hear it. It didn't know you were here. Element of surprise. Closed the door.' Amy Pond could be astonishingly efficient when she was under stress. Right now, she was under stress, but you wouldn't have known it, if it wasn't for the squiggly whatsit, which she was holding between her hands and was bending and twisting into shapes that defied the imagination and seemed to be wandering off into peculiar dimensions.

'Did they say who they were?'

She thought for a moment. '"You are now entering Kin space. This world is the property of the Kin."'

He said, 'Could be anyone. The Kin. I mean . . . it's like calling yourselves the People. It's what pretty much every race-name means. Except for Dalek. That means *Metal-Cased Hatey Death Machines* in Skaronian.' And then he was running to the control panel. 'Something like this. It can't occur overnight. People don't just die off. And this is 2010. Which means . . .'

'It means they've done something to Rory.'

'It means they've done something to everyone.' He pressed several keys on an ancient typewriter keyboard, and patterns flowed across the screen that hung above the TARDIS console. 'I couldn't hear them . . . they couldn't hear me. You could hear both of us. Limited telepathic broadcast, but only on human frequencies. Hmm. *Aha!* Summer of 1984! That's the divergence point . . .' His hands began turning, twiddling and pushing levers, pumps, switches and something small that went *ding*.

'Where's Rory? I want him, right now,' demanded Amy as the TARDIS lurched away into space and time. The Doctor had only briefly met her fiancé, Rory Williams, once before. She didn't think the Doctor understood what she saw in Rory. Some days, *she* was not entirely sure what she saw in Rory. But she was certain of this: nobody took her fiancé away from her.

'Good question. Where's Rory? Also, where's seven billion other people?' he asked.

'I want my Rory.'

'Well, wherever the rest of them are, he's there too. And you ought to have been with them. At a guess, neither of you were ever born.'

Amy looked down at herself, checking her feet, her legs, her elbows, her hands (the squiggly whatsit glittered like an Escher nightmare on her wrist; she dropped it on to the control panel). She reached up and grasped a handful of auburn hair. 'If I wasn't born, what am I doing here?'

'You're an independent temporal nexus, chrono-synclastically established as an inverse ...' He saw her expression, and stopped.

'You're telling me it's timey-wimey, aren't you?'

'Yes,' he said seriously. 'I suppose I am. Right. We're here.'

He adjusted his bow-tie with precise fingers, tipping it to one side rakishly.

'But, Doctor. The human race didn't die out in 1984.'

'New timeline. It's a paradox.'

'And you're the paradoctor?'

'Just the Doctor.' He adjusted his bow-tie back to its earlier alignment, stood up a little straighter. 'There's something familiar about all this.'

'What?'

'Don't know. Hmm. Kin. Kin. *Kin* . . . I keep thinking of masks. Who wears masks?'

'Bank robbers?'

'No.'

'Really ugly people?'

'No.'

'Halloween? People wear masks at Halloween.'

'*Yes!* They *do!*' He flung his arms wide in delight.

'So that's important?'

'Not even a little bit. But it's true. Right. Big divergence in time stream. And it's not actually possible to take over a Level 5 planet in a way that would satisfy the Shadow Proclamation unless . . .'

'Unless what?'

The Doctor stopped moving. He bit his lower lip. Then: 'Oh. They wouldn't.'

'Wouldn't what?'

'They couldn't. I mean, that would be completely . . .'

Amy tossed her hair, and did her best to keep her temper. Shouting at the Doctor never worked, unless it did. 'Completely what?'

'Completely impossible. You can't take over a Level 5 planet. Unless you do it legitimately.' On the TARDIS control panel something whirled and something else went *ding*. 'We're here. It's the nexus. Come on! Let's explore 1984.'

'You're enjoying this,' said Amy. 'My whole world has

been taken over by a mysterious voice. All the people are extinct. Rory's gone. And you're enjoying this.'

'No, I'm not,' said the Doctor, trying hard not to show how much he was enjoying it.

The Brownings stayed in the hotel while Mr Browning looked for a new house. The hotel was completely full. Coincidentally, the Brownings learned, in conversation with other hotel guests over breakfast, they had also sold their houses and flats. None of them seemed particularly forthcoming about who had bought their houses.

'It's ridiculous,' he said after ten days. 'There's nothing for sale in the town. Or anywhere around here. They've all been snapped up.'

'There must be something,' said Mrs Browning.

'Not in this part of the country,' said Mr Browning.

'What does the estate agent say?'

'Not answering the phone,' said Mr Browning.

'Well, let's go and talk to her,' said Mrs Browning. 'You coming with, Polly?'

Polly shook her head. 'I'm reading my book,' she said.

Mr and Mrs Browning walked into town, and they met the estate agent outside the door of the shop, putting up a notice saying 'Under New Management'. There were no properties for sale in the window, only a lot of houses and flats with Sold on them.

'Shutting up shop?' asked Mr Browning.

'Someone made me an offer I couldn't refuse,' said the estate agent. She was carrying a heavy-looking plastic shopping bag. The Brownings could guess what was in it.

'Someone in a rabbit mask?' asked Mrs Browning.

When they got back to the hotel, the manager was waiting in the lobby for them, to tell them they wouldn't be living there much longer.

'It's the new owners,' she explained. 'They're closing the hotel for refurbishing.'

'New owners?'

'They just bought it. Paid a lot of money for it, I was told.'

Somehow, this did not surprise the Brownings one little bit. They were not surprised until they got up to their hotel room, and Polly was nowhere to be seen.

4

'1984,' mused Amy Pond. 'I thought somehow it would feel more, I don't know. Historical. It doesn't feel like a long time ago. But my parents hadn't even met yet.' She hesitated, as if she were about to say something about her parents, but her attention drifted. They crossed the road.

'What were they like?' asked the Doctor. 'Your parents?'

Amy shrugged. 'The usual,' she said, without thinking. 'A mum and a dad.'

'Sounds likely,' agreed the Doctor much too readily. 'So, I need you to keep your eyes open.'

'What are we looking for?'

It was a picturesque little English town, and it looked like a little English town as far as Amy was concerned. Just like the one she'd left in 2010, with a village green and trees and a church, only without the coffee shops or the mobile-phone shops.

'Easy. We're looking for something that shouldn't be here. Or we're looking for something that should be here but isn't.'

'What kind of thing?'

'Not sure,' said the Doctor. He rubbed his chin. 'Gazpacho, maybe.'

'What's gazpacho?'

'Cold soup. But it's meant to be cold. So if we looked all over 1984 and couldn't find any gazpacho, that would be a clue.'

'Were you always like this?'

'Like what?'

'A madman. With a time machine.'

'Oh, no. It took ages until I got the time machine.'

They walked through the centre of the little town, looking for something unusual, and finding nothing, not even gazpacho.

Polly stopped at the garden gate in Claversham Row, looking up at the house that had been her house since they had moved here when she was seven. She walked up to the front door, rang the doorbell and waited, and was relieved when nobody answered it. She glanced down the street, then walked hurriedly round the house, past the rubbish bins, into the back garden.

The French window that opened on to the little back garden had a catch that didn't fasten properly. Polly thought it extremely unlikely that the house's new owners would have fixed it. If they had, she'd come back when they were here, and she'd have to ask, and it would be awkward and embarrassing.

That was the trouble with hiding things. Sometimes, if you were in a hurry, you left them behind. Even important things. And there was nothing more important than her diary.

She had been keeping it since they had arrived in the town. It had been her best friend: she had confided in it, told it about the girls who had bullied her, the ones who'd befriended her, about the first boy she had ever liked. She would turn to it in times of trouble, or turmoil and pain. It was the place she poured out her thoughts.

And it was hidden underneath a loose floorboard in the big cupboard in her bedroom.

Polly tapped the left French door hard with the palm of her hand, rapping it next to the casement, and the door wobbled, and then swung open.

She walked inside. She was surprised to see that they hadn't replaced any of the furniture her family had left behind. It still smelled like her house. It was silent: nobody home. Good. She hurried up the stairs, worried she might still be at home when Mr Rabbit or Mrs Cat returned.

On the landing something brushed her face – touched it gently, like a thread, or a cobweb. She looked up. That was odd. The ceiling seemed furry: hair-like threads, or thread-like hairs, came down from it. She hesitated then, thought about running – but she could see her bedroom door. The Duran Duran poster was still on it. Why hadn't they taken it down?

Trying not to look up at the hairy ceiling, she pushed open her bedroom door.

The room was different. There was no furniture, and where her bed had been were sheets of paper. She glanced down: photographs from newspapers, faces blown up to life-size. The eyeholes had been cut out already. She recognised Prince Charles, Ronald Reagan, Margaret Thatcher, Pope John Paul, the Queen . . .

Perhaps they were going to have a party. The masks didn't look very convincing.

She went to the built-in cupboard at the end of the room. Her *Smash Hits* diary was sitting in the darkness, beneath the floorboard, in there. She opened the cupboard door.

'Hello, Polly,' said the man in the cupboard. He wore a mask, like the others had. An animal mask: this was some kind of big black dog.

'Hello,' said Polly. She didn't know what else to say. 'I . . . I left my diary behind.'

'I know. I was reading it.' He raised the diary. He was not the same as the man in the rabbit mask or the woman in the cat mask, but everything Polly had felt about them, about the *wrongness*, was intensified here. 'Do you want it back?'

'Yes please,' Polly said to the dog-masked man. She felt hurt and violated: this man had been reading her diary. But she wanted it back.

'You know what you need to do, to get it?'

She shook her head.

'Ask me what the time is.'

She opened her mouth. It was dry. She licked her lips, and muttered, 'What time is it?'

'And my name,' he said. 'Say my name. I'm Mister Wolf.'

'What's the time, Mister Wolf?' asked Polly. A playground game rose unbidden to her mind.

Mister Wolf smiled (but how can a mask smile?) and he opened his mouth so wide to show row upon row of sharp, sharp teeth.

'Dinner time,' he told her.

Polly started to scream then, as he came towards her, but she didn't get to scream for very long.

5

The TARDIS was sitting in a small grassy area, too small to be a park, too irregular to be a square, in the middle of the town, and the Doctor was sitting outside it, in a deckchair, walking through his memories.

The Doctor had a remarkable memory. The problem was, there was so much of it. He had lived eleven lives (or more: there was another life, was there not, that he tried his best never to think about) and he had a different way of remembering things in each life.

The worst part of being however old he was (and he had long since abandoned trying to keep track of it in any way that mattered to anybody but him) was that sometimes things didn't arrive in his head quite when they were meant to.

Masks. That was part of it. And Kin. That was part of it too.

And Time.

It was all about Time. Yes, that was it . . .

An old story. Before his time – he was sure of that. It was something he had heard as a boy. He tried to remember the stories he had been told as a small boy on Gallifrey, before he had been taken to the Time Lord Academy and his life had changed forever.

Amy was coming back from a sortie through the town, looking for things that might have been gazpacho.

'Maximelos and the three Ogrons!' he shouted at her.

'What about them?'

'One was too vicious, one was too stupid, one was just right.'

'And this is relevant how?'

He tugged at his hair absently. 'Er, probably not relevant at all. Just trying to remember a story from my childhood.'

'Why?'

'No idea. Can't remember.'

'You,' said Amy Pond, 'are very frustrating.'

'Yes,' said the Doctor happily. 'I probably am.'

He had hung a sign on the front of the TARDIS. It read:

SOMETHING MYSTERIOUSLY WRONG?
JUST KNOCK! NO PROBLEM TOO SMALL.

'If it won't come to us, I'll go to it. No, scrap that. Other way round. And I've redecorated inside, so as not to startle people. What did you find?'

'Two things,' she said. 'First one was Prince Charles. I saw him in the newsagent's.'

'Are you sure it was him?'

Amy thought. 'Well, he looked like Prince Charles. Just much younger. And the newsagent asked him if he'd picked out a name for the next Royal Baby. I suggested Rory.'

'Prince Charles in the newsagent's. Right. Next thing?'

'There aren't any houses for sale. I've walked every street.

No *For Sale* signs. There are people camping in tents on the edge of town. Lots of people leaving to find places to live, because there's nothing around here. It's just weird.'

'Yes.'

He almost had it now. Amy opened the TARDIS door. She looked inside. 'Doctor . . . it's the same size on the inside.'

He beamed, and took her on an extensive tour of his new office, which consisted of standing inside the doorway and making a waving gesture with his right arm. Most of the space was taken up by a desk, with an old-fashioned telephone and a typewriter on it. There was a back wall. Amy experimentally pushed her hands through the wall (it was hard to do with her eyes open, easy when she closed them), then she closed her eyes again and pushed her head through. Now she could see the TARDIS control room, all copper and glass. She took a step backwards, into the tiny office.

'Is it a hologram?'

'Sort of.'

There was a hesitant rap at the door of the TARDIS. The Doctor opened it.

'Excuse me. The sign on the door.' The man appeared harassed. His hair was thinning. He looked at the tiny room, mostly filled by a desk, and he made no move to come inside.

'Yes! Hello! Come in!' said the Doctor. 'No problem too small!'

'Um. My name's Reg Browning. It's my daughter, Polly. She was meant to be waiting for us, back in the hotel room. She's not there.'

'I'm the Doctor. This is Amy. Have you spoken to the police?'

'Aren't you police? I thought perhaps you were.'

'Why?' asked Amy.

'This is a police call box. I didn't even know they were bringing them back.'

'For some of us,' said the tall young man with the bow-tie, 'they never went away. What happened when you spoke to the police?'

'They said they'd keep an eye out for her. But, honestly, they seemed a bit preoccupied. The desk sergeant said the lease had run out on the police station, rather unexpectedly, and they're looking for somewhere to go. The desk sergeant said the whole lease thing had come as a bit of a blow to them.'

'What's Polly like?' asked Amy. 'Could she be staying with friends?'

'I've checked with her friends. Nobody's seen her. We're living in the Rose Hotel on Wednesbury Street right now.'

'Are you visiting?'

Mr Browning told them about the man in the rabbit mask who had come to the door a fortnight ago to buy their house for so much more than it was worth, and paid cash. He told them about the woman in the cat mask who had taken possession of the house . . .

'Oh. Right. Well, that makes sense of everything,' said the Doctor, as if it actually did.

'It does?' said Mr Browning. 'Do you know where Polly is?'

The Doctor shook his head. 'Mister Browning. Reg. Is there any chance she might have gone back to your house?'

The man shrugged. 'Might have done. Do you think –?'

But the tall young man and the red-haired Scottish girl pushed past him, slammed shut the door of their police box, and sprinted away across the green.

6

Amy kept pace with the Doctor, and panted out questions as they ran.

'You think she's in the house?'

'I'm afraid she is. Yes. I've got a sort of an idea. Something I heard when I was a boy. A sort of a cautionary tale. Look, Amy, don't let anyone persuade you to ask *them* what the time is. And if they do, don't answer them. Safer that way.'

'You mean it?'

'I'm afraid so. And watch out for masks.'

'Right. So these are dangerous aliens we're dealing with? They wear masks and want you to ask what time it is?'

'It sounds like them. Yes. But my people dealt with them so long ago. It's almost inconceivable . . .' He looked worried.

They stopped running as they reached Claversham Row.

'And if it is who I think it is, what I think it – they – it – are . . . there is only one sensible thing we should be doing.' The worried expression vanished as rapidly as it had appeared on his face, replaced by an easy grin.

'What's that?'

'Running away,' said the Doctor, as he rang the doorbell.

A moment's silence, then the door opened and a girl looked

up at them. She could not have been more than eleven, and her hair was in pigtails. 'Hello,' she said. 'My name is Polly Browning. What're your names?'

'Polly!' said Amy. 'Your parents are worried sick about you.'

'I just came to get my diary back,' said the girl. 'It was under a loose floorboard in my old bedroom.'

'Your parents have been looking for you all day!' said Amy. She wondered why the Doctor didn't say anything.

The little girl – Polly – looked at her wristwatch. 'That's weird. It says I've only been here for five minutes. I got here at ten this morning.'

Amy knew it was somewhere late in the afternoon. Without thinking, she said, 'What time is it now?'

Polly looked up, delighted. This time Amy thought there was something strange about the girl's face. Something flat. Something almost mask-like . . .

'Time for you to come into my house,' said the girl.

Amy blinked. It seemed to her that, without having moved, she and the Doctor were now standing in the entry hall. The girl was standing on the stairs facing them. Her face was level with theirs.

'What are you?' asked Amy.

'We are the Kin,' said the girl, who was not a girl. Her voice was deeper, darker and more guttural. She seemed to Amy like something crouching, something huge that wore a paper mask with the face of a girl crudely scrawled on it. Amy could not understand how she could ever have been fooled into thinking it was a real face.

'I have heard of you,' said the Doctor. 'My people thought you were –'

'An abomination,' said the crouching thing with the paper mask. 'And a violation of all the laws of time. They sectioned us off from the rest of Creation. But I escaped, and thus we escaped. And we are ready to begin again. Already we have started to purchase this world –'

'You're recycling money through time,' said the Doctor. 'Buying up this world with it, starting with this house, the town –'

'Doctor? What's going on?' asked Amy. 'Can you explain any of this?'

'All of it,' said the Doctor. 'Sort of wish I couldn't. They've come here to take over the Earth. They're going to become the population of the planet.'

'Oh, no, Doctor,' said the huge crouching creature in the paper mask. 'You don't understand. That's not why we take over the planet. We will take over the world and let humanity become extinct simply in order to get you here, now.'

The Doctor grabbed Amy's hand and shouted 'Run!' He headed for the front door –

– and found himself at the top of the stairs. He called 'Amy!' but there was no reply. Something brushed his face: something that felt almost like fur. He swatted it away.

There was one door open, and he walked towards it.

'Hel*lo*,' said the person in the room in a breathy, female voice. '*So* glad you could come, Doctor.'

It was Margaret Thatcher, the Prime Minister of the United Kingdom.

'You *do* know who we are, dear?' she asked. 'It would be such a *shame* if you didn't.'

'The Kin,' said the Doctor. 'A population that consists of

only one creature, but able to move through time as easily and instinctively as a human can cross the road. There was only one of you. But you'd populate a place by moving backwards and forwards in time until there were hundreds of you, then thousands and millions, all interacting with yourselves at different moments on your own timeline. And this would go on until the local structure of time would collapse, like rotten wood. You need other entities, at least in the beginning, to ask you the time, and create the quantum superpositioning that allows you to anchor to a place–time location.'

'Very *good*,' said Mrs Thatcher. 'Do you *know* what the Time Lords said, when they engulfed our world? They said that as *each* of us was the Kin at a different moment in time, to kill any one of us was to commit an act of genocide against our whole species. You cannot kill *me*, because to kill me is to kill *all* of us.'

'You know I'm the last Time Lord?'

'Oh *yes*, dear.'

'Let's see. You pick up the money from the mint as it's being printed, buy things with it in time, using the same money over and over, return it moments later. Recycle it through time. And the masks . . . I suppose they amplify the conviction field. People are going to be much more willing to sell big important things, places that belong to the country, not to an individual, when they believe that the leader of their country is asking for them, personally . . . and eventually you've sold the whole place to yourselves. Will you kill the humans?'

'*No* need, dear. We'll even make reser*v*ations for them: Greenland, Siberia, Antarctica . . . but they *will* die out, nonetheless. Several billion people living in places that can barely support a few thousand. Well, dear . . . it *won't* be pretty.' Mrs Thatcher moved. The Doctor concentrated on seeing her as she was. He closed his eyes. Opened them to see a bulky figure wearing a crude black-and-white face mask, with a photograph of Margaret Thatcher on it.

The Doctor reached out his hand and pulled off the mask from the Kin.

The Doctor could see beauty where humans could not. He took joy in all creatures, but the face of the Kin was hard to appreciate.

'You . . . you revolt yourself,' said the Doctor. 'Blimey. It's why you wear masks. You don't like your face, do you?'

The Kin said nothing. Its face, if that was its face, writhed and squirmed.

'Where's Amy?' asked the Doctor.

'Surplus to requirements,' said another, similar voice from behind him. A thin man, in a full-faced rabbit mask. 'We let her go. We only needed you, Doctor. Our Time Lord prison was a torment, because we were trapped in it and reduced to one of us. You are also only one of you. And you will stay here in this house forever.'

The Doctor walked from room to room, examining his surroundings with care. The walls of the house were soft and covered with a light layer of fur. And they moved gently, in and out, as if they were . . . 'Breathing. It's a living room. Literally.'

He said, 'Give me Amy back. Leave this place. I'll find you somewhere you can go. You can't just keep looping and re-looping through time, over and over, though. It messes everything up.'

'And when it does, we begin again, somewhere else,' said the woman in the cat mask, on the stairs above him. 'You will be imprisoned until your life is done. Age here, regenerate here, die here, again and again. Our prison will not end until the last Time Lord is no more.'

'Do you really think you can hold me that easily?' the Doctor asked. It was always good to seem in control, no matter how much he worried that he was going to be stuck here for good.

'Quickly! Doctor! Down here!' It was Amy's voice. He took the steps three at a time, heading towards the place her voice had come from: the front door.

'Doctor!'

'I'm here.' He rattled the door. It was locked. He pulled out his screwdriver and soniced the doorhandle.

There was a clunk and the door flew open; the sudden daylight was blinding. The Doctor saw, with delight, his friend, and a familiar big blue police box. He was not certain which to hug first.

'Why didn't you go inside?' he asked Amy, as he opened the TARDIS door.

'Can't find the key. Must have dropped it while they were chasing me. Where are we going now?'

'Somewhere safe. Well, safer.' He closed the door. 'Got any suggestions?'

Amy stopped at the bottom of the control-room stairs and looked around at the gleaming coppery world, at the glass pillar that ran through the TARDIS controls, at the doors.

'Amazing, isn't she?' said the Doctor. 'I never get tired of looking at the old girl.'

'Yes, the old girl,' said Amy. 'I think we should go to the very dawn of time, Doctor. As early as we can go. They won't be able to find us there, and we can work out what to do next.' She was looking over the Doctor's shoulder at the console, watching his hands move, as if she was determined not to forget anything he did. The TARDIS was no longer in 1984.

'The Dawn of Time? Very clever, Amy Pond. That's somewhere we've never gone before. Somewhere we shouldn't be able to go. It's a good thing I've got this.' He held up the squiggly whatsit, then attached it to the TARDIS console, using crocodile clips and what looked like a piece of string.

'There,' he said proudly. 'Look at that.'

'Yes,' said Amy. 'We've escaped the Kin's trap.'

The TARDIS engines began to groan, and the whole room began to judder and shake.

'What's that noise?'

'We're heading for somewhere the TARDIS isn't designed to go. Somewhere I wouldn't dare go without the squiggly whatsit giving us a boost and a time bubble. The noise is the engines complaining. It's like going up a steep hill in an old car. It may take us a few more minutes to get there. Still, you'll like it when we arrive: the Dawn of Time. Excellent suggestion.'

'I'm sure I will like it,' said Amy, with a smile. 'It must have felt so good to escape the Kin's prison, Doctor.'

'That's the funny thing,' said the Doctor. 'You ask me about escaping the Kin's prison. By which, you mean, that house. And I mean, I did escape, just by sonicing a doorknob, which was a bit convenient. But what if the trap wasn't the house? What if the Kin didn't want a Time Lord to torture and kill? What if they wanted something much more important? What if they wanted a TARDIS?'

'Why would the Kin want a TARDIS?' asked Amy.

The Doctor looked at Amy. He looked at her with clear eyes, unclouded by hate or by illusion. 'The Kin can't travel very far through time. Not easily. And doing what they do is slow, and it takes an effort. The Kin would have to travel back and forth in time fifteen million times just to populate London.

'But what if the Kin had all of Time and Space to move through? What if it went back to the very beginning of the Universe, and began its existence there? It would be able to populate *everything*. There would be no intelligent beings in the whole of the space–time continuum that weren't the Kin. One entity would fill the Universe, leaving no room for anything else. Can you imagine it?'

Amy licked her lips. 'Yes,' she said. 'Yes I can.'

'All you'd need would be to get into a TARDIS and have a Time Lord at the controls, and the Universe would be your playground.'

'Oh yes,' said Amy, and she was smiling broadly now. 'It will be.'

'We're almost there,' said the Doctor. 'The Dawn of Time. Please. Tell me that Amy's safe, wherever she is.'

'Why ever would I tell you that?' asked the Kin in the Amy Pond mask. 'It's not true.'

7

Amy could hear the Doctor running down the stairs. She heard a voice that sounded strangely familiar calling to him, and then she heard a sound that filled her chest with despair: the diminishing *vworp vworp* of a TARDIS as it dematerialises.

The door opened at that moment and she walked out into the downstairs hall.

'He's run out on you,' said a deep voice. 'How does it feel to be abandoned?'

'The Doctor doesn't abandon his friends,' said Amy to the thing in the shadows.

'He does. He obviously did in this case. You can wait as long as you want to, he'll never come back,' said the thing, as it stepped out of the darkness and into the half-light.

It was huge. Its shape was humanoid, but also somehow animal. (*Lupine*, thought Amy Pond, as she took a step backwards, away from the thing.) It had a mask on, an unconvincing wooden mask, that seemed like it was meant to represent an angry dog, or perhaps a wolf.

'He's taking someone he believes to be you for a ride in the TARDIS. And in a few moments reality is going to rewrite. The Time Lords reduced the Kin to one lonely entity cut off from the rest of Creation. So it is fitting that a Time Lord restores us to our rightful place in the order of things: all other things will serve me, or will be me, or will be food for me. Ask me what time it is, Amy Pond.'

'Why?'

There were more of them now: shadowy figures. A cat-faced woman on the stairs. A small girl in the corner. The rabbit-headed man standing behind her said, 'Because it will be a clean way to die. An easy way to go. In a few moments you will never have existed anyway.'

'Ask me,' said the wolf-masked figure in front of her. 'Say, "What's the time, Mister Wolf?"'

In reply, Amy Pond reached up and pulled the wolf mask from the face of the huge thing, and she saw the Kin.

Human eyes were not meant to look at the Kin. The crawling, squirming, wriggling mess that was the face of the Kin was a frightful thing; the masks had been as much for its own protection as for everyone else's.

Amy Pond stared at the face of the Kin. She said, 'Kill me if you're going to kill me. But I don't believe that the Doctor has abandoned me. And I'm not going to ask you what time it is.'

'Pity,' said the Kin, through a face that was a nightmare. And it moved towards her.

The TARDIS engines groaned once, loudly, and then were silent.

'We are here,' said the Kin. Its Amy Pond mask was now just a flat scrawled drawing of a girl's face.

'We're here at the beginning of it all,' said the Doctor,

'because that's where you want to be. But I'm prepared to do this another way. I could find a solution for you. For all of you.'

'Open the door,' grunted the Kin.

The Doctor opened the door. The winds that swirled about the TARDIS pushed the Doctor backwards.

The Kin stood at the door of the TARDIS. 'It's so dark.'

'We're at the very start of it all. Before light.'

'I will walk into the Void,' said the Kin. 'And you will ask me, "What time is it?" And I will tell myself, tell you, tell all Creation, *Time for the Kin to rule, to occupy, to invade. Time for the Universe to become only me and mine and whatever I keep to devour. Time for the first and final reign of the Kin, world without end, through all of time.*'

'I wouldn't do it,' said the Doctor, 'if I were you. You can still change your mind.'

The Kin dropped the Amy Pond mask on to the TARDIS floor.

It pushed itself out of the TARDIS door, into the Void.

'Doctor,' it called. Its face was a writhing mass of maggots. 'Ask me what time it is.'

'I can do better than that,' said the Doctor. 'I can *tell* you exactly what time it is. It's no time. It's Nothing O'Clock. It's a microsecond before the Big Bang. We're not at the Dawn of Time. We're before the Dawn.

'The Time Lords really didn't like genocide. I'm not too keen on it myself. It's the potential you're killing off. What if, one day, there was a good Dalek? What if . . .' He paused. 'Space is big. Time is bigger. I would have helped you to find a place you could have lived. But there was a girl called

Polly, and she left her diary behind. And you killed her. That was a mistake.'

'You never even knew her,' called the Kin from the Void.

'She was a kid,' said the Doctor. 'Pure potential, like every kid everywhere. I know all I need.' The squiggly whatsit attached to the TARDIS console was beginning to smoke and spark. 'You're out of time, literally. Because Time doesn't start until the Big Bang. And if any part of a creature that inhabits time gets removed from time ... well, you're removing yourself from the whole picture.'

The Kin understood. It understood that, at that moment, all of Time and Space was one tiny particle, smaller than an atom, and that until a microsecond passed, and the particle exploded, nothing would happen. Nothing *could* happen. And the Kin was on the wrong side of the microsecond.

Cut off from Time, all the other parts of the Kin were ceasing to be. The It that was They felt the wash of non-existence sweeping over them.

In the beginning – before the beginning – was the word. And the word was 'Doctor!'

But the door had been closed and the TARDIS vanished, implacably. The Kin was left alone, in the Void before Creation.

Alone, forever, in that moment, waiting for Time to begin.

8

The young man in the tweed jacket walked round the house at the end of Claversham Row. He knocked at the door, but no one answered. He went back into the blue box, and fiddled with the tiniest of controls: it was always easier to travel a thousand years than it was to travel twenty-four hours.

He tried again.

He could feel the threads of time ravelling and re-ravelling. Time is complex: not everything that has happened has happened, after all. Only the Time Lords understood it, and even they found it impossible to describe.

The house in Claversham Row had a grimy *For Sale* sign in the garden.

He knocked at the door.

'Hello,' he said. 'You must be Polly. I'm looking for Amy Pond.'

The girl's hair was in pigtails. She looked up at the Doctor suspiciously. 'How do you know my name?' she asked.

'I'm very clever,' said the Doctor seriously.

Polly shrugged. She went back into the house, and the Doctor followed. There was, he was relieved to notice, no fur on the walls.

Amy was in the kitchen, drinking tea with Mrs Browning. Radio Four was playing in the background. Mrs Browning was telling Amy about her job as a nurse, and the hours she had to work, and Amy was saying that her fiancé was a nurse, and she knew all about it.

She looked up sharply when the Doctor came in: a look as if to say, *You've got a lot of explaining to do.*

'I thought you'd be here,' said the Doctor. 'If I just kept looking.'

They left the house on Claversham Row: the blue police box was parked at the end of the road, beneath some chestnut trees.

'One moment,' said Amy, 'I was about to be eaten by that creature. The next I was sitting in the kitchen, talking to Mrs Browning, and listening to *The Archers*. How did you do that?'

'I'm very clever,' said the Doctor. It was a good line, and he was determined to use it as much as possible.

'Let's go home,' said Amy. 'Will Rory be there this time?'

'Everybody in the world will be there,' said the Doctor. 'Even Rory.'

They went into the TARDIS. He had already removed the blackened remains of the squiggly whatsit from the console: the TARDIS would not again be able to reach the moment before time began, but then, all things considered, that had to be a good thing.

He was planning to take Amy straight home – with just a small side trip to Andalusia, during the age of chivalry, where, in a small inn on the road to Seville, he had once been served the finest gazpacho he had ever tasted.

The Doctor was almost completely sure he could find it again . . .

'We'll go straight home,' he said. 'After lunch. And over lunch I'll tell you the story of Maximelos and the three Ogrons.'

THE TWELFTH DOCTOR:
LIGHTS OUT

HOLLY BLACK

1

Space is so dark that looking out at it confounds the brain. The more you stare at the vastness of it, at the hanging stars and the swirling galaxies, the more you start to notice how imprecise words like 'dark' and 'black' and 'endless' are. There are so many gradients of shadow, all of them terrifying to me. That's why I keep the lights on.

I know that it's silly. I'm many years away from the cramped spaces of my childhood in the crèche on the Collabria Research Colony. But in the dark there's always the possibility of *things* being close by: stalking, mask-wearing things, with cold hands and sharp needles. Nasty hiding things that I can't see. Lately, even my dreams are full of monsters.

That's why I like to travel alone. Here, in my own ship, I can track heat signatures to make sure I'm the only one on board. I can keep everything as super-bright as I like. I can view my cargo hold – currently empty and waiting for a new shipment of freshly roasted coffee beans from the Intergalactic Coffee Roasting Station (or the ICRS, pronounced 'Icarus' by long-time transporters) – right here from the control-room console. But, no matter the precautions, I'm still always looking over my shoulder. My heart hammers in my chest, my skin feels clammy and rippling and stinging-goosefleshy. Thank goodness I rarely have to leave my ship.

After leaving Collabria, I lived in a lot of places, hand-to-mouthing it. I even did a contract term with the Galatron Mining Corporation. I've always been big for my age, so they didn't question me signing the contract, even though I'm not sure it was strictly legal. Three whole years I worked for them, sifting red sand and breathing in poison, but in the end I saved up enough to buy a second-hand ship.

It was towards the end of my time in the mines when the fear started. There was a collapse and I was trapped deep under the earth. No air. Incredible heat. Terror ballooned inside me in the dark.

At first, I worried that being on board a ship would feel like being trapped under the earth or in one of the cage-cribs of the crèche, but instead it felt a lot closer to freedom. I repaired it myself, teaching myself from a big old book. Now my ship runs well enough for me to have a steady gig – my first – transporting coffee.

My route between the ICRS and the Planet of the Coffee Shops is a slog. I spend my time watching holovids, spraying myself with fiction mist, exchanging messages with 78342 and 78346 from the crèche (lately, 78342 spends hours complaining because her secondary antennae finally came in and, ever since, boys have been paying her more attention) and avoiding sleep. It should have been dull, swimming through the same old sea of stars in the same old ship, but I don't feel that way at all. I feel hounded, like I don't want to slow down for fear of a nameless, suffocating something nipping at my heels.

The past is hard to outrun. You have to go faster than my run-down ship can manage.

Fiddling with the controls, I see the reflection of my face in the polished glass surface – my mottled grey skin and the forked tongue that tastes the air around me without me even noticing I'm doing it half the time. My eyes are red-veined. I look like I could use more sleep.

What I really need is more coffee.

The Intergalactic Coffee Roasting Station orbits the planet Chloris, which has an ideal climate for growing the super-caffeinated coffee beans that make it famous. People say that the ICRS is the most caffeinated place in the universe. Just breathing the air is supposed to wake the newly dead, make hair grow on your eyeballs and recharge depleted batteries.

I like it there. Oddly, I actually feel less twitchy when I'm on the station, although I might be the only one. The caffeine calms me. I worry that I'm becoming an addict, but maybe that's a hazard of a job like mine.

By the time I dock, my chronometer says that I am running a little ahead of schedule. I go outside and fingerprint a bunch of official forms for a spiky Vinvocci, while robots load my cargo hold with bags of beans that shine like mahogany, sticky with oil. Even through the airlock, I'll be able to smell the stuff on the ride back. That's always a bonus.

The Vinvocci says something to me, and when I turn to reply he takes a step back. I guess I'm a little intimidating when you don't know how young I am: large, slightly hunched and too shy to smile when I should. Growing up the way I did, I don't know how to talk to people or put them at ease. I sign his datapad, go back to my ship, eat my

dinner out of a packet and get ready for bed. As I stare up at
the ceiling above my bunk, I have the pleasant thought that
tomorrow, before I leave, I'll go to get a cup of coffee – real
coffee, scorching hot and brewed on the station by baristas
who know what they're doing, not made in my ship's old,
rust-stained pot.

My mouth waters at the thought.

I don't like sleeping because no matter how bright the
room is, when my eyes are closed, I'm in the dark.

I don't like my dreams, either. Lying there, I find myself
wishing I could sneak out and grab a quick coffee, but the
shop will be closed. Maybe I could find some loose beans?
No, I tell myself, forcing my thoughts to focus on how
impressed 78342 will be when I've saved up enough for us to
get a place of our own in one of the nicer star systems. And
78346 too. We'll live all together and then I won't have to be
nervous about anything any more because they'll always be
looking over my shoulder for me.

When I wake up, the lights are off and my heart is pounding.
For a long moment, I think I am still in the same old nightmare, plunged into darkness, skin crawling. I fumble for the
computer screen on the wall. Gradually, the room brightens.
I blink rapidly. I must have hit the light switch in the night.

Groggily, I stumble out into the electroshower, turn the
heat up as high as it will go, and let the night's dirt and flop-
sweat burn off my skin.

There's a legend that drinking enough coffee at the
Intergalactic Coffee Roasting Station will make a person stay
awake for a week at least. Right now, I like the sound of that.

I get dressed and make my way through the corridors to

the little coffee shop. They keep it small, grubby and only open for limited hours because they don't want the transport staff – like me – to consume too much of the good stuff. It's filled with workers from inside the station too, along with a few travellers stopping because they felt the need for coffee strong enough to bench-press a star system. Behind the bar, by the bubbling, steaming machines, is a purple-skinned barista with six arms. She's making espressos and frothing milk faster than I can follow.

Glancing around the room, I see a tiny Graske borrowing money from a Terileptil in a cloak. I think I've seen them on the station before. A Blowfish with an eye patch sits in a shadowed back corner, scanning the shop with a sinister look on his face. At one table, a group of workers in overalls are kicking back, laughing together. At another, a soldier stares gloomily into the depths of her cup.

The queue is short: I'm at the back; at the counter is a woman wearing a military uniform; between us stands a whippet-thin man in a navy-blue coat with a scarlet lining. He turns to look at me with piercing, hollow-set grey eyes, then furrows his impressive silvery brows.

'I'm buying a coffee,' he says. 'For a girl.'

'Ah,' I say, wondering if her secondary antennae came in. It sure sounds like it. 'Great.'

'She thinks I'm just buying her a twenty-first-century Earth coffee,' he goes on, rocking back on his heels. 'Won't she be surprised? Turns out I'm the fetching sort after all. I mean, this isn't as good as the incredible coffee made by Elisabeth Pepsis, of course, or that amazing stuff Benton used to make – what was his first name? Oh yes, Sergeant.

Sergeant Benton. Something to do with the temperature of the water, he said. But this is still good.

'Clara's a bit annoyed with me, but once she tastes this her mood will be much improved. Or possibly not, but at least she'll have coffee.'

'Clara?' I echo. He's said a bunch of names, but that seems to be the important one.

He nods. 'She's *impossible*.'

'You seem so familiar,' I say, before I think better of it. The man he reminds me of looked very different, but spoke in the same dizzying, joyful rush. I understood less than half of what that man said, but he'd saved my life, so I was determined to pay attention to anyone who was even a little bit like him.

This man's frown deepens. His eyebrows do things I didn't even know eyebrows could do. 'I don't get that a lot.'

'He was called the Doctor and he saved –'

'Ahhhhh, right,' he says, interrupting me. 'I remind you of *me*. Oh, well, that makes much more sense.'

'What?'

At that moment, a nondescript human dressed in grey joins the queue behind me. He's wearing a respirator mask over the lower half of his face – the white, paper kind that scientists always wore in the crèche. Even though I can only see his eyes, he looks hideously, uncomfortably familiar. Might he really be one of the scientists?

'I *am* the Doctor,' the man with the eyebrows says, looking quite puffed up about it. 'I bet we had some good times, didn't we?'

I don't know how to respond to that because it doesn't

make any sense. If he really *is* the Doctor, then surely he must remember coming to Collabria, must notice the resemblance of the masked figure behind me to the scientists there. I open my mouth to ask, when the coffee grinders shudder to a halt, blades crunching metallically against each other in the sudden absence of beans.

Astonished words slip out of the barista's mouth. She even looks surprised to have said them. 'There's no more coffee!'

The beans have stopped automatically feeding down into the machines from a chute in the ceiling. On the Intergalactic Coffee Roasting Station, that's the worst thing that could ever happen.

Then the lights go out.

To me, that's even worse.

Everyone around me is screaming. I feel that familiar terror, so intense that I am unable to think beyond it. I want to run, but I feel cold and hot all at once and I can't seem to control my feet. Just as I think I might be able to move, the lights flicker back on. I gasp.

The man with the respirator mask is gone, but lying on the metal floor is the body of the female soldier who was ahead of the Doctor in the queue. A cup is still in her hand, spilling out its precious contents on to the greyish floor tiles. The fumes of the freshly brewed coffee do not seem, as the legends would have it, to be bringing her back to life.

She's dead.

It's not the first corpse I've seen, but it's the first since the mines. I had kind of hoped never to see one ever again.

2

I just stand there, not sure what to do. I'm frightened —
everyone's frightened — but at least, for the first time in
months, I'm not the only one who's scared.

The purple barista has three of her six hands covering her
mouth, staring down at the corpse in horror.

'The last cup of coffee!' the Graske yells, throwing itself to
the floor to lap up the spreading puddle. Coffee does different
things to different creatures. For most of us, it wakes us up,
makes us more alert, gives us focus. For some, though, it's a
sedative, sending them into a gentle sleep. For others, it's a
hallucinogen. And for a few, like the little Graske who now
staggers off with a stupid grin on its face, it seems to actually
induce a jolt of pure happiness.

The Doctor looks down and seems surprised to find the
body still there. 'Hello? Someone ought to do something
about that.'

'Call a doctor!' the barista says.

He sighs. 'Oh well, that's me then. The Doctor, at your
service. I suppose she didn't die of natural causes.' He
suddenly appears to have had a thought. 'Unless *you* poisoned
her. Did you poison her?'

The barista looks as flummoxed as I feel.

Overhead, a speaker springs to life, intoning: 'ATTENTION. A LIFE FORM IS NO LONGER TRACKING. ERROR IN THE CONTROL CENTRE DETECTED. THE SPACE STATION IS CLOSED UNTIL DATA IS COLLECTED. NO SHIPS ARE TO LEAVE OR LAND WITHOUT PERMISSION. ACCESS TO COFFEE-PROCESSING AREA IS RESTRICTED.'

The other coffee-shop patrons seem to be suddenly thrust out of shock and into panic. A few are trying to comm their ships. Several rush out, only to return a few moments later to report that the corridors have been sealed. People pull out various communication devices. The Terileptil draws a conch shell from beneath his cloak and shouts into it, sounding annoyed.

'Isn't someone coming to investigate?' a pig-nosed man asks.

The barista is speaking on a comm. She turns to him, clearly frustrated. 'There aren't that many people on the station. It's mostly robots. They're sending someone from the planet, but it's going to take hours.'

'That's ridiculous,' says a Silurian woman in worker's overalls.

'Poisoning isn't *natural causes*,' I point out to the Doctor, because someone should.

The Doctor looks surprised. 'There's something about you that I like. And you've met me before, which speaks to the good company you keep. So you'll have to be my companion while we solve this mystery.'

'I'll be your what?'

'Yes, it's easy stuff. Just help me, remind me how brilliant I am, notice things that I've already noticed, ask me questions whose answers are so blazingly obvious that it would never have occurred to me to explain. Up for it?'

'Uh,' I say. Above us, the lights flicker. 'Are you really the Doctor? The same one that came to the Research Colony on Collabria? To the crèche? Because you seem a little different . . .'

He peers at me with clear, bright eyes framed by those disturbingly unruly eyebrows. 'I am absolutely sure that I'm the Doctor. Are you sure that you're . . . whatever your name is?'

'So you remember me?' I ask hopefully. '78351?'

He looks at me quizzically. 'I'm afraid not. Did you change your hair?'

I touch one hand to my bare head and frown.

'No matter.' He whirls towards the body, pulling out a device from the inside pocket of his coat.

I stumble back, until I realise it's not a weapon. He waves it over the body until it emits an odd sound.

'Hmmm,' he says, muttering to himself. 'Most humans – even newly dead ones – emit a dim light. Something to do with free radicals. But this body doesn't.' He runs his glowing thingamajiggy over the body. 'No light. No heat. Did you know that, even in the year one hundred trillion, people still drink coffee?

'Is it the shadows that did this? No, not the Vashta Nerada; they'd take *everything*. Might be a Plasmavore; there are plenty of bendy straws in here. But the body hasn't lost blood, just adrenaline – cortisol. Its adrenal glands are completely stripped.

No, no, this has to be something else, something *new*.'

'What does all that mean?' I ask.

'Right,' he says. 'Really settling into your new role. Good. Something took all her delicious, freshly caffeinated energy.'

'You were the one standing right next to her,' says the Blowfish with the eye patch. 'Maybe you're the one who killed her.'

People draw closer, some of them vibrating slightly, clutching cups that hold only the dregs of coffee. Everyone wants a scapegoat and the Doctor – even I notice – is behaving a little oddly.

He doesn't help his case by moving around with his thingamajiggy, scanning everyone. 'Sonic screwdriver,' he says, when people try to back away. 'Just checking.'

'Checking for what?' asks a Tivolian with tiny brass glasses. He appears annoyed by the murder and prepared to be even more annoyed by the investigation.

'There was a scientist here . . .' I start, but I don't know how to explain the man in the hospital mask. Besides, I have no evidence that he had anything to do with the murder. I couldn't even prove he was in the room. It's probably for the best that no one pays me any attention.

The lights overhead flicker again and a chorus of stifled screams rises from a dozen mouths.

'We have to keep the lights on,' I say faintly, but the Doctor continues ignoring me. He's scanning the Tivolian in the brass glasses.

'I may be a *suspect*,' the Doctor informs the crowd finally. 'But we're all suspects. The question is, *which one of us had a motive?*'

'Well, she *was* holding the last cup of coffee,' says one of the onlookers.

The Doctor's eyebrows twitch. I don't think he considers that a motive, although it sounds pretty convincing to me.

'Which of you knew her?' asks the Blowfish with the eye patch. 'She wasn't here alone.'

Several of the beings in the room turn to one another. After a few moments, it becomes clear that they're mostly looking at a soldier in a military uniform similar to the one the deceased is wearing.

'I knew her,' the soldier says, clearing her throat. She looks nervous, which makes her seem guilty. I remember seeing her staring gloomily at her beverage. 'We were on the same ship. She'd come over to get a second round of mochas.'

'I heard them arguing,' a Cat Woman says, claw pointing accusingly.

'It wasn't about anything important. We were talking about shift changes. She kept taking the plum hours – that's all. She was going to get me an extra shot of espresso to make up for it.'

Now everyone is paying attention to the soldier. The whole jittery, over-caffeinated crowd. Everyone – except the Doctor. He waves his screwdriver-thing in the air and then looks at some kind of read-out. He continues talking to himself, under his breath.

'What does coffee *do*? Raises your heart rate. Widens blood vessels. Boosts brain activity. *Neural excitation* – yes, that would make for a lot of energy.' Then, after a few moments, he turns to the barista and raises his voice. 'When the lights came back on, what exactly did you see? Be precise.'

'I don't know,' she says. 'I guess it seemed like she was clutching her chest – up by her heart. Or maybe higher – closer to her neck.'

I want to ask the barista if she saw the scientist in the hospital mask, but I don't think I should interrupt.

'Interesting,' says the Doctor, pulling away a bit of the victim's collar to peer at her skin. 'Yes, I see. So either someone stabbed her with two very tiny swords or something bit her. Which changes the question somewhat. OK, who has a motive and also two tiny swords? Everyone turn out your pockets.'

'Doctor,' I say.

He looks up at me placidly. 'Yes?'

At that moment, the lights go out again.

3

In the darkness, everything is different. The air feels thick. My skin itches. I close my eyes, but that just plunges me deeper into nothingness. It's like being out in space, drifting, without even the comfort of stars. It's like being buried in the earth, buried in my past, buried and trying to dig my way out.

When the lights come back on, the Blowfish is lying on the ground not far from where I'm standing. His patch has slipped, revealing a gem in the hollow socket where his eye ought to be. Everyone is screaming. I think I might be screaming with them.

'Fifty-one,' the Doctor says, bringing his hand down on my shoulder hard enough that I shut up and turn towards him. I'm shivering all over.

Then I realise the Doctor's calling *me* 'Fifty-one'. He's given me a nickname. I've never had a nickname before.

'S-sorry,' I stammer. 'The dark. It b-bothers me.'

'Is it because whenever the lights go out, someone dies?' the Doctor asks, his fierce eyebrows contracting. His eyes look a little sunken, ominous. 'Because that bothers me too. But good idea!'

'What idea?'

'I had one and it was excellent, and I had it because of you.' He looks at me as though expecting me to be pleased. Then he walks quickly towards the exit.

I follow him. Glancing back, I see that several of the patrons are crying. Someone is eating coffee grounds straight from the machine and two people are shouting at each other.

'Where are we going?' I ask.

'Like you said. We're going to keep the lights on,' he says, pointing his screwdriver at the door. It opens and he continues on into the corridor. 'All we have to do is find the master control centre, figure out what's broken and fix it.'

Relief fills me. 'Yes, the lights. I can help. I'm good at figuring out how things work.'

As we walk, the bulbs overhead flicker, and I shudder, even though it's just us in the corridor. 'When we were in the queue, Doctor, did you see a scientist?'

'A scientist?' the Doctor echoes, clearly distracted. He's holding out his sonic screwdriver, monitoring the air.

'In a respirator mask,' I say, thinking of the marks that the Doctor claimed could have come from two tiny swords. Needle marks might look like that too. 'He'd gone when the lights came back on, but he was there in the queue with us. Right behind me.'

'Interesting,' he says, frowning in concentration. I'm not sure if he's actually paying attention to what I'm saying.

After the laboratory on Collabria was destroyed, I didn't know where all the scientists went. I wondered if they started again somewhere, on some other planet.

When I was a child, I lived in a cage-crib. We all did in the crèche – well, the ones who were like me did, anyway. Not the scientists. I don't know where they lived but I imagine it was somewhere big and open and clean. But those of us in the cage-cribs, we charted time by the fluctuations of the dim amber light, the beep of monitors and the drip of fluids. 78346 was in the cage next to mine and he would put a tentacle through when I was super-scared and I'd sneak him food when they wouldn't give him enough. We'd whisper to one another until the scientists made us stop. 78342 was in a cage above me. She would lie on her stomach and peer down at us with bright yellow eyes. She couldn't speak until they grafted a mouth on her, and when they did they gave her two, both a little too big for her face; she claims that's why she won't stop talking now.

There were others, all of us different from each other, but we three were the ones still alive when the Doctor came. He took us away in his blue box. He spoke to us as though we were normal children. We liked him.

I want to tell him that, to tell him how grateful we were; how grateful we will always be. I want to thank him for choosing me to be his assistant, for giving me the chance to watch his great mind at work up close, but something in his manner tells me he wouldn't appreciate hearing it.

'This seems to be it,' says the Doctor, pointing to a door with a graphic representation of switches on it. 'The control centre of the station.'

It's then that the flickering lights go out entirely. We are plunged into darkness.

I am terrified.

I feel as though something is with us, something huge and awful, something nearly on top of me, breathing on my neck. Somehow, I know it must be the scientist. He's come looking for me. And now he's going to get me. I brace myself for the sting of a needle.

Then the lights come back on and everything's fine – I'm still alive and so is the Doctor. He's staring at me with fierce, narrowed eyes and I'm staring back at him, my relief draining away. In that moment, he scares me almost as much as the dark.

4

The control-room door opens when I push it, which doesn't seem right. A room like that should be locked. When I look down, I see that it probably was locked once, but there are scorch marks around the locking mechanism, as though someone fried it. It's cool to the touch, though.

Inside the room, I can barely see. The wash of light from the corridor reflects off the central control panel and for a moment I think I am looking at a masked face reflected back at me in the shining metal. I turn, but there's no one behind me, no one else in the room.

Except the two bodies lying on the floor.

They're sprawled out as though asleep. But I know they're not. I know they're dead.

I take a step closer and fumble with the light panel. Overhead, the fluorescents flicker on, illuminating the pale faces of the technicians. All their blood has congealed beneath them, purpling the backs of their necks. Their eyes are cloudy and pale, their bodies stiff.

The Doctor has followed me in. He flares a single nostril the way another person might arch an eyebrow. 'I think we can agree this room has been tampered with.'

Behind the bodies, a wall-sized control panel flashes red and yellow lights. A hole gapes in the middle, between labels marked COFFEE DISPENSER and LIGHTING SYSTEM. Wires stick out like messy curls and shards of twisted metal protrude from the hole like jagged teeth. The whole thing is hot enough that the air ripples around it. Above the mess is a timer, the numbers reading 00:00. A bomb, rigged to go off when we were in the coffee shop.

The scientist, I think. *The scientist did this.*

I reach out and tug a piece of metal shrapnel free. It's warm in my hands, my skin being engineered to be resistant to heat, but, when I drop it, it makes a scorch mark on the floor.

The Doctor waves his sonic screwdriver over the bodies. 'They've been dead for about fourteen hours. Which means this started before it began.'

'What?'

'I mean the beginning began before the start – when that girl collapsed in the queue, she wasn't the first victim. So the new question is, *who was the first?*' A single long finger taps the cleft above his lip.

'Do you know?' I ask. I'm honoured he chose me to be his companion. I believe he can solve this. I believe he's going to turn round and tell me what to do about the scientist.

'You have a ship here, right?' he says, pointing to a sign indicating the direction of the docking bay. 'Take me to it.'

He starts down the corridor. I run to catch up, puzzled. 'We can't go down there.'

'Of course we can,' he says. 'We're not *allowed* to, but that just makes it a bit more exciting, doesn't it?'

'I'm not sure I can deal with any more excitement,' I say,

trying to keep up with him. His coat is flapping around him like he's some tall, angular, sinister bat.

We are approaching the docking bay by now and he goes up to the large double doors and runs his sonic screwdriver over the entry panel. It sizzles a little and the lights dim.

'Doctor!' I yell.

'Just a second. I've almost got it.'

And with that the doors begin to open. In the next room are robots and a few techs. They look over at us.

'Identify yourselves,' one demands in its tinny voice.

'Just passing through,' the Doctor tells the room, then turns back to me. 'Which one of these is yours?'

'Um, that one.' I point towards the hangar door where my little ship is docked.

He pushes me towards it. 'Go! Go!'

One of the techs gets in front of me. 'You aren't supposed to be in here. There was a murder at the coffee shop and there's going to be an investiga—'

'Already done. Found the murderer,' the Doctor shouts, grabbing me and racing past. 'Got to go!'

The tech starts yelling at the robots to stop us. They chug in our direction, but they're too late. I'm already keying my code into the ship.

We tumble aboard and I seal the door. The robots pound on the other side.

'Open up!' the tech shouts. 'You're breaking the lockdown.'

'What now?' I ask, a little out of breath.

'We take off,' the Doctor says, as though this is obvious. He's at my control console, tapping keys and flicking switches. I don't like it. He's scaring me and he's making all the decisions and he's touching my stuff. But I'm too frightened to tell him to stop.

'And leave all these people? But you're the Doctor. You help people! You don't abandon them.'

'Not this time,' he says, sounding positively jolly. 'Nothing we can do. We have to go. Right now!'

'Wait!' I say, surprising myself, because there's nothing I want more than to run away. I'm always running. Even this job – shipping coffee – has been a kind of running. 'If you know who the murderer is, then we should at least –'

'RIGHT NOW,' he shouts, and there is a command in his voice that makes me move before I can even think better of it. His pale eyes are blazing. I feel like I am looking at a creature who has stepped out of time. A god is staring out at me from behind the crack in his mask.

I unlock the anchoring system and engage the engines. The techs back off once those roar to life. They're probably going to report me, which means I'll be blacklisted at the Intergalactic Coffee Roasting Station and I'll have to find another way to pay for the upkeep of my ship. I feel guilty even worrying about that when we've abandoned all those people at the coffee shop and I feel even worse that we've left them behind. I think about all of that as we blast off into the endless sea of space.

Then I slump down on to the padded seating area – the one that can fold out into a bunk when I want to sleep. It's been patched with fibre-tape and is half covered in the manuals I've been studying. To one side is a collage of pictures, arranged around the computer inset into the wall, images of warm, bright places that I think 78342 and 78346 would like.

'I do remember you now,' the Doctor says, turning to look in my direction. 'Time is occasionally difficult for me. Most times it's ridiculously easy, but that can make me miss things. Important things. You're practically grown up, aren't you, but not nearly as old as you look?'

'I guess,' I say, because I'm not sure how old I am. An unhappy childhood is supposed to make you grow up fast, but I still feel like a kid a lot of the time. Lately, though, it's been weird. We were all always growing, but not in so many directions at once.

'Well, you're enough of an adult to hear this. You're the one who killed those people, Fifty-one. You're the one who drained their energy.'

I stare at him. It's impossible. I was there when it happened. I was in the dark, afraid. I wanted to run. I didn't want to hurt anyone. I start shuddering all over.

'What about the scientist?' I ask. 'The one in the mask? I saw him before the first attack in the coffee shop. And then I thought I saw him again reflected in the panel in the control centre.'

'What did you call it? The place where I found you? The crèche. But that's not what it really was, did you know that? It was a laboratory, where they experimented on you children from the moment you were born. I don't know if you ever understood, if they ever explained, but you were patched together from bits of this and that – to be monsters. They wanted to make monsters out of children. They wanted to use you against their enemies and colonise all the galaxies. You think you're seeing one of the scientists, but that's your mind's way of explaining the thing you don't want to accept – that a different part of yourself, a hungry part, is emerging in the dark to feed. Sometimes we need to tell ourselves something important, something so important we don't tell ourselves in a very straightforward way. Sometimes we can only do it with a new face. Sometimes even a face we don't like. The scientists did terrible things, but they didn't do this.'

I flinch. I think of my pallid reflection, of my dreams, of how tight my skin feels as he speaks. I think about how I'm almost as tall as the Doctor and how I'm pretty sure I still have more growing to do.

I think about whether or not I could hurt him.

I shake my head, to push away the vision I have of grabbing him in my over-large hands, of pulling him apart like taffy.

'I understand how you feel more than you might think,' he goes on, waving his long fingers in a gesture that seems to indicate many things. 'Monstrousness can sneak up on you. One day you're faffing around through the universe and the next day you realise you're responsible for the murder of seven people. I let you out. I'm responsible for the murder of seven people too.'

'Seven?' I gasp, feeling sick.

'Three people died at the ICRS, several months apart. I bet if I checked your logbook I'd find you were on the station each time. I heard about the deaths; that's what got me interested. After all, who goes for the *third* best coffee in the universe?'

That was right – he'd told me he came to the ICRS to get a coffee for a girl. Clara. But I guess he'd mostly come here looking for the murderer. I did recall the other deaths on the

station. The ICRS had been abuzz with talk about them
when I was leaving with my last shipment. I hadn't thought
much about it. People die. I've seen lots of people – kids –
die for no reason at all. Failed experiments.

'Humans and some humanoids,' the Doctor says, 'produce
cortisol and adrenaline. You need both, don't you? People
with coffee in their systems produce more adrenaline. The
station must be an irresistible source of energy. The scientists
made you as best they could for their purpose, but they gave
you an enormous appetite.'

I don't bother shaking my head. I'm too scared now.

'I worked it out from your adrenaline levels.' The Doctor's
gaze is pitiless. 'In the coffee shop, the read-outs on my
screwdriver were extraordinarily high. At first I supposed
that you were a very nervous person – you are a bit twitchy,
you have to admit – and, as such a rich source of energy,
you'd be the next victim. When I pulled you into the corridor
to find the control centre, I thought the murderer would
come after us. But, when the darkness lifted, neither of us
was dead and your adrenaline levels were *lower* instead of
spiking the way they should have at a moment of such peril
– I realised you were using it up in the darkness. By
transforming. And you're storing energy for some kind of
further transformation, aren't you?'

'No! That's not possible. If I was the murderer, why didn't
I attack you?' I am reaching for anything that might disprove
what he is saying. I need him to be wrong. My heart slams
against my chest with a fear of myself that's worse than any
fear of the dark.

'I'm not human enough, I imagine.' The Doctor looks at

me with something like pity. 'I understand not wanting to remember all the terrible things you've done. I understand locking all those memories away, but sometimes it's imperative to remember.'

He's talking about himself, but it's impossible to believe he understands what I feel. A horrible weight settles on my shoulders and I sag underneath it, because I can no longer argue. 'If I'm doing this, you have to stop me! I don't want to hurt anyone.'

'I believe that,' the Doctor says.

'The others aren't like me, either. We're all different. They're not monsters.'

'I believe that too,' he says. 'Now, Fifty-one, let's talk. Let's really get to know one another.'

He reaches over, hits a key on the console and plunges us into darkness.

5

I open my eyes, expecting to be blind, but everything is glowing with a gentle light. Predator instincts flood me – urges of hunger and violence. Memories flood me too: all the stuff my weaker self doesn't want to recall, the pain and fury of needles and scalpels, the stench of bleach and rot. I hunch forward; my body has grown larger, my back has split open to reveal spines running down it. The forks of my tongue have become pointed and needle-sharp, perfect for puncturing skin. I have a second set of eyes too, newly opened. It's with those eyes that I am seeing in the dark. It's with those eyes that I see the Doctor.

An instinct presses down on me to let my consciousness, the part of me that's in control, drift away. I fight against it. If I don't stay focused, I'm going to try to hurt him. And he is going to hurt me.

Now I can recall skulking through the ICRS in the early hours of this morning, entering the control room. It is with some satisfaction that I think about the terrified looks the faces of the engineers wore when I found them, just before I . . .

Before I killed them. Before I fed on their energy.

I overheard the scientists talking about it once, about what I was made from, before they knew I could understand them. Before I was aware what the words meant: a pinch of Axon, a bit of Ogron, a dash of Pyrovile.

'We all have things inside ourselves we can't kill,' I say, not sure which part of me would be better off dead: this monster self, or the normal one who wants nothing more than a little place on a little planet with his friends, the one who will have to live with being a killer.

'Yes,' he says, and I can hear in his voice that, again, he isn't just talking about me when he speaks. 'Which is why I worry that some of us can't be saved. That some of us *shouldn't* be saved.'

'Back at the crèche, they'd tell us that the things they did in the dark didn't matter because no one could see them,' I inform the Doctor. Even my voice sounds different, deeper.

'And you believed it. Some part of you must have believed it, because you hid yourself in yourself, bottled yourself up until you burst,' says the Doctor. 'I thought about sending you to Boukan. It's in a planetary system that has three artificial suns. It would always be bright there and you could live a good life. But . . .'

'But one day the stars will die and I'll be in the dark again?' I ask. With Pyrovile in my genetic make-up, who knows how long I might live?

'That's one way of putting it,' says the Doctor. 'So then I thought –'

'You thought you would have to kill me,' I finish for him.

'Did you know that when human boys enter puberty, their voices change?' His voice is light again, as though we aren't talking about living and dying. As though I wasn't a murderer. As though he wasn't wishing he hadn't saved me in the first place. As though, in a few moments, we weren't going to fight and one of us wasn't going to die.

'What does that have to do with anything?' I ask.

He moves around the room, fingers trailing over my control panel. I watch him warily.

'Their voices change, but not all at once. They go back and forth – deep one moment and high the next. Mortifying stuff. Try to chat up a girl and all of a sudden you go all squeaky, new hormones just showing up and humiliating you. But that's not all that puberty does. It makes you aggressive and temperamental. All that hate for all the things that happened to you – all that fear.'

I think about 78342 and her talk about boys. We're about the same age; maybe we're both changing because this is when it happens. But, if so, puberty doesn't seem very fair – she got antennae and I got this.

'I'm not scared,' I say. 'That's the other me. He's scared.'

The Doctor brings up his hands, fingertips pressing against each side of his head. 'It's amazing how we hide from that, isn't it? How much of the violence of the universe comes from the unwillingness to say those two little words: "I'm scared." Everyone gets scared. Every last one of us. But have you ever admitted it, ever said it aloud? Go ahead. Just say it: "I'm scared."'

'I'm scared.' I grit the words out.

'Good,' the Doctor says. 'You should be. That's the first step. You're going through a growth spurt, Fifty-one, a transformation. It hasn't stabilised yet. The question is, what are you going to do to stop yourself from killing until it does?'

'You mean that, once I'm transformed, I will be able to control myself?' I ask.

The Doctor shrugs. 'It depends on what kind of adult you turn out to be.'

The lights all around the cabin flash on, making me stumble back and cover my face because the bright lights hurt my second set of eyes. The Doctor must have turned them on while we were talking. I recall him touching the control panel, but I haven't been paying close enough attention.

By the time I'm able to figure out how to shut my night-time eyes and open my regular eyes, he's standing very close. 'Time to decide.'

I blink at him and then look down at myself. My hands are huge mottled-grey claws. I move towards the control panel and see myself, my almost-adult self – if the Doctor is correct – for the first time, reflected in the glass.

I am enormous, hunched over on two stocky legs, bony ridges and spines running down my back, sharp teeth to match the sharp forks of my tongue.

'When will it stabilise?' I ask.

'You've just killed four people in quick succession and taken their energy. You might have enough to make the full transformation now. Your body is still processing what you've ingested,' the Doctor says.

I punch some coordinates into the computer. 'Get to the escape pod,' I say. 'It will take you back to the ICRS. I know what I have to do. I know where I can get the energy I need.'

He looks out at the darkness of space and down at my coordinates. 'That's a sun.'

'Heat doesn't hurt me,' I tell him. 'I've got a cargo hold full of coffee. It could provide me with a last blast of energy – maybe that will stabilise me enough to get control.'

'And what if it doesn't? You'll be burned to ash and scattered on solar winds. Roasted like a coffee bean.'

'Then at least people will be safe. That's what you would do, isn't it? Keep the people safe, even if it means getting roasted by the sun. You got into a spaceship with a monster, didn't you?'

'If that's what I taught you, it was an awful lesson.' The Doctor's expression is one I haven't seen on him before. He looks very serious and very sad.

'Do something for me,' I say. 'Will you?'

'If I can,' he tells me.

'I have a . . . friend. From the crèche. You might remember her from when she was little. She's got these two mouths and she talks a lot.'

'The little mite,' says the Doctor, looking a bit unnerved. Sometimes 78342 had that effect on people. 'Who could forget her?'

I smile. 'She's beautiful, isn't she? And I never got to tell her that. You said you were buying coffee for a girl. Buy my girl a coffee too. Tell her I thought – no, just tell her I think she's beautiful.'

He nods solemnly, and I believe that he will. I watch him head for the escape pod. He gives me one last look, as though he's waiting for me to back down, to chicken out. But I don't and, a few moments later, he's heading back towards the Intergalactic Coffee Roasting Station and his blue box.

Then it's time for me to go on my own journey.

I lock the screens so I can't have second thoughts.

I go over to my bunk and pull down my pictures, studying all the little places I imagined buying. Living all together again seems like a kid's dream, but not a bad one. Once I'm permanently changed, I hope I can remember dreams like that. I hope I can be the kind of grown-up that doesn't lose the good part of being a kid, even if I'm a grown-up monster.

I hope I get to be a little bit like the Doctor.

As I hurtle towards the sun, everything else burns away. The bunk smoulders, fibre-tape catching on fire. The paper pictures blacken in my hand. Hot molten energy fills me, licking at my skin, burning up the coffee beans in the hold into a cloud of energy. I am the creature I was always meant to be. Wings break free from my back. A cry rises from my throat.

All around me, everything is light and bright. And, for the first time I can remember, no part of me is afraid.

THE THIRTEENTH DOCTOR:
TIME LAPSE

NAOMI ALDERMAN

Earth, 2019

In April 2019, very suddenly, the Earth lost the year 2004.

The first recorded instance of loss was on a BBC television programme — *SportsWatch* — where the hosts were asking Olympic silver medallist Mallika Montgomery what the experience of competing in the long jump in 2004 had been like. Did all the crowds put her off? Had she been nervous?

Mallika drew breath to speak. She paused. She frowned. 'I can't remember,' she said.

The host of *SportsWatch*, Ian Glendennis, laughed. She must be joking. But she wasn't.

'Do *you* remember what happened?' said Mallika.

Ian Glendennis had been a BBC commentator for the 2004 Olympics. He smiled. Of course he could remember, he'd been right there in . . . Just a second. Where had the 2004 Olympics taken place? He scrabbled around in his memory. 2004. There must be something in there. His son was fifteen. He must have been born in 2004. He must remember the birth. He must remember *something*.

But he couldn't.

And nor could anyone else.

★

It was very clear from the start that the year 2004 had definitely happened. There were fifteen-year-old people. If you cut down a tree planted in 1989, it had thirty rings. A woman in Omaha who had been knitting the world's longest scarf since 2001 could count the number of rows she'd done (one and a half million, give or take), divide it by the average number of rows she did a day and feel reassured that a year wasn't missing.

It was just that no one could remember anything that had happened in 2004. There was no mention of it on Wikipedia. No one had any photos. No books – feverish searches of libraries confirmed – recorded any events from 2004. Even gravestones and plaques put up in 2004 had vanished.

All over the world, people racked their brains. They searched for diaries and letters. Keen astronomers asked themselves what they'd been doing during the Transit of Venus. Music fans were convinced that, if they tried hard enough, they'd remember the death of Ray Charles – he'd been alive in 2003, but not alive any more in 2005. Military historians told themselves they must surely remember the aftermath of the Iraq War. But no.

No one could remember anything.

A great and profound sense of unease fell over the people of Earth.

The Time Vortex

In the TARDIS console room, the Doctor was trying to teach Graham to solve Janganarthi visual riddles.

'If you like puzzles, you'll love this one,' she said, holding up a small, squishy blue ovoid ball with three orange dots on it. No – red dots. No – green dots.

'I don't know about love it, Doctor. I love the quick crossword and a digestive. *That* is making my eyes go weird.'

'Yeah!' said the Doctor. 'It's supposed to do that. Go on, stick with it. What does it make you think of?'

'Is this supposed to be like *Catchphrase*? Say what you see?' asked Graham.

Ryan glanced over. 'It's one of them . . . things, isn't it?'

'Yeah? Yeah?' said the Doctor. 'One of what things? Go on, you've nearly got it. I can feel it!'

Ryan held his head in his hands. 'Give me a second, give me a second.'

The spots started to change colour more quickly.

'Look, Ryan,' said the Doctor, 'it's giving you a hint. Focus on what you're seeing.'

'How can it give him a hint?' asked Graham. 'It doesn't know what he's thinking, does it? Just a sec, it doesn't, does it?'

'Ah, interesting you ask that, actually,' said the Doctor. 'They have a very rudimentary form of intelligence. Not enough to qualify for full sentience, but there *was* a court case on Janganarth about a set of self-reproducing puzzles that started asking to be allowed to travel freely around the galactic hub. But no, these ones are just responding to the words we're saying. Go on, Ryan, you've almost got it.'

'Spots that change colour. Blue like those hot pools we saw on . . .'

'Ah, you're red hot, Ryan. You are practically on fire.'

'It's the cat eggs in the hot pools on Malbior Seven!' Ryan shouted triumphantly, as the blue ovoid winked into a live video stream of the hatching cat eggs and a *WEE-WAW-WEE-WAW* klaxon rang out around the TARDIS.

'Huh,' said the Doctor. 'That's never happened when I've solved a Janganarthi riddle before. Did I install a Janganarthi-riddle triumph alarm when I was a bit wibbly after the last regeneration?'

Yaz walked through a side door, towelling her hair dry. 'What's up? Burglar alarm? Can you get burglars on here? How do they find a window?'

'Er, Doctor,' said Graham, staring at the TARDIS's door, 'I didn't see anything come through the door, but I think you've got a letter?'

And there was one. Sitting on the floor by the door. For all the world as if it had dropped through a letter box in the middle of space.

'A letter! Yes. That is the letter alarm. Rigged that up after the whole Kerblam business, just to be on the safe side.'

The Doctor pulled a wooden lever on the TARDIS console. The alarm cut out. She stooped down, picked up the letter. It looked normal. Boring, even. Official. A typed envelope reading *The Doctor, The TARDIS, Ex-Gallifrey* followed by a long string of numbers, letters, and things that probably were letters but looked like they came from about eight different languages.

'Look at this! Someone got hold of my TARDIS serial number. Didn't know anyone even had that any more.'

She opened the letter. Inside was a single sheet of

paper with a few words written on it. It said:

DO YOU REMEMBER THE YEAR 2004?

'2004? Course I do,' said the Doctor.

Except, when she came to think of it, she didn't.

National Air and Space Museum, Washington, DC, 2004

Maria Hackett paused as she walked into the staff cafeteria. It was tortilla day. But she'd had tortillas for breakfast. So if she had some now, that'd make it a *two*-tortilla day. Could she be that person? Would she miss out on some vital food group? Could you – and this is the kind of thing Maria worried about – get a tortilla overdose?

'Excuse me,' drawled a man's Southern accent behind her. 'I'm new here. You couldn't help me out, could you?'

Maria turned. Standing behind her was a tall, well-built man. Handsome, you might say, actually. Dark hair, tan. Sunglasses half concealing his eyes. Something *kind* about him.

She glanced at his badge and saw that he was an airman. 'You just transferred here?'

'Something like that,' he said. 'I'll be here for a little while. Helping with collection of artefacts after the Iraq War. I'm the Air Force liaison, here to make sure they don't put anything classified on display.'

'Oh! That's great! We'll be working together. I'm the curator of new collections. I'm Maria.'

'Richard Somerset. Pleased to meet you.'

She shook his hand. He was warm, his skin was smooth. He seemed . . . yes, nice.

'You're in luck,' she said. 'They make the *best* tortillas in this cafeteria.'

What the heck. It could definitely be a two-tortilla day.

The Time Vortex

You wouldn't expect Ryan or Yaz to remember 2004, not so much, at least. They'd only been in primary school then – their memories were blurry anyway, though they were a bit upset to work out that there was definitely a teacher's name *missing* from their mental lists of teachers. It was Graham who was most upset. 2004! It wasn't even that long ago, and he must have done *something* that year that he could . . . But no, he couldn't.

'What's weird,' said the Doctor, 'is that there are other years that *correspond* with 2004 on Earth that I remember. It's the year 7818 in the Huskix Cycle and I'm not going to forget *those* moon eels in a hurry, I can tell you! Not to mention the battle of Ygnbnbby.'

'How d'you spell *that*, then, Doctor?' said Yaz.

'Just like it sounds. No, this must be an Earth-specific phenomenon. What could do it?'

'Isn't there anything else in that envelope?' asked Graham.

Ryan opened it up, peered inside. Looked at the letter again. 'Nah,' he said, 'but look, there *is* something on the back of the letter. Small letters. Easy to miss.'

And they were. Tiny capital letters round the edge of the back of the letter. Like someone had got their printer settings wrong when they'd printed it out.

They all read it together.

I DON'T KNOW WHO ELSE TO CONTACT. THE

BOOK SAYS IT'S YOU, IN AN EMERGENCY. THIS IS AN EMERGENCY. I'M THE ONLY ONE WHO REMEMBERS 2004. AND I THINK I KNOW WHERE IT'S GONE.

There was a woman's name at the bottom.

Maria Hackett.

And the words *British Museum* with a date, 28 April 2019.

British Museum, 28 April 2019

The TARDIS materialized with a rasping *vworp-vworp* sound in a high-ceilinged, marble-lined room.

Graham marched out and looked around. The room was hung with plastic sheeting and full of decorating equipment. There were high scaffold ladders resting up against half-hung gallery signs that said things like *Celtic Tiger* and *Dubstep*. And there were rows and rows of shiny glass cases, some of them empty and some already filled.

'If this is the British Museum,' Graham said, 'it looks like they're redoing it.'

'New wing,' said Yaz. 'Remember? It was on the news. They're doing a big building funded by that hotel guy – what's his name?'

'Robertson,' said Ryan, 'the Robertson Wing. Yeah, I saw it on the news. It's supposed to be, like, things that exist right now that they think *will* be in a museum in a hundred years' time. So it's like a museum from the future. Plus stuff from the past to compare it all to, like, look at that stuff, a real Egyptian mummy covered in hieroglyphics!'

Graham looked at one of the glass cases. 'What, they've put a record player in a case? I've still got a record player.

Sound quality is beautiful.'

The Doctor stood with her hands in her pockets, looking around in wonder.

'Oh no, *this* is someone who really gets *time*, I mean *really* understands it. Why would you try to remember the past, but not the future? It's just really *weird* to do that. This is a museum of the future of museums. And look at those pillars! D'you see that?'

Yaz went to look at the pillars holding up the huge, high roof. The closer she got, the more she saw that what she'd taken for a decorative pattern circling each pillar was actually words – millions of words, scrolling round and round, spiralling up to the ceiling. She leaned forward, until her nose was almost touching the pillar, and read: *March 2017: North American blizzard; the United Kingdom triggers Article 50 of the Lisbon Treaty of the European Union; SpaceX conducts reflight of orbital class rocket* . . .

As she looked, she saw it went on and on. Events stretching back and forth along the pillars, the writing tiny, a line for each month of each year. There must be – Yaz quickly added it up in her head – a thousand years of history in this room.

'Yeah,' said Graham, 'they should have made *that* pillar over there a bit longer, shouldn't they? Look! If that scaffolding wasn't still there, that bit of the roof would have nothing to hold it up.'

They all looked where he was pointing. There was, indeed, one pillar that was just a bit shorter than the others. Despite the scaffolding, the roof was sagging slightly.

'Yeah,' said the Doctor, 'that's where 2004 used to be.'

They stood and looked at it for a long moment.

'Right then,' said Graham. 'We should try and find this woman, Maria Hackett.'

There was a cough from behind them. They all turned. A tall, apologetic-looking man was standing next to one of the pieces of hanging plastic sheet, just in front of a sign reading *Kardashians*. He was wearing a slightly scruffy American air-force uniform.

'I'm so sorry,' he said, 'I didn't want to interrupt. You're looking for Dr Hackett?'

'We think she's looking for us,' said Ryan.

'Oh, then do please follow me,' said the tall man. 'I'm Richard Somerset. I'll take you straight to her.'

Richard Somerset led them down several long corridors through the building, which was – they saw – enormous. Outside of the vaulted central hall, there were dozens of smaller rooms, libraries of the modern book, study rooms, offices.

'How far *is* it to Dr Hackett?' said Yaz. 'Only, I feel like we've been down this corridor before.'

Richard laughed jovially. 'Yeah, the building's a little like that. Until we have all our exhibits on display, it looks kinda *samey*. Do tell me, though – why is it that you believe Dr Hackett wants to see you?'

'Oh, it's *really* interesting,' said the Doctor. 'Did you know that everyone on Earth has forgotten the year 2004?'

Richard Somerset looked at them, raising a quizzical eyebrow. 'Everyone knows that. It's on the news all over the world. Or have you . . . not been around much lately?'

Yaz was starting to have a funny feeling about Richard Somerset. She couldn't have said precisely what it was.

Maybe something about how he'd just somehow turned up to find them in an empty wing of a museum. Maybe it was the strange watch on his wrist – the glass on the front was cracked, and it just looked a bit 'Doctor-stuff'. (Yaz was starting to get an eye for things that didn't come from Earth.) Maybe it was the way he hadn't commented on the TARDIS. She knew they'd landed in a bit of the museum dedicated to the recent past, so perhaps he'd thought it was just a new exhibit, but still . . .

'Do you work here?' asked Yaz.

'Do I work here?' echoed Richard.

'Yeah,' said Yaz, 'just, you're taking us to Maria Hackett as if you work for her, but you haven't said what you actually, you know, do?'

'Oh, my apologies,' said Richard. 'Just a moment, I've got my ID around here somewhere, if I just . . .'

He started to reach into his trouser pocket at the very second that Yaz started to think she shouldn't have let him reach into his trouser pocket at the precise moment that Ryan saw him pulling a small, dull grey globe out of his jacket pocket with the other hand at the exact instant that the Doctor shouted, 'No!'

And then Richard Somerset threw the dull grey globe on to the floor, while leaping backwards. And suddenly they were all – Ryan and Yaz, Graham and the Doctor – covered in something sticky and gleaming, stuck so they could hardly move.

And Richard Somerset was giving a gracious bow and saying: 'I'm so sorry. But when I saw your TARDIS I knew it was just the thing to sort this whole stupid mess out. Don't worry. I won't damage her. I just need the puncture repair kit.'

He took off at a sprint, back in the direction of the TARDIS.

Graham looked at the Doctor, and the Doctor looked at Ryan, and Ryan looked at Yaz, and Yaz . . . Well, Yaz was the first to realise what they were stuck in.

'It's spiderwebs,' she said. 'Thousands of sticky metal spiderwebs.'

'Not spiders,' said the Doctor. 'I've seen these before. Moth webs, from Exabin Seven.'

'Moths don't sound too bad,' said Ryan. 'What are they going to do, eat my jumper?'

From out of the dull grey globe on the floor came scuttling hundreds of small black-and-red caterpillars.

'Well, you know, it's interesting,' said the Doctor, 'there are a lot of different species of moth on Exabin Seven, and I never did learn how to tell one type of web from another. If we're lucky, they just want to use our body warmth to incubate their young.'

'That doesn't sound lucky,' said Ryan.

'And what if we're unlucky?' asked Graham.

'If we're unlucky, they're the ones that want to . . . eat the flesh from our bones?'

'Oh, triffic,' said Graham.

'I mean, there's some good news,' said the Doctor. 'All species of moth on Exabin Seven are completely blind. They'll only be able to find us if we move.'

'But if we don't move, we're not getting out of these webs,' said Yaz.

And the silence in the empty hall suggested that everyone else agreed she had a point.

A few minutes passed. And then a few more.

'Yeah, it's not very comfortable, this, you know,' said Graham. 'My elbow's pinned right against my back.'

'None of us are comfortable,' said Ryan. 'Look, I'm half bent over.'

'Well, we can't stay like this. There must be someone around. How about we try shouting for help?' said Graham, and without waiting for permission he started to yell, 'HELP! HELP!'

'Yeah, don't do that,' whispered Ryan. 'Look at those caterpillars right next to me.'

Red-and-black heads were rearing up, antennae tasting the air. A few caterpillars crawled nearer to Ryan's boot.

'What else are we going to do? One of us is going to have to move eventually,' said Graham.

'Doctor,' said Yaz. 'There's one crawling up the inside of my trouser leg right now. I didn't want to say anything, and it's just one. If I can move my arm a bit, I can squash it when it gets up to my thigh. I just . . . wouldn't want it crawling any higher than my thigh, Doctor. Do you know what I mean?'

The Doctor had the look on her face she got when she was thinking very intently.

'What do you reckon, Doctor?' said Yaz. 'Just squash the one on my thigh?'

'What would he want with the puncture repair kit? That's the question, really. It's only meant to repair the time circuits enough to get the TARDIS to a qualified engineer.'

'*Doctor*,' said Yaz. 'It's on my knee right now.'

'Look, Yaz,' said Ryan, 'maybe if I just move the back of my wrist that's right next to your knee, I can get it.'

Ryan started to move his arm towards Yaz, but that only sent shockwaves through the sticky webs. More caterpillars emerged from the dull grey ball. A few found Graham's shoe, raised their front feet in obvious delight, then began to climb.

'Don't do that!' said Graham.

'Well, you shouldn't have shouted!' said Yaz.

'Just keep quiet!' hissed Ryan. 'Doctor, you need to *stop* thinking about the puncture repair kit and work out how we get out of here!'

And they might have gone on arguing like that, while more caterpillars got ever closer to them, if it hadn't been for the gentle *pop* that echoed around the room as an enormous three-headed vulture appeared in the corridor.

It landed a few metres away from them on the marble floor. Its wing-span took up the whole width of the corridor – four metres, at least – and its three heads peered around in three different directions at once, all three beaks clicking open and shut, all six of its eyes red and angry. Its breath smelled *awful*. The worst Ryan had *ever* smelled, and his friend Hussain had once dared him to smell his dog's breath after it had been eating straight from the bins.

The good news was that the caterpillars immediately stopped crawling towards the webs, and went for the source of the greatest vibration and noise instead: the angry, stomping three-headed vulture.

The bad news was . . . that there was a three-headed vulture attacking them, and they were still trapped in the sticky webs.

'I think *now* is the time to start struggling to get free,' said the Doctor. 'We're all going to pull together towards that door over there. OK? When I say "heave", heave. *Heave.*'

They pulled as hard as they could. The webs gave way on one side.

'Come on!' said Ryan. 'One more big pull will get us out of here.'

The vulture's three heads were snapping viciously at the air and at the caterpillars around its feet. It seemed to be composed mostly of annoyance; its heads even got annoyed with each other if two of them were going for the same caterpillar. They started hissing and trying to bite each other.

'Pull when I say,' said Ryan. 'One, two, three . . .'

As one, they yanked, and the webs suddenly came loose. They toppled to the floor together – Ryan on top of Graham, the Doctor on top of Yaz – with a loud yell. One of the vulture's heads swung round, beady red eyes searching for them through the haze of webs.

'We have *got* to get out of here,' said the Doctor. 'Run!'

Two of the vulture's heads had now turned their attention away from the crawling caterpillars and homed in on the four running figures. The creature started to lurch forward. It was ungainly in the space, its shoulders rubbing up against the walls of the corridor. Its third head was still trying to gobble up some of the caterpillars that were crawling up the wall, and along the empty shelves, so the other two heads couldn't drag the body away very fast. But even so it was slowly, unmistakably gaining on them.

'Doctor,' Graham puffed. 'That door . . . at the end . . . of the corridor.'

'Yeah?' said the Doctor.

'It looks . . . very . . . closed,' panted Yaz.

'Yeah,' said the Doctor. 'If you give me a minute, I can open it with the sonic.'

Ryan chanced a glance behind him. 'We might not . . . have . . . a minute.'

The vulture had managed to get its third head to turn its attention to running, and it was now approaching even faster.

The Doctor reached the big metal door first. She immediately pulled out her sonic screwdriver, but before she could aim it at the lock, the door pinged open.

'Wow,' said Yaz. 'That was fast.'

'I didn't do it yet! Must be a super-danger-sensing door!' said the Doctor.

But, as the door opened wider – and while the vulture drew closer and closer – they saw a short, plump woman standing behind it. She was holding a smartphone.

'Get down!' she shouted.

They all ducked and dived through the door. The woman pressed a button on her phone. It started to play the most angry music any of them had ever heard. It sounded like someone taking a car to pieces with a chainsaw while screaming their throat raw. The Doctor looked at the phone.

'It'd be better if that was louder, wouldn't it?'

The plump woman nodded.

The Doctor spun her sonic screwdriver around her fingers, aimed it at the phone and suddenly the sound of the awful discordant music was so loud that Graham wanted to cover his ears, but he was too busy trying to get the door shut.

The vulture was almost on top of them now – there was no way even this big metal door would hold if the creature barrelled into it at full tilt.

The woman hurled the phone through the door, and the vulture's three heads suddenly turned towards it. The vulture skidded to a halt. Pivoted. Headed towards the phone.

The woman slammed the door and bolted it shut.

'That should stop it for now,' she said.

The Doctor looked at the woman, impressed. 'That was a Corpse Gipe, right? I've heard of them, but I've never seen one in the flesh. Why did you play that music on your phone?'

'I don't know why it works,' the woman said. She had an American accent and spoke softly. 'But I've seen something like it done before, with music.'

'Was that in 2004?' The Doctor ventured a guess.

The woman laughed. 'You must be the Doctor,' she said.

'And I just think it could possibly be that you're Maria Hackett?'

Maria nodded.

'We need to talk,' said the Doctor. 'I need to know how you knew to contact me. I need to understand how Richard's Time Adjuster got broken. But, first of all, I need to know *everything* about what happened to you in 2004. Right now.'

National Air and Space Museum, Washington, DC, 2004
Richard Somerset was trouble. It was never the same sort of trouble, Maria noticed, but there was always something.

He was supposed to be working on creating a new collection, like her. It was a great job. When she'd taken her course in museum studies, she'd never thought she'd get to work on anything like this. Maria loved old things – always had. She got a huge kick out of holding an object that had been used by people centuries or even millennia ago – an Ancient Egyptian pen, or a knife used by a Native American person three hundred years ago, the handle worn smooth by use. But *this* job was something else. It was the other side of museums – not working out how to interpret old things, but trying to figure out which *new* things would be precious one day.

'Of course,' she told Richard during one of their long lunch conversations, 'in a way, the answer is that everything will be precious one day. The milk carton you drank from this morning, for instance. If we had a milk container from nine hundred years ago, that'd be precious. Or the note you passed to your friends in class when you were at school. If we had notes passed between kids in school from three hundred years ago, they'd be precious.

'So the question is more: which things should we keep now to tell a story about who we are, who we want to be, the ways we succeeded, how we fell short?

'Like me,' said Maria. 'If you wanted to tell a story about my life, you wouldn't pick this milk carton. You might take a page from one of my notebooks about putting the exhibit together. A photograph of me with my mom and dad. But that wouldn't be the whole thing – you'd also need a recording of me talking about who they were and what they meant to me. You'd need a breath from me to make it come alive.'

Richard had smiled. 'That's beautiful. Your job is to make inanimate objects come alive. I get it. I . . .' He paused. 'I've done some work with things that are inanimate but also alive.'

'Well, my job is to find objects that we can keep alive. Maybe for hundreds or thousands of years. And *your* job is to make sure they're not classified. So, how about your life? What objects would tell *that* story?'

Richard shrugged and changed the subject.

She noticed that he didn't seem to want to talk much about himself. Maria had asked him more than once how he'd ended up in the air force, but he always gave her some kind of jokey answer. 'Just passing through,' he'd say. Or, 'I just filled out my forms and let the auto-psych-machine pick for me.'

So maybe he'd come from a hard family or a tough life. Maria had met those guys before.

It was the amount of trouble Richard managed to get into that was new.

Like: you'd think that a pilot with the US Air Force would know how to greet a senior officer, and that, 'Hey, how're you doing?' wouldn't cut it with a lieutenant colonel. But, for all that he had the flashy paperwork and a letter of commendation from the President, Richard Somerset apparently *didn't* know that – and got a week's latrine duty for it. Then there was the regularity with which he got through his uniforms – something always seemed to happen to them. He'd turn up with his uniform covered in some kind of sticky oil that didn't match anything Maria had ever seen used anywhere. Or his jacket would be missing one arm, sheared clean off like he'd cut it with a laser. Or, one time, Maria was pretty certain it was a *shredded* uniform she'd seen him shoving down the garbage chute next to the kitchen. Like something with claws had ripped it to pieces.

Plus: even though he was supposed to be just looking over all the artefacts Maria had chosen for the collection to represent the Iraq War, all he seemed to do was play with these silly little toys he'd gotten from somewhere. It was weird – they'd just *appear* in his hand like magic. They'd be working on a crate full of objects the sweeper teams had shipped from Iraq, and one moment Richard's hands would be empty, and the next he'd be holding something new and fun. Like, he had a musical instrument that was a sort of self-playing bamboo flute, which could rearrange itself into different configurations; he said it was a sort of plant that he had to put in water overnight, but Maria knew she'd seen something just like it in the Sharper Image catalogue. Or, he had a battery pack for charging his cellphone that he said would never run down; it had a little screen on the front that showed a silly cartoon of tiny yellow furry beetle-creatures running around and around. He had a weird kind of yo-yo that hovered in mid-air and let out a stream of silvery-gold petals. That one was fun. Maria had wanted to buy it from him for her niece, but he'd said it was 'a rare fungus from Gaxagori' and if he gave it to her it'd 'seed', and all life on Earth would be dead within the week.

He was always kidding around like that – especially when he should have been working with her on the collection. That was the kind of thing that could get a guy into serious trouble. *Firing* trouble.

★

'You don't know,' said Richard to Maria over lunch one day, 'maybe I do things while your back's turned that are *very* important.'

'Aha,' joked Maria. 'In the thirty seconds I turn away to log a new artefact, that's when you make your brilliant discoveries! But you have to keep them secret . . . because reasons.'

He laughed.

Maria liked his laugh.

They had lunch together most days – and not just because he was handsome and friendly, but also because she liked his goofy sense of humour and the way he pretended not to know really obvious things like what money was for or that Kermit was not, in fact, a 'sentient frog species with an unusual epidermis'.

'Hey,' said Richard, 'you like to travel, right?'

'Sure,' said Maria, 'I love travel. Not that I've ever been anywhere much. The US and Mexico, a few weeks in Europe.'

'Not even Asia? Africa?'

She shook her head. 'Not so far.'

'But you'd jump at the chance if it came? To travel? Maybe even quite far away?'

Maria looked at him curiously. A thought crossed her mind. She dismissed it.

Then there was a gentle *pop*, and an enormous vulture with three heads burst, screaming, into the cafeteria.

British Museum, 28 April 2019

Ryan laughed softly when Maria mentioned the three-headed vulture. 'Yeah,' he said, 'I think we know what that was.'

There was a small porthole window in the metal door. Peering through it, they could see the three-headed vulture rustling around and squawking in the corridor on the other side. Maria's phone was still playing the car-chainsaw-screech music. The vulture looked weirdly contented, though – it was hunched over the phone, and its squawks were more melodious than when it had been attacking them.

'A Corpse Gipe,' said Maria. 'It came right through the window of the cafeteria at the Air and Space Museum. I think people would have died if Richard hadn't brought out that weird little bamboo flute and whispered something to it.'

'Ohhhh,' said the Doctor. 'That flute is a semi-sentient Zazool. I spent a few weeks with them once. You know their "music" is actually a kind of digestive gas? Farting, basically.'

Ryan and Yaz exchanged a look.

Maria carried on with her story. 'The flute started playing this horrible angry, discordant music, and it distracted the Corpse Gipe. That's what gave me the idea with my phone.'

National Air and Space Museum, Washington, DC, 2004

It happened too quickly for Maria to be sure, afterwards, what came first. There was a hot wind at her back; there was a snarling sound; there was a smell like someone had left two tons of garbage rotting in the sun and then covered it in melted Camembert.

She turned and saw the vulture. At first she thought it was several vultures, bodies the size of the desk in her office, before she realised it was just one enormous, shrieking bird, with three snapping, biting, red-eyed heads.

It had smashed through the window of the cafeteria, bringing chunks of wall and broken glass with it. It shook its great furniture-sized body, sending shards of glass flying.

People started to run away, screaming. A couple of air-force personnel stood, drew their sidearms and took aim.

The vulture breathed out a hot, rasping breath which smelled exactly like a five-day-old bean salad that had been left on a countertop in the sun while Maria went away for a long weekend.

Richard Somerset, meanwhile, was still sitting beside Maria, quietly munching on his lasagne. 'Those guns aren't going to work,' he said to her, pulling out the self-playing flute from his pocket.

The flat cracks of gunfire filled the room. And, as Maria watched in horror, the vulture creature half dissolved into the air, becoming just slightly transparent. The bullets flew through the creature . . . and embedded themselves in the wall behind it. It was horrifying. The vulture could attack, but it couldn't be attacked.

'Come on,' Maria said to Richard. 'We have to get out of here.' She tugged on his arm.

He just smiled at her. Then he whispered to his flute, and threw it across the room. It started playing angry, discordant music.

The vulture turned its heads, and took a pace or two towards the flute.

'Hey,' Richard said to Maria, 'wanna see a trick?'

He tapped the watch-like gadget on his wrist. (Maria had once asked him what it was, and he'd said 'a hyper-intelligent exercise trainer', so she'd just thought it was some fancy watch with too many features that he'd picked up at the mall.) Richard did one final tap on his watch, then raised his hand with a flourish, and said, 'Hey presto!'

And time stopped.

All around the cafeteria, everyone was frozen in mid-movement. One of the vulture's heads was reaching forward towards a young man with red hair, its beak open, its purple tongue stuck right out. Another head was turning towards the flute, caught halfway through a blink, like someone photographed with a stupid expression on their face. The third head was suspended leaning down to peck at the floor. All the people were frozen, too – running away, or falling backwards, or firing a pistol. Several bullets were frozen mid-flight.

Maria blinked. Everyone in the cafeteria was frozen, except for Richard and her.

Richard took a deep breath. 'OK,' he said, 'I guess you have some questions. I can answer them. But first we need to get rid of the Corpse Gipe.'

British Museum, 28 April 2019

'OK!' said the Doctor, 'we are getting somewhere! You met a Time Agent on Earth in 2004 posing as a member of the military – Richard Somerset is an officer of the Time Agency. Given his interests in technology that's also partly living – you've all noticed that, haven't you?'

She was met with a set of blank stares. 'Everything he has is partly biological. The Zazool flute. The grey moth-caterpillar orb he used to control us. I'm betting that he was *especially* interested in some of the artefacts that were coming through your office, right, Maria?'

'I mean, that was his job, Doctor, to look at the artefacts . . . But yes, there *were* a few he was especially interested in. Sometimes, we'd be going through those crates from Iraq, and he'd just stop and wouldn't let me touch something half buried in a bag full of sand. And the next time I looked . . . it wasn't there.'

'Hold on,' said Ryan, 'a Time Agent? What's that?'

The Doctor grinned. 'I'm so glad you asked me that. They are *total* amateurs with time travel, Ryan. I mean, they think you can *control* time, which is the first sign of someone trying to be professional about time, which is the *absolute* sign of a complete amateur.'

'Yeah,' said Graham, the Corpse Gipe crooning happily to itself, 'but what actually are they?'

The Doctor wrinkled her nose. 'All right, this is a bit complicated to explain. After the Hexbane treaties of the forty-first century, the Intergalactic Council – well, one of the Intergalactic Councils, there were three back then. Or maybe four. But one of them turned out to be another one from the future that had gone back in time. Anyway, there was a lot of messing around with the time stream in a way that made stuff go unstable. Like, really unstable. Planets popping in and out of reality, species going in and out of sentience. So . . . OK. First of all, before Hexbane, you need to know about the Treaty of the Nine Suns. Hang on.'

The Doctor pulled a notebook and a stub of pencil out of her pocket, and started drawing a complicated diagram with lots of spiral squiggles.

Yaz looked at Maria. 'Do *you* know what a Time Agent is? Since you met one.'

Maria said, 'He told me he was a sort of police officer. From space.'

National Air and Space Museum, Washington, DC, 2004

'Not a police officer,' said Richard, as he heaved on the Corpse Gipe, pulling it back towards the smashed window of the cafeteria. 'A law-enforcement official. Hey. Is there any chance you can help me with this? I think one of its claws is stuck in that chair.'

Maria stepped gingerly round the frozen tableau of terrified people about to be eaten by the Corpse Gipe.

'Oh, it's fine,' said Richard, noticing her concern. 'You can touch them. We're going to reset this whole room, anyway. You wanna put them in funny poses? I do that sometimes.'

Maria gave Richard a hard stare.

'Yeah no, I've never done that. You're right.'

Maria unhooked the Corpse Gipe's talon from the wooden chair, and Richard gave another long heave on it. It skidded a few metres across the room, before falling over, straight on to one of its outstretched beaks, with a painful cracking sound.

'At least it's moving,' Richard said cheerfully. 'We just need to get it out that hole it made coming in, and we can start to put this all right. That's my job. Putting it all right.'

'OK. Because you're a law-enforcement official. From space.'

'You're making it sound weird.'

Maria actually felt she was dealing with all this surprisingly well. It was like she'd always kind of half known that something like this was probably going on in the world. She already knew that there were government secrets, state secrets, military secrets. Why wouldn't there be space secrets, too?

'I've been dying to tell you for weeks,' Richard said. 'I mean, weeks in my subjective time. Obviously I've been stopping and starting time a lot to deal with the anomalies – pieces of tech that shouldn't be here.'

'Obviously,' said Maria.

They were hauling the Corpse Gipe through the hole in the wall. Richard had said it'd be 'easier to do clear-up' if they 'erased it outside', none of which had made a whole lot of sense.

Outside, the people walking around the concourse were also frozen but, she noticed, not *quite* as frozen as the people inside the cafeteria. There was a man in a half-running step heading away from the cafeteria. As she watched, his front foot was descending, a millimetre every few seconds, towards the ground.

'Oh, yeah,' said Richard. 'I don't need to freeze the whole planet just to deal with this one Gipe. There's a gradient setting on my Time Adjuster.'

He pulled out the watch to show her. The face was covered in symbols in a language she didn't read. Though, looking at it, the museum curator in her had a sudden yearning to get it into the archive room so she could examine and categorise it properly.

'People in the building aren't quite as frozen as people in the cafeteria, people across Washington, DC, are a bit less frozen than that, people in Maryland are less frozen than that. And so on. Do the minimum needed, that's the Time Agency motto.'

'Won't people notice,' asked Maria, 'if this museum's time

runs a bit slower than everywhere else?'

'Nah,' said Richard. 'We fix the clocks. And no one really notices losing fifteen or twenty minutes. I mean, you've had that happen to you, right? You were sure it had only been ten minutes doing something, but it turned out to have been half an hour?'

Maria nodded slowly.

'That was a Time Agent, doing their job properly,' said Richard proudly.

The Corpse Gipe was in the concourse now, lying flat on its front, one of its heads pointing up, its wings ruffled, feathers facing in every direction.

Richard checked a dial on his Time Adjuster. 'That's only taken us eight minutes of subjective time. No one will even notice.'

'You . . . haven't done this to *me*, have you, Richard?'

Richard looked a bit sheepish.

'That's my job. Look. The Iraq War was a large-scale conflict with significant loss of life. I mean, not large-scale compared to the First World War. That's why we only need one agent here. But. There are a lot of trans-dimensional and intergalactic species attracted to conflict – the Hopthens, the Grey Sizers, the 3toil Collectives . . . I mean, those are just the big ones. They turn up to get whatever it is they want – energy, life force, anger residue, fluids, whatever.'

'Fluids?'

'Humans are full of fluids. Anyway. These races leave stuff behind. Stuff that's come through from different times, sometimes, things that no one on Earth should be seeing yet.

So, when something comes through your office . . . I just pause you for a few seconds, erase your memory of it, on you go. And if there's stuff that's really interesting – I love those things that are plants, or kind of alive somehow – then I show it to you!'

'How . . . many times have you done that?'

Richard shrugged.

'Only a few. Twelve? Thirteen?'

Maria went hot and then cold. It was not a good feeling. Thinking of Richard pausing her, in her office as they went through boxes of artefacts together. Thinking of herself like these people around them, frozen and unable to defend herself.

Richard picked up on her mood. 'I don't want to do it any *more*. That's why I'm showing you this. I've had to deal with a few Corpse Gipes this time around. No idea why they keep showing up. They usually leave when all the conflict is at an end. They like fighting-energy – something to do with hormones, I think, they want to eat creatures that are in the middle of fighting.'

Maria looked at the Corpse Gipe. 'No one was fighting in the cafeteria,' she said.

'Yeah,' he said. 'It's weird. Anyway. Off you go, Corpse Gipe, back to the void between dimensions.'

He aimed the face of his Time Adjuster directly at the Corpse Gipe and pressed a button. There was a gentle flickering in the air around the three-headed vulture. Like the light was being filtered through the slow-moving blades of a fan. And as she watched, the creature began to phase out of reality, each flicker of light making its real-ness a little less solid. She could see the grass through its body. Then there was more grass than body. And then there was just grass.

'Cool, right?' said Richard. 'Man, there are so many things I've been wanting to show you! You're going to love this stuff so much.'

Maria followed Richard back through the hole in the cafeteria wall.

'I'm just going to wind this building back until a moment before the Corpse Gipe arrived,' he said, and rotated a dial slowly on the outside of his Time Adjuster.

As Maria watched, the people around her moved slowly backwards. People fell upwards from the floor back into their chairs. Tables flew back across the room to their rightful places. The wall built itself together brick by brick, the window unsmashed itself, the pieces flying back into place and the cracks healing until the cafeteria was peaceful again.

Richard looked around. 'All looks good, right?'

'Yeah, I guess so.'

'Here we go, then. Let's rejoin the time stream.'

Richard pressed a single button on his Time Adjuster. And Maria *felt* the bump as they started moving forward through time together with the rest of reality again. It was like getting on to a moving escalator or walkway, suddenly feeling yourself carried along by something larger than yourself. How funny. She'd never felt the flow of time before.

She and Richard were sitting together again, as they had been a few minutes before in her subjective time. Eating lasagne. A gentle hubbub of conversation among museum staff all around them. Everything was the same, but everything was different.

Maria put her fork down. 'Why did you show me?'

Richard said, 'Because I want to show it all to you.'

He put his hand on hers. She looked down at it. She didn't say anything. The moment felt much longer than the suspended minutes when the world had been frozen.

Richard took his hand away. He unfastened a clasp at the back of his Time Adjuster and put it round Maria's wrist. He tried to fasten the clasp.

'I want to show you what you can see. In the universe.'

And suddenly Maria felt a bit disgusted, a bit afraid, something overwhelming she could hardly name. She pulled her hand away. The Time Adjuster fell hard on to the concrete floor and – just like one of the vulture beaks – there was a cracking sound. But Richard barely seemed to notice. He scrabbled to pick it up.

'Look,' he said, 'I like you. I *really* like you. I mean, my friends can hardly believe it when I talk about you. You know, it's the kind of thing Time Agents do on their first assignment, falling for a stump.'

'A *stump*?'

'Yeah, sorry, that's what we call people who are rooted in one time period. Like a stump. You see?'

Maria knew her face was showing that she did not see.

Richard laughed nervously. 'Ha, sorry, when I say it I can see it sounds a bit rude. But yeah, I mean, it's such a cliché – going on an operation, falling for a girl – but, you know, you're my thirty-fourth assignment, and obviously I've had a lot of attention along the way.'

'I'm a *cliché*?'

'No. No. Sorry, that's not coming out right.'

Maria just kept thinking of herself frozen in her office while Richard reached into the crate to pull out the bamboo flute or the yo-yo with petals. 'Did you ever . . . put me in funny positions? When I was frozen? Like you said?'

He looked at her. 'I've done this all wrong. I'm really sorry. This isn't what I meant. What I mean is that you're incredible. The *things* you've kind of managed to half understand. I mean, when I first met you I thought you seemed nice but dumb, and it's not like you dress like anything special, but the more I've got to know you, the more I've thought . . . well, you are. You are special.'

'Nice but dumb?'

'Look. Would you like to be with me? In a relationship, I mean. Or . . . dating? Just dating? See how it goes? I could take you to the fifty-second century right now – you'd *love* it there. The parties and the music. You'd love it.'

Through the chatter of the cafeteria, the silence between them was audible.

Maria said, 'Um. No thank you.'

Richard opened and closed his mouth a few times. And he walked out of the cafeteria, leaving his lasagne still half eaten.

British Museum, 28 April 2019

'Oh man,' laughed Ryan. 'Crash and *burn*. He called you dumb, and a "*stump*", said you don't dress well, told you you've "half-understood" stuff and expected you to go out with him?'

Maria shrugged. 'I've heard worse. Well. Not often.'

'And so he just walked out?' said Yaz. 'And then what?'

'And then nothing,' said Maria. 'I mean, and then I didn't see him for fifteen years. Didn't hear anything from him. Didn't catch a glimpse of him. Until yesterday.'

'When he turned up at your office looking exactly the same as he had fifteen years ago? Even down to his uniform?' asked the Doctor.

'Yeah,' said Maria. 'He just asked me some question about . . . whether I remembered that day, which of course I did, every detail. He asked me if I'd ever thought of him as more than a friend. It was really weird. I said no, I hadn't. And he got really flustered, and stammered and then just turned and walked away. He left his coat on the chair, but when I went out into the corridor to find him, he was gone. I looked through the pockets . . . and I found this.'

Maria pulled a black book from her inside jacket pocket. It looked like a list of contacts. On the first page was written: *TIME AGENT EYES ONLY: REGISTERED EMERGENCY CONTACTS BY PLANET AND ERA.* On the very back page, there was a red notice stuck into the inside cover. It read: *IN CASE OF EXTREME EMERGENCY, CONTACT THE DOCTOR. WARNING: DO NOT CONTACT UNLESS IN CASE OF ABSOLUTE NECESSITY.* There was a number there too, the TARDIS serial number they'd seen on the letter that had arrived at the TARDIS. And a set of instructions about how to use 'local devices in the relevant time period' including a postal address, a fax-machine number, a 'telex' and advice on reprogramming a 'Space Station Servo-Robot' to issue a distress call. And an email address. Maria had sent an email to that. It had seemed like an extreme emergency. She hadn't known what else to do.

'And just a little while after he left, 2004 went missing? And you started to realise that you were the only person who still remembered it?'

'How did you know?' said Maria.

But before the Doctor could reply, there was an ominous sound from the corridor behind them. First, the music stopped. And then there was a gentle *pop*, like someone had broken the seal on a vacuum. And then another one. And then another one. And another. And then there was the shrieking. Just like six, or seven, or maybe no – *pop, pop, pop* – eight or nine or ten three-headed vultures had all landed in the corridor.

Ryan looked through the small window in the metal door.

'Yeah,' he said, 'that corridor is, like, totally *filled* with those things now. Completely, totally filled.'

'Maria,' asked the Doctor, 'is there a back way round to the gallery with all the history pillars in it? Because we need to get there *right now*. Before Richard Somerset makes something very, *very* bad happen.'

The screeching got louder. And there was banging too. The vultures were taking runs at the door, crashing into it. The door was making ominous creaking sounds.

Maria motioned with her head towards a glass security door.

'Locked,' she said, 'by the builders. But we might be able to barge it?'

The Doctor waggled her sonic screwdriver.

'No need. I'm access all areas, me.'

The sonic pulsed. The glass security door lock clicked open. There was no time to pull it shut. There was a crash behind them.

They ran. And there were a dozen or more three-headed vultures loping and flying after them.

The hall of pillars was long and wide. At the far end, there was the TARDIS, still just where they'd left it, half-concealed by flapping plastic sheeting. Ryan could just make out the figure of Richard Somerset doing something by the TARDIS door. He'd got a little panel open on the front of it – he'd never seen anyone do that before – and there was a fine cable or tube running from the TARDIS to a large-faced watch on Richard's wrist.

'No!' shouted the Doctor. 'Richard! Don't do it! Your Time Adjuster is unstable! Putting extra energy into the system will just make the effect worse!'

Richard looked up, saw them coming and redoubled his efforts to do whatever it was he was doing. He tapped furiously at the device on his wrist. A faint line of orange energy particles began to glitter between the TARDIS and his wrist. He smiled.

And then several Corpse Gipes burst through the brick wall to the Doctor's left. And the ceiling started to fall down.

'No!' shouted the Doctor. She rubbed her hand across her forehead.

They were still running, but Graham was getting puffed out and the Corpse Gipes were getting nearer and nearer. The closest one's leftmost head could almost snap at the back of the Doctor's coat. She thrust her hand into her pocket and brought out a handful of marbles. She chucked them behind her – the three-headed vultures skidded and slid with the marbles underfoot. Two of them crashed into each other, another two into a pillar, which collapsed in their path. As Ryan watched, another pillar started to shake.

'Those vultures are going to bring the whole roof down!' shouted Graham.

'It's not the vultures,' said the Doctor. 'Look.'

She pointed to the far end of the hall, near the TARDIS. Up near the roof, a block of stone in one pillar shook, trembled gently, as if the light around it was being filtered by the blades of a slowly turning fan, and then it . . . popped out of existence.

'What year was that, Maria?' said the Doctor.

'Up that end of the hall? Near the ceiling? 1963.'

'Any of you remember anything that happened in 1963? Anything at all? Anything from history lessons? Culture? Any music? Any events?'

They shook their heads.

Another block disappeared. Low down, so the pillar banged down unsteadily, almost toppling as the roof sagged.

'He's using the TARDIS energy to try to repair his damaged Time Adjuster. But it's not working. The energy is just making the rift larger. He's going to end up wiping the whole of Earth's history.'

Already, Ryan could see that there were far fewer signs and exhibits in this room than he remembered there being. He tried to make himself remember what had been here before, but he couldn't. Something . . . some kind of thing about a civilisation? Somewhere important? He tried to remember anything about history. He could *feel* the gaps in his brain.

There had been 'the Second World War', hadn't there? So why couldn't he remember a 'First' one?

The Doctor took careful aim at the TARDIS with her sonic screwdriver. There was a small pulse of energy, and then . . . it looked like Richard Somerset's arm was encased in a sort of bubble. The Doctor dashed behind a large display case and beckoned the others to shelter with her.

'That won't hold for long,' the Doctor whispered, 'the TARDIS energy will build up inside that time-safe bubble and crack it open. History will start vanishing again. But, for now, this building's not going to collapse. We've got a few minutes.'

Graham squinted down the hall at Richard's Time Adjuster. 'Can't you just get that thing off him, Doc? Make him stop?'

'I can,' said the Doctor. 'But it'd probably kill him, and I won't be able to repair everyone's memory of history unless I know exactly what he's done. Which he might not want to tell me.'

The Doctor flicked her attention to the Corpse Gipes, which had stopped comically falling over and into each other, but several of them had got their heads tangled together and several of the others were pecking at them irritatedly. As more Corpse Gipes barrelled into the hall, they seemed almost irresistibly drawn to the pile of battling Corpse Gipes at the entrance, and started biting at each other with their beaks.

'Fighting-energy,' she muttered to herself. 'Did you all notice when the first one appeared?'

'Couldn't fail to notice it, Doc,' said Graham. 'It was when we were stuck in those caterpillar webs.'

'Yeah,' said the Doctor, 'but it didn't turn up until we started arguing, did it? Because it's attracted to fighting-energy. So, what's attracting them all here now?'

She looked at the seething pile of Corpse Gipes, their necks so intertwined now they looked like a particularly complicated bit of woven textile. 'Furry yellow beetles . . .' she muttered to no one in particular. And then, decisively: 'Come on, keep calm. No fighting-energy at all and the vultures won't bother us.'

'That just leaves history, Doctor!' said Yaz. 'We want it back.'

'Yeah, well,' said the Doctor. 'I think I have some leverage over Richard Somerset now.'

At the TARDIS, Richard Somerset was sweating visibly. The TARDIS's energy was coursing over his wrist and arm. He was jabbing at the device on his wrist. Whatever it was he wanted to happen, it wasn't happening.

'Do you know what the punishment is for the violation of the Hexbane Treaties?' said the Doctor, conversationally.

Richard Somerset looked at her, then at Maria, then back at his Time Adjuster.

'Look,' he gabbled. 'I'm really sorry, but it was the only way. I just need to repair my Adjuster and I'll leave you alone.'

'You're not just repairing it though, are you?' said Yaz. 'You're deleting Earth's history. All those pillars falling down around us? They're years we're losing.'

Richard Somerset gave a pathetic kind of yelp.

'Hexbane Treaties,' said the Doctor again. 'I believe the

statutory minimum sentence is twenty thousand years for a violation like enslaving a sentient species. A Time Agent – who should have known better – would get *considerably* more. Ryan, have you got your phone? I can tell you how to get the reporting form. Internal Affairs will be here in moments, I should think, after we file the report on your indentured life-forms, Richard.'

'What are you talking about?'

'The "battery pack" you carry around with you – the one with the furry little yellow bugs that power it? They're a sentient creature, Richard. Namarkians. Maybe you didn't know – it's only recently been discovered – but if you leave them alone in a confined area, they start to develop sentience. The Corpse Gipes certainly knew it – they keep being drawn to that battery pack and to you, because the Namarkians inside your "battery" are so angry. There are probably a billion of them in there. Can you imagine how angry you'd be – stuck inside a battery for decades, not able to get out? Thinking, feeling, talking. Whole generations being born knowing nothing but the inside of a prison cell?'

Everyone went very quiet at that. Yaz had been locked in a cell once – they all had at police training college, just so they'd know how it felt. So that when they locked someone up, they'd know what they were doing, why it could affect people like it did. She remembered the sound of the door clanging shut. Knowing that she could only get out if someone let her out. The hopeless despair that rose up in her, even though she knew it was only part of the training.

'No wonder they were angry enough to bring down a horde of Corpse Gipes,' she said.

Richard looked aghast. 'I didn't know. I wouldn't have kept them if I'd known.' He fished the battery pack out of his pocket and handed it to the Doctor. They all looked at the beetles inside it with new eyes. 'You can take them. You look after them. Look, I didn't mean any of this. I didn't mean this to happen. I just . . . I liked Maria, and I wanted to spend more time with her. With you.' He looked at Maria. 'Believe me. I just . . . I didn't want it to go like this.'

'We believe you,' said the Doctor. 'But you have to tell us what happened. Exactly what you did. Or tried to do. There is no way for me to make all of this right unless I know *exactly* what you did.'

Richard flicked his eyes between them, as if looking for some secret way out he hadn't thought of before.

'Ryan,' said the Doctor, 'put this code into the browser in your phone. Eight slash per cent slash –'

'All right!' said Richard. 'All right!'

National Air and Space Museum, Washington, DC, 2004

Richard Somerset walked out of the peaceful cafeteria, his face burning. He really *liked* Maria. He had really thought that she liked him too. Those endless conversations working together on the boxes of artefacts pulled from the desert in Iraq. The way she talked about the past and the future, as if she could see them both as one – he'd kind of started to believe she might know he was a Time Agent already. He'd just thought that, when he told her who and what he was, she'd be so impressed she'd *have* to agree to come with him, explore time and space together.

Right, he thought. *Let's see how she feels in a few years.*

When she realises the chance she's given up.

He manipulated the face of his Time Adjuster – he barely noticed the crack in the glass – and set it to find her, wherever she was, in fifteen years' time.

British Museum, 27 April 2019 – the day that 2004 disappeared

She'd aged a few years, but her face was still the same, her demeanour sitting at her desk in the British Museum just as he'd known her back in Washington, DC. Richard felt touched, for a moment, that she had clearly managed to travel. She'd seen something of the world. She'd want to see space now. She'd have had years and years to mull over what she'd lost by not leaving with him. As soon as she looked up and saw him, she'd be his.

He coughed lightly.

She looked up. She knew him at once. She smiled.

Yes. Yes. This was going to work.

'I need to ask you,' he said, 'did you ever think of me as more than a friend?'

She paused. She frowned. She gave a tiny laugh.

Richard's heart felt like it was melting inside his chest.

'No,' she said. 'What a funny question. We were good friends.' She chuckled. 'Ha, do you remember that day you tried to ask me out? And managed to call me stupid *and* ugly at the same time? God, I have a good laugh thinking about that sometimes. I bet you do too, don't you?'

She would have asked more, but he'd already walked back out. *Right*, he thought. *That's it. I'm going to erase her memory of 2004. No more memory of me. She'll be fine. She'll hardly notice it.*

He twisted the dial on his Time Adjuster. He tapped the button. And the crack in the face got a little wider.

And something was very, very wrong indeed.

British Museum, 28 April 2019

'That's *it*?' said Ryan. 'You lost half of human history because you didn't want her to remember you asking her out?!'

Richard looked as if he was going to protest. He opened his mouth. He closed it again. He nodded sadly.

'I could see what had happened as soon as I'd done it,' he said. 'It had sort of . . . sprung a leak in time. It did the opposite of what I wanted: Maria kept on remembering 2004, but everyone else forgot it. I've been here for a day trying to work out what to do. When my temporal radar showed a time vehicle was on the way, I thought it was High Command coming to arrest me. I couldn't believe my luck when I saw your TARDIS. I thought I could just use the puncture repair to patch it up, fix it, everything good as new.'

'Yeah, you did trap us with those flesh-eating caterpillars though,' said Graham.

'Flesh eating? No! No! They'd just have made you giggle.' He paused. 'Sorry, yes, they do *look* quite a lot like the flesh-eating ones. Sorry. Again. Sorry.'

'Give me your Time Adjuster,' said the Doctor. 'Now I know what you've done with it, I can sort it out.'

She aimed her sonic screwdriver at the broken face and, as the others watched, the crack slowly started to heal itself.

★

Richard looked at Maria. Maria looked at Richard.

'I feel a total idiot,' he said.

'You'll get over it,' she said.

'I thought it was so much more . . . and when you said we were just friends . . . I just wanted you not to remember it.'

Maria took a deep breath. She was fifteen years older now than the last time she'd seen him. She'd been married for a few years. Had a daughter, a house, a life. And yet, she still remembered liking him. If it hadn't been for the time-freezing, if she'd had time to talk to him about it, if he'd understood why it had upset her so much . . .

'Richard. There's no "just" about friendship,' said Maria. 'I really would have been your friend. That's a lot. It doesn't ever have to be more than that.'

'There!' said the Doctor. 'Fixed! Now I can reverse the last few commands . . .'

One by one, the blocks in the pillars of the hall rematerialised back in place. The roof was standing again.

'Who remembers 2004?' said the Doctor.

'Oh my word,' said Graham. 'I do! I remember it all! Arsenal won the Premier League, floods in Boscastle – those were terrible.' He paused, blushed and gave a little laugh. 'And a few personal things I don't think I need to go into.'

Ryan made a face. 'Didn't need to start imagining what you meant by that actually, Graham.'

At the other end of the hall, the Corpse Gipes were still fighting among themselves. The Doctor pulled Richard's battery pack out of her pocket and looked at it. Inside the device, the furry yellow beetles were running in orderly lines. It almost looked as if they were dancing – or trying to communicate.

'Poor things,' she said, 'trapped in there for so long. There's a rescue centre set up for them on Dwolo Beta. I'll just pop them into the TARDIS for now to take them out of the time stream.'

She opened the TARDIS door and gently placed the box on the floor.

Almost at once, the Corpse Gipes started to look up and around, bemused. Their heads talked to each other in a soft chirrup. And, one by one, they vanished from reality with a gentle *pop*.

'As for *you*,' the Doctor said to Richard, 'I am not going to report you to the Time Agency. But I am keeping this Adjuster. You've shown yourself incapable of using it correctly, and you need a bit of time to think about what you've done.'

Richard looked like he might be about to protest. He frowned, took a breath. And then he thought better of it. He sighed. 'That's fair enough,' he said. 'Might be quite nice to live through time at a normal pace.'

'You never know,' said the Doctor to Maria, 'he could make himself useful around the museum. I noticed at least one object on display that definitely isn't from Earth. But only if you fancy having him around. Otherwise I can drop him off somewhere else.'

Richard looked at Maria. 'What do you say,' he said, 'to trying out that "friends" thing? Properly?'

'You'll have to show me you're worth it,' she said. 'I'm not friends with just anyone, you know.'

THE FOURTEENTH DOCTOR:
FLEETING FACES

STEVE COLE

PART 1

DESTINATION: SKARO

'Ahhhh, nice big red planet!' cried the Doctor, looking up at the TARDIS scanner. As the world grew larger, he noticed pinprick blooms of fire erupting on the surface. 'Or possibly, *nasty* big red planet,' he concluded. 'Wonder where I'm going?'

It was a question weighing heavily on the Doctor. Life had been a blur in this new body, and he'd only had it an hour. A poem popped into his head:

> *If you can fill the unforgiving minute*
> *With sixty seconds worth of distance run . . .*

'Ha! And then some!' The Doctor frowned. 'Who wrote that? Kipling! That's it! What a fella! What cakes . . .'

The planet was still fast approaching, filling the asymmetrical screen. The Doctor tutted, feeling his fingers across the TARDIS console towards a switch.

The wrong switch.

As he flicked it, the planet suddenly zoomed closer at six times the speed. The Doctor staggered back, clung to the nearest crystalline pillar and whooped with laughter.

★

In a bunker, deep beneath the war-strewn surface of the planet Skaro, Jonas Castavillian stood in a cold and fumy workshop, though to him, it felt more like a royal reception hall.

Despite being the most junior member of the Kaled Propaganda Council, he had been handed this most prestigious assignment: to engage with Davros – the greatest scientist of the Kaled race – on what some were calling his Ultimate Breakthrough. Well, all right, only Jonas was calling it that for now. But perhaps Davros might like the name, he thought. Just imagine if it catches on –

With an oily shift of gears, the outer door to the workshop slid open. Jonas straightened his uniform, his heart thumping. The war against the Thals had endured for a thousand years, and to most, it seemed inconceivable that it could ever end.

But not to Davros. Davros had invented a means to end it, and Jonas felt giddy with the privilege of being the first person outside of the Bunker to witness its unveiling.

Davros stalked into the room, tall and gaunt, an almost-spectral figure haunting the high-tech surroundings. His face was severe, his skin stretched taut over high cheekbones as he looked down at Jonas.

'Greetings,' said Davros cordially, a faint metallic rasp to his voice. Jonas had heard that Davros had been injured by a Thal shatterbomb early in his career; those things inflicted all kinds of internal damage. 'Mr Castavillian, I take it?'

Jonas nodded eagerly. 'Yes, Davros! It's an honour to work for you, sir.'

Davros nodded as if certain this was the case. 'Then allow me to show you the future of our beloved Kaled race.' He produced a remote control from his pocket and placed a skeletal thumb on a switch.

SCHUNK!

Intense red lighting flooded the room, and steam and hydraulics hissed. The entire lab pulsed with threat and energy as a bulky, conical shape rose into view on a metal platform.

'Behold,' Davros hissed. 'My Mark Three Travel Machine.'

The thing was impressive, Jonas thought. Much more so than the leaked images the council had gotten hold of. Its grey metal surface was adorned with grooves and ridges, slats and mesh. At the apex of its form, a domed head housed a single, glowing eye at the end of a flexible shaft. There were two more appendages at the thing's midriff – one slim, short and sleek, the other ending in a formidable claw.

'The war has caused the Kaled race to mutate,' said Davros with eerie reverence. 'But within this casing, we can evolve. We can start anew. We can become stronger than ever!'

At that, the thing stirred. It looked up, twitching with movement. And in a harsh, synthesised voice, it articulated its intentions with chilling clarity: 'We will become the supreme race in the universe!'

'Led by me,' Davros added softly.

Hmm, Jonas thought. That's one to run past the focus groups.

'Observe. A bonded polycarbide shell . . .' Davros strode forward to survey his creation, like a proud father at the incubation tanks, gesturing to the smaller metal rod extruding from the creature's shell. 'This ruby-ray blaster is capable of exterminating a million Thals without recharging. And *this* . . .' He stroked his finger along the machine's large, powerful grabbing tool – 'This is a multi-dextrous claw, capable of lifting great weights, with electrified poison darts and a multi-omni-port to hijack any form of electronic communication. My ultimate masterpiece of design!'

The machine glared down at Jonas as if challenging him to disagree.

'Yes . . .' Jonas could hear his bosses in his ear: Remember, a man like Davros respects strength; you must have no qualms over pressing your own agenda. He took a deep breath and dived in. 'I did some research on the name, sir,' he said brightly. 'Since we're called Kaleds, I thought our future selves could be an anagram of Kaled. Like . . . Lekad.'

Davros blinked. 'No,' he said.

Jonas tried again. 'Adlek?'

A look of disdain. 'No.'

Jonas felt sweat drip down his back. He suddenly realised just why he had received this 'prestigious' assignment: because Davros was terrifying, and no one else wanted to be on the receiving end of this withering glare. Jonas reckoned Davros could end more than just your career if he took against you.

'Klade?' he tried again with a winning smile.

This time, Davros turned away. 'No.'

Jonas had been so sure that 'Klade' would win Davros over – lucky number three on the list – that he hadn't thought up any better alternatives. 'Er . . . Ed-l-ka?'

Davros winced. '*No.*'

Over the intercom, a cold, nasal voice intruded on the awkward discussion. Jonas recognised it as belonging to Security Commander Nyder and rolled his eyes. Nyder had blocked Jonas's debut PR campaign to rehabilitate the Mutos' public image and recruit them into the army; after all, why shouldn't the warped, genetic relics of their own race fight the Thals in their own regiments? But, no, Nyder had steamrollered both the idea and his complaints, insisting repeatedly, '*Your views are not important.*'

'Davros,' Nyder said, 'I need your confirmation to begin the next bombardment, sir.'

'One moment,' said Davros, and crossed to the door. He turned briefly and held up a warning finger to Jonas. 'And, touch nothing. Is that understood?

'Yes, sir.' Jonas nodded smartly as Davros left, the door shuddering shut behind him.

Jonas almost relaxed. But the Mark Three Travel Machine (argh, Klade would make such a good name!) was still scrutinising him. The iris of the eye seemed to shrink as if in disgust. And had that ruby-ray blaster thing twitched a fraction?

Then, in an instant, a large blue box hurtled into the workshop – insubstantial one moment, hard as diamond the next. It flew across and sliced past the front of Davros's creation, almost knocking it off its base. Then, with a quivering *CLANG*, it smashed to a halt, jammed at a thirty-degree angle against the left-hand wall.

Jonas's jaw dropped so far it nearly brushed his jackboots. Was that meant to happen? he thought numbly. Is this some sort of test? Should I sound the alarm, or –?

Jonas's blood ran cold as he saw the Not-a-Klade's claw arm – bent and broken – sticking out of the side of the big blue box.

The big blue box had doors, and one of them opened.

★

The Doctor peered out into a smoky haze. It smelled like a garage – oil and grease and a bonding agent of some sort. It felt familiar, and so did the gravity. But not in a happy way. He felt familiar hairs prickle on the back of his familiar neck.

Then he saw the young man staring across the room at him.

'Hello!' The Doctor beamed and stepped outside. 'Just passing by, cos I got a bit lost. It's funny, sixty minutes ago, I was this really brilliant woman. And now I've got this old face back again! I mean, why? Why? I ask of you, my brand-new friend, why? It's all a bit of a puzzle, and –' He broke off as he saw a sleek metal device sticking out of the side of the TARDIS and winced. 'Ohhh . . . I'm sorry, I'm so, so, sorry; I think I've broken this multi-claw adaptable . . . what is it?' He looked around in the hope of finding a clue.

He found one.

There, on a plinth, stood an all-too-familiar figure. Wires and cables trailed uselessly from a socket that clearly once had held the metal appendage.

'That's a Dalek!' he declared. He'd seen enough of them lately. The shock of impact as the TARDIS had swung through in partial phase must have knocked it inert. But for how much longer? he wondered.

'Good word!' His brand-new friend was typing on a tablet. 'Dalek! Yes, that's it!'

The Doctor frowned. 'I'm lucky I wasn't exterminated . . .'

'Oh, exterminated! Good word!' The young man typed again. 'Great!'

'Wait a minute.' The Doctor looked at his new friend more closely. He was wearing the austere black uniform of a Kaled officer from the last days of Skaro's thousand-year war. 'D'you mean to say . . . this is the genesis of the Daleks?

His new friend was furiously typing. 'Oh, this is the stuff!' he said, his smile widening. 'Thank you!'

'No, no, no, stop it!' the Doctor protested. By coming here to so pivotal a point in history – a point he might be patrolling in an earlier body right now – he could risk untold carnage to the web of time. 'Look, I was never ever here,' he said. 'Never. The timelines and the canon are rupturing, I'm just going to go, and you're not going to say a word, OK?'

The young man looked unimpressed. 'No, but you broke the multi-claw-adaptable-thingummyjig!'

'Oh, yes, right. Hold on!' The Doctor grimaced, then dashed back inside the TARDIS.

He knew what he needed to do and took the plunge.

Or rather, the *plunger*.

There was one kept behind the TARDIS door, left long ago by a passing plumber. (Even the most incredible of trans-dimensional crafts got a clogged drain sometimes.) He tossed the sink plunger to the young man, who caught it with his free hand.

'Never here!' the Doctor reminded him. And he slammed the door shut.

As the blue box vanished as impossibly as it had arrived, Jonas might have imagined the whole visitation had been a dream. Except he was left standing before a broken Klade – no, a Dalek, he knew that name would fly – with some sort of plastic stick that ended in a rubber suction cup. He stared at it. It looked like it might be handy for drawing out the juicy bits from the giant clamshells that roamed the under-city tunnels, but besides that . . .

Focus, Jonas told himself. Davros would soon be returning. When he saw the missing claw-thingummy, he would surely explode.

What can I do, thought Jonas. What can I do?

He looked down at the strange appliance in his hand.

Less than a minute later, Jonas heard a smart tattoo of footsteps outside the workshop. The door grumbled open.

He stood to attention as Davros entered, feigning as much innocence as he could muster.

'Now, where were we, Mr Castavillian?' Davros said airily. 'Ah, yes, the splendid design of my secondary arm —'

He broke off and stared as he noticed the change to have befallen his creation: in place of the gleaming, perfect multi-dextrous claw, the plastic and rubber tool protruded.

As if waking at its master's presence, the travel machine shifted on its plinth. Its eyestalk looked down at this unexpected alteration, then up again at Davros.

Silence filled the workshop.

Davros kept staring at Jonas's hamfisted handiwork.

Jonas tried not to cringe, holding himself with an assurance he didn't feel.

Finally, Davros looked back at Jonas.

'Mr Castavillian,' he said, a smile chiselling its way into his face. 'I like it.'

PART 2

UNDER CONTROL

'Whoa!' The Doctor had wasted no time resetting the TARDIS flight controls. 'There's lost, and then there's *get* lost!' He raised his voice, addressing the whole control room. 'Let's go somewhere we've never been before, shall we?'

In answer, the crystalline controls glowed, glittering with power. The Doctor caught sight of his reflection – at the old face staring back at him. And he looked quickly away as the TARDIS warped and *vworp*ed into existence a little more calmly this time.

But who needs calm? The Doctor thought. He burst out of the TARDIS, and into a dank, rocky gloom, grinning as he stared about. 'It's a cave. I love a cave!' The only dim light came from seams of gleaming silver in the stone. 'Natural phosphorescence? Or has someone given nature a hand? Or a Skarosian claw, or a tentacle, or –?'

A scream, deep and despairing, echoed from somewhere in the blackness beyond the cave's mouth.

The Doctor's eyes widened. 'Someone to save, inside a cave.' He froze for a moment, every sense working to pinpoint the source of the scream. Then he set off at a sprint.

The cave opened on to a tunnel. Soft, silvery light blossomed over the bare rock walls as the Doctor raced forward – was it responding to vibration? Movement? Body heat? The scream sounded again, more desperate this time, and the question was forgotten as he rounded a corner.

Ahead of him was a deep fissure in the rock. Wedged inside it was a powerful, white-furred creature easily twice his size. *A Strombok!* thought the Doctor. *Must have landed on Strombokkaccino.* The Strombokk's shaggy limbs were braced against the rock, its face twisted in effort.

The Doctor stared. 'Are you stuck?'

'Trapped.' The creature's groan was deep and rumbling.

'Let's have a look,' said the Doctor, darting straight into the fissure.

It was then that he realised the walls were closing in.

'Whoa! All right, then!' The Doctor added his strength to the Strombok's, making a concertina of his body between the two walls. 'Squeeze past me. Quickly!'

'No good.' Sweat was wetting the Strombok's furry face. 'Can't get out.'

'You can! Same way I got in.' The Doctor pulled his new sonic screwdriver from inside his coat pocket and buzzed it about the crevice. There was some sort of technology in the rock walls, but he couldn't get a clear reading.

The Strombok groaned as rock dust showered down from above. 'Leave me.'

'Nah, don't want to do that. A-ha!' The Doctor pointed the sonic up at the ceiling. 'If I can hit just the right resonance where the wall meets the roof . . .' The pitch of the sonic snaked in and out of hearing, then hit a note so high even

Time-Lord ears couldn't hear it. A huge slab of rock – very nearly the width of the fissure itself – started to detach itself from the ceiling overhead.

Yellow eyes bulged in the Strombok's face. 'We'll be flattened.'

'Not yet we won't!' The Doctor tugged down on the creature's right arm, dislodging it. Then with a grating, grinding sound, the unsupported wall closed inward – until it came up against one end of the slab of rock about to topple from the roof. With the rock wedged in place, the walls could no longer squeeze shut.

The Doctor dragged the Strombok out of the crevice, and they tumbled together to the cold ground. 'Now that we've rocked each other's world,' he said, panting for breath, 'why don't you tell me what's going on? I'm the Doctor. You are . . .?'

'Trapped.' The Strombok stared at him. 'Can't get out.'

'You *are* out.' The Doctor peered into the creature's clouded yellow eyes. 'But you might be in shock . . .'

There was another grating noise, and the slab of rock fell loose from the ceiling with a terrific *crump* as the walls now began to slide apart. The Strombok pushed the Doctor away and then scrambled back inside the widening fissure.

'Oi!' The Doctor stared as the Strombok disappeared through a gap in the rock at the back. Then, another, near-identical Strombok emerged from inside and stepped forward to stand in the same spot as his predecessor. The walls of the fissure began to shudder and close in again. This second Strombok flexed his arms mechanically, ready to brace against the wall.

The Doctor got up and crossed to the Strombok. 'Who's doing this to you? How many of you are in there?'

Suddenly, another scream of terror tore through the tunnel – this one higher pitched, almost bestial. The Doctor turned to his right and saw silvery glints sparkle along the length of the dark passage, like a trail of luminous breadcrumbs leading the way. He hesitated a moment, conflicted, as the Strombok grunted with the effort of holding back the vice of the enclosing rock. But as more screams came from the same direction, he made the decision and ran off, yelling over his shoulder as he did so, 'I'll be back!'

The screams bounced off the rock in confusing echoes, and more than once the passageway branched into multiple tunnels leading in different directions. He let instinct guide him, and when he discovered a den of mole-like creatures, clustered and quivering together in a filthy cavern, the relief he felt was like a physical weight had been lifted from him. As the Doctor skidded to a stop, coat tails flapping about his legs, he recognised three things at once: Firstly, that the creatures had curved tusks for digging and wide, bulbous eyes for seeing in the dark, which could only mean they were a mining race from Vega Raptos. Secondly, the Vega Raptons seemed too terrified to have noticed his dramatic entrance. And thirdly, that the focus of their fear appeared to be a small pig.

'I'm the Doctor,' he announced. 'Who can tell me, are we on Strombokkaccino? The gravity feels off for Vega Raptos . . .' The miners ignored him, but the pig spared him a glance, and a morose oink. The Doctor approached it, making soothing noises. The pig shifted its meagre weight, skinny and sad looking – the Doctor noticed the poor thing had been roped to a nearby stalagmite. 'You're not so scary, are you?' the Doctor murmured. It looked to be a genuine Earthling pig, but as he reached out a hand to touch it, the Vega Raptons started screaming again.

'It will destroy you,' one shouted shrilly. 'Destroy us all.'

'Yeah?' The Doctor turned to face them. 'How's it gonna do that? I mean, you can never rule out a twist in the tail – not with a pig, anyway – but, still . . .'

'If we take our eyes off the beast, it will kill us,' a Vega Rapton said hoarsely. 'It will tear us apart.'

The Doctor stooped to untie the rope and scooped up the bony pig, which barely struggled. 'This poor animal's been too badly treated to do anything,' he said angrily. 'Look!'

'The armoured beast!' One of the miners was gibbering with fear, while its neighbours gouged at the rock in terror. 'Its bristles are tipped with poison; its tusks will tear your flesh . . .'

What are they seeing here? The Doctor wondered. With the pig under one arm, he scanned again with the sonic. And again, he picked up an unclear reading of technology somewhere in the walls that might not be technology at all.

The Doctor cast an accusing look at the sonic and pushed it back in his pocket. 'It's fine!' he told the Vega Raptons. 'Honestly.' The Doctor backed away with the pig under his arm, holding up his free hand in a placating gesture. 'Look, I'm taking it away. You're free to do what you want.'

But though the Vega Raptons quietened, they remained huddled together, tearful eyes still sharp and suspicious.

'Where is this place?' the Doctor asked. 'I've seen Stromboks, you lot and now a pig . . .'

'We travel to the place of offering,' someone said.

'Travel? To somewhere else in the caves, you mean? Where? I'll help you find it if you like.' There was no response, so the Doctor tried again. 'What place of offering? Offering what?'

'Ourselves,' came a whisper from the crowd.

The Doctor was about to question them further when he heard another hoarse scream from somewhere. 'Wait. Really?' He narrowed his eyes in sudden suspicion. 'Do you hear screams a lot around here?'

There was a rustling in the gloom as a hundred heads nodded.

'They travel with us,' someone said.

'Sounds like someone's in trouble,' the Doctor said. 'Who wants to help me help them?'

No one moved. The shouts started up again, multiple tones, and then the pig gave a short but plucky squeal.

'Come on then, Alfredo,' said the Doctor, disquieted. 'Let's leave this lot to it, shall we?' The pig didn't answer, but as he moved away with the pig in his arms, he wished that someone would. *What is happening here? Two wildly different races living side-by-side, trapped by their own fears. Two failed interventions. And now, a third species?* The Doctor felt a sense of urgency at the back of his mind, driving him to find whoever was in trouble.

That's who you are, he thought. *That's what you do – whatever you can.*

He paused for a moment to set down the pig. 'Nothing personal, Alfredo,' he apologised, 'I just don't know how dangerous it's gonna be through there and I might need both hands to . . .'

He trailed off as the pig scurried on ahead of him. 'They never listen,' he muttered, and hurried after it.

Another cavern opened up to his right, lit with torches that burned infernal red. In the hellish light, people writhed helplessly on the floor, transfixed by a platform of stalactites with sharpened points which hung overhead. Alfredo snuffled up to one of the humans and licked his face. The man recoiled. 'What on Earth . . .?'

'Earth, is it?' the Doctor said. 'Well, sort of makes sense. Twenty light years on from Vega Raptos and maybe forty from Strombokkaccino. It's like a join the dots in space!'

'Christmas.' The man was staring at Alfredo. 'They came back for us at Christmas.'

'Christmas?' The Doctor frowned. 'Don't tell me the place of offering is Santa's grotto? Who came back for you?'

'They found the sword,' someone said.

'Found *us*,' said another.

'Whoever "they" are,' the Doctor replied, 'they're gonna find trouble. Who's with me?' He was unsurprised by the lack of response. 'Don't tell me, you'd rather lie on the ground feeling helpless . . .'

Alfredo nudged his ankle. The Doctor saw that the vicious spiked platform was held up by a heavy chain wrapped around a pulley. He studied it for a moment, then switched on the sonic. At the bright blue buzz, the chain jumped and unwound to its full extent. A collective scream went up from the humans as the stalactites dropped a half-metre lower, then stopped.

'That's as far as the trap can go,' the Doctor announced. 'Look. It's run out of chain.'

'You'll kill us all!' someone shouted. 'Get away from those controls.'

The Doctor waved the sonic and the chain rewound itself, hauling up the stalactites. With another buzz, they chuntered noisily free again, well away from their would-be victims. 'Not wanting to make you feel silly or anything, but you're not in any danger,' the Doctor insisted. 'I have a feeling the Stromboks' closing walls can't close all the way either, and Alfredo's no bother at all. But you're all being kept in a state of hypervigilance, focusing so much on your fear that you can't do anything about anything else. Come on, up you get.'

'You don't understand,' a man sneered.

'They'll spear us if we move away,' a woman said, 'and spare us if we don't.'

'Ahh, the mysterious "they" that you can't seem to name,' said the Doctor. 'Either you don't know, or it's some kind of hypnosis.' He blinked. 'They came *back* at Christmas. I wonder . . .'

A deep, rumbling bellow shook the ground and ploughed straight through his thoughts.

'Not again,' The Doctor sighed. 'Cue Doctor, off into the dark again, trusty pig by his side . . .'

But Alfredo had wandered off somewhere. The Doctor couldn't blame him – a strong reek of spice and decay was filling the corridor. He ran on towards it, aware of that same strange pressure at the back of his mind, trying to push him on. He stopped for a few moments, just to be sure he could resist the impulse, wary of a trap. But the sound of anyone in despair set his teeth on edge, and teeth were troubling enough at the best of times. He ran on along the tunnel . . . which ended in a huge circular chamber with six passages leading off from it. The chamber was dominated by a pool of dark fluid where vast octopods thrashed and quaked in a frenzy of motion.

'Sarnsquids!' The Doctor shook his head. On their native world, they were a gentle race of scientists and philosophers, their great bulk and clumsy appendages at odds with the elegance of their thought. 'What a menagerie . . .'

'The bile-pit burns!' shrieked one of the Sarnsquids, its single eye blood-red and rolling. 'Burns like fire!'

Of course, the Doctor realised. *The stench is the Sarnsquid's physical pain and fear.* 'What can I do?' he muttered. 'Got to be something . . .' A strong vibration hummed through the ground around the pool, and the Doctor saw the silver veins in the rock thread upwards like powerlines towards a giant porthole in the roof. Stars glowed beyond and, as he stared, gobsmacked, a pale ringed planet passed by.

The Doctor remembered the words of the Vega Rapton: *We travel.* 'This isn't just a cave system,' he breathed. 'It's a cave system inside a spaceship.' The howl of another Sarnsquid snapped him back into action. He waved round the sonic around, tracing the silver powerlines. The same unclear readings showed that he was scanning something that either was or wasn't technology. The sensors he'd detected in the walls of the cells all fed into this arterial network. They reminded him of a humanoid nervous system pinned down in two dimensions – as if the Boneless were on board. But as the sonic did its work, these powerlines seemed to culminate in a decidedly three-dimensional crimson panel in the dark stone wall, where strange symbols danced and shook. The Doctor stabbed at the design with his fingers, directing the squiggles with short, precise movements until the panel cooled to blue and the thrashing of the Sarnsquids died down.

The Doctor crossed back to the edge of the giant pool and crouched down to address the octopods. 'I'm sorry. So sorry for what's been done to you.'

'Thank you.' A Sarnsquid reached out a quivering tentacle and pressed it to the Doctor's arm. 'The scale of our pain turns the psychic turbines that power this craft.'

'Yeah. Scream if you want to go faster,' the Doctor said grimly. 'The systems here were designed to torture whoever's in the pool in perpetuity. I shouldn't think there are many races who could withstand such a punishment.'

'No.' Another Sarnsquid panted, eyes closed. 'There are not many.'

'We are all slaves,' said another. 'Everyone on this vessel faces that fate.'

'Yeah, to be brought to the place of offering,' the Doctor agreed. 'And I'm being brought there too . . .' He couldn't hear the Sarnsquids' response over a new clamour – hundreds of raucous cries and screams. *More people needing help, that's what I'm meant to think.* 'Turn the shouting up to eleven!' he yelled up at the ceiling. 'It's not gonna do you any good.' He walked out of the chamber through the nearest tunnel. The walls pulsed about him with thick red light. The atmosphere grew hot and oppressive. The Doctor heard groaning, keening, calling. Stromboks, Vega Raptons, humans, Sarnsquids. Other voices, taunting him with their pain. So many prisoners on this ship. He had to help them.

'Come on, then!' he yelled. 'Let's do this.' The Doctor marched on, spying light at the end of the tunnel ahead through the red haze. 'Who needs me most? Who needs help first? He emerged into stone-cold whiteness, like a winter dawn, with a chill in the air to match. The ground was stained dark as if with blood. The screams fell silent. He stumbled to a stop, gazing round at a rocky arena. And now he realised who needed the help so badly.

Me.

PART 3

INTO CONTROL

He was surrounded by hundreds of stark, imposing figures in crimson robes. Charms of rope, braid and ivory hung about their necks and wrists. Some held whips; others long, twisted staffs of wood that they slammed against the ground in jeering applause. Their faces looked to be bare skulls with blazing red eyes. But the Doctor knew what lay underneath the intimidating masks – faces of raw, bloody bone and muscle.

'Sycorax,' the Doctor said simply. 'Should've known.'

'Sycorax strong!' the rasping chant hacked at the cold air. 'Sycorax mighty! Sycorax rock!'

'Sycorax ought to know better!' the Doctor called back, shoving his hands in his pockets. 'Abducting tribes from different planets; using your blood rites to influence their minds; keeping the poor things wracked with fear and pain until you reach the "place of offering" – your sick slave auction. You even use their terror and hurt to drive your motors.' He shook his head. 'Nah. Not having that for a second.'

Again, the Sycorax sounded their clamour, hissing and calling and slamming staffs against the ground. It was deafening, intended to intimidate. 'Yeah, yeah, yeah,' the Doctor jeered over the din; 'Spare me the self-promotion – if you wanted me dead, you've had long enough to do something about it. So, I'm here for something else. Let's cut to the chase, shall we? Who's in charge?'

The braying died away, and the ranks of Sycorax parted as a massive figure strode out into the blood-black arena. She stood a good half-metre taller than those around her, vermillion robes puckered at the shoulders where thick strands of stray vertebrae poked through. But it was the huge mask of bone that rooted the Doctor's attention – threaded with veins and arteries that still pulsed with ghostly life. As she loomed over the Doctor, she pulled away the mask to reveal a cadaverous half-face of congealing flesh. Plates of rusting armour were bolted to the skull, etched with runes and symbols. The purple eyes were ringed with yellow, and two tongues licked lasciviously at her thin, cracked lips.

'The Queen of the Sycorax.' The Doctor inclined his head. 'It's an honour, I'm sure.'

'Only a fool cares for honour.' She spoke in a voice that was sticky and slow and rich as molasses. 'And what a fool are you. See how you have come here alone, unarmed, seeking to threaten us in our home, like a *cranak pel casacree salvak*.'

'Not exactly like that,' the Doctor said, as the roar of the onlookers renewed – until the queen raised one arm, and hush fell. 'So, what is this, mothership of the armada? Sorry for turning up unannounced.'

'We knew you from the first whisper of your craft,' she said. 'Doctor. Time Lord. Sworn defender of the planet Earth. Betrayer who bathes in blood as he humbles and kills.'

'You after some tips?' The Doctor knew he couldn't show a hint of weakness to the Queen of the Sycorax. He looked up, unflinching, into her hate-filled eyes. 'It wasn't me who destroyed your scouting party as it left Earth. I bested the Leader – your *Fadros Pallujikaa* – according to the Sycorax's own sanctified rules of combat. The Leader brought his death down on himself. I had every right to order the Sycorax to accept that Planet Earth is defended and to leave it in peace.'

'Every right?' The Queen hissed, her two tongues darting out between her lips. 'After what you did, you speak of rights!'

'And wrongs, too, cos you've broken your oath and sneaked back to Earth, haven't you? Another Christmas invasion, was it? Yeah, I met the humans you took, along with those other races you've enslaved, and poor old Alfredo the pig. Good name for a pig, don't you reckon? Alfredo! Has a certain *sty*-le –'

'You prattle to delay the inevitable.' The Sycorax queen leaned closer, and her protruding vertebrae trembled as if with anticipation. 'You will pay for your crimes, Time Lord.'

'And you will pay for yours.' The Doctor stood on tiptoes, gazing up into the darks of the queen's eyes. 'No one on this ship will be a slave for you or anyone else.'

'You cannot stop us.' She smiled, revealing rows of twisted yellow teeth, and reached inside her bright red robes. She pulled out a hefty broadsword stained dark with blood. '*Fadros Pallujikaa* hacked off your hand with this blade. It fell to Earth and was taken for a trophy by the same creatures who destroyed our ship. Your allies.'

'Torchwood?' The Doctor shrugged. 'Not really my allies. Though I s'pose you could say I lent them a hand once.'

'Your blood marks the blade. Through it, we charmed and twisted your will according to the dark rites of Astrophia.'

'Blood control.' The Doctor raised his eyebrows. 'You thought you could use blood control on *me*?'

'That is what has brought you here to us.' The queen snapped her teeth together, crocodile-quick, and the Doctor blinked. 'Your body and soul belong to the Sycorax.'

'Ah. You want revenge. To kill me.'

'The Sycorax are not simple, vengeful wastrels!' the queen spat. 'It is simply bad luck to allow an enemy to prosper when he can serve our cause.' She swung her huge and horrible head from side to side. 'You have come to us at a useful time.'

'Lovely little Christmas present for you, is that it?'

'See.'

The Doctor held still as the golden glow of a teleport beam throbbed about him. The rock of the arena faded, and he suddenly stood on the stone floor of the Sarnsquid's prison-pool. The octopods cowered from the queen as she appeared beside him.

'I've already clocked what you're doing here,' the Doctor said. 'Congratulations. I've seen so many kinds of ship propulsion systems. The fastest, the cleanest, the most powerful. Congrats! Yours are the most relentlessly horrible.'

'They are efficient,' the queen contended. 'Such a simple principle: pain into propulsion.'

'It's sick,' said the Doctor. 'There's no possible justification for it.'

'We stride the long darkness,' said the queen. 'Our supply of fuel must be inexhaustible.'

'These Sarnsquids are exhausted for a start!' the Doctor shot back. 'The sensors you've set up in the walls transmit the pain and fear of every locked-up life-form into their minds.

Add that to their own pain and suffering and they're half-dead with the effort. There are so many ways you could power your craft, but *this*?'

'What was it you said, Doctor?' The queen raised the pitch of her voice in a mocking impersonation of his own. ' "*There are not many races who could withstand such punishment.*" ' She laughed. 'However . . . I am certain that the last of the Time Lords can.'

The Doctor stared at her. 'You want to use me?'

'Blood control cannot compel others to act contrary to their spirit – but then, that is not necessary, is it? You wish to help the helpless, to rescue the weak. You would give your life to save them – and so you shall. You will take the place of these pitiful beasts and push our homeship through the dark desolations.'

'I won't serve you,' the Doctor told her.

'You must. Your blood compels you, Doctor. As your pain and anguish will compel this craft to voyage onward.' The queen pressed her bony fingers against symbols on the blue control panel, and new symbols hatched and danced there. The lighting changed to a strong but sickly yellow. The deep moan of an alarm reverberated around the chamber. 'I have altered the psychic warp-field settings so that if this craft does not maintain cruising speed, it will self-destruct.'

'With you and your subjects on board?' The Doctor snorted. 'I doubt that.'

'We are quite safe. But will you let so many innocents die?' The queen swung the broadsword down and sparks flew from the rock – a demonstration of power and control. 'Enter the bile-pit, Doctor. Feed your pain to our great engines . . . abase yourself for the lives of the cattle on board. End your days a slave in the service of the Sycorax – *uscok fra shakkra*!'

The Doctor stiffened. Then he took a jerky step forward, towards the edge of the pool. The queen grinned, teeth bared and eyes wide, caressing the blade of the sword with her bony fingers. The Doctor gritted his teeth and took another step closer to the foul, bubbling liquid.

And then he changed direction and waved his arms. 'BOO!' he yelled. 'Made you jump.'

Reflexes sharp and violent, the Sycorax queen raised the sword. The Doctor grabbed her hands around the hilt and the pair struggled for control. She brought up her knee and pushed him away. But as he fell backwards, the Doctor tore the sword free from her grip, performed a shoulder roll and jumped back to his feet, wielding the weapon.

'Here we are again,' he said mildly. 'Sword fight at Christmas.' The knell of the alarm thundered on. 'Aren't you gonna turn that thing off? Can hardly hear myself think. Love hearing myself think!'

'The blood charm was strong.' The Sycorax queen pulled a whip from a belt beneath her robes and took a careful step towards him. 'How could you have resisted?'

'You can't use ancient rites to charm a Time Lord,' the Doctor said, brushing down his blue and burgundy tartan suit. 'Specially not this one. Specially not now.'

The queen's eyes narrowed to burning slits. 'You mock the Sycorax.'

'Do I? Is that the kind of man I am now?' As the queen cracked out her whip, the Doctor parried with the sword, sending energy sparking. 'Don't feel bad, Your Highness. Your blood control could never have worked. *Because . . .*' He ran a finger along the bloodstained sword, tasted it, and grimaced. 'Yeah, no. I'm just not that Doctor.'

The queen bellowed with rage. 'Impossible!'

'I know I *look* like him, but, nah! That Doctor and me, we're nothing alike on a cellular level. There are whole bodies between us!' He blocked another whipcrack and jumped nimbly to one side, his navy trenchcoat brushing around his knees. 'Still, cheer up, Your Highness! I must have felt a residual buzz of the blood control. The TARDIS brought me here, and my subconscious maybe, just maybe, pushed me to see what was going on –'

'It has pushed you to your death.' With a devastating crack of the whip, the queen swiped the sword from his hands. Electricity shocked through the Doctor, and he shouted out as he fell to his knees. The queen flew for him, talons outstretched.

And a small, scrawny pig ran across her path, making her stumble to a stop, off-balance.

'Nice one, Alfredo!' roared the Doctor. 'Here, Your Majesty . . .' The Doctor grabbed the fallen sword and tossed it to the Sycorax queen. 'Happy Christmas!'

Caught off guard, she tried to bat away the sword, but the impact pushed her backwards . . . and into the bile-pool. She hit the filthy liquid with a splash, and rose up, spluttering, screaming. Her heavy robes weighed her down, and the Sarnsquid tentacles pushed and pulled at her, dragging her into the mire. The octopods crowded in; furious and exultant to have their persecutor in their power at last.

But then a golden glow bled murkily through the fluid in the pool, and suddenly the queen was gone. The mournful boom of the alarm rose in pitch. The yellow light darkened. Alfredo the pig scurried over to the Doctor, who patted him on the back then scrambled over to read the control panel.

'The Sycorax queen's no longer on board,' the Doctor reported. He played the sonic over the symbols but they refused to shift. 'Self-destruct has been locked down.'

'We'll keep the ship going,' a small Sarnsquid said shrilly. 'We can do that.'

'It's not tied to the engines now. She *wants* the whole place to go up in flames. Why should she care? Her and her entourage, they've beamed away to safety.' The Doctor banged a fist against the panel in frustration. 'Think! *Think.* There's got to be a way to stop the countdown.'

'The ship is powered by a psychic under-grid,' said the largest Sarnsquid. 'If we could divert and channel the mental energy from the other prisoners into the mainframe –'

'It might burn out the self-destruct protocols – brilliant!' The Doctor warmly shook its tentacle. 'But, first, we have to be able to get to the grid links. Which means bypassing this panel.' He sonicked the glowing edges of the controls, but the metal seemed rusted into the rock. 'Come on . . . come *on* . . .'

A huge white arm pushed past him, and thick fingers gripped the edge of the panel. The Doctor turned to find a Strombok beside him. 'Whoa! Where'd you come from?'

'The pain in our heads has gone,' she said, using brute force to peel back the metal and prise it off. 'We are free.'

'And no longer afraid,' added a Vega Rapton scurrying into the chamber.

A human man had entered too, looking anxiously at the Sarnsquids in the pool. '*Trying* not to be afraid,' the man admitted.

'Good. Brilliant. Try and hold on to that thought.' The Doctor sonicked the controls. With a slew of sulphurous sparks, the inner workings were revealed, and the alarm finally wound down. But there was no silence in the aftermath. A rising rumble was filling the air. The ground was trembling as some huge and hideous force strained to break free and destroy the sanctuary of rock.

'All right.' The Doctor wiped sweat from his forehead and opened a communications link to the whole ship. *I just hope the TARDIS translation circuits can handle it*, he thought. 'This is an urgent message to all on board,' he announced. 'The Sycorax have gone; you don't need to be afraid anymore. Be glad! *Happy*. Happiness is stronger than fear, beats it hands down . . .' With another buzz of the sonic, he brought the wall sensors back online. 'You can all go back home. It's possible. You just have to want it enough. Think how much you want it . . . all of you. Think it together!'

The Strombok beside him closed her eyes. 'Strombokoccini,' she breathed. 'The snow. The lights that dance and play in the southern skies . . .'

'London,' said the man. 'Grimy, overcrowded, beautiful London Town . . .'

The psychic under-grid began to glow with a warm, pulsating light.

'It's working!' squealed a Sarnsquid. 'I can feel it working.'

'All my people!' the Vega Rapton said hoarsely. 'Imagine digging our way out of here . . . burrowing a path to safety!'

'Keep going,' the Doctor urged them, as the power continued to build. Other life forms were entering the chamber too, drawn here, perhaps, by the focussing of energies. 'You're free, all of you! How good does it feel?'

'To divert the power into the mainframe,' a Sarnsquid piped up, 'the mental wavelengths must be channelled on a precise frequency if we're to silence the self-destruct. A *precisely* precise frequency . . .'

Alfredo squealed and ran away as the octopod pulled itself from the pool and sidled over, tentacles twitching and questing over the controls. Its weeping red eyes closed as it concentrated, in concert with its friends and fellows in the room. The Doctor could feel the ether crowd with the psychic spoor of different races, and tried to add his own strength to the task. *Home*, he thought. *Freedom*. The image of the TARDIS burned bright blue behind his eyes, and he exhaled deeply. *Got to find out why I'm wearing this old face again. Got to get the bottom of things . . .*

Then the thrum of power built to a crescendo before descending into a quenching hiss. The vibration beneath his feet began to fade. The lights flickered as the sickly yellow drained from them, and a steady blue glare asserted itself.

'Well.' The Doctor grinned. 'That seemed to work.'

He retraced his steps back to the arena. The hordes of Sycorax had gone, of course. As a race they were smoke-and-mirrors as much as blood and bone; it was hard to know if they'd really been present or if the queen had conjured avatars to cow him. Perhaps she even had the power to conjure herself into any of the ships in her armada whenever she chose.

'Not into this one,' the Doctor muttered. 'Not anymore.'

The Sarnsquids had already placed mental barriers around the ship to protect it from Sycorax intrusion. Now they could retrace their path through the planets and return all the prisoners home.

And I should leave, too, the Doctor thought. *Time to take control of my days.*

Can't lose yourself forever.

He heard a quiet snort behind him. Alfredo was looking at him, expectantly.

'Good point,' said the Doctor. 'The Sycorax are still out there. There'll be a reckoning, some day. Till then, let's all make the most of our second chances . . . shall we?'

THE FIFTEENTH DOCTOR:
THE DALMATIAN TERRAIN

FARIDAH ÀBÍKÉ-ÍYÍMÍDÉ

'Duck!' Ruby Sunday yelled, as a colony of birds came swooping down from their ivory rooftops, wings flapping wildly as they eagerly plunged towards her steaming parcel of fried haddock and chips. She managed to dive behind a lamppost, obscuring herself from the beady, watchful eyes of the *enemy* – which, in this case, were the predators that resided in the skies of Brighton Beach.

'Look, Ruby,' the Doctor replied, staring up at the sky. 'I know I'm not from this planet, but that is definitely *not* a duck. Even a Time Lord could tell you that's a seagull . . .' he said, tossing a chip in his mouth. He observed the cawing gulls encircling him, seemingly unaware of their murderous intent.

'Yeah, I know you know what a seagull is! I meant duck down before they bite your fingers off and steal your fish!' Ruby yelled, a small laugh erupting from her lips as she watched the clueless Time Lord slowly begin to realise that he was indeed the seagulls' prey. The birds began their descent and the Doctor shuffled from side to side like a crab stuck in a fishing net.

'*Oh*, this is *not* good!' the Doctor exclaimed as one gull managed to peck him in the ear.

'Don't you have an anti-seagull setting on that screwdriver of yours?!' Ruby asked, as she attempted to hide her lunch beneath her jacket.

'My screwdriver can do many clever things, but, unfortunately, it isn't programmed to ward off murderous gulls . . . which is a real shame . . . I might have to look into fixing that.' He trailed off as he rushed to the corner Ruby was in, attempting to hide behind the lamppost with her. Given that lampposts were not historically reliable for their cloaking abilities, this was, of course, unsuccessful.

'I've got an idea,' the Doctor exclaimed, as the caws increased in volume.

'What's that?' Ruby asked, wide-eyed and breathless.

'On the count of three, I say we run,' the Doctor replied, laughing.

'Run?' Ruby began to question, but the Doctor had already started counting.

'Three . . . two . . . RUN!' he yelled, taking her by the hand and yanking her along the cobblestone pathway that led away from Chippy Chippy Bang Bang, the delightfully named fish shop they'd gotten their meals from. Ruby almost dropped her parcel as she ran, stumbling a little as they wove between streets filled with rows of brightly coloured buildings and crowds of families dressed in beach wear, blissfully unaware of the dangers that lay ahead at the shore.

If Ruby had anticipated that visiting Brighton would result in their near untimely deaths, she might've thought twice about the decision.

She hadn't been to Brighton since she was a little girl. Her mum, Carla, had brought her to have what she had promised

Ruby would be *the* best fish and chips in the entire world. Ruby was sceptical, but in the end, her mum was right, as she tended to be about most things. Now, she was passing the baton on and introducing the Doctor to the wonders of earthly cuisine, though things hadn't gone quite as she'd planned.

'I think we've lost them,' the Doctor declared once they were on a quieter path – a dank alleyway on a random street corner. He was still catching his breath as he looked up at the skies suspiciously. 'You know, if it wasn't for the fact that I'm quite well-versed in this planet's Laridae species, I'd suspect those gulls were from someplace else . . .'

'Where else would they be from? Planet of the seagulls?' Ruby asked with a breathless laugh.

The Doctor laughed along with her at the ridiculousness of it all. 'I've never come across any planets like that and honestly, thank haddock I haven't!' He gestured towards his papered parcel.

'If there was actually a planet of seagulls, I think it would be called the planet of dangerous, evil birds . . .' Ruby said. 'Although now that I'm saying it, it doesn't quite roll off the tongue, does it?'

'Maybe it could be the planet of fish and chips, seeing as you don't seem to be able to have gulls without the presence of fried potatoes,' the Doctor added thoughtfully.

'Maybe both. Maybe fish and chips is the code word for danger there. FISH AND CHIPS! BIG SCARY BIRD COMING! RUN AWAY!' Ruby mused.

The Doctor nodded in agreement. 'I have confronted some very impressive creatures in my time, but nothing like these gulls. Everyone should be warned of this murderous, mavity-defying species. Actually, fish and chips should be the code word for danger *everywhere*.'

Ruby bit back a laugh at the Doctor's genuinely horrified expression. She found it hilarious that the Doctor, who had probably fought off more aliens than she could ever count, had been bested by a bird. Despite his very accomplished life as a Time Lord, meeting all sorts of creatures from across the galaxy, it was *seagulls* that had truly shaken him.

She didn't blame the guy though – seagulls were indeed dreadful creatures.

'What, like you'd shout fish and chips and everyone would just understand that something bad was gonna happen?' Ruby asked in response to the Doctor's suggestion.

He nodded. 'Yes, exactly. Let me demonstrate,' he cleared his throat. 'Fish and chips! Murderous species around, run for your lives!'

Ruby smiled at that. 'Fish and chips! Someone forgot to make Cherry a cuppa and will now be on the receiving end of her infamous death glare!'

The Doctor laughed out loud. 'Oh, I would *never* dream of forgetting to make Cherry a cup of tea. I value my life, thank you very much,' he said.

Before Ruby could add another ridiculous example of when they might use their code word, she was interrupted by the familiar yapping of a dog nearby.

Ruby and the Doctor snapped out of their stupor and turned towards the sound. Standing behind them in the dark, winding alleyway was a spotted dog.

Ruby's grey-green eyes lit up. 'Oh my God, is that a

Dalmatian?' she asked no one in particular, as she walked over to the blue-and-white hound. She kneeled beside the dog, staring right into its wide, pitless eyes as she reached out and gently petted its ears.

The Doctor narrowed his eyes at the creature. 'Hmm. It looks like one. Something isn't right though. I can give it a quick scan, just to be sure of its intentions . . .'

Ruby laughed. 'It's a dog, Doctor, not an evil drone.'

'You're right. I guess anything is better than a seagull at this point,' the Doctor said with a smile.

The Dalmatian yapped again, this time up at the Doctor, who looked rather elated by the excitable sounds it was making, his grin widening.

'Doctor, it's . . . she's . . . got these blue spots. Is that a thing? I've never seen a dog like this. I mean, how cool is that though?' Then Ruby cooed at the dog. 'Isn't she the sweetest?'

'Very cool indeed. But you're right. Blue spotted Dalmatians aren't right for this point in Earth's history . . .' he trailed off. 'You know, she sort of reminds me of K9,' he said, regarding the hound warmly.

'What's a K9?' Ruby asked, looking back at the Doctor over her shoulder.

The Doctor waved the question off. 'Just a robot dog I used to know.'

Ruby raised her eyebrows at the mention of a robot dog. She wasn't sure why she was so surprised that such a thing could exist. She had been travelling with the Doctor for a while, and yet she still found herself perpetually shocked to hear about the vast technologies and alien wonders that existed so casually in his exciting life.

Ruby turned back to the dog, her hands moving instinctively down its neck to where a collar should be, but wasn't.

'It doesn't have a collar. It's been left out here all alone,' Ruby said quietly, with a frown.

Oddly enough, the hound seemed to be wearing a small, metallic protective vest. An indication that someone had been looking after this dog at some point.

The Doctor was taking in all of the details he could about this strange dog they'd stumbled across.

'Maybe there's a shelter somewhere . . . or . . .' Ruby continued, too enamoured by the creature to take note of any strangeness.

She stood up and took her phone out of her jacket pocket. 'I'll look up what's around here, see if I can call some –' but Ruby did not get to finish her sentence. Suddenly, the dog's yapping rang out once again, followed by the sound of paws scuttling across cobblestone ground.

Their new friend had taken off.

The Doctor and Ruby Sunday had already spent much of their day running around the crooked, winding streets of Brighton, and now they found themselves yet again jetting off – but this time in pursuit of the spotted hound.

At present, the chase was both alarming and tense, but it was the sort of ridiculous thing the pair would joke about later on when reflecting on the day. For now, there was hardly any merriment, just the sound of shoes hitting the ground as the two held on tightly to their parcels of fish while sprinting through the town.

Finally, they came to a stop at a familiar clearing. Ruby spotted the TARDIS in the corner of the street, exactly where they'd parked it earlier in the day. The Dalmatian had come to a halt and was now seated casually next to the TARDIS, staring up at the Doctor and Ruby with a blank expression on her spotted face.

Out of breath but glad to no longer be running, the pair looked from the Dalmatian to each other and burst out laughing.

'I didn't know I could run that fast,' Ruby giggled between breaths.

The Doctor grinned. 'Me neither! Light work I'd say . . .' he laughed.

'I bet we could give Usain Bolt a run for his money,' Ruby replied.

The Doctor's eyebrows furrowed. 'Who's that?' he asked.

'You don't know Usain Bolt? The fastest man on the planet?'

He shook his head. Ruby had so much she still needed to teach the Doctor.

'For a lord of time, you are seriously lacking in the pop-culture history department,' she said. 'Do you even know who Beyoncé is?'

The Doctor looked outraged, placing his hand on his chest to demonstrate his grave offence.

'*Of course* I know who Beyoncé is!' he exclaimed. 'There isn't a person in the entire universe who isn't familiar with *the* alien superstar herself.'

'So, you know who Beyoncé is . . . but not Usain Bolt?'

'Well, yes,' he said, as though it were a perfectly normal thing to admit to.

Ruby looked at the Doctor in disbelief and awe. 'You are very, very . . . strange, Doctor.'

The Doctor grinned down at her, taking that to be the highest of compliments. 'You too, Ruby Sunday,' he said, glancing at their canine companion, who was still patiently waiting by the TARDIS. 'On to more pressing matters. What on Earth are we to do with it?'

'Oh yes! I was going to look up shelters. Could you hold on to my fish and chips while I look?' Ruby asked. The Doctor nodded, taking the parcel into his hands while Ruby got to work, tapping away at her phone.

She scrolled down a page that listed all of the local animal shelters, clicked on the one that seemed to be the closest and began reading more about the organisation, ensuring that it was legitimate.

Ruby was so preoccupied with her search that she didn't register the ominous sound of squawking overhead. But the Doctor did.

'Oh no . . .' he groaned, glancing at the gulls flying around by the rooftops. He looked down at the parcels in his arms, swathed like newborns. 'Ruby . . .' the Doctor warned cautiously as one seagull, who'd now spotted the Doctor, swooped down towards him.

'Just a second! I'm almost done . . .' she said, copying the details for the shelter.

'Ruby –' the Doctor began again, but was cut off by the tremendous sound of more cawing as even more seagulls swooped down from the blue skies.

'Ruby! Fish and chips! Fish and chips!' he yelled, and Ruby finally glanced up, away from her phone screen. Her eyes were as wide as saucers as she watched the feral birds descend.

'The TARDIS!' he exclaimed. 'Let's get in!'

Ruby nodded, not needing to be told twice, and the two of them quickly rushed over to the doors of the blue telephone box. The Doctor managed to manoeuvre the door open while holding the two parcels in his arms. The pair rushed inside before the birds could swoop down and devour their lunch.

Ruby slammed the door of the TARDIS shut behind her.

When she stepped away from the door, she felt herself slip back a little, something slimy sticking to her shoe. She glanced down at her boot to find that she had accidentally trodden on some rogue chips that had slipped out from the parcels, littering the entrance to the TARDIS.

That's unlucky, Ruby thought, glaring down at the pristine TARDIS flooring.

'Do you reckon the Goblins put the seagulls up to this?' Ruby joked, as she walked up the slope to where the Doctor was standing, right in the centre of the spacious room by the control console.

'Those Goblins seemed to only have eyes for babies, luckily, and I sent them packing! So, I don't think so . . .' he replied, turning to the ship's console. 'Should we head off? Or is there more of Brighton I need to see?'

Ruby shook her head. 'We have our food. We can always come back to Brighton another day to see the sights,' she said.

And the Doctor let out a strange yelp of agreement. Only, his mouth hadn't moved at all. The two turned around suspiciously to find that the Dalmatian they had just chased was seated on the sloping floor of the TARDIS.

'What the . . .' the Doctor started, as the dog got up on to its hind legs and began spinning round frantically as if it was chasing its tail. Although, this did not look as adorable as when other dogs usually did it. The Dalmatian looked more possessed than anything. Weirder still, the dog's vest seemed to glimmer and flash brighter with its frantic movements.

Suddenly, out of nowhere, the TARDIS began to shake violently, as though someone had triggered the ship to launch.

'OK . . . not Goblins . . . but maybe something . . .' the Doctor muttered under his breath. He rushed to the console to assess the situation close up.

'What's happened?' Ruby asked, her voice raised in alarm as the lights in the TARDIS began to flicker in different colours, flashing on and off as though the ship itself was hyperventilating.

'We've taken off. We're somehow travelling some*where* . . .' the Doctor said, as he began tracing the dog's steps, trying to figure out where the ship would land.

'Taken off? What do you mean taken off? Did you ask it to do that?' Ruby asked.

'No, it appears that the TARDIS is piloting itself, which happens sometimes . . .' the Doctor replied, glancing at the console wearily.

Ruby's eyes widened. She didn't know the TARDIS could fly itself. 'Where is it taking us then?'

'I'm not sure . . . the TARDIS is taking us wherever it deems fit, which could be anywhere!'

'Well, can't you control it? Reverse it, tell it to take us back to Earth?'

'Not without potentially disrupting something major in the space–time continuum. I do *not* want a repeat of twelfth-century Tuscany, that's for sure.'

'Why, what happened in Tuscany?'

'Well, I assume you've heard of the city of Pisa and its famous tower?'

'Yeah, the one that leans?'

'Exactly,' the Doctor replied, tapping on buttons, trying to calm the TARDIS down. 'Let's just say the tower didn't always have a slant to it . . .' he said with a wink.

Yet again, her mind filled with a flurry of questions, but given their current predicament, she thought her questions could wait for a less chaotic time.

She held on to a metal bar nearby as the TARDIS flung itself through time and space. She peered over at the hound in the corner, unbothered by the lights, the movement and the panic. It sat calmly and obediently as though waiting for its next instruction.

Something was unnerving to Ruby about the Dalmatian's sudden stillness now it was no longer twirling around like a possessed thing.

After a few moments, the TARDIS finally settled. The lights stopped blinking and Ruby could finally stand up straight.

The Doctor turned back to his companion, sweat gleaming off his shiny forehead. 'I believe we've landed . . .' he said nervously, dusting off his jacket.

'Where?' Ruby asked.

'I don't know,' he replied. 'But we'd better go and find out . . .'

The new TARDIS trio exited the ship one by one, the Doctor leading the pack as Ruby and the dog followed.

Ruby held her breath as they stepped out into unknown territory. In the seconds it had taken them to leave the TARDIS, her mind had already imagined one million ghastly scenarios. She'd thought about the possibility of being suspended in the deep, vast webs of space, or falling through the cracks of time, lost to history forever.

But when she stepped out, she wasn't met with overtly scary terrain like she had suspected they might be. Instead, they seemed to have landed in some kind of bustling city, much like the one they had just come from. She looked up at the sky. It was similar to Earth's, with only slight differences. The clouds were more pronounced and brighter than London's grey, miserable skies, and they seemed to follow a pattern of polka dots across the brilliant blue backdrop.

She looked at the Doctor, who was taking in their surroundings and wearing a serious expression on his face. She wondered if he found the normalcy of the place to be strangely comforting as it was to her. But then again, what was normal for the Doctor anyway?

His face began to screw up and she quickly realised that the comfort she felt was not shared by her travelling companion.

She could see cars speeding off down the street and flashy billboards fitted on to high-rise buildings.

It was like being in London's Piccadilly Circus. Always busy, the city never asleep, not for one second.

From the looks of it, she might have thought they'd landed someplace close to home but still far away, like Paris or Aberdeen. But something about the Doctor's demeanour told her they had travelled much further than that.

The Dalmatian suddenly leaped forward, passing the Doctor, who seemed not to notice that their companion had slipped away again. He was much too busy staring blankly ahead.

'Well, we're certainly not in Brighton any more,' the Doctor muttered. 'It's not even Hove . . .'

She moved from behind the Doctor and gasped when she saw what he was looking at. Ruby wasn't sure how she hadn't noticed it before – maybe it was that everything was too familiar, so her brain hadn't yet picked up on all the tiny details: the billboards surrounding them were almost completely made up of images of dogs – Dalmatians, to be exact – except for a single billboard in the centre with a glamorous-looking woman on it. The cars she'd seen whizzing past were also driven by Dalmatians, with more dogs in the passenger seat. Spotted hounds surrounded them everywhere: crossing the streets; sitting in the windows of cafés; waltzing in and out of department stores; handling shopping bags in their mouths. They seemed to have landed on a planet populated solely by dogs!

'Uh . . . Doctor, we're –' Ruby began, but was cut off by a loud siren of yapping and barking.

She winced at the volume of the alarm as the dog howls rose to an uncomfortable level.

Everything stopped suddenly. The cars stopped driving, the dogs stopped walking, and all eyes were now on the

Doctor and Ruby. Thousands of spotted faces were carefully watching the pair.

'That alarm . . . it's saying, "intruder . . . intruder alert",' the Doctor revealed to Ruby.

'What? I can't hear any words! Just loud barking!' Ruby yelled back, feeling the urge to cover her ears.

'There are words, just not in English. I translated it,' the Doctor said.

'You speak dog?' Ruby asked. 'I thought the TARDIS translated for us?'

'I speak space dog. The TARDIS can't translate space dog. It's an ongoing fault. It's also not my strongest language, but I can get by . . .' he replied. Then his eyes widened, and he pointed up at the sky. 'Do you hear that?' he asked.

Ruby shook her head. Nothing had changed about the sound for her. There was still that loud, dizzying siren and the annoying yapping sounds surrounding it.

'The message . . . it's changing,' he said. 'It's saying . . . alert . . . contacting . . . the Dame?' The Doctor closed his eyes for better concentration. 'Yes, that's definitely it – *alert, contacting the Dame.*'

'Who in the world is the Dame?' Ruby muttered to no one in particular, not expecting a reply.

'That would be me.' A shrill, feminine voice rang out from the cluster of frozen Dalmatians, who moved obediently as she made her way through the sea of blue-and-white spotted dogs. Ruby's eyes followed the moving figure as her face came fully into view.

It was a woman. A very familiar one at that. It was the woman from the billboard.

She had a crown of bouffant-style curls forming a halo around her head. Her smile was wide and stained a deep auburn colour, and her eyes were covered by a large pair of circular sunglasses. She wore a poofy green gown with tulle sage-coloured gloves. The Dame looked like she'd stepped out of a magazine from the 1950s.

The alarms stopped ringing, but everything remained still. All were eyes on the woman gliding towards them.

The woman extended a gloved hand to the Doctor. 'Charmed,' she said.

The Doctor took her hand in his. 'I take it you're the Dame?' he asked.

She nodded, lowering her glasses and revealing her eyes. Ruby involuntarily let out an astonished breath.

The Dame's eyes were unlike any Ruby had ever seen. They were a bright blazing orange, with slits for pupils, like that of a reptile. And those weren't the only reptile-like things about her: Ruby noted a pattern of translucent scales along the small sections of exposed skin that her clothes could not veil.

'And you are?' the Dame asked, her gaze dancing lazily between the two of them.

'I'm the Doctor and this is –'

'Amethyst. Amethyst Monday,' Ruby interjected. She didn't trust the Dame and didn't feel like handing over her name just like that. She suspected the Doctor's name was an alias, so she'd have an alias too.

She could feel the Doctor's eyes shift to her briefly, but he didn't say anything.

The corner of the Dame's mouth quirked up, as though

she could somehow see through Ruby's lie with those snakey eyes of hers.

'Pleasure to meet you, Doctor, and you too, Amethyst,' she said, her gaze finally settling towards the space behind them, on what Ruby was certain was the TARDIS. She swallowed hard, not liking the hungry way the Dame looked upon it.

'Welcome to Maculosus,' the Dame said.

Ruby heard the Doctor mutter, '*Maculosus . . . the spotted planet,*' under his breath, his eyes darting to and fro as though he was trying to figure out something internally.

'It's been a while since we've had any outsiders come and visit. And by a while, I mean *never*. Which makes your arrival all the more interesting,' the Dame continued.

The Doctor's head snapped up and he nodded. 'We aren't guests at all, actually. We weren't meant to land here,' he began. 'This was all one big mistake. We found your dog wandering the streets of our planet and wanted to help, but somehow found ourselves here instead. Which I think is a good thing, seeing as we've now returned the hound back to its rightful owner –' the Doctor paused, gesturing down at the Dalmatian seated by the Dame's feet that the pair had spent the better half of the morning chasing – 'we'd better be on our way back. Don't want to trouble you any more than we already have.'

The Dame merely blinked at the two of them, seemingly unimpressed by the Doctor's explanation. 'I take it that is your . . . transportation device?' she asked, ignoring everything the Doctor had just told her while gazing gluttonously at the TARDIS. When neither of them answered, the Dame turned sharply to the Dalmatian at her feet and then, to the horror of both the Doctor and Ruby, kicked the hound hard in its shin with the rough edge of her boot. Ruby gasped as the Dalmatian gave a loud howl. The Doctor's expression hardened and twisted into one of grave disgust. Ruby froze, feeling something inside of her instantly break.

'Why'd you do that?' Ruby asked, feeling her chest tighten as her eyes grew heavy with tears.

The Dame twisted towards her with a curious arch of her eyebrow. 'Do what?'

'Harm that dog, it did nothing to you and you –'

'Oh don't be silly girl, this is not a dog as your people may see it.'

'It's still a living being,' the Doctor said, his jaw set and his eyes shimmering. 'No one deserves that abuse.'

The Dame considered them for a few moments.

'All right, it won't happen again . . .' she said, but clearly was not at all the slightest bit apologetic.

The Dame then turned to hiss out something at the dog, who suddenly began to bark out a sentence that neither of them could decipher.

The Dame let out a soft *ahh* after the dog had finished *speaking*.

'I've been reliably informed that this is indeed the transportation device that has brought you here all the way from Earth,' she said, gesturing towards the TARDIS. The Doctor hesitated before nodding.

'But as I was saying . . . your ship is rather small for a powerful transportation device ,' the Dame mused out loud. The dog barked again. 'What was that? It's much bigger on the inside, you say? How fascinating. I look forward to exploring all of its . . . capabilities,' the Dame said with a wicked smile, showing off the razor-sharp edges of her teeth.

The Doctor stepped forward, holding his hand up now. 'What exactly do you mean by exploring its *capabilities*?'

Ruby had an inkling that whatever she had meant by this, it had to be bad.

The Dame's orange, reptilian eyes slowly scanned over their cautious expressions, and then she let out a rather disarmingly jolly chuckle. 'You both look as though you've seen a Humroid grow legs and dance!'

'A Hum-what?' Ruby began.

'A species of tree,' the Doctor clarified in a mumbled response, his eyes narrowed as though he was quietly contemplating something.

'There's no need for you to look so worried! We will take good care of your transportation device and return it to you in no time. This is just the standard procedure with non-native objects.'

'Sorry, Dame, but *what* is the standard procedure?' the Doctor replied.

'Just a simple scan of the foreign device. We need to make sure it isn't harmful to this habitat, that's all!' she replied.

'And *you're* not harming the habitat? You're clearly torturing these poor creatures!'

'I have a feeling she doesn't care, Ruby,' the Doctor said, which was verified by the Dame's unbothered expression. 'And how long does this *scan* usually take to complete?' the Doctor asked the Dame, continuing his line of questioning, his tone levelled.

'Oh! It is very quick, it won't take us more than . . . three to four. Give or take.'

'Three or four what? Seconds? Minutes? *Hours?*' Ruby asked, exasperated. It was like the Dame was purposely holding back information to annoy her specifically.

'Sorry, earthly tongues are not my natural mode of speaking. Three to four months. Maybe sooner if we get started right away! I'll get a team of my best to begin work later this evening.'

Ruby felt her heart plunge into the hollow depths of her stomach. *Three to four months?* She couldn't be stuck on this dog planet with this strange reptile woman for *three to four months!*

'We must take all precautions to ensure that this device is safe here. We wouldn't want to risk causing harm to the civilians of Maculosus now, would we, Doctor?'

The Doctor glared at her. 'Because you haven't harmed them at all?' he seethed. 'You're not going anywhere near my ship.'

'Oh really?' the Dame remarked, her smile wide and brilliant as she began clapping her hands together.

Then, to the surprise of the Doctor and Ruby, the Dame began barking. It was a loud, shrill noise, like that of a chihuahua. This snapped the other dogs out of their daze as they glanced up at their master, who was clearly barking commands at them.

Ruby did not understand what it was, but as the pack of them circled around herself and the Doctor, she could take a pretty good guess that it was something along the lines of 'capture them!'

Ruby felt the panic that had already begun to bubble under the surface reach the precipice and spill over. Before the dogs could follow the blind orders of their maniacal leader, the Doctor did something that stopped them all in their tracks.

He brought out his sonic screwdriver, the circular device he always kept on him, and pointed it directly at the Dame's head.

The Dame's eyebrows shot up in surprise. 'What are you doing?' she hissed out, but the Doctor did not pay her any mind, concentrating instead on the metallic device in his hand.

A blue ray shot out from its tip, spreading into several beams of light and painting the Dame in sapphire luminous stripes. The device began to make a low-pitched thrumming sound that Ruby had never heard before, much like a trumpet with a sock stuck in its aperture.

The Dame gave a shrill, panicked scream, which made the hounds surrounding them stand up on high alert. Ruby felt her heart hammering abruptly in her chest.

'Doctor . . .' Ruby began, stepping back instinctively.

'Interesting . . .' the Doctor mumbled as he stared intently at the Dame, who was growing angrier by the second.

'*Fish and chips, Doctor! Fish and chips!*' Ruby muttered through gritted teeth, but the Time Lord did not appear to hear her at all. He just continued threateningly sonicking the woman who would most likely maim them now or, at the very least, get her dogs to do it for her.

Then, the Doctor decided to make matters worse by moving his target from the Dame to her herd of hounds.

'Very interesting indeed,' the Doctor repeated just as the Dame barked out an order. A large, spotted dog leaped into the air and knocked the sonic screwdriver squarely out of the Doctor's hand with one swoop of its jaw.

'No!' Ruby yelled as the device flew into the air and landed in the Dame's iron-claw grip.

Everything seemed to move in slow motion. Ruby watched in horror as the Dame began viciously barking once again, and then, before either of them knew it, the dogs were moving in until there was no place to turn. They slowly shuffled the pair away from the TARDIS and towards a building across the street. On the front was the billboard Ruby had noticed earlier – the one with the Dame's gigantic face plastered on it. The building seemed to be the Dame's headquarters, which explained how she got to them so quickly in the first place.

The Dalmatian they had chased through Brighton had landed them right in a hornet's nest.

Ruby looked at the Doctor, hoping to read any sign of how dire this situation was on his face. But his features revealed nothing.

He looked calm and collected as they were herded off to their potential doom.

The Doctor and Ruby Sunday were ushered into a dim, windowless room in a dank basement and backed into claustrophobic dog cages.

The Dalmatians that had terrorised them earlier stood guard outside the cramped quarters of their cages. One of the guard dogs held the Doctor's sonic screwdriver hostage between the slobbery coating of his canine teeth.

The Doctor sighed loudly, leaning back against the walls

of his cage in an awkward, scrunched up position. At first, there was nothing but a sterile silence, which was then disrupted by a low, grumbling sound. 'Sorry, my stomach,' he said. 'It's a pity I never got to finish my fish and chips.'

'I think fish and chips are the least of our problems at the moment, Doctor,' Ruby said, peering over at him through her own cage in a similarly contorted position. 'Right now, we're IN fish and chips. We're stranded on a strange planet, in who knows what galaxy, and our only transportation has been confiscated by an evil reptile woman. This is not how I thought the day would go. Or the next four months, for that matter.'

'OK. You're not wrong . . .' the Doctor replied. 'I probably should have predicted this, considering how often we end up in the middle of fish-and-chips-like situations . . .'

Ruby wasn't sure how the Doctor could have known that they'd end up on a dog planet, but she knew there was nothing that could be said to convince him otherwise. He'd still place all the blame on himself. The Doctor always seemed to be carrying the weight of the entire universe on his shoulders.

'Do you reckon the gulls are behind this? Maybe they brainwashed her or something,' Ruby said with a forced smile, trying to bring some light into the darkness of their current situation.

'As much as I would love to blame the gulls for this, I'm afraid there is something even more sinister at play,' the Doctor said. 'Though you were right about brainwashing being a factor here.'

Ruby slowly tried to sit up. 'So the Dame *is* brainwashed?'

The Doctor shook his head. 'No, not the Dame. If anyone is brainwashed it's the Dalmatians – or, as this spotted species are *actually* called, the *Macula* of Maculosus. I scanned the Dame and her dogs.'

'Wait, so you're telling me that Dalmatians *aren't* really Dalmatians? They're all this . . . alien dog species?' Ruby asked.

The Doctor shook his head. 'Not quite. Dalmatians on Earth are like . . . distant relatives of the Macula. From my scan, it seems that the Macula were once Earth dogs. Something must have brought them here. A wormhole or a species collector. Or, maybe one of them fell through a time corridor . . . and they eventually evolved into this. They're very similar appearance-wise to the Dalmatians back on Earth, but on an evolutionary level, the two species couldn't be more different.'

'Right, and the Dame? What did you learn when you scanned her?' Ruby asked, quietening her voice.

'No need to whisper – the dogs can't understand you,' the Doctor said.

'I know, but the Dame could still be listening,' she replied.

'Good point,' the Doctor said, bringing his voice down a few octaves. 'The Dame has a high security trace placed on her.'

'A trace?'

The Doctor nodded. 'Yes, like those ankle monitors that prisoners wear to ensure they can't escape their cells. The Dame has a really strong one placed on her by the Shadow Proclamation, which could only mean one thing.'

'OK. The shadow what?' Ruby asked, her eyes wide.

'I don't usually love it when you say "which could only mean one thing" . . .'

'Space police. Old acquaintances of mine. We're dealing with a highly dangerous and, likely, unpredictable criminal,' the Doctor said. 'I didn't get to see where exactly she's from, but for whatever reason, the Shadow Proclamation thought it would be wise to keep her here on Maculosus as a prisoner. They've put the lives of the Macula in danger. Honestly, they can be so useless sometimes,' the Doctor muttered, kissing his teeth as he did. A short silence followed as the mavity of their situation finally sank in.

'How do you plan on cleaning up their mistake in this instance? How are we even going to get out of here?' Ruby asked.

The Doctor surveyed the space through narrowed eyes. The basement was cave-like, with its stone walls and arched ceilings, and it seemed there was only one way out.

'Well, it the fastest and most reliable way out of here would be using my TARDIS . . . which is obviously not currently on my person. *But* if there was a way to get to my TARDIS, I could easily get us out of here in no time. We just need a way out.'

A way out. Meaning a way past these Dalmatians, who looked like they were on a cocktail of protein shakes and steroids. Ruby noticed the one on the left side of the cage wagging his tail excitedly, his tongue sticking out and his ears twitching. The dog reminded Ruby of her old neighbour's Labrador. His name was Liam – and Ruby loved playing with him. He was always excited, and she often tried to match his energy. The world could do with more

Labrador's like Liam. Ruby might've thought the guard dog to be just like any other dog on Earth if it weren't for the fact that she knew otherwise.

Unless . . . Ruby thought. *They were.*

'Doctor, I think I might know how to distract the guards,' Ruby said, nodding towards the two guard dogs beside them. 'Do you happen to know the rules of the game *fetch*?' she asked with a calculating smile.

Suddenly, the Doctor's eyes lit up and his lips stretched wide into a grin. 'Oh, Ruby Sunday, you genius!' he exclaimed. 'I'd bet these two would love a game of fetch, don't you think?'

'I think they would!' she replied excitedly. 'But we'd need, like . . . something for them to fetch.'

'Give me one moment!' the Doctor said, as he dug into his coat pocket for something small and needle-thin, straightening up as much as he could in the limited space. Ruby watched as he leaned forward, hovering over the lock to the cage. His tongue poked out the corner of his mouth as he wriggled his fingers around, smiling triumphantly when a small click sounded, indicating that the cage door had been successfully unlocked.

She heard a muttered thank you to Houdini before the Doctor reached into his jacket again, producing what appeared to be a bright yellow plastic dog toy.

Ruby's eyebrows furrowed.

'Is that a –'

'Dog toy? Yes, it is indeed,' the Doctor said with a grin.

'And you just happen to keep that on you?' Ruby asked.

'I keep all sorts of important things on me, Ruby! You never know what you might need,' he said.

Ruby wasn't sure why she was so surprised. She'd once seen him casually pull out a freshly baked Jamaican patty from this very coat after Cherry had complained about feeling peckish. His jackets seemed to have an unlimited number of capabilities, much like the Doctor himself.

Once he'd carefully crawled out of his cage, he quietly shuffled over to Ruby's and helped her out of hers. When they were both freed, he glanced at his companion expectantly. 'Would you like to do the honours, Ruby Sunday?' The Doctor held the dog toy out to Ruby, who grabbed it with a nod. He positioned himself, ready to spring up when the time called for it. Then he looked at her and nodded. Ruby began banging the plastic device gently against the cage bars, triumph singing through her as the dogs both turned sharply to the source of the noise. She let out a breath before raising her hand and yelling, 'Fetch!'

Disappointedly, the dogs did not stir or seem to get giddy at the mention of the game, and Ruby felt her heart sink. Maybe dogs on Maculosus didn't enjoy fetch like their earthly counterparts after all.

'Ah. I don't think they understand what you're saying . . . I think "fetch" in dog would be –' The Doctor started, hesitating before making a yipping sound.

This time, both dogs straightened up, their ears pointing upwards and their tails wagging eagerly. Ruby waved the toy in front of them, and their hungry, dark gazes followed her. She took off, running out of the basement with her heart beating wildly as she heard the galloping hounds from behind. When it seemed they were close to tackling her, she finally skidded into a clearing and hurled the toy as far as she could into the distance. The dogs leaped ahead of her, yapping as they chased the soaring yellow object through the building's exit.

Ruby ran back into the room, wild-haired and wide-eyed. 'We don't have long before they come back with the toy,' she said between breaths.

In the frenzy, one of the guard dogs had dropped the sonic screwdriver from its canine-toothed grip. The Doctor picked it up, pleased to be reunited with his screwdriver but not so happy about the saliva now dripping from it.

'We better get going then,' the Doctor said.

Without taking another breath, the Doctor and Ruby were off again, out of their temporary prison and to what would hopefully be their permanent freedom.

It didn't take the pair long to locate where the ship was being held captive.

This was a) because they could hear the TARDIS making a peculiar ringing noise, and b) because the Dame had not done a good job at trying to hide the TARDIS in the first place, seeing as they'd found it in a nearby room with glass walls and a glass door.

'What is that? Is the TARDIS ringing? It sounds like a bell tolling!' Ruby asked as the sound grew louder.

The Doctor nodded. 'My clever ship! It rings when the TARDIS senses danger,' he said grimly, as they glanced up at its hiding place – a spacious glass-panelled room on the second floor of the headquarters. 'It normally only tolls during the darkest of emergencies, though. So that's not reassuring . . .'

They stood at the centre of the ground floor but could see the room clearly.

'Let's head up,' he said, before moving forward swiftly towards the spiral staircase that would deliver them to the TARDIS. Ruby followed behind hastily, glancing over her shoulder for any signs of lurking alien dogs.

When they got to the room, the sound coming from the TARDIS was even more laboured, almost screaming at them.

'Wait,' Ruby said as the Doctor reached for the glass door handle.

'What?' he said, pausing and turning to face his companion.

'What if this is a trap? It all feels really convenient, doesn't it? Why would the Dame just leave the TARDIS here, where we easily might find it? She doesn't seem like the generous sort. For all we know, that door might be booby-trapped.'

The Doctor turned back to the room that housed the TARDIS with a curious glance.

'You make a good point, Ruby,' he said, and then he held his screwdriver up to the glass door just like he'd done before with the Dame. And like before, a bright blue light shot out from the mouth of the screwdriver, followed by another strange sound, as the Doctor scanned the entrance to the glass room.

'All clear, no booby-traps,' the Doctor said with a satisfied nod, before pulling the door open and stepping over the threshold.

For some reason, the all-clear did not make Ruby feel any less nervous. They were dealing with a dangerous alien criminal, and she suspected that getting out of this would not be an easy task.

She seriously couldn't wait to be back home, eating fish and chips. She'd had enough of the Dame.

The noise from the ship shook the entire room as they entered, the sound rising to an unbearable volume.

'What's wrong with it? Why is it still making noise?' Ruby yelled over the urgent ringing.

The Doctor began walking towards his ship, his eyebrows furrowed and his senses on high alert. 'I don't know . . . it's trying to tell us something,' he replied as he placed his palm on the dense exterior of the blue police box he called home. 'It thinks we're still in danger,' the Doctor finished, using some of the functions on his screwdriver to soothe the ship.

'We should get out of here then. You know, away from the danger?' Ruby said.

The Doctor nodded, wanting just as much as Ruby to get off of Maculosus and never be graced by the Dame or her Dalmatians again. He would, of course, have to alert the Shadow Proclamation to their ineptitude in dealing with the Dame as soon as possible and work out a way of detaining her before they left, but he could figure all that out from the safe confines of his TARDIS.

The pair had been so distracted by the sound from the ship and their need for an imminent escape plan that they didn't hear the distant chime of heels clicking against marbled ground, followed by the scuffling of paws on the floor. Nor did they sense her dark presence looming.

It wasn't until the Doctor reached for the door to his ship that they were finally made aware of the presence of others in the vicinity. Loud barking echoed from wall to wall, the sound coming from the space behind where the Doctor and Ruby were standing.

When they turned, they found the Dame standing outside

the glass room, blocking the only exit with her arms crossed, her expression pinched and a look of abject irritation on her face, which Ruby had now noticed was as scaled as her arms. At her feet were the two larger Macula Dalmatians she had been playing fetch with moments before. The Dame now gripped the dog toy in her taloned grasp.

Ruby could hear the TARDIS starting up again, shaking the room. The ground beneath her felt uneasy, and she couldn't tell if it was her own impending panic causing this or if it was really just the ship. *Perhaps it was both.*

The Dame stepped into the room, her dogs trailing behind her, and when the glass door slammed behind them, Ruby realised that they were stuck.

It hadn't occurred to either of them until that point that while the room was not booby-trapped, they'd essentially walked themselves into yet another prison. *At least it's not a dog cage this time*, Ruby thought.

It seemed that they had celebrated prematurely. *We're in a hotbed of fish and chips now.*

'Hello Doctor, Amethyst,' the Dame said in a way that felt faintly threatening.

'Dame,' the Doctor replied in an icy manner.

Ruby said nothing.

The Dame suddenly barked loudly, and the two Macula guards moved closer to Ruby and the Doctor, now baring their teeth.

Ruby swallowed as the Dame eyed the big blue box behind them.

'I see you both managed to escape,' she said.

The Doctor nodded. 'That we did,' he said brusquely.

'I would be more displeased by your trickery if it wasn't for the fact that I was planning on bringing the transportation device to you to open anyway, which it would be in your best interest to do. I must remind you that I have complete and total control over these hounds, and it is only a short walk to the great cliffs of Maculosus, and then over the edge,' the Dame replied.

Ruby swallowed and glanced over at the Doctor, who did not look worried about the prospect of being pushed over a cliff. Instead, he just looked puzzled.

The Dame clearly sensed the Doctor's confusion and went on. 'It seems your transportation device is locked. We used the best of our materials to try and crack the entrance open, but it is impenetrable. I'm assuming you know how to open it?'

The Doctor suddenly understood the context behind her threats. 'Ah yes, the TAR – I mean, the transportation device, only opens for me. I could open it for you and quickly show you that the device is perfectly safe, and you can let us go.'

The Dame did not look pleased at his suggestion. 'I'm afraid that is not possible,' she said.

'Why not? You'll get your guarantee that the transportation device is safe, we can leave, and everything can go back to how it was – back to normal,' the Doctor said, clearly lying through his teeth. Things would not go back to normal, especially now that they knew she was a criminal. But the Dame didn't have to know that. Ruby still didn't know what crime the Dame had committed, and for some reason, the not knowing made everything feel worse.

'Back to normal for *you*, perhaps,' the Dame started in a low hiss. 'But *not* normal for me.' Her voice boomed over the sound of the ringing ship and echoed around the panelled walls of their glass prison. The dogs beside her cowered back as though they could sense the impending doom before it happened.

'What do you mean *not normal for you*?' Ruby questioned, feeling an icy chill as the Dame's venomous gaze pierced through her. In the bright fluorescence of the room's lighting, her scales almost looked like feathers, and with her squished features, Ruby thought the Dame had some resemblance to a seagull.

'Well, Amethyst, do I look spotted or hound-like to you? Do I resemble any one of these foolish creatures?' the Dame asked, glowering at her.

'Uhm, not at all, Mrs Dame. You look . . . er . . . as majestic as a tree! No that's not right, sorry. You look great! Grand!' Ruby replied, stumbling clumsily over her words.

'Grand?' the Dame asked in a prickly voice. Ruby felt like the Dame was a ticking time bomb that could go off at any moment and braced herself for the inevitable explosion. She swallowed hard as her snake eyes slowly narrowed at her, but before she could explain that *grand* was just earthly slang for good, she was distracted by the sound of a gentle murmur from beside her.

'*Humroid* . . .' the Doctor said suddenly, repeating it under his breath softly.

Ruby looked at him as if he had grown two heads.

'Doctor?' she whispered.

Just then, the Doctor's neck snapped up, and he looked at the Dame with a new-found curiosity. 'Earlier, you mentioned the Humroid tree,' he said.

'I did, yes,' the Dame replied, looking more than a little bit ticked off.

'Not many know of its existence, unless they have a particularly fond interest in rare tree species or have been fortunate enough to see it in person, as I have. I actually happen to favour the apples that particular tree sprouts. But, as I imagine you would already know, Dame, it is extremely difficult to find Humroid apples. Firstly, because that tree only produces apples once every ninety-seven and a half years and secondly, because the Humroid tree can only be found on one specific planet in a far-reaching galaxy. A planet known as Zoron,' the Doctor said, and then he tilted his head at the scaled woman. 'You aren't from Maculosus, are you?'

The Dame's frown slowly morphed into a grimace. 'Smart man you are, aren't you, Doctor?' she said.

The Doctor shrugged. 'I have been told that from time to time, yes. But the more pressing matter here is . . . what is a Zoronese prisoner doing on Maculosus anyway?' he asked no one in particular. The question felt more rhetorical than anything because moments after, his eyes had lit up with the tell-tale signs of recognition.

'Zrominag!' He exclaimed suddenly in a way that made the Dame flinch backwards. Then he turned to Ruby. 'That's "*dame*" in Zoronese,' he continued delightedly. It was the voice he had whenever he figured out a particularly troublesome puzzle. He clapped his hands together. 'You're *that* Dame! The one who obliterated almost all of the timelines in the Zoronese historical index! Nasty stuff. I knew the guy who had to process the paperwork for that.'

'She did *what*?' Ruby said, her eyebrows raised so high they almost flew off her face.

'She deleted several large chunks of history. It was massively devastating, I heard – it must be why she was imprisoned here on Maculosus. Maculosus is a planet where timelines are stagnant and can't be manipulated!' the Doctor said, looking very pleased with himself.

The Dame did not look happy at this reveal, but there was also something in her expression that looked oddly like relief. It seemed she was glad to be seen for exactly who she was by the Doctor.

'You're right, Doctor, I am *that* Dame,' she said, standing taller now. 'Though you mustn't believe the rumours about what led to my exile. I was imprisoned here, not because of my supposed crimes, but because the Shadow Proclamation are stuck in an ancient age of rules and legislation,' she continued. 'They deny brilliance whenever it is handed to them. I wanted to fix the Zoronese timeline and cleanse our history of all the ills our forefathers had polluted it with. Make Zoron great again.'

The Dame seemed so convinced by her mission that she didn't see what was wrong with erasing history.

'But aren't mistakes in the timeline important? To remind us of how not to repeat wrongdoings of the past?' the Doctor said. 'Surely getting rid of all that just makes us vulnerable to bad things repeating, seeing as there was no chance to learn from the previous erased mistakes?'

The Dame's snake eyes filled with venom as she looked down upon them. 'You don't know what you're talking about, boy. My plan was brilliant! It would have saved Zoron from its ghastly fate. But the Proclamation did not agree and banished me here, to a land with no pretence for time travel in their history,' she continued angrily. 'But the thing is, they underestimated me. They underestimated Maculosus. It took me years, but I finally built a prototype using the planet's resources. I made several transportation devices that would be able to track down the closest advanced technology in the universe. The first few models failed. I didn't have enough resources to create a large enough model that would fit and transport myself. But, with the last version, I managed to make a compact vest suit small enough for a Macula to wear. This vest had enough engine power to take one hound to you and then transport the hound back to me. I sent out one of my best, with the instruction for her to bring back anything that could aid in future attempts at building a similar device. Only I got more than I asked for, and for that, I am grateful. I thought it would take me aeons to escape, but thanks to you, Doctor and Amethyst, I can be free, at long last.' The Dame looked elated.

'Free?' Ruby asked, not liking the sound of this at all.

The Dame curled an eyebrow up at her as if she were dense. 'I will be using your transportation device. To get away from here,' she said, gesturing to the TARDIS, which had now stopped ringing out.

'And how do you plan on doing that if you can't even unlock the device?' the Doctor said.

'Hopefully by enlisting your help.'

'Why would we help you?' Ruby asked.

'I can offer you what I believe to be a fair deal in these circumstances. I will set you both free, but only after you take me to where *I* want to go. Drop me off first, then you are free to go anywhere else you'd like,' the Dame said. 'And I get to keep this transportation device after.'

'You want to *keep* the T– um . . . travel device?' Ruby said, her voice rising.

The Dame nodded as though it were a perfectly reasonable request.

'Yes, I think it is only fair. You both return to your home, and I to mine, where I will put this device to good use. Fixing holes in time. I will say, blue has never really been my colour, so I will have to give this a nice paint job. Maybe add a pattern to liven it up, make it less drab.'

It was no fair deal. And to make matters worse, It was clear to Ruby that the Dame had no intention of actually letting them go freely. *She would ask them to do her bidding, then she'd probably leave them stranded, or worse.*

There was no way they would let her do this.

'It's a deal,' the Doctor said.

Ruby's mouth hung open in shock and horror. How was the Doctor seriously considering this?

The Dame looked delighted. 'Wonderful. I knew you'd come around somehow. Now, take me inside. I would like to leave this place as soon as possible.'

'Of course,' the Doctor said with a smile and nod.

The Dame barked loudly, and the growling guard dogs stepped aside obediently as she walked towards the big blue ship.

Ruby shot him an anxious glance that he didn't seem to notice. It seemed, to Ruby at least, that the Doctor had finally lost the plot. But the Time Lord always managed to get them out of various scrapes. So, despite the fear and the uncertainty she was feeling at present, somewhere inside her, she plucked up the courage to trust him.

Moments later, they were all stepping into the TARDIS, the Dame following the Doctor's lead as he escorted her to the console.

She had a dazed look on her face as she took in the large, luminous interior.

'Magnificent,' she whispered, breathless, and then her gaze met the Doctor's once again. She walked up to the console, her eyes scanning over the many buttons.

'How does this all work then?' the Dame asked.

'Well,' the Doctor began, pointing at a large panel in the console's centre. 'You'll need to press a few buttons here and there, which will compute the location into the TARDIS's system, and then you'll need my sonic device to pilot the ship through the function and control feature. The F n' C programme.'

Ruby's heart leaped. She did not recall the Doctor *ever* using his sonic screwdriver to pilot the TARDIS, or an *F n' C programme* for that matter. Where was he going with this?

'I see,' the Dame said. 'Well, I'll need the Amethyst girl to do the piloting for me.'

Both Ruby and the Doctor looked shocked at the suggestion.

'Me? Why Me?' Ruby asked.

'Well, for one, I don't trust him,' the Dame said, looking pointedly at the Doctor. 'He has a cunning look to him, and I don't believe he'll follow my directions as intended. And two, my hands are not *button* friendly,' the Dame finished, removing a glove and revealing her scaly, slimy-taloned hands.

Ruby shook her head. 'I don't know much about the technology . . . and I –'

'It wasn't a question, little girl. You will do it, and you will do it now,' the Dame hissed, her voice rising.

Ruby swallowed and looked over at the Doctor, but his expression was blank.

'Doctor –' Ruby started.

But the Doctor shook his head.

'Do as she says, Amethyst. Dame, I'll have to begin, and then I'll hand over to Ameythyst. We work as a team,' he said.

'Very well,' the Dame replied, her eyes suspicious.

Ruby hesitated. Panic was rising in her chest. She didn't want the Dame to ruin more lives or keep corrupting the history of her people. She tried to stay calm, knowing that the Doctor almost definitely had a plan, but her thoughts were muddled with anxiety. 'But –'

'Just trust me, OK? I'll get this all started, and then you can use the sonic screwdriver to pilot,' the Doctor said in a measured tone. His expression shifted from neutral to something she couldn't quite read.

She turned to the Dame, who was grinning from ear to ear, and decided she would just have to trust him. Maybe an eternity spent as the Dame's prisoners on Zoron wouldn't be too bad after all. Maybe she'd grow to love the Humroid tree apples the Doctor seemed so obsessed with.

She thought about what she would miss back home. Playing music with her band. Her mum and her nan. The idea of never seeing either of them again made her chest constrict. She'd miss fish and chips. She'd honestly miss it all, even the seagulls. Ruby took a deep breath in and nodded.

The Doctor stepped towards the console and began the TARDIS's take-off sequence. He whisked around, executing his usual pattern of pulling levers and pressing buttons with effortless flair, and Ruby waited for the rumble of the ship beneath their feet, the usual sign that the TARDIS was ready to take off. But instead, the ship didn't stir. Everything was weirdly . . . quiet. *Too quiet.*

'All done! And now for the last bit,' the Doctor said.

Ruby's heart hammered in her chest as the Doctor tossed the sonic screwdriver over to her. She looked up at the Doctor through bleary eyes.

'Activate the F n' C programme, Ruby. The ship cannot take off without it,' he said levelly, a small smile on his face, his eyes darting subtly to the Dame next to them.

F n' C programme . . . Ruby thought. *What does that mean?*

'Any day now,' the Dame said with an exasperated sigh.

She looked back up at the amused face of the Doctor, and just then, realisation smacked into her.

'Right . . . the F n' C programme,' Ruby said, finally understanding. F n' C. Fish and chips. She scanned the screwdriver for the button she'd seen the Doctor use countless times before. She always wondered how one button had so many functions, and had no idea what was going to happen. She took a deep breath and pressed down . . .

It all happened in a matter of seconds.

A brilliant blue light shot out from the tip of the screwdriver for the third time that day, and Ruby aimed it in the direction of the Dame.

Unlike earlier, when the sonic scanned for information, this time was different. The rays from the light formed blistering blue beams around the Dame like a jail cell . . . or a *cage*.

The Dame's reptile pupils rattled, her eyes widening as she looked around at the cell, now trapping her in one spot in the TARDIS.

'Brilliant work, Ruby!' the Doctor said, as he held out his hand for the screwdriver.

'What are you doing, you foolish girl!?' the Dame exclaimed, as she tried to exit her fluorescent blue cage, hissing when the bars scorched her skin.

Ruby felt relief spread through her at the confirmation that the Dame could not escape this prison.

'Release me this instant!' the Dame said. When no one stirred, her scowl morphed into a meaner expression. She let out a shrill scream. 'I said release —' she began, but was cut off by the Doctor, who had raised his sonic device once again in her direction.

'You were wrong earlier, by the way,' the Doctor said. 'I think blue *is* your colour.' He spun a dial on the screwdriver and the Dame was zapped away instantly.

'Where did she go?' Ruby asked.

'I sent her to a different spot on Maculosus in her new cage. This way, she won't be able to get out and harm or control any more of the Macula.'

'I don't think I tell you enough how truly amazing your mind is,' Ruby said, awestruck by how seamlessly the Doctor had executed his plan.

'I think you're amazing too, Ruby,' he replied with a kind smile. 'Now, I just have to send the Shadow Proclamation a strongly worded message to tell them to pick up their prisoner, and then we can be on our merry way.'

A few minutes later, the Doctor had finished sending a few choice words to the Shadow Proclamation through his sonic screwdriver.

Ruby was relieved to be back inside the TARDIS.

The Doctor began toggling with buttons on the console. 'Should I drop you off at your mum's?' he asked.

Ruby shook her head, suddenly thinking of a better idea. Despite missing home, she wasn't quite ready to give up on her original mission for the day.

'Well . . . I was wondering if you were still up for one more adventure?' she asked.

The Doctor raised an eyebrow at her, looking intrigued. 'What sort of thing did you have in mind?'

After a long day of alien dogs and a criminally deranged Dame, Ruby was glad to be back in the sunny seaside town of Brighton.

'That'll be fifteen pounds, please,' the monotone server at Chippy Chippy Bang Bang said. Ruby slid three fivers across before handing the Doctor his parcel of fish and chips. They sat under a parasol on the beach and ate their supper in *relative* peace.

'Ruby, I must say, this is truly the *best* thing I have eaten in a very long time,' he said when he had finished.

'Really?' Ruby asked.

The Doctor nodded. 'Really.'

It was music to her ears.

'By the way, I meant to ask you earlier – how did you programme your sonic with the F n' C programme?' she asked her Time Lord friend. They'd barely had time to breathe, let alone programme anything. She'd been wondering how he'd done it ever since they'd arrived back in Brighton.

The Doctor tossed the empty newspaper wrappings into a nearby bin, and then sat back with his hands splayed behind him, his midnight-blue hair and deep-brown skin glistening in the blazing sun. He smiled at his companion. 'I programmed it in just before we landed on Maculosus. It's a new feature I've been trialling. I figured we might need to detain the dog and thought it would be an apt name for such a function. I think it'll definitely come in handy.'

Ruby was never not amazed by the Doctor and all his curiosities and capabilities.

'Who would have guessed that fish and chips would save the day?' she said with a laugh.

In the distance, unbeknownst to the young girl and her centuries-old time-travelling companion, there was a threat lurking in the overcast sky. They had not yet heard the foreboding flapping of wings, or the menacing squawk that followed, or seen the glaucous gulls encircling and glowering down at them from above, as Ruby offered the rest of her chips to a very elated lord of time. The Doctor was much too busy trying to convince Ruby that this fish meal would pair well with custard to take notice of the predicament they would soon find themselves in yet again.

That was for future versions of themselves to worry about. Right now, all that mattered was this.

ABOUT THE AUTHORS

THE FIRST DOCTOR: A BIG HAND FOR THE DOCTOR

EOIN COLFER was born and raised in the south-east of Ireland. *Artemis Fowl*, his first book of eight featuring the young anti-hero, was an immediate international bestseller and went on to win several prestigious international awards and be made into a feature film by Disney Studios. He has written a number of other successful books for both adults and children, including *Airman*, *Plugged* and the W.A.R.P. series. For theatre, Eoin has written the plays *My Real Life* and *Holy Mary*, as well as the book for the Christmas musical *Noël*.

From 2014 to 2016 Eoin served as Ireland's third Children's Laureate. He lives with his family in Dublin.

Find out more about Eoin at www.eoincolfer.com. You can also follow him on Twitter: @eoincolfer

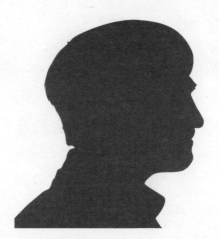

THE SECOND DOCTOR: THE NAMELESS CITY

MICHAEL SCOTT is one of Ireland's most successful and prolific writers for both children and adults. Michael has over 100 titles to his credit, has written in a variety of genres including fantasy, science fiction and horror, and is considered an authority on mythology and folklore. In 2007, *The Alchemyst: The Secrets of the Immortal Nicholas Flamel*, the first in a groundbreaking young adult fantasy series, launched straight into the *New York Times* bestsellers list, spending sixteen weeks in the top ten. All six books in the series have been *New York Times* bestsellers and the series is now published in thirty-seven different countries. Michael lives in Dublin.

Find out more about Michael at www.dillonscott.com. You can also follow him on Twitter: @flamelauthor

THE THIRD DOCTOR: THE SPEAR OF DESTINY

MARCUS SEDGWICK was born and raised in East Kent in the south-east of England. He now lives in the French Alps. He is the winner of many prizes, most notably the 2014 Michael L. Printz Award for his novel *Midwinterblood*. Marcus has also received two Printz Honors, for *Revolver* in 2011 and *The Ghosts of Heaven* in 2016, giving him the most citations to date for America's most prestigious book prize for writing for young adults.

Other notable award-winning books include *Floodland*, Marcus' first novel, which won the Branford Boase Award in 2001, a prize for the best debut novel for children published in the UK each year; *My Swordhand is Singing*, which won the Booktrust Teenage Prize for 2007, and *Lunatics and Luck*, part of The Raven Mysteries series, which won a Blue Peter Book Award in 2011.

His books have been shortlisted for over forty other

awards, including the CILIP Carnegie Medal (seven times), the Edgar Allan Poe Award (twice) and the Guardian Children's Fiction Prize (four times). He has been nominated for the Astrid Lindgren Memorial Award three times, in 2016, 2017 and 2018.

He has illustrated some of his books, and has provided wood-engravings for a couple of private press books.

His website is www.marcussedgwick.com and you can follow him on Twitter: @marcussedgwick. He is probably currently working on a new book of some kind . . .

THE FOURTH DOCTOR: THE ROOTS OF EVIL

PHILIP REEVE was born in Brighton and worked in a bookshop for many years before becoming a full-time illustrator and then turning to writing. His first novel, *Mortal Engines*, won the Nestlé Smarties Book Prize Gold Award (2002), the Blue Peter Book of the Year Award (2003), and was shortlisted for both the Branford Boase Award and the Whitbread Children's Book Award. A movie version by Peter Jackson was released in December 2018. He has since won many more awards and accolades for his works including the Guardian Children's Fiction Prize in 2006 and the Los Angeles Times Book Prize for *A Darkling Plain*, and the 2008 CILIP Carnegie Medal for *Here Lies Arthur*. His most recent titles are *Night Flights* (a Mortal Engines collection), *Station Zero* (the third part of the Railhead series) and *The Legend of Kevin*, co-created with illustrator Sarah McIntyre.

He lives in Dartmoor, England, with his wife and son, Sam.

For further information and to explore the author's own curious world visit www.philip-reeve.com

THE FIFTH DOCTOR: TIP OF THE TONGUE

PATRICK NESS was born in Virginia, USA, and is the author of the Chaos Walking trilogy. The third book of the trilogy, *Monsters of Men*, won the CILIP Carnegie Medal, with previous accolades for the series including the Guardian Children's Fiction Prize and the Booktrust Teenage Prize. The film adaptation of the first instalment, *The Knife of Never Letting Go*, is currently in post-production with Lionsgate, starring Tom Holland and Daisy Ridley.

Patrick's sixth book, *A Monster Calls*, became the first book ever to win both of the prestigious CILIP Carnegie and Kate Greenaway Medals. *A Monster Calls* was adapted into a 2016 film of the same name starring Liam Neeson and Sigourney Weaver, and in summer 2018 a theatre production was staged at The Old Vic as part of its bicentenary celebrations.

Patrick has written three works for adults and eight YA novels, and is published in forty-three languages. His latest novel *And the Ocean Was Our Sky*, with illustrations by Rovina Cai, is out now.

Find out more about Patrick at www.patrickness.com. You can also follow him on Instagram: patricknessbooks

THE SIXTH DOCTOR: SOMETHING BORROWED

RICHELLE MEAD is the bestselling author of the Vampire Academy, Bloodlines, Glittering Court and Age of X series. Her love of fantasy and science fiction began at an early age when her father read her Greek mythology and her brothers made her watch *Flash Gordon*. She went on to study folklore and religion at the University of Michigan, and, when not writing, Richelle spends her time drinking lots of coffee, keeping up with reality TV and collecting 1980s T-shirts. Richelle lives with her family in Seattle, USA.

Find out more about Richelle at www.richellemead.com. You can also follow her on Twitter: @RichelleMead

THE SEVENTH DOCTOR: THE RIPPLE EFFECT

MALORIE BLACKMAN has written over sixty books for children and young adults, including the Noughts & Crosses series, *Thief* and most recently her science-fiction thriller *Chasing the Stars*. Her work has also been adapted for TV, with the six-part adaptation of *Pig-Heart Boy* winning a BAFTA and Noughts & Crosses currently in production for the BBC, with Roc Nation (Jay-Z's entertainment company) on board to curate and release the soundtrack as Executive Producer. A stage adaptation of the book, by Pilot Theatre, ran from February 2019, under the direction of Sabrina Mahfouz.

In 2005, Malorie was honoured with the Eleanor Farjeon Award in recognition of her distinguished contribution to the world of children's books, in 2008 she received an OBE for her services to children's literature and, between 2013 and 2015, she was the Children's Laureate.

Malorie is currently writing for the new *Doctor Who* series on BBC One, and the fifth novel in her Noughts & Crosses sequence, *Crossfire*, will be published by Penguin Random House Children's in summer 2019.

Find out more about Malorie at www.malorieblackman. co.uk. You can also follow her on Twitter: @malorieblackman

THE EIGHTH DOCTOR: SPORE

ALEX SCARROW used to be a graphic artist, then he decided to be a computer-games designer. Finally, he grew up and became an author. He has written a number of successful thrillers and several screenplays, but it's young-adult fiction that has allowed him to really have fun with the ideas and concepts he was playing around with when designing games.

He currently lives in Norwich with his family.

Find out more about Alex at www.alexscarrow.co.uk and www.time-riders.co.uk. You can also follow him on Twitter: @AlexScarrow

THE NINTH DOCTOR: THE BEAST OF BABYLON

CHARLIE HIGSON started writing when he was ten years old. After university he was a singer and painter and decorator before he started writing for television. He went on to create and star in the hugely successful comedy series *The Fast Show*.

He is the author of the bestselling Young Bond books, and the horror series, The Enemy. His Fighting Fantasy interactive gamebook, *The Gates of Death*, came out in 2018.

Charlie doesn't do Facebook, but you can tweet him @monstroso

THE TENTH DOCTOR: THE MYSTERY OF THE HAUNTED COTTAGE

DEREK LANDY hates to brag. He positively blushes whenever anyone mentions the awards he's won, such as the Irish Book of the Decade, the Red House Children's Book Award, and numerous regional honours in Ireland and the UK – all for his Skulduggery Pleasant series (which is, incidentally, published in over thirty-five languages around the world). He wouldn't want to point out that the eleventh book of the series, *Midnight*, was released in 2018, and heaven forbid anyone should mention that he also found time to pen the Demon Road trilogy. Modesty demands that he refrain from pointing out that, on occasion, he also writes for Marvel Comics.

If you really must, you can follow him on Twitter @DerekLandy and Instagram: dereklandyofficial

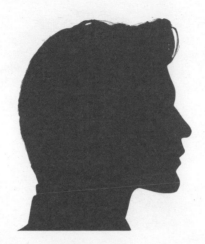

THE ELEVENTH DOCTOR: NOTHING O'CLOCK

NEIL GAIMAN is the bestselling author of more than twenty books for adults and children, including the novels *Neverwhere*, *Stardust*, *American Gods*, *Anansi Boys*, *Coraline* and *The Graveyard Book*, the Sandman series of graphic novels, and two episodes of *Doctor Who* ('The Doctor's Wife' and 'Nightmare in Silver'). He has received numerous literary honours including the Locus and Hugo Awards and the Newbery and CILIP Carnegie Medals. Neil has written and is the showrunner for a mini-series based on *Good Omens*, the book he co-authored with Terry Pratchett. *American Gods* has also been adapted into an Emmy-nominated TV series.

More than two million people follow him on Twitter: @neilhimself. You can find out more about Neil at www.neilgaiman.com

Born and raised in England, he now lives in the USA, with his wife, the rock star Amanda Palmer. He is Professor of the Arts at Bard College. His hair is ridiculous.

THE TWELFTH DOCTOR: LIGHTS OUT

HOLLY BLACK is the author of bestselling contemporary fantasy books for kids and teens. Some of her titles include *The Spiderwick Chronicles* (with Tony DiTerlizzi), the Modern Faerie Tale series, the Curse Workers series, *Doll Bones*, *The Coldest Girl in Coldtown*, the Magisterium series (with Cassandra Clare) and *The Darkest Part of the Forest*. She has been a finalist for an Eisner Award, and the recipient of the Andre Norton Award, the Mythopoeic Award and a Newbery Honor. Her latest young-adult novel, *The Cruel Prince*, begins a new series, The Folk of the Air.

Holly currently lives in New England with her husband and son in a house with a secret door.

Visit Holly's website for up-to-date news: www.blackholly.com. You can also follow her on Twitter: @hollyblack

THE THIRTEENTH DOCTOR: TIME LAPSE

NAOMI ALDERMAN is a novelist, broadcaster and video-game designer. Her novels include *Disobedience* (2006), *The Liars' Gospel* (2012) and the bestselling *The Power* (2016), which won the Baileys Women's Prize for Fiction and was named by Barack Obama as one of his ten books of the year. Her work has been published in more than thirty countries. She was mentored by Margaret Atwood as part of the Rolex Mentor and Protégé Arts Initiative, was one of Granta's Best of Young British Novelists in 2013 and is Professor of Creative Writing at Bath Spa University. She presents *Science Stories* on BBC Radio 4, and is the co-creator and lead writer of the smartphone audio adventure *Zombies, Run!* She is currently working on the TV adaptation of *The Power*.

Her website is www.naomialderman.com and you can follow her on Twitter: @naomiallthenews

THE FOURTEENTH DOCTOR: FLEETING FACES

STEVE COLE is an editor and bestselling children's author whose sales exceed three million copies. Among over 200 published titles he has written many Doctor Who books, four Young Bond novels, acclaimed eco-adventures for reluctant readers, such as *Tin Boy* and *World Burn Down* and created several young fiction series, including Astrosaurs, Cows in Action and Adventure Duck. He lives in Buckinghamshire.

THE FIFTEENTH DOCTOR: THE DALMATIAN TERRAIN

FARIDAH ÀBÍKÉ-ÍYÍMÍDÉ is the instant New York Times- and international-bestselling, award-winning author of *Ace of Spades* and *Where Sleeping Girls Lie*. In 2024 she was a World Book Day author with her title *The Doomsday Date*, and she also has a Marvel Spider-Verse story coming out this year where she writes a new Spider-Verse character known as Spider-UK/Zarina Zahari. Faridah is an avid tea drinker, a collector of strange mugs and a graduate from a university in the Scottish Highlands where she received a BA in English Literature. She also has an MA in Shakespeare Studies from Kings College London. When she isn't spinning dark tales, Faridah can be found examining the deeper meanings in Disney channel original movies.